Held in Moonlight's Favor is the first in a why choose romantasy duet and is intended for mature readers, 18+. It contains past infidelity (not between the romance pairings), infidelity accusations, social ostracization, cruel fae bargains, and background themes of coercion/enthralling (not between romance pairings).
It also contains multiple love interests, graphic intimacy, and explicit MM romance within the harem, and ends on a cliffhanger. Read responsibly.

JADE BONES

HELD IN MOONLIGHT'S FAVOR

Contents

1. Bailey 1
2. Bailey 13
3. Bailey 32
4. Bailey 45
5. Bailey 57
6. Sebastian 68
7. Bailey 77
8. Bailey 97
9. Bailey 114
10. Bailey 125
11. Bailey 137
12. Bailey 152
13. Bailey 170
14. Sebastian 188
15. Bailey 194
16. Bailey 210
17. Bailey 224
18. Bailey 234
19. Bailey 245
20. Sebastian 262
21. Bailey 274
22. Bailey 280
23. Bailey 300
24. Bailey 311
25. Bailey 323
26. Bailey 340
27. Bailey 354
28. Sebastian 370
29. Bailey 384
30. Bailey 396
31. Bailey 413
32. Bailey 432

33. Sebastian   440
34. Bailey   448
35. Bailey   457
36. Bailey   464
37. Bailey   475
38. Bailey   486
39. Bailey   498
40. Bailey   503

Acknowledgments   507
About the Author   509
Also by Jade Bones   511

This one is for the exiles who loved too much and were never loved in return.
Exile's over, darlings. It's time to come home.

AELOR
TO CRIERA...
WHISPERING FIELDS
Springbreach
Crow's Foot Hollow
Golden Nest
HOLLOW PLAINS
Stillhaven
Ylsgul
THE SORCERERS' WILDES
Felsrun
Mountain's Drift
GODS' CROWN
Misthale
Crystal Hill
No Man's Vale
GIANTS' MARSH
Bellrun
THE FORGOTTEN VALLEY
Ferntide
Silent Tower
SILKEN HILLS
Riverhone
Sunholde
Broodshire
VIRA'S SECRET
Mosswilde
Belle's Gift
Cavern's End
SLEEPING WOODS
Silvermorne

To every generation born

A luckless child of grief and scorn

A bargain laid, a promise made

Of health and fortune thus repaid

- Prayer to the Fae
(The First Bargain)

CHAPTER 1

Bailey

> *To every generation born*
> *A luckless child of grief and scorn*
> *A Bargain laid, a promise made*
> *Of health and fortune thus repaid*

> *- Prayer to the Fae*
> *(The First Bargain)*

THE MAGIC HAD RUN OUT OF MY ENCHANTED MIRROR AGAIN, AND NOW the voices streaming from it sounded like they were underwater.

"*Did he trade the... or his memory of...*"

"*No! Are you serious? For just a—*"

"*Swear on my ma's life. All for the love of... you know her? That prissy bitch who... at the last Fair...*"

"*A handful of bloody seeds!*"

"Stupid bastard. The fae will be back for more before the season's through."

I poked the frame, where the glass met the wood; my reflection wobbled and distorted. The reflections of my three friends, arranged in floating bubbles along the top of the mirror, winked out completely.

"Huh," I muttered. My face stared back at me, alone. Eyebrows flat, expression blank and unimpressed. "Someone needs to ban me from visiting stores run by little old women. My heart can't take the empathy. I keep buying things that are destined to explode the second I'm home."

No one answered. Even the audio spell had vanished, and since I wasn't a Spell Master of any description, that meant I could do sweet, juicy *nothing* to fix it.

That would teach me not to ignore the Council's wishes and bring gaudy city magic into our village, I supposed.

I leant forward, my shoulders hunching as I gripped the edge of the dressing table and allowed myself a quiet moment to lose my shit. What had they been saying? Luke Tanner traded his *what* for the love of *who* at the last Fair? Or had it been for seeds?

Well, Luke was never going to be winning awards for his ability to think, I supposed. Still...

My nerves were already sizzling ahead of our plans tonight, and I really didn't need the reminder about how important those Bargains were. Sacred. Unbreakable.

Potentially devastating, with a side of unfathomable mortification.

My friends and I were meant to be visiting the Lumière tonight—the fae circus that visited twice a year from Criera, the fae land across the water. The fae stayed for the seven nights between the quarter and the full moon, delighting us mortals with their illusions and acrobatics.

It had been years since the circus was close enough for us to visit, and since I'd been a child the last time, I hadn't gone. It was far too dangerous for children. Not because of the acts, or even the performers themselves, but because of the entry fee.

The Lumière didn't take payment in coin; they asked for a Bargain.

The unofficial deadline for making your Bargains was a seven-day ago, but I'd put it off, unable to think of the right thing to trade. It was hard enough for the average person to make such a choice, but since I was the Offering, it was practically impossible.

Merelda—an imp who'd taken a fancy to me for reasons unknown and made a nest somewhere in my rafters—pranced about on top of the mirror while I sulked. The face swayed within the stand, its ornate wooden carving sending curved shadows across the walls. As she pranced, she began waving her hands around and fluffing her bright blue hair while chattering high-pitched words at the wall, as if she were giving a speech.

It was incomprehensible to me, since I couldn't speak imp. I'd tried to learn for a while, but the more I'd researched their language in increasingly older and dustier books, the more those ancient scholars told me they were just animals. Smart animals, but animals nonetheless.

However, even with the language barrier and the dubious title of magical creature, I was fairly certain she was doing an impersonation of Stacey.

"That isn't kind," I pointed out with a wry smile. "She might still be able to hear you, you know. And then where will you be when she decides to pick up her new hobby of spear the tail on the imp?"

In response, Merelda stuck out her tongue and blew me a raspberry. Her pink tongue was a vibrant contrast against her blue skin, and the sight was almost enough to pull me out of my misery. Almost.

My smile fell as quickly as it had appeared. I should just end the spell and go to bed, forget about tonight and whatever wild plans the girls had made. I wasn't ready for this, and besides, I was no fun to be around. I hadn't been for six moons, ever since Hayden left and I'd finally been forced to accept my inherited destiny.

I glanced across my dressing table at the silver chain and pendant I'd taken off while I showered. It was a simple enough design: two overlapping circles with a wavy line down the center where they joined. The symbol of the Offering, created in homage to the mismatched colors of my eyes that had marked me for the position from birth.

The Offering Bargain had been made centuries ago—the first Bargain Aelor ever made with the fae, and it was made here in Broodshire. Its legacy continued long after those who made it were gone, one child for every generation, and I was the lucky one for mine. The village's Offering, in name and in duty, until the day I died or was lost.

I wore the necklace every day, both in deference to my sacred duty, and as an aide to warn me if I was about to step a toe out of line and risk breaking my oath. I'd ignored its dull, residual heat for a year with Hayden, telling myself it was only the lingering warmth of my body.

Lesson learned: I wouldn't ignore it again.

With a grimace, I traced my fingers over the cool metal, waiting for it to burn me. A beat passed, and then a second. My shoulders lowered; nothing. My plans tonight weren't off limits to the Offering, then. I had the village's blessing to be a block-head and trade my life away to the fae. But daemons damn my soul if I took an extra helping of pudding. Go figure.

I drew my hand back from the necklace, unwilling to put it on just yet.

With a whistling sound like a kettle, the three mini portraits reappeared. The magic spilled over its bounds as the spell revived, sending rainbow colors dazzling across the glass.

"It's too much money, Sadey. You've been ripped off. You should take it back."

Murmurs of agreement followed.

They hadn't even realized I'd disappeared.

My stomach dipped, but I dismissed the sensation quickly. *Let it go, Bailey*, I told myself. *It doesn't matter.*

Piece by piece, inch by inch, I relaxed the muscles of my face into a graceful, calming smile. After a few seconds, my mind followed, as if it, too, had muscles that could be let go of one by one. I looked at the faces of my friends, reflected in the glass, reminding myself of the joy we'd shared and the kindness of their hearts. Soon, that was all I remembered.

I'd always been good at that: seeing the beauty hidden inside people. Finding the truth in their hearts and focusing on that rather than whatever emotional outburst my body was having. People were complicated, and I never liked to judge from one thing alone.

I turned my attention to my own reflection, ignoring the three faces at the top, and began to style my hair. The spell was still fritzing, so there was no point trying to contribute to the conversation. Besides, we'd all be ready soon enough, and we could finish chatting in person. Preferably while eating copious amounts of street food and drinking fae wine.

I squinted at my reflection. There was a spot across the bridge of my nose where a light cluster of freckles was visible in the light. Hayden used to call it my sugar dusting. Bile rose at the back of my throat, and with a slow, practiced exhale, I willed it away, focusing on my task. A few gentle twists in the upper half of my hair, a quick brush through the locks that remained free, two shining metal clips to decorate, and I was finished. Ready to meet the mystical fae and marvel at their magic.

If they didn't lock me away for a hundred years first.

Urgh, why couldn't I make up my *mind*?

"Oh, Bailey!"

I startled, looking up at one of the portraits—Sadey. She waved at me, her image remaining crystal clear even as she moved. The spell must have stabilized.

"Yeah?" I asked, my smile softening again. My voice was a light, unaffected drawl—the laid-back tone I'd cultivated my entire life, and then perfected in recent moons. "Sorry, I drifted. Were you talking to me?"

Sadey waved her hand with an easy laugh. "Don't worry about it, hun. I was just gonna ask if there was any chance I could borrow your mirror in the next few days?"

I frowned. "Is yours not working?"

Maybe they were all on the fritz.

"It's not for me! It's for Hannah. She's coming to stay at Jackson's for the winter, and it'd be really cool if she could join in our chats."

The others made noises of agreement, sighing as they reminisced about how long it had been since Hannah was in town.

The churning feeling sliced in my gut, sinking lower.

"For... the whole winter?" I asked. No matter which way you did the math on that one, it didn't add up in my favor.

No one heard me. I waited a second and then asked again.

Sadey nodded enthusiastically. "You know how far away Jackson's is. It'd be so much easier to have her in the mirror than to walk over there all the time. And you're just down the street, so I can fill you in on anything you miss." She blinked, adding quickly. "Or you can come over and join in with mine! It'll be fun!"

Right.

"Uhh," I trailed off, looking at their eager expressions.

My heart twisted. I knew how long it had been since they'd seen Hannah, and with the new baby, it was hard for her to leave the house on a whim. Being able to chat with her in the mirror would be so much easier.

I opened my mouth, intending to ask whether one of the other girls should give up their mirror instead—I was the one who'd bought them, after all—but I closed it again without speaking. I knew the answer. Didn't know why I even bothered questioning it. It wasn't like they were doing anything wrong.

Most of the time, being the Offering was a passive existence. My duty lay in everything I *didn't* do, rather than what I did. But in moments like these, it was a living, breathing snake coiled around my throat.

Over the back of the mirror, Merelda chittered angrily, her little face growing bright red as she tried to catch my attention. I ignored her.

"Sure thing," I answered, slow and breezy. "Do you want to pick it up before we leave tonight?"

Sadey blinked. "Tonight?"

"Yeah... The circus?"

You know—that small, insignificant yet wildly magical thing that we're all getting ready for?

Silence descended, and even though we couldn't exactly make eye contact like this, it was suddenly obvious that everyone was avoiding mine.

Merelda wasn't even yelling now; she was just staring at me —all four inches of her stretched onto indignant tippy toes. Distantly, through the haze of welling sadness, I acknowledged the funny side of things—if it could shut up my loquacious imp friend, it had to be pretty shocking.

"Shit," Christine stuttered. "We've double booked!"

A flurry of explanations layered over each other, each one sharp and strident, like breaking glass. I pieced it together somewhere in between—they were going to the theater. A dance troupe I hadn't enjoyed last time they were in town, or something.

I didn't remember saying I didn't like them, but sure. It was possible. It could be true.

"The circus could be fun, though," Ella said cautiously. "It hasn't been to our village in over ten years…" She lowered her voice to a whisper. "It's the *fae.*"

"Ella!" Sadey whined. "We've had these tickets forever. We can do the circus next season. It's only ever a few villages over. Besides, it's way too late to think up a safe Bargain."

I cleared my throat. The sound of her words—*we've had these tickets forever*—whirling in my mind. Unexpectedly, something hot and fierce burned in my throat. I didn't recognize it, and I didn't like it.

"What did you think I was getting ready for if I wasn't coming?" I asked, one eyebrow raised in disbelief. My voice came out sharper than I meant it to, and, in my reflection, the shining silver hair clasps flashed angrily in the setting sun.

Sadey's eyebrows shot up in surprise. "We thought you were just joining in the pre-game!" she answered, slightly breathless. "You know we'd never leave you out, even if you weren't joining in the show."

"Yeah!" Christine agreed enthusiastically. "We still wanted to see you!"

"We're so sorry you couldn't come this time," Ella added, a little softer than the others.

Right. Because they'd asked, and I'd said no, and I was just here for the chatting and the drinks. Which I'd absolutely been part of, and not just a fly on the wall.

"Maybe you can use this time to visit the town hall," Sadey suggested. The sun hit her eyes at an angle that made them glint, like my hair pins. I winced as the light flared. "You've been saying the Oath needs you to swear anew, ever since Hayden, well... you know." She pulled an apologetic face.

All of a sudden, the fire fizzled out of me, leaving me hollow in its absence. The wooden walls of my cottage bedroom, filled with cozy paintings, seemed abruptly to loom in the rising shadows of dusk.

I flicked a glance up at the shocked imp, now perched on the edge of the mirror, her legs dangling over Sadey's face. I looked away after only a second.

"I have been saying that, haven't I?" I agreed mildly, having no intention of renewing the Oath of the Offering. Not tonight, anyway. Perhaps later, when I could stomach the thought of looking at the ancient glass ball that ruled my life.

"Well, I'll drop the mirror off in a couple of days," I said, adopting a serene smile while Merelda shrieked obscenities at me in her little high-pitched voice.

The conversation picked up with barely a stutter. I let the words wash over me, drifting in and out of focus, until eventually everyone signed off with blown kisses and promises to have lunch soon.

The sudden silence was deafening.

By now, the setting sun in the window behind me had turned the light in my bedroom golden, and it was that golden light which caressed my face as I studied my reflection. Even knowing what I was thinking, feeling, my face was impossible to read. Unnaturally still, some had said, among other things. I focused on my hair instead; the sun had highlighted my red-tinted blonde curls, turning them into a gleaming crown, which I tugged gently with one hand.

The effect in the mirror was ethereal—my hair lit up like magical royalty. The gentle shadows lining my face gave me an air of mystery, like I was someone important. Like I was about to step out into a life of adventure.

It was a lie. This world didn't hold adventure. Not for me.

I was the opposite of adventure. The opposite of a chosen one. The Offering who, in a twist of cruel irony, offered nothing.

I dropped my hand, fingers finding a perfume bottle that I turned absentmindedly this way and that, distracted by the sensation of the glass rolling along the wood. It didn't matter, of course. I knew the Bargain that ruled my life was fair, and I was happy to play such a vital role for my village, even if I hadn't taken that first oath myself. The one that bound me to my destiny centuries before I was even born. It was still my duty, and I was honored.

But ever since Hayden left, I'd struggled to remember that. Every now and then, I caught myself feeling... off. Like a fire burned inside my chest. Or vicious words hovered on the tip of my tongue.

It was all just mixed up together. That was all. Six moons wasn't long enough to grieve a breakup, no matter that Hayden had been right to leave. My relationship with him had gotten out of hand, and everyone had been relieved when it ended. I *should* be relieved. I just couldn't quite think straight yet. My feelings were tainting everything else.

Daunting or not, I'd hoped the circus would be an escape from that. A thrilling night of adventure that eclipsed all my murky feelings. But now the others had changed plans, I had no idea what to do. I knew I shouldn't go alone. It was... well, foolish didn't even begin to cover it. I didn't even have a Bargain ready to trade.

Rushing one now, on my own, would mean I missed loopholes. Clauses. Things the Lumière could and would use against me.

But... what was the alternative?

Another night home alone, with my thoughts, and my feelings, and... silence. Alone.

I set the perfume bottle straight on the counter with a resounding slam.

So what if the girls weren't coming with me? I'd go alone. And okay, I wasn't the brightest, but I could be clever if I tried, and occasionally shrewd, and most importantly: I was worthless.

The fae had nothing to gain by tricking or trapping me, and so I had nothing to lose by walking through those gates. They probably wouldn't even notice I was there.

I spun around, facing the rest of the room, with its soft yellow glow and cozy lace curtains. Now, I just had to think of a Bargain I could trade for entry. But everything I came up with felt like either too much or not enough.

The fae traded in memories, favors, and feelings: pieces of ourselves that either gave off an energy they wove into their magic—not that anyone knew exactly what that meant—or literally offered a trade of service.

I was the Offering. I existed to balance the ledgers of my village's good fortune, and my sacred duty determined that I would be as unremarkable as leaves falling in the autumn. Forgettable in every manner, and honor bound to stay that way.

What could I possibly trade that was valuable enough for the fae to want, but useless enough that I didn't risk the scales of fortune by losing it?

A thought hit me.

A wild, impulsive, ridiculous thought. The kind my mother

had always chastised me for, and my sister had always hated because she couldn't control it.

I turned slowly, staring at the cupboard.

Without thinking—barely breathing—I crossed the floor and opened the tall, wooden doors to my bedroom cupboard. On the top shelf, tucked at the back, was a velvet lined, metal trinket box, approximately eight inches across.

I took it down, lifting the worn lid and gazing at the contents. They didn't look like much. A couple of well-thumbed notebooks. Some letters. A handful of photographs, their silvery images haunting in the near dark of my room.

Each item was charged with so much emotion, so much pain, that a single one would be a worthy trade in any fae Bargain. The energy they could siphon from these memories. The magic they could cast...

I dropped the lid and slid the entire trinket box into my satchel before running out of the house.

The door slammed shut behind me.

CHAPTER 2

Bailey

THE GARDEN PATH WAS OVERGROWN WITH VINES, SWEEPING UP OVER the arched trellis and reminding me how long it had been since I'd put any care into my house. But my neglect was useful now; the shadows concealed me from nosy neighbors as I raced toward the gravel lane that ran along the houses on this side of the forest.

Merelda chattered somewhere behind me, her wings buzzing extra loud as she fought to keep up, but she wasn't fast enough and the sound soon faded.

I squinted against the setting sun, counting the minutes as it slipped further below the horizon. The unofficial deadline had passed days ago, but the real one could still be met. Bargains had to be made and accepted by the last ray of light and the first footfall of fae along the bridge. I'd thought all four of us would be racing along by now, giggling, with our Bargains tucked in our bags or held carefully in our palms. But instead, it was just me.

At least I was faster this way.

The twisting trunks of the towering paperbark trees faded behind me, white flowers glinting orange in the sun, and up ahead the path forked in two. I took the lower path, crashing beneath drooping branches and thick vines that smelled like honey. Soon, my boots landed in soft soil, and then softer still, until I had to hop from stone to stone to avoid sinking into the mud.

The river ran from the ocean, far, far in the distance, to Stone Lake, where the Lumière would cross the invisible bridge in under an hour. But the Bargains were done here, downstream from the lake, at our altar beneath the water.

We weren't like the larger cities, where magic flowed freely, spilling out from every corner. My Talking Mirror set was an anomaly in Broodshire, and the Village Council hadn't been happy when I'd brought it back from Mosswilde after one of Hayden's business trips.

Not just because I wasn't a Spell Master, and so I couldn't work magic of my own to maintain it. Or even because, as the Offering, I wasn't allowed to have anything remarkable. But because there had always been a resistance to that sort of showy magic in my village.

In the city, magic poured from the witch lanterns that lined the cobblestone streets, gathered in glittering clouds around the Spell Masters' towers, and hummed beneath the wheels of every cart. You couldn't walk two steps in the city without being caught up in a blissful whirlwind of enchantment. Out here in the countryside, with no Order to maintain the spells and only two aging witches located within an hour's ride, we didn't have that luxury. But that didn't mean we had no magic.

It meant the magic we had was older.

Stronger, but more sparse. Rooted in ritual, steeped in danger.

We honored and served that magic, trading in Bargains of prosperity and abundance. And while we bought spells from the Spell Masters in the cities to keep our services running, and indulged the roaming Order when their hearth witches came to peddle their wares, we didn't play with magic for the sake of it.

Perhaps that had been the first way that I'd truly known I was different. Where my neighbors scoffed at human attempts to mimic the fae's command of Aelor's power, I had never been able to get enough of it.

From the very first strass beetle I'd chased down with my sister, its cuticle glowing with hidden magic, I'd wanted everything magical I could get my hands on—gaudy or ancient, I didn't care. I would walk the steps to the underwater altar like the rest of my neighbors and honor our gods for their good fortune, but if someone offered me an enchanted brooch that sang like a nightingale, they'd have to fight me before I'd give it up.

Finally, I reached the stone steps at the edge of the river. Someone had been by recently to scrub them; the cracks in the worn stone were free from even a speck of dirt. Unless that, too, was magic. I paused at the edge, looking around into the shadows. The only sound came from the soft trill of distant birds preparing for the night. The quiet trickle of water against rock.

No other humans were in sight. Everyone who was visiting the circus tonight had been and gone well before now, and it was a rare Bargain that was made outside of the Winter Fairs.

I took a deep breath, let it out slowly, and began to descend. The water lapped at my ankles, folding over my boots and squelching to pool at the bottom of the leather. It soaked the edge of my riding breeches, cropped at mid-calf, and still I kept walking. Deeper, I went, as it rose above my waist and sank into the home-knit sweater I'd thrown on in haste.

I kept walking until only my eyes were left above the surface. In the darkness on the other side of the bank, I swore another pair of eyes were watching me, but I knew from experience that if I were to investigate that shadow, there would be nothing there. My heart pounded in my chest, screaming *danger*. My body trembled with fear. The river water rushed against my nostrils, threatening to invade my lungs the moment I gave in.

For a second, I wanted to.

And then I took the final step and it all cleared away. The river, the trees, the muddy bank. They all vanished, and I was left standing in a cave below the surface of the water.

The air rushed back into my lungs, leaving me gasping as I braced myself on my legs and stared.

"Phew," I muttered into the silence. "Made it."

Well. I made it *here*. That didn't mean I would make it out with my Bargain in time.

Before me, a simple stone altar rose from the cragged rock. The space below the water couldn't be more than four meters across, and yet the presence emanating from that altar was vast. Infinite. A statue rose above it, twisted into formless shapes—an ear, a tail, a wing.

And above my head, the world I'd just left was visible through a flowing stream of water, perfectly poised as if it ran over glass.

The Council said this place was a pocket realm, tucked away somewhere between Aelor and Criera. A hidden dimension, kept separate by the surface of the water.

You only had to step foot in here to believe every word.

I cleared my throat, brought the flat of my palms to my neck, as if choking myself, and bowed. With my fingertips gently pressed against my skin, so the vibrations of my words could be felt through them, I offered the words of prayer.

"In the spirit of fairness and honor, I offer to you a memory of pain, that it may fuel an immortal winter in the passing to spring. In exchange, I ask for entry to the circus of the Lumière, for seven nights, and safe passage home as many times as I will. There is no gate, key, or exit to this offer. Humbly, I wait."

Then I dropped my hands and reached for the box inside my satchel. With the lid open, I paused over the contents. Which memory did I want to trade? My fingers brushed against sepia photographs of Hayden, smiling up at my face behind the camera. Photos of the two of us dancing in a field. A single photo of the wedding dress I'd worn for the briefest of moments.

The photographs fell to the side, revealing older trinkets.

I touched the notebooks full of my private heartsore musings, and the impersonal letters written in response to me begging my sister to come home from the city for my latest achievement. Promotions, recitals, and announcements skimmed past in faded ink, each one barely acknowledged. Sometimes, they weren't acknowledged at all, and simply returned unread.

They were modest accomplishments that the Offering was allowed to have, never greedy or more successful than anyone else, but apparently all that meant was that they were too modest for anyone to care.

My heart clenched, my teeth digging into my lower lip as I flicked past those letters in search of more memories of Hayden. I wasn't here for the rest of my life, only him. A couple of pink rose petals fluttered past; they must have fallen in from last year's prayers.

Which one should I choose? Which one could I *possibly* choose when they all amounted to the same thing? A breakup that never should have made it that far. The naïve hope of a woman who'd never learned to accept her destiny.

Words raced through my mind, swirling faster and faster as I searched.

> *To every generation born*
> *A luckless child of grief and scorn*
> *A Bargain laid, a promise made*
> *Of health and fortune thus repaid*

The first Bargain. The trade that dictated my destiny and all that I would have in this life. If I hadn't been so selfish, if I wasn't seduced by pretty words and faces so badly that I never thought about the consequences, I might have realized the danger of marrying the village's golden boy. Of course, Hayden and I would never last. Of course, our relationship would shatter in the worst way possible.

The Offering had nothing, so that the rest of the village would have everything.

It was a small price to pay, to secure abundance for so many.

I paused, my fingers playing over the top of the papers, fidgeting. Maybe it was wrong of me to trade any of these memories at all. Even though Hayden tore my heart out and left me standing there alone, it was right that he'd done it. It was fair. The fact that I'd let it get that far at all was the problem; he'd only corrected it.

I shouldn't lose these memories. They were a reminder that I was the Offering. That I had a role to play, and that role came with certain responsibilities. Ones I had never taken seriously.

My body moved of its own volition, and before I could think, I threw the entire box down onto the altar.

Immediately, I froze. My heartbeat sounded too loud; what the hell was I thinking? That wasn't a fair trade. That was... wild. Mad.

Stupid. Utterly, utterly stupid.

I caught my breath, searching the shadows for more eyes—teeth, talons.

"Bailey?"

I startled, leaping where I stood, and spun around. But before I could find whichever fae had decided to teach me a lesson for my completely unbalanced Bargain, I recognized the voice.

I looked up, toward the ceiling of running water. On the other side, back on the surface, an elderly man knelt by the river, frowning down into the depths.

"Stefan?" I called as quietly and respectfully as I could, hoping not to disturb the guardians of this place while they were busy deciding my fate.

But I also didn't want my friendly, elderly neighbor walking into the middle of this. It seemed those vines down my path hadn't been strong enough to hide me after all. He tilted his head, looking unnervingly in my direction, as if he could somehow see me through the water. It was impossible. This place was concealed by magic.

"Bailey, what are you doing down there?" Stefan asked urgently. "Compacts aren't until mid-winter."

Our village renewed the fae Bargains that brought us success and prosperity every winter, leaving gifts for the fae and making new trades. Each year, I attended wearing a woven coronet, threaded with the dried, pressed rose petals from my nightly prayers. A symbol of the Offering's sacrifice and continued blessing.

But I'd only attended the Fair to make my own Bargain twice; once, when I needed help academically to get accepted as a research assistant to the only apothecary in town. And a second time, far earlier...

The memory of that time was strangely muddled, but I

supposed I was distracted. Focusing was difficult when the fae were midway through judgment.

"I'll be right out!" I called, fighting to keep my voice calm and gentle, so he didn't do something foolish like try to enter.

The stairs would keep him out—at first. But if he insisted...

I didn't want him to be hurt. I wouldn't want anyone from our village to be hurt like that, but he was one of the few people who actually showed me kindness, even when I forgot myself and shirked my duties.

"Bailey," he insisted, quieter yet more urgent. "You can't trust them. They *lie*."

So does everyone, I thought.

I turned back to the altar. Something had shifted, although I couldn't name what it was. A whisper on the breeze. A scent.

There was a presence in the cave with me, and I knew that if I disrespected it, it would wipe me from this earth like nothing more than a strass beetle.

I slowed my breathing, bowing my head in respect. The light from the setting sun glowed like fire, skimming over the stone floor and shimmering through the refraction of the water. It was almost gone. Only a few lingering rays remained to mark the day.

There must have been only seconds left for my Bargain to be approved.

Above me, I could hear Stefan softly calling; I begged him silently to shut up, and perhaps I had some luck with me this day—or Stefan's luck overrode my ill fortune—because after a few seconds, he did. As I glanced upward, I caught a final glimpse of him, kneeling among the muck, shadowed by the drooping trees. My breath caught. It must have been something to do with the magic separating us, but he didn't look right. It was as though I'd never truly seen him before; his face had become alien and strange.

Was this what fae magic did to us? Was this what I was inviting into my life? A tremble raced through me.

Then a voice spoke, startling me back into the present.

"It is fair. Go, and be blessed."

I almost choked on horrified laughter. Fair? *Fair*? I had to have paid more than five times what anyone else had for entry. Every memory of Hayden, completely undone. But then, as the Offering, perhaps that was my price. Perhaps it was fair.

And I didn't even want the memories. Perhaps they'd taken that into consideration.

Whatever the reason, I caught the laughter in my throat, bowed low to the darkness, and held out my hand. After a moment, a small glass sphere appeared in it, its center glowing softly with a blue flame. It was the Bargain Orb, sealing my trade.

For just a second, as I stared into that flame, I felt a wave of revulsion and fear so strong it nearly sent me to my knees. There was something wrong with this Bargain. I'd given too much, offered too much. And they'd deemed it fair.

It was wrong, wrong, wrong.

But as my fingers folded over the glass, my mind—softened.

For the first time in my life, the tension in my shoulders eased. I straightened, my brow smoothing out, and my heart felt... lighter. I blinked, looking around the cavern as an almost giddy sensation overtook me. I hadn't known what to expect by trading those memories, but I thought there would be an absence of something. A hole. A sense of loss, even if I didn't want what was gone.

But I could still remember them. I could still remember Hayden's touch and my sister's cruelty. Could still remember how he'd looked at me in a way no one should have—like I was a prize he had to win. Something worthwhile. I could still remember all the words I'd scribbled in those notebooks as a teenager. The tear-soaked pages.

But I didn't feel anything. There was no pain, no heartache, no agonizing weight pressing down on my shoulders.

I began to laugh, the sound echoing strangely in the space. Stefan called out again, more urgently this time as the last rays of light faded from the cavern.

"Oh shit," I hissed and raced back up the stairs as darkness finally fell.

Stefan caught me as I stumbled to the surface, the water beading off my skin and leaving me completely dry. He looked the same as I'd always known him this time—kind, quiet, and sincere.

"Bailey," he rasped, the wrinkled furrow of his brow deepening. "What did you do?"

"It's alright," I assured him, clasping his shoulders and trying to soothe his fears. "It's only entry to the circus."

If anything, the worry on his face etched in sharper, harsher. "The Lumière?"

He leaned closer, studying my expression, but I gave nothing away. I never did. Calm, serene, composed—that was me.

"Of course. It's harmless. I didn't trade anything I didn't want to lose, and there were no loopholes. I followed the script perfectly."

But Stefan was shaking his head. "It doesn't matter. You were reckless—that's how they catch you. Recklessness, impulsivity. Thoughtlessness. They'll find a way to use it against you, Bailey. Especially the Lumière. Fae, well, they can be kind or they can be cruel, just like anyone else. But not the Lumière. It's a certain temperament of fae that are drawn there, and they will only be cruel."

A hint of fear bubbled up in my chest, but then I remembered what I had traded. I remembered curling in on myself in bed for days while tears poured down my cheeks, my chest breaking open with pain. I remembered the guilt and shame that had torn through me, knowing that I had brought it all on myself because I wouldn't listen to the warnings that came from all sides.

But instead of falling to my knees from the weight of those images, I watched as if from a distance. I felt no guilt, no shame, no sadness. The memories were visible if I searched, but they were also lost—unreachable in any way that mattered.

Whatever the Lumière did to me, it couldn't be worse than taking them back.

"Well, it's done," I said as gently as I could. "And I have to go, or I'll be late."

Already, the silvery touch of the moon was brightening the river. That glow would carry down the channel until it reached the lake, and then they would arrive. I had to leave now if I wanted to see them arrive on that shimmering invisible bridge.

As I turned to the west, the sound of crashing branches made us both startle. Seconds later, Merelda burst from the trees and rocketed into my neck. She latched on, tiny fingers digging into my skin, and chattered up at me. Apparently, someone else had come to offer their opinions on my bad choices.

"Sorry," I murmured, tugging gently on the foot that dangled from my shoulder in apology. "I had no choice."

She cut off mid sentence, but instead of reacting with her usual anger, she looked sad. Something shifted in my gut, but it was distant and hard to grasp. I remembered that strange sense of wrongness down in the cave, before I'd accepted the Bargain Orb, and my hands flexed by my side.

But just as quickly, that wrongness dissolved and I was left with the strangest feeling: light, airy, almost giddy with possibility. It was probably the adrenaline pumping through my veins, and the relief of having made it in time.

After a beat, Merelda rose and nestled in among my curls, where she liked to hide. I suspected she'd disappear once I reached the circus grounds, darting off into the night to hunt lightning bugs or something. Not much was known about imps, even though they were one of the few fae creatures to migrate across the water and stay here. But while the old scholars hadn't been able to piece together the imp language for me—especially frustrating, given that I was quite good with languages—they had made it clear that imps held no love for the fae.

I glanced at the moon again and pulled away from Stefan, giving him a final pat on the shoulder as I turned to follow the river's path. But to my surprise, he fell into step beside me.

I raised a brow. "What are you doing?"

"Keeping you company, of course," he said in that gruff, kind manner he had. Like he was trying to act pained but couldn't manage it.

Warmth unfolded within me, and for once, there was no accompanying sadness. Someone was showing me a kindness, and there was no hidden cost or ledger to be balanced. I blinked away my surprise, sweeping my hair off my face for something to do. The sensation of gratitude felt utterly new.

Probably because it was.

The giddiness lifted a few notches, as if I were already tipsy off fae wine.

"Just to the entrance, you mean?" I confirmed, rolling my shoulders out and stretching.

Gods, I'd never realized how stiff my body was. Was it always like this? With the light, warm sensation growing, it was impossible to keep holding all that tension, and the sudden release spreading through me was intoxicating.

"Nope. I'm coming in."

My eyebrows flew up. "But you didn't make a Bargain in time." I let my lips quirk into a smile. "I draw the line at lifting you over the fence. They'd probably transform me into a padlock, and I can't handle being door hardware for the next three centuries. I don't have the temperament for it."

He gave a quiet chuckle at my joke, but it faded quickly as something complex crossed his expression. "Sure I did. Years ago—I Bargained my life away to the Lumière, don't you know? I can enter whenever I like." He added quietly, "It's leaving that's the hard part."

Silence stretched between us. All of a sudden, his warnings didn't seem so silly.

"What did you trade?" I asked before I could stop myself.

He gave me a look and said nothing. I let the conversation fall.

Beside us, the silvery thread of moonlight in the water grew brighter. It was as though the moon was leading us to Stone Lake, its reflection slowing until we caught it and then skipping just beyond our reach. Like it knew the fae were coming, and it was telling us to hurry.

We quickened our pace, darting glances at the river and weaving through increasingly thicker vines and trees. Soon, we were running, barely keeping pace with the silvery stream.

And then, we burst out into the clearing by the lake and barrelled to a halt. The shock of returning to civilization made everything appear in sharp contrast. Too loud, too bright. The memories of the underwater altar and its magic began to fade as I stared at the pockets of humans waiting for the fae to arrive. A low hum of anticipation wove through the crowd, and Stefan and I quickly found a spot by the shore to wait.

Even knowing the fae were minutes from arriving, I couldn't look away from the humans; I'd rarely seen so many people in one place. They'd come from several villages over, judging by the differences in clothing and how few faces I recognized. And each person carried a small glass orb, held protectively in the palm of their hand.

None of them appeared to have had the same reckless, terrifying experience I had in obtaining it.

In fact, by contrast, most people were flushed with excitement. Small groups of teenagers giggled and pretended they didn't have flasks concealed in their jackets. Adults passed by in pairs or groups, walking down the middle of the path where the light from the moon's reflection was brightest. The only kinds of people we didn't see were families with young children. No one in their right mind would Bargain for a child to enter, no matter how safe the trade seemed.

As we passed some people from our village, they caught sight of me and stiffened. Their eyes roamed my face, studying it and dismissing it in a single glance. The nearest's lip curled into a familiar sneer—I caught Hayden's name being whispered—and they turned away.

I waited for the tight squeeze of pain in my chest, but it didn't come.

Huh. How odd.

Just as we'd settled in a quiet corner and caught our breath, the last of the racing moonlight flooded into the lake. It spread, rippling out on itself and growing until every edge was alight. The laughter of the crowd hushed, and a sense of exhilaration rose, spreading from one end of the crowd to the other.

I stared across the lake, into the shadows there, my body taut. Would we see them first? Or hear them? Would they appear on the water, or on the other shore?

The fae lived on the other side of the water—*any* water. If it was large enough, and you had the means to cross it, you could reach Criera. I'd heard that in the bigger cities, to the west of the mountains, it was even common to find the fae walking among the people like tourists.

But those were the cities where buildings towered above the ground, taller than trees, and they traded wares with foreign lands. Criera counted itself among such trading countries, and the fae visited through every season, traveling in their glittering boats from across the sea.

Here in the countryside, locked by the mountains in all directions, with our only source of water being the lakes and streams, only the Lumière bothered to visit. This was our one chance to see such raw magic. Something more wondrous and beautiful than the subtle strangeness of the Compact Fairs or the imitation Bargains we humans made among ourselves using the glass shell of the strass beetles.

No one made a sound. No one wanted to miss their arrival.

Anticipation hovered in the air, in the quiet breath of wind. And then, after a few suspenseful seconds, something appeared above the water. Step by step, the boards of a bridge lit up, as if it had been there all along. Lanterns appeared from the gloom, coming closer and closer until the final step met the shore. Beside me, Stefan sucked in a breath.

I glanced at him, concerned by the hint of fear that rang within the sound.

"You know, you really don't have to come," I reminded him, urgency making my voice sharp.

But he merely turned that shrewd gaze my way, sparking another flood of guilt, and shook his head. "As if I would let you come here alone."

A fresh shiver of warmth ran through me, and once more I felt a flicker of surprise when no pain followed. No bitter memories. Just simple, honest kindness. Selfish though it was of me, I could get used to such a thing.

I squeezed his arm again, and together we stepped toward the bridge.

The crowd shuffled in, cautious but eager. A gasp rippled through, traveling from one person to another as the Lumière's magic unfolded before our eyes. Small lanterns caged in metal rose from the earth, sprouting one by one like fast-growing trees. In seconds, they had illuminated a winding pathway that stretched from the bridge to the fairground.

The fairground that hadn't been there before.

Merelda hissed, her claws digging into my earlobe, and launched into the air to fly back the way we'd come. I waved to her, biting my lip to keep from laughing at the middle finger she threw in response.

The crowd whispered louder now, their excitement making them bold, and that's when they appeared.

A troop of glittering fae.

Their pointed ears drew my attention first, but not for long —there was just so much to look at. Their costumes dazzled with a thousand glimmering stones, fabric wrapped tight around lithe, lean muscles. They appeared from the shadows as if they had always been there, as if they'd been poised halfway along the bridge, ready to step free the second the moon's light touched the earth.

Their eyes glittered strangely in the darkness, swallowing the light whole.

My first reaction was fear, but then the shadows faded away, and I didn't know what I'd been afraid of.

They were laughing, dazzling their audience with brilliant smiles and beautiful faces. Welcoming us with wide arms as they danced and strolled and cartwheeled down the illuminated path and into the circus bounds.

I held up my Bargain Orb, marveling at the blue flame inside. With this, I would pass through their gates and experience the wonders of their magic. Just for the joy of it—not for practicality, or fairness.

The center of my orb twisted the bridge and its occupants around, distorting their image into tiny shadows. One shadow stood apart from the rest.

I frowned, lowering the orb to study the solitary figure that had drawn my attention. He had shoulder length dark hair, slightly curled, and was dressed in the same glittering black leggings and loose, flowing shirt as many of the others. And yet, while he stood in the center of the bridge, surrounded on all sides by dancing, acrobatic fae, compared to them, he was still.

Where all the other fae were aiming to be watched, he was watching us.

I tilted my head, studying the lines of his body for a clue as to what he did. Was he the ringmaster? Or the head of the Lumière, perhaps? Why else would he not be performing?

But no, the thickly corded muscle of his arm suggested a performer's strength, and yet he was too quiet compared to the others.

Without warning, he turned. Our eyes met. The air grew still, as if the wind had just vanished and left me behind in a pocket of nothingness. Everything in me stilled as well. This fae... there was something familiar about him... Something I almost recognized, even though I had never seen him before.

His lips parted, as if in surprise, but then the wind returned to catch my hair, blowing it over my face and hiding him.

By the time I'd shoved it back, he'd turned away.

When the last of them brushed past us, I let out a breath for the first time in what felt like minutes, my lungs suddenly heaving in fresh air. Beside me, Stefan was shaking his head, eyes wide.

"Bloody hell," he muttered under his breath, scrubbing a hand over his mustache. He took a deep breath, raising his eyebrows at me as he gestured to the fairground gates, lined on either side with torches. "Well, then... Shall we?"

But before I could leave, he reached out to clasp my shoulder, making me halt in the middle of the path.

His expression was unusually serious as he said, "I know why you did it, Bailey. I know what you traded."

My stomach jolted, and a brief note of pain soared within me. But it was only an echo of a memory I no longer had, easily forgotten.

"It hurts to be left out in the cold," he continued, his words threatening to slice me open anew. "It hurts to be unwanted. But being wanted is no picnic, either. Just look at the Lumière. They want you. They'd snatch up every human here in a heartbeat if they could. Their desire to own us knows no limit." The pressure of his fingers deepened, painful now. "It doesn't matter who wants you; what matters is what *you* want, Bailey. You're allowed to want things of your own. You're allowed to get them. Try to remember that."

All my life, I'd been told the opposite. The Offering couldn't want things, couldn't have desires or ambitions or skills. That was the whole point—we had nothing, so that the others in the village would have everything. One child's loss for all to gain. And if the Offering ever failed, ever took something that wasn't hers to take... Well, death would be kinder than what awaited those caught in the crossfire.

It was a fair trade. Beyond fair, when you considered how our small village had prospered for generations. But Stefan hadn't grown up in our village. He didn't understand.

Still, I didn't want to argue, so I simply laid my hand over his and squeezed, smiling. Reluctantly, he dropped his hand back to his side.

"I'll be okay, I promise," I said.

For a moment, the sense of wrongness I'd felt at the altar as

I made my Bargain returned. It felt like a tidal wave when it should only be a ripple. Too much. Too strong.

On reflex, I lifted my hand to my throat, where the Offering necklace lay.

It wasn't there.

My eyes widened. In my haste to leave, I'd forgotten to put it on. Holding my breath, I waited for the rush of grief and guilt to hit me. I couldn't forget the necklace; it kept me in line. It was *vital*.

But the wave of guilt never came. Instead, the sense of wrongness faded, as did every memory of guilt or grief that I'd ever had. They shimmered, dissolving in patches until the memories were there but so distorted they had no meaning.

There was only joy. Possibility. A lightness of being that was as foreign as it was addicting.

I lowered my hand to my side, and felt, for maybe the first time in my life, as though I were free.

From the look on Stefan's face, he wasn't happy with my answer. But it didn't matter; ultimately, there was only one truth. I couldn't want things, and nobody would ever want me. Not even the Lumière. I'd forgotten that once, forgotten my place, but I wouldn't again.

It was strange, but, as I walked toward the gates without the pain of Hayden's memories weighing me down, that thought didn't even hurt.

CHAPTER 3

Bailey

WE JOINED THE QUEUE FOR THE GATES, AND IT DIDN'T TAKE LONG before we were standing before a long-haired, glittering fae. She regarded me with bright eyes—too bright, too interested in the humans before her. As if she caught my thought, she burst into laughter.

With jittery movements, I placed the Bargain Orb into her outstretched hand. She held it before her, examining it from all angles. The light from the blue flame within cast strange shadows over her face, deeper and darker than those stretching from the willow trees along the lake shore. After what felt like an eternity, she glanced at me, her expression unreadable as she seemingly took in every feature on my face.

Too much. Too strong.

An echo of something forgotten stabbed through my chest, making me wince. But it faded so quickly, it took all memory with it. I rubbed dully at my sternum, wondering what had just happened.

Beside me, Stefan had grown very still, his affectionate grip on my arm now clenching hard enough to hurt.

Then, the fae smiled and twisted her hand; the orb vanished.

"Welcome to the Lumière," she said in a musical voice.

She turned to Stefan and held out her hand, only to freeze halfway through the motion. The smile curved on her face once more, but this time, it was distinctly predatory.

"And welcome back to you," she purred, a vicious gleam in her eye that made me wonder once again what the hell Stefan had traded for lifetime entry.

And why.

Before I could ask, he softened his grip and whirled us through the gates and into the circus grounds.

It was like entering a whole other world. I forgot the murky, dangerous path that had led us here, and simply stared around in awe. More lanterns sprouted from the ground, covering the fair from one end to the other, and dotted between them were strings of lights that connected like a golden web. Except I couldn't see any string; the lights were simply floating.

I turned in a slow circle, admiring the moody shadows and silvery dapple of moonlight among the lanterns. The fairground was encircled by streamers, and if memory served, no fae were allowed to leave that circle. Neither were any new humans allowed to enter after tonight. Any section of the fairground that didn't butt up against impenetrable forest was clothed in fabric, like a curtain. A curtain that I had no doubt would strangle any attempted visitors who had not paid their way.

Returning to the center, I gazed out over the grounds, taking in the finer details now I'd adjusted to the magic. I was used to human circus tents, with their inelegant red and white stripes, but the Lumière was something different altogether. Deep emerald fabric stretched well above our heads, with silver thread woven through in a dozen occult symbols I didn't recognize. They could have meant anything. They could have been ritual sigils designed to trap us here forever and we'd be none the wiser, us foolish humans ensnared in their web.

A laugh bubbled free at the thought. This world was like nothing I'd ever seen. So new, so raw.

So magical.

Best of all, with such a mix of villagers in the crowd, no one knew me. I could be anyone here. I could have anything. I could *live* and no one would stop me.

I wasn't sure why, but that thought filled me until I could think of nothing else—wanted nothing else.

A soft sound fell from my lips, almost incredulous. From the corner of my eye, I saw Stefan turn in surprise before giving me a warm smile. I took another step further in, and another, losing myself as the music began to echo over our heads—a lilting melody played on something similar to a lute. It both relaxed and invigorated me, filling me with the need to move, to dance. To take one of the cups that were appearing out of thin air and drink and drink, losing myself for the night.

I blinked as my fingers closed of their own volition around a silver cup hovering in the air beside me. The liquid inside smelled delicious, but I didn't remember deciding to drink it. Pausing for only a beat, I shrugged and took a sip.

It tasted exactly as it smelled, and the last of my nerves faded away.

Arm in arm, we began to roam. I sipped from my silver cup every few steps, but Stefan never accepted one. Instead, he kept his stern, kind gaze fixed on me and our surroundings, watching for danger. But with each step we took, I became more convinced there wasn't any.

Just like on the bridge, there was so much to look at, it was easy to get lost. Golden butterflies flew past our heads, morphing into tiny dragons as we watched. I was only ninety percent sure they were all illusions. Every corner was filled with a dazzling performance—smoke and mirrors, light and magic. Magnificent acrobatic feats, and exhilarating displays of swordsmanship and magic.

The drink in my hands was tasty and light, the air was touched with a crisp autumn breeze, and the crowd around me was full of laughter. I'd never been so carefree.

I'd traded terrible memories and insurmountable pain to get in here, and I'd never have to hold them again. Warmth bubbled within me as another chunk of memory faded into the distance, almost completely out of reach.

Something good was going to happen tonight; I could feel it.

"Where to first?" Stefan asked after we'd made a meandering circuit of the fairground.

"Hmm," I tapped my finger on my lower lip, rising on my toes to glance over the heads of the crowd.

Strange noises hovered by my ear, like physical creatures, whispering words that sounded like my own thoughts. Soft, crooning caresses that promised me everything I craved. I closed my eyes and let the desire wash over me, filling me from head to toe.

Something about the words felt strange. As though they were coming from a place two steps to the left of where they should have been.

I squinted, tilting my head and trying to hold the words in my mind long enough to make sense of. Were they a different language? I knew they were offering me what I desired, but... I couldn't hear what they were saying. Even if they were speaking in the fae tongue, that shouldn't have mattered to me. I'd spent long enough in my own company, pouring over translations and books written in Criari until they made sense. Another language was no barrier.

An echo of sensation flooded my chest, followed by a wave

of want so deep I staggered. But I didn't know what I wanted. It was like my body remembered, but I didn't—or perhaps couldn't.

The smile on my face faltered.

One of the performers, busy juggling beads of water, glanced my way. He never stopped juggling, but his gaze was fixed on me, his eyes appearing eerily dark in the shadow. Too dark.

"I can hear a siren singing," Stefan said, brow furrowing as he stared into the distance. "Likely performing a ballad where the audience become the unwitting clowns who act it out."

I squinted at the fae juggler, but the shadows were too thick for me to understand what I was looking at. What was it about his face that looked wrong?

Was his glamor lifting?

As the seven nights wore on, the fae's faces would shift. Their glamors would fade until we caught more and more glimpses of their true faces hidden beneath. Rumor said that those hidden faces were cruel. Full of gleeful malice that revealed the wearer's true intentions.

Any foolish human caught lingering after the final dance of the closing festival, when those faces appeared, would run the risk of becoming ensnared in the worst kind of Bargain. Perhaps this was the warning: a glimpse of the faces hiding beneath the glamor, and a hint of what was to come.

But I shouldn't be seeing that so soon, on the first night.

Maybe it was just the siren song, like Stefan said. It had muddled my thoughts, ready to enchant me, and this fae was waiting for the show to start. There was no need to be frightened.

As my thoughts eased, the fae turned back to his crowd, laughing brightly as he threw the balls above their heads and around again, calling them back to him with ease. Light bathed his face, catching on his green eyes. I hovered on the edge of his circle, searching for a sign of those coal-edged irises, but they weren't there.

"Let's go the other way," I said to Stefan, shaking off the odd experience. "Away from the siren."

My smile widened again. The night was young, and I was untouchable. I'd never been hurt or rejected in my life—all was well.

We began browsing the smaller tents that dotted among the large performance spaces like glittering jewels. I paused at one by my right, its sweetly scented smoke curling free and forming shapes before my eyes.

The smoke settled in the air, roughly a foot before my face, and twisted into a canopy of trees. I stared, spellbound, as the trees moved to the side, parting as if I were running through them. It wasn't just an illusion; I could feel the cold depths of the forest and the breeze on my skin.

They shifted, moving faster and faster until my stomach was churning, my heart racing as if I really were on a mad dash through the forest. And then—

Eyes, glowing in the darkness.

I yelped and staggered backward, catching myself on Stefan's shoulder to remain upright. The eyes disappeared with a flash of laughter, the smokey trees collapsing and fading away.

I stared as the sign behind the smoke became slowly clear.

No humans after midnight, on pain of death.

Pain of death. Huh.

In my experience, there were things in this life that hurt far more than death.

I froze. Where had that thought come from? As quickly as it appeared, it was already fading. The sign swayed in the gentle night breeze, glinting as the moonlight caught on its ominous words. An unfamiliar sensation stirred in my gut, spilling outward as I read the message again and again. It was heavy, like sand, and sharp as a knife between my shoulder blades.

I thought it might be a memory—once intrinsic to every breath I took. Now, out of reach.

For a long moment, I didn't move. I barely breathed.

This sign wasn't personal; it was directed to every human here, and yet... the harshness of it struck me in a way that didn't just threaten my joyful thoughts; it pierced them right through, popping a bubble I hadn't even noticed was there.

You don't belong.

You aren't welcome.

A bitter taste thickened on my tongue, and I wondered at the unfamiliar feeling that still swirled in my stomach. Distant memories churned, oddly numb no matter how much I poked them. I chewed on my lip, trying to recapture the light, joyful sensation I'd had since we first entered the carnival.

It returned as soon as I recalled it, and the memories that had threatened to overwhelm me became like dreams.

Humming, I shook my head to clear the fog of my thoughts and turned away from the sign.

Only to find I once again had an audience, only this time, it wasn't made of smoke. Every fae in a five meter radius was staring at me. Pitch black eyes, eyes tinted red, eyes that glowed in the darkness... All were watching me, and not one of them looked harmless.

Terror surged, mixing horrifyingly with the rising swell of joy that wouldn't be quenched. What was happening?

What had I forgotten?

Something important. Something vital. I couldn't trust these faces, but I couldn't hold on to my slippery thoughts long enough to know who I *could* trust.

In a moment of vulnerability, it felt like no one.

I grabbed Stefan's elbow and led him through the crowd, away from those faces. My heart hammered in my chest, and yet I still had the impulse to laugh. To grab another silver goblet from the air and drink my problems away.

"What's happened?" he asked, his voice low and urgent.

"I'm not sure." I wove us through the crowd, toward the entrance. I wasn't sure yet if we should leave, but I wanted the gates in sight, just in case. "Something isn't right."

He glanced at me, studying my face silently. "We're leaving then," he said, a gruff note entering his voice. I'd never heard him sound like that before.

"Maybe," I hedged.

"Yes."

Pursing my lips, I looked at him sideways. The furrow of his rough, gray eyebrows deepened.

"Fine," I hissed. "But you owe me a really impressive back-bend if you're going to make me miss the contortionist on the posters."

Stefan barked a laugh but wasted no time bee-lining for the gates.

Even though part of me still resisted, I knew leaving was the smartest choice. I'd made a good Bargain—given away something I hated, even if I couldn't remember what that was—seen the sights, and enjoyed more than my share of fae wine. Maybe it was foolish to ask for anything more.

The exit appeared before us, its finely wrought archway glittering in the light of the bulbs strung above. We quickened our pace, maneuvering around the final performance space between us and freedom—the archers, who were shooting arrows at increasingly smaller targets and clearly didn't give two hoots about what was happening outside of the bullseye.

Until, it seemed, the bullseye changed.

A tall fae with long, straight auburn hair stepped before us, smiling with false charm as he swept a low bow and held out his hand to me.

"Just in time, my lady," he called, loud enough for the crowd to turn. "We are accepting volunteers."

"But I didn't—" I began, but he was already leading me to the stage.

Stefan's protest rang out across the crowd, but the sound was cut short. I whirled around, dragged backward by my elbow for several steps as the fae refused to let go, but Stefan was still standing. He glared mutely at the fae woman before him, but he was standing.

The threat that he may not be if I didn't comply was heard loud and clear.

Meekly, I followed the fae male to the stage and stood in the center. Most of the archers lounged against the barrier at the other end, all lazy arrogance and grace.

All of them looked hungry.

"Gather round, dear friends," the one who'd grabbed me called, parading up and down the stage as assistants scurried behind him to remove the targets.

They did not replace them.

"Who among you would like to see a *real* display of skill?" He turned to me as the final words resounded through the audience, his eyes glinting.

The iris was completely gone, leaving only black in its wake.

The crowd went wild. Spurred on by drink and awe, they cheered so loudly that I had to cover my ears. Walking slowly now, almost predatory, the fae returned to me and halted face to face.

"Arms up," he said, his voice a low purr.

My heart pounded like crazy, and every instinct told me to run. More than that—there was a feeling in my gut, the same feeling that had been burning all evening, that told me something was missing. Some warning system, or piece of knowledge that would tell me how to navigate this threat. But it was only a dull ache, its details lost to forgotten memory, and I had no path but forward.

I lifted my hands. He bound them quickly to the leather cuffs held at shoulder height. The position was docile enough that I looked vulnerable and scared; not enough that it became obscene. The Lumière had this down to an art. Just before he stepped back, he leaned in, and I swear to the gods he was smelling me.

I waited for him to stick an apple on my head, silently praying it was a big one.

Instead, he balanced a coin.

My mouth fell open. The movement was sharp enough that I felt the cool disc on my head slip over and land flat. The fae *tsked* me, reaching out to adjust the coin once more. It remained upright by some piece of magic, but the magic only aided it. If I moved. If I breathed... The coin would fall.

What would the archers aim for then?

A hush spread over the crowd as the fae stepped back. Several of them squinted, struggling to even see the target atop my head. The fear in my chest began to spiral. I couldn't do this. I'd been an idiot to make that Bargain tonight; something was wrong with it. And I couldn't even remember what the damned thing was to fix it.

The fae had been onto my mistake from the moment I stepped through the arch. They were making me pay for what I'd traded, and I hadn't even seen it coming because something had been taken from me. Something that kept me on my toes, alert to danger. It was gone, and without it, I'd walked right into the open maw of the beast.

Frantically, I scanned the crowd for a familiar face. Someone who might help me. Stefan hovered at the back, his expression anguished as he spoke quickly and desperately to the fae woman beside him. Whatever he was saying wasn't working, and I wouldn't risk him further by letting him know how frightened I was. I kept searching.

There, at the front: Anameya and Gertrude. Two women who frequently bought their tinctures from the apothecary.

I didn't dare call out in case the coin fell, but maybe if they knew I was in trouble, they could make a distraction. Wetting my suddenly dry lips, I widened my eyes at them, silently pleading for them to understand me. Anameya caught my eye and blinked, clearly surprised.

Then she turned away.

My heart sank as the two of them whispered together. Gertrude laughed quietly and looked my way, but whatever desperation shone on my face—and I knew it was there—it wasn't enough to persuade her to act.

And why would it? I was exactly where I was supposed to be, getting the raw end of the deal every time, so that they might enjoy the circus without fear.

The thought slipped away as soon as I had it—a distant memory without any details—but it couldn't hide the feeling any longer. The tidal wave surged, and even though I couldn't remember why, I knew that it was a wave of pain.

The hot prick of tears threatened the corner of my eyes, and I wondered how long it had been since I let myself cry.

At the other end of the space, the archers nocked their arrows. My handler muttered something from the side of the platform to another fae—whispering in Criari.

"Her scent will be stronger once she bleeds. We'll know then."

My breath caught, even as I stilled my expression so no one knew I understood their words. It wasn't common to speak fae. Truthfully, I'd never met anyone else who could. But then, no one else had been blessed with quite as much time alone in their childhood as I had been, and I had been desperate to talk to someone. Anyone. Even if they were only foreign words on a page, prattled into forest clearings that didn't talk back.

Why had I been so desperate? I wondered, frowning as the memory drifted out of reach.

I waited for the fae to speak again, but he said nothing more, and their conversation hadn't given me anything I could use against them. This was the end, then.

I forced my eyes to remain open so I could at least say I'd faced down my defeat.

"Hold up," a lazy, arrogant voice called from the opposite side of the stage, and then a new fae stepped into view.

He was tall, with flowing blond hair that fell just a little too long to be called short, although it was still above his shoulders. As it shifted in the wind, I caught sight of a beautiful silver and blue earring dangling from his right ear. He wore the emerald jacket of the entrance fae, who guided visitors into the tents and performance spaces.

When he reached the top of the platform, his bright blue eyes fixed upon me, but for once, there was no hint of a broken glamor. No dark sclera, no glowing red irises. He was simply fae—charming and exciting, like all the other dozen performers we'd seen leaping along the bridge.

One corner of his mouth crooked into a grin as he stepped casually between me and the archers. "I'm afraid the lady has an appointment."

With a twist of his hand, the leather cuffs opened. My hands dropped to my sides, and I practically ran from the wall, stopping only because he was in the way of the stairs.

The fae who'd snatched me leaped the stairs in one bound, coming nose to nose with the newcomer. His pretty face twisted into a snarl. "*Listen here*," he muttered in Criari, lifting an arrow from the quiver by the stage and waving it beneath the new fae's chin. To the audience it must almost look playful. Theatrical. I knew better. *"You can't ruin the show. Heillon will have your head."*

"Oh, that?" the fae asked cheerfully. "I'm sure you'll think of something."

He pressed a finger against the point of the arrow and pushed it slowly, deliberately aside. Despite the drop of blood that welled on his skin, he didn't flinch.

From this angle, I couldn't see his face, and neither could the audience. But whatever expression was written there stopped the other fae in his tracks. He swallowed, and then turned and barked an order at the others. Before he'd even finished speaking, he threw his hand toward the sky, and a mighty dragon made of light and darkness erupted from his fist.

The crowd screamed, ducking for cover as the dragon roared and breathed its fire skyward, singing the treetops. The archers took aim as my previous captor leaped to the center of the stage and cried out: "A terrified damsel, a valiant rescue, and now—"

The archers let loose, piercing the lightning flesh of the beast and sending its neck arching back in pain.

"A daring defeat," the announcer finished, sweeping forward into a bow as the dragon burst into stars, each one cascading down into the now cheering crowd.

In the chaos, the fae with jewels in his ears took me gently by the elbow and whisked me away.

CHAPTER 4

Bailey

WE WOVE THROUGH THE CROWD, LEAVING BOTH THE ARCHERS AND THE exit behind us. The fae only turned to look at me once, remaining silent throughout his assessment. In that brief moment, the glittering lights made the blue of his eyes look like jewels of their own.

Finally, we paused before a tent. The absence of a guard at the door made me think it must be his own abandoned post. Which begged the question—why had he abandoned it?

He regarded me, one arm propped against the silver pole at the entrance. "You," he said softly, after a pause that lasted approximately five thousand years, "have been very foolish."

In the face of his sheer arrogance, I forgot to be scared.

"Excuse me?" I asked, gaping at him.

He shrugged one shoulder. "You're excused, just don't do it again."

Was it possible to pop a blood vessel after sharing ten words with someone? "Do *what* exactly?"

The casual air faded, and the fae's eyes narrowed as he pushed off the pole and leant into my space. "Bargain your gods damned life away for a circus ticket," he hissed. "You've stunk out the whole grounds with your deal. I'm shocked they hadn't already taken you."

My breath caught. "Taken me?"

"Yes," he said, gentler now, though still with a bite of anger. "I suspect the only thing that saved you was the fact they couldn't quite believe their luck and had to prove it before they pounced."

Prove it?

Oh—the blood. They'd wanted to make me bleed, so they could smell me better. I shuddered.

"Okay, well…" I trailed off, looking over my shoulder. No one was watching us—yet. "I'll leave then."

"It won't save you."

The ice cold sensation of fear slid down my throat. "Why not?"

"The Bargain has been made, and you gave into our possession the key to your downfall." The fae's eyebrow quirked upward, telling me without words this time that I'd been a complete idiot. "Never give someone the means to destroy you," he said quietly. "Surely that's obvious, whether you're dealing with the fae or a human."

"The means to destroy me?" I asked, my brow furrowing. "I don't know what you're talking about. I only Bargained a handful of memories away. It was unfair, I know, but not for *you*. I got the better end of that deal by far!"

I didn't need the pitying expression on his face to know I was wrong; I could feel it. I'd known it since I walked through the gates.

My thoughts threatened to slip away, replaced by the now-familiar, intoxicating swell of joy. I was meant to forget. I'd Bargained for it. The joy would lead me deeper into the wondrous circus of the Lumière, and all that remained was for the memories I'd given up to drift out of reach.

I didn't let them. I clung to those forgotten memories—to the sign threatening death for the unwelcome, to Anameya and Gertrude, who had laughed and turned away when I needed them most. I clung to the hurt that threatened to drown me, and I didn't let go.

As the ache of discomfort churned within my bones, determined to make me forget it had ever existed, I finally put words to the wrongness I'd sensed while standing before the altar: I'd given away more than my memories of Hayden. I'd given away everything. Anger. Terror. Grief. Memories I hadn't even known were hurting me, all twisted up in the words of my diary, the letters returned unanswered by my sister.

I hadn't given away Hayden; I'd given away my pain. All of it.

And yet...

"If the pain is gone, why does it still hurt?"

My voice sounded completely incongruent to the utter desperation I felt. Outwardly, I sounded bored, my expression no doubt fixed into its usual unreadable stillness. Inwardly, I was coming apart at the seams.

The fae tilted his head to the side, thinking. "In what way does it hurt?"

"It's like—" I broke off, picturing that tidal wave of wrongness that had threatened to drown me ever since I made the Bargain. "I get the feeling of it, but none of the memories. And yet, most of the time, there's nothing there at all. It's like... I'm floating. Giddy." As I described it, I realized how true it was. I'd been in pain, and now I wasn't—the statement was so simple, but the effect was astronomical. "And then suddenly it will slam into me." I took a deep breath. "But I don't see it coming, or even understand it. I can't."

His expression flickered. "You offered a memory of pain,

didn't you? Rather than the feeling itself," the fae said, his voice oddly gentle.

"Of course." I drew myself up, jaw tight. "How could I let it go if I still remembered every horrible detail?"

The pity in his expression deepened. "The old pain is gone, yes, but the knife is still stuck in the wound. And where your memories once gave you a map to avoid fresh pain, you're now walking blind. Every time something triggers that wound, the knife twists in a little deeper."

A knife stuck in a wound... The sign from earlier flashed into my mind. No humans allowed after midnight on pain of death.

You aren't welcome here.

Was that pain? I'd always just called it fact. Truth. Life.

There was a word... one that was slipperier than all the rest... A kaleidoscope of memory spun through my mind, and I reached into the center of the whirlpool and plucked that word free.

Offering.

I flinched, my teeth grinding together as I turned away and leant against the silver tent pole.

"This is how it will be used against you," he continued, relentless even in his softness. "A knife twisted in where you will never see it coming until step by step they walk you off the edge of a cliff. You have to take the memories back."

I startled, coming awake from the fog. "I don't want them back."

I hadn't meant to say the words. They just slipped out, bringing an echo of that lost hurt with them, broken and raw. The fae's expression stilled, his bright blue eyes seeming once more to glitter like jewels.

"There is more than one way to get what you want," he murmured. "Whatever you gained by losing this pain, there will be another way to obtain it."

I couldn't stop the bitter laugh that escaped me. My words turned caustic, fear making me wilder than I should be. "Sorry to disappoint, but humans live much simpler lives than your twisted riddles suggest. There was pain; now it's gone. I don't want it back. End of story."

A flash of what I swore was interest crossed his face. I pressed my lips tightly shut.

After a beat, the fae said, "Are you sure there's nothing else you want?"

"Of course I'm—" I broke off. He was fae—an expert in deals and desires. Did he know something he wasn't telling?

What was he offering?

"Tell me about it," the fae said persuasively, startling me. I'd almost forgotten he was there. "Perhaps I can help."

I rocked back on my heels, studying him cautiously. Tell him about the hurt I carried... like that was something I could just do. Like it was something I even understood.

Perhaps he could help me understand. I opened my mouth to form the words, but—they didn't come. I didn't want them to. If what he said was true, then I was like the girl from the fairytale, Ashonwy, who danced with the prince until midnight, when her dress turned back into the vines of a pumpkin and her painful reality smacked her in the face.

If this night was to become the forgotten memory, I wanted it to last as long as it could.

"Or not." He held up his hands in easy placation, studying my face as if he could read all the answers from it. "But you have to acknowledge the truth in what I'm saying. You can't keep this Bargain. They'll destroy you."

"Gods above," I muttered, gritting my teeth. Tonight, my reality had spun itself around, shattered into a thousand pieces, and then landed on its head for good measure. But before I could make sense of that, I had to get out of this mess. "Okay, fine. Shit. I'll just—" I broke off.

What would I do? Broker a new deal in return for my lost memories?

Even if the cavern's guardian agreed, it was like the fae had said: I'd given them the key to my downfall. They knew what made me tick. What made me fall.

They owned me, and they would use it against me.

"Make a Bargain with me."

The low, lazy drawl snapped me out of my spiraling thoughts. I looked up to find him watching me, only this time the humor was gone.

"What?"

He held out his hand, and in the center was the orb I'd traded for entry. It looked exactly as all the others did, but this one called to me. I could feel the soft, familiar hum of my memories inside.

"They haven't been processed yet," he said. "That's why you can still find the memories if you try. There's time to make a new deal."

Not once did he so much as glance at the glass sphere in his palm. If he did, he would catch glimpses of the Bargain inside, and if he looked for longer than a glimpse, he would be able to watch my memories play out in crystal clarity.

"But I'm not at the altar," I began, but the fae was already shaking his head.

"The altar bridges the gap between human and fae." With a curl of his lips, he reached out and let his hand hover just above my arm, where he'd held me earlier. I could feel the warmth from his near touch. Eyes fixed to mine, he let his palm rise along the length of my arm, never closer than an inch. He traced the line of my shoulder up to my neck, then withdrew. "No need to do that now."

I could Bargain with him, and he'd give back the original orb before anyone saw it. There would be no more fae hunting me down, no more threatening smiles or hungry looks...

Only pain.

But it was pain I'd held for nearly thirty years without crumbling, apparently. Besides, as much as it killed me to take it back, the other option was death. Or worse.

"What's the catch?"

His smile deepened. "Not so foolish after all, perhaps." He chewed his bottom lip, studying me, even though I was sure he already knew exactly what he wanted. "I'm offering an Open Bargain."

"What's that?" I asked, frowning.

"You don't pay me now. You pay me later."

My stomach dropped. "No deal."

There were a handful of rules when it came to dealing with the fae, and the first among them was to never say thank you. It indebted you to whoever you thanked, and they could ask you for anything in return. This Open Bargain sounded far too close to that.

He held up his hand, his voice lowering once more to that lazy drawl. "Hear me out. If you walk away, every single fae in this fairground is going to hunt you down before the night is over, and by the time dawn rises, they'll have worked out a way to use what you've given freely to own you. Body and soul."

I swallowed. He wasn't finished.

"And since that Bargain is sealed, there are no rules. One of us will use you, and then another will take over, do you understand? This is not a give and take. You gave us your pain, and the possibilities for what we can do with that are endless."

As he spoke, an illusion of light twisted into existence: a knife, buried deep in someone's chest, just as I'd imagined earlier. Hands emerged from the darkness, clasping the hilt and twisting. Many, many hands. The illusion vanished in a puff of smoke.

Hopelessness swirled low in my gut, spurned on by the hoarse sincerity in his voice.

"But if you trade with me now, before anyone sees precisely what this Bargain holds..." He held up the orb, still without looking at it. "Then all we know is that you are hurt." He smiled bitterly. "And who in this life isn't?"

They wouldn't know the source. Wouldn't be able to use it against me. He was offering me that—he would give back my Bargain without ever looking at it.

"And what will you trade me in return?" I asked, forcing my voice to remain steady.

"A simple Bargain. Seven nights entry in exchange for one word from you—to be uttered when I call for it."

"What word?" I asked slowly. It would have to be 'yes', or something equally insidious. Possibly even 'thanks'.

"My name."

Around us, I could hear the fairground full of chattering people, but it was as though they were at a distance. We were separate from that world, caught in a bubble together where nothing made sense.

"Your name," I repeated.

"That's it." He spread his hands wide. "When I ask you to, simply say my name and the Bargain will be concluded."

I stared at him. There were still so many ways that could be used against me. He could ask me to say his name as an answer in a new Bargain—like, perhaps, 'to whom will you give all your money and undying servitude forevermore?' and I'd be bound to answer 'him'.

And yet... there was so much freedom within this Bargain. Because I could answer his name and then add caveats. I could say 'Him, so long as he hand-picks me a thousand bluebells every seven-day for the rest of our lives'. And then we'd be caught in some kind of stalemate, where he had to waste every daylight hour picking bluebells or let me go.

That, or we'd drown in flowers, I supposed.

But either way... there was room within it to breathe. To have a little control.

And there was no room within my current Bargain. It was sealed. Concluded. And, apparently, the worst possible thing I could ever have traded.

I opened my mouth to answer, but he cut me off. "You haven't yet heard the catch, only the terms."

His eyes glinted, but oddly, I was almost relieved. It seemed too easy so far, but if there was more to it, maybe I could trust him.

"Of course I haven't," I said dryly. "Out with it then."

"Fae will be able to sense there is something wrong with your Bargain, and if they find out that it has been left open, they can use that to step within the confines of the magic. It will mean they can ask you for anything, and you will have to give it to them, the same as if you had thanked them," he said, his gaze holding me captive.

My heart sank. I was right; this *was* the same kind of folly, all wrapped up in a glittering bow. He was wasting my time.

"How is that any different from now?" I snapped, casting a glance over my shoulder.

I should have run; my chance to escape was slipping through my fingers. Where in the hells was Stefan?

"It's entirely different, because now, they can sniff out exactly what you've done, and all they need to do is get their hands on this"—he waved the orb—"to control you. But with an open Bargain, no fae can know what you've done unless you tell them; the magic is hidden. The Bargain Magic protects you until the debt is paid."

My nose wrinkled, all the tricks and clauses of their world looping around and tangling in my head. I supposed what he was describing did sound safer. Barely, but enough.

An open Bargain wasn't like the danger of thanking a fae, or of trading something as potentially destructive as the memories of my painful life. It was wild—utter madness. But if I didn't take it, I was already lost.

"No fae will be able to guess or discover the Bargain is open by any means?" I confirmed.

The fae shook his head. "They might try to get the answer out of you, but so long as you keep your mouth shut, you'll be safe." He raised an eyebrow. "And what's life without a little risk?"

A shiver raced down my spine. Something darkened in his gaze, but he didn't move, didn't push.

All I had to do was keep my mouth shut and my wits about me when the time came to pay. I may not have been very smart, but I could do that much.

"It's a deal." I held out my hand.

The fae took it, his palm warm as he clasped mine in a firm caress. When he lifted his hands to his throat in supplication for the Bargain, he didn't let go.

I felt the vibration of his words through the tips of my fingers, unable to keep from shivering at the intimacy of the gesture.

"In the spirit of fairness and honor," he intoned quietly, eyes fixed to mine. "I offer to you seven nights entry to the circus of the Lumière, and safe passage home as many times as you will. In open exchange, I ask for my name to be uttered a single time at my request. There is no gate, key, or exit to this offer. Humbly, I wait."

My breath caught. Two Bargains in one night; Merelda was going to skin me alive. And once again, I'd made them with no gate, key, or exit that would let me break the Bargain early. They were only used in the larger deals, where more than a memory or two was at stake, so it should have relieved me. It really didn't.

Taking a breath, I said with a steady voice, "It is fair. Go, and be blessed."

His lip twitched as he lowered our joined hands from his collarbone and let go. Then, in a sleight of hand gesture, he slid the orb into my palm and folded my fingers over it. Only then did he look down at it, watching as I took the concealed orb and slid it into my pocket.

"Shatter it in privacy," he said. "All that was lost will be returned."

"Noted," I answered, a touch breathless.

The look he gave me had my mind racing in ways it shouldn't. I'd sworn off men; I knew that much, even though the memories wouldn't hold still for long enough that I could understand why. I shouldn't be noticing the way his hair fell around his face, softening it. Or the quiet glint of amusement in his eyes—even, possibly, of attraction. I shouldn't feel my body betraying me, leaning toward him, tingling from head to toe at the first hint that a man might be interested.

I chewed on my lip, studying the sharp lines of his features and the soft pout of his mouth. Even without my full memories, I knew I was a sucker for a pretty face. That I fell for men who said all the right things, and then did all the wrong ones. If it had caused me even a fraction of the pain I'd given up tonight, then it was time I broke the pattern.

But then, he wasn't a man.

I forced myself back to the present—to what mattered— and left the rest behind. "What *is* your name, by the way?"

The fae grinned, bright white teeth gleaming in the darkness. "Fynn."

"I'm—"

"There you are!" Stefan's breathless wheeze from beside me had me turning in a wild mixture of panic and relief. "I thought they'd taken you."

I clasped his hands, running my thumb soothingly over his knuckles. "I'm right here. Everything's fine."

He straightened, eyeing Fynn suspiciously. But before he could ask any questions, Fynn stepped back and gestured toward the tent opening.

"I was just telling the lovely lady that I think this performance will be *just* what she's craving."

I tilted my head, wondering if it was a complete lie to soothe Stefan, or if he really did want me to see this one. It almost sounded like he did.

"Well," I said, trying to mask the shakiness of my voice. "I could do with sitting down for a minute, that's for sure."

Stefan gave me a piercing look, but I could see from his own unease that he needed to rest as well. We'd watch the show and then leave. It would give the fae who'd been hunting me time to back off, and hopefully we could slip out unnoticed.

"If you're sure," Stefan agreed, nodding firmly.

"The night is still young," Fynn insisted in a voice pitched low enough that only I could hear. "Enjoy one final gift for your foolishness." He lowered his voice to a whisper. "See what you could become if you found another way."

I blinked at him. One final gift?

A wave of exhaustion hit me, and all of a sudden I really needed to hide in a dark tent and sit down for a few minutes. I nodded and gestured for him to lift the flap. The cool air from inside rushed out, soothing my flushed face.

"Until next time," I murmured.

He replied just as quietly: "Until next time, Bailey."

CHAPTER 5

Bailey

THE DARKNESS FOLDED OVER US, LIT ONLY BY TINY, FIREFLY-LIKE creatures that bobbed around our heads. I thought, for a minute, of Merelda, and how if she were here she'd buzz around and torment these strange insects with her incessant fascination.

It had been such a wild, unexplainable evening so far, that the mental image of Merelda being so utterly normal made me snort laugh loud enough that several people looked over at the sound.

I steadied myself against the silver tent pole and smiled in sheepish apology. The expression felt foreign on my face, but I warred against the urge to smooth it over. Unfortunately, distracted by the difficulties of arranging the same face I'd had for twenty-eight years, I realized too late that I knew one of the women.

She'd been on the groom's side. I didn't know her name.

The second our eyes met, she stiffened. Her gaze swept over me from head to toe before she sniffed and turned away.

I waited for the pain to hit, but with the Bargain Orb still whole in my pocket, it was only an echo. The wedding itself was barely within reach—just as Fynn had said, if I tried to find the memories, I could. But why would I want to?

I shut my eyes until I couldn't even remember her face, basking in the lingering shred of joy and ignorance. It wouldn't last after tonight, so for these remaining hours I would be free. At the thought, Fynn's words echoed in my mind.

See what you could become if you found another way.

My brow furrowed. It was ludicrous, but what if he was right? I'd had one small taste of this, of freedom from... something... *Offering*. A word that had no meaning now, but that threatened to mean everything if I followed those memories to their source. The idea that I would have to let this freedom go by dawn was unbearable.

I stilled, realization hitting me: I couldn't let it go, not now that I knew what it felt like.

We found our seats—unfortunately right next to the familiar woman—and settled in to wait. The audience was growing quickly, the lights twinkling across more and more filled spaces than empty ones. Conversation hummed, the sound dotted through with quiet laughter, and everywhere I looked I saw faces spilling over with wonder.

I wondered whether we should catch our breath and then slip out while the audience was captivated, or if we should stay for the whole show. Had Fynn been telling the truth when he'd said I'd enjoy it? Or was he only selling the story for Stefan's benefit?

I was still mulling it over when the lights illuminated, flickering from a dull yellow mood light to a strange silvery glow tinged with blue. In the center of the light stood a man.

No, not a man, I reminded myself—a fae.

With a jolt, I realized it was the one whose eyes I'd caught on the bridge, what felt like a lifetime ago now. The one who seemed different from the others. But before I could think much more about what that might mean, the fae began to move.

My breath left me in a rush.

There was no way a body should be able to move like that. One leg stretched upward casually, as if he were only warming up, as the music began to ring out through the tent. But there was nothing casual about it. He arched back, muscles rippling like water, while the movement of his leg kept going and going until he was twisted around himself like vines.

Stefan leaned toward me. "We should leave while they're distracted," he whispered. "This is the main performance."

I waved him away, distantly hushing him as I stared. Stefan was right; this was the main performance, and we *should* leave. But I couldn't. Whether Fynn had been serious or not, I couldn't look away from this fae.

He eased out of the position to awed silence and continued the illusion of stretching—but none of us were fooled this time. We watched in mute rhapsody, already spellbound.

The accompaniment was a different sort of music to the wild chaos outside. This was deeper, more sorrowful—a cello, I thought, mixed with some kind of wind instrument I didn't recognize. I looked around the tent, searching for the source of the sound. There might have been a quartet hidden in the back corner, but I didn't bother searching long because the fae's movements drew me back in again.

I was enraptured. Caught by the fluid, water-like grace with which he spun and writhed, casting golden illusions around him with each new movement. Birds and vines and waves appeared from nothing, crashing against the barrier as his performance rose toward the crescendo. One second, he was diving through silvery hoops too fast to follow. The next, climbing a rope suspended by nothing as the two of them spun around one another—both the rope and him moving like magic.

It *was* magic.

No human could move like that, or, if they could, they couldn't also manipulate the rope beside them. Couldn't twist like a snake upon themselves and wrap that rope up in a bow around their torso—a maneuver that sent an unexpected shock of heat coursing through me. Heat I hadn't felt in moons, not since...

I broke off the thought with a thick swallow. I only had a handful of hours left, each one sliding through my hands like water. One night without pain; I wouldn't ruin it. Tonight, I had no memory of what had come before. There was only this.

Abruptly, the music paused, sliding to a suspenseful halt with only the wind instrument still quietly trilling. The lights above the audience faded back in.

The performer stood upright for the first time in minutes and stretched out his hand toward the audience. When he spoke, I forgot how to breathe.

"Who will join me tonight for the crescendo?" he asked.

His tone was a lilting, tender caress, sparking with just the briefest hint of fire—fire that I knew I should run from. My place was the shadows, the corners. My place was silent and forgotten. I knew that truth deep within my bones, no matter what memories were hidden from me.

But the only thing I couldn't remember in that moment was why the hell I should stay there.

His eyes—casually roaming our illuminated faces and the dozens of eager, reaching hands—landed on me, and I froze. Something jolted between us. Something more than fire, more than the spark of recognition on the bridge but born from that same place... This was an awareness that sank deeper than names and faces. A soul-deep knowing.

And it was one that terrified me, because it reminded me of everything I wasn't meant to want.

His body stilled, hand outstretched, now, toward me.

"Lovely lady with the golden crown of curls," he called. "Will you join me in the ring?"

I swallowed thickly, and even though I knew I had to refuse, there was a part of me that ached so deeply to take that outstretched hand that I could hardly breathe from the force of it. But it would be foolish—something I'd already been warned against once tonight. I'd barely escaped one audience participation; another would surely kill me.

Besides, even if I couldn't remember my place right now, that didn't mean it didn't exist. There was a voice at the back of my head that screamed at me to hide, an instinct twenty-eight years in the making. I wasn't allowed to accept this beautiful man's hand, no matter what I wanted. And taking it anyway would have devastating consequences.

My tongue darted out to wet my lips as I prepared to say, '*oh no, not me, but this woman beside me is willing*'. She was practically jumping out of her seat, more than eager to take his hand and have her night of pretend romance with the fae.

But when I opened my mouth, I saw the look on her face. The sneer in her wrinkled nose, the twist of her lip.

The judgment that she was bestowing upon me.

As we stared at one another, the sneer curved into a smile and she stood. Smoothing her dress, she turned to the fae male, the picture of sweet innocence. Almost in slow motion, I watched her companions urge her onward. It was good and right—the reward should go to her, not me. Never me.

I reached instinctively for a necklace that wasn't there and froze as the touch of cool skin met my fingers. Another Bailey would have sat back down immediately. But tonight, I wasn't another Bailey. Tonight, I was *this* Bailey.

Enjoy one final gift.

A churning pit of guilt and anger and shame writhed in my stomach, and all of a sudden I wasn't in this circus tent at all. I was in another kind of tent, one with lacy white walls, an altar, and me—standing alone for shamefully too long. Longer than anyone should have waited.

I swallowed down the bile, and beneath it anger rose. How dare she? How dare any of them, with their whispers and their taunts? Their constant suggestions that I wasn't good enough. How dare she think that no one would ever want—

Before I knew it, I was stepping forward, angling my body in front of hers until she was covered by my shadow.

"Are you talking to me, handsome?" I said, my voice a low, confident lilt I barely recognized.

The woman beside me bristled, and for the first time, I reveled in it.

The corner of the fae's mouth twitched, then curled into something that fell just the right side of wicked. Just as quickly, he smoothed his expression over and raised an eyebrow, beckoning me closer.

The crowd parted before us like magic, even though no one rose from their seats. A clear line formed from me to him. I stepped through, my body moving almost like a trance, that fire surging within me as our eyes met and held...

Leaving me powerless to look away.

I slid my hand into his, and he whirled me to the center of the ring. The music surged again, the audience falling back in shadow. It was just me and him.

The silver rope twisted around us, somehow multiplying until there were more threads—spinning together until they became like one mass. A moving curtain of rope concealing us from the audience.

"I can't help but feel we've made a faux pas," he said, raising an eyebrow.

Another mortifying snort of laughter escaped me, thankfully hidden from anyone else by the rising music. His smile widened, becoming more genuine than performance.

"You don't know the half of it," I murmured. "I've stepped foot outside my box, you see."

Gods, and wouldn't I pay for it? As soon as this night came to an end, reality would crash back down in more ways than one. Memories and consequences would return like a brick to the face.

But for now... I was seeing what I could become.

The fae lifted his eyebrows but didn't comment. As the music rose, he gently guided me into position. My lips parted in shock at the familiar touch, and I raced to follow his movements so I didn't mess his performance up and embarrass the hell out of myself—not that I was any stranger to public mortification.

On the other side of the curtain of ropes, I could hear the awed gasps of the audience. His magic was obviously entertaining them as it concealed us, building to a crescendo like he'd promised.

"Are you okay?" he whispered, making me startle. "You only have to stand there, I promise."

"I think so," I said, eyes wide as I glanced at him. We stood so close within the silver whirlwind that our breath skimmed each other's cheeks.

Agitated and distracted, my fingers twirled an errant strand of the silvery rope in on itself. But to my shock, the rope tugged itself back, flying free and shaking me off, like a cat that didn't want to be touched. Then, it caressed the fae's cheek and shot back to join the others.

Amusement glinted in his eyes at the expression on my face. "Hold still, then," he cautioned me.

He slid my hand into the final position and stepped away.

One of my hands rested upon a lantern that had grown from the earth while we were talking, while the other lay at its center, so it looked like I was holding the lantern up. To sell the illusion, my foot was placed in a way that concealed how all the strength was in the metal. He could have done it all with magic, I was sure, but he hadn't.

It was a beautiful illusion, one without magic, which blended human and fae seamlessly together.

For once, I didn't feel out of place; I felt essential. As he leaped over my hand, passing me by with a wink, and landed upon the center of the lantern, I, along with the audience, gasped. The sound trickled like water as the ropes fell away and revealed him balanced on one hand, legs stretching above him, curved backwards and twisted like an 'S'.

And with one final flourish, he produced a box from the air, which opened to reveal a pretty, golden dove—who flew toward the ceiling and was free. His eyes slid to mine and he winked, and I somehow knew then that this final move was improvised. For me.

The music rose to a final, stunning clash of sound, but I didn't move. I didn't respond at all to the roaring sound of the audience, because that would mean looking away from him. And when something in his expression flickered—something a little breathless, a little shocked and unexpected—I didn't move then either.

Once again, I found myself noticing things I shouldn't. The gentle twist of his curls over his neck. The dark mystery of his gaze. The way his eyes dropped, ever so briefly, to my lips.

He was beautiful—stunning, even—and with the orb still whole in my pocket, Hayden felt so very far away.

With a bound, he leapt down, twisting his hand so that the lantern pulled back into the earth. Then he stood before me, clasping my hand in his, lifting it above us both and sweeping me into a bow alongside him.

It was a bow I didn't deserve, but the giddy feeling that rose in my chest made me want to take it all the same.

Then he turned and bowed to me, lifting my hand into a gentle kiss—the barest brush of his lips—as he thanked me and gestured that I could return to my seat.

I didn't want to return to my seat.

I didn't want my dress to become vines again.

The lights faded in, bright as day, and the audience began to file toward the exits. The conversation was a deafening roar of excitement now, as each member of the audience cooed over what they'd seen.

I blinked at the performer, noticing the pause that now stretched between us—especially when his eyes flicked to my hand, where I still hadn't let him go. I couldn't begin to identify all the churning, writhing emotion in me. My memories felt obliterated after that performance; I was an entirely new person.

"My name's Bailey," I said, offering the first words I could think of.

His eyes widened in surprise. For the second time in one night with this man, I'd apparently done the unexpected.

Then he softened, letting my hand go slowly—reluctantly —as he said, "Sebastian."

His voice still rang with that low, gentle melody. I could happily listen to that voice read my shopping list, for gods' sake. As we stared at one another, he tilted his head to the side, brow furrowing slightly.

Oh—the Bargain.

He could sense the open Bargain.

Just like that, reality crashed back into me. No matter what illusions I'd indulged tonight, I'd sworn off men, and the fae had never been an option in the first place—not when they already had me ensnared in dangerous Bargains. Tonight had been a dream, and the dream was over.

I nodded, took one final look at the beautiful man who had made me a star, if only for one night, and turned away.

Stefan rushed to me, eyes frantic with fear, and I didn't make him wait any longer. We ran from the fairground, well before the final performer had taken their bow. The forest closed around us, ominous and frightening, but we didn't stop. Not even when Merelda barrelled into us and chattered away.

I kissed Stefan's cheek goodnight at the garden gate and hurried inside to the safety of my bed. Acting on instinct rather than true memory, I crossed to a small altar by my bed and opened a blank notebook. Between its pages were layers of dusky pink rose petals. When I looked at them, I thought of oaths and offerings, but I couldn't grasp the thoughts for long enough to remember. More to the point, I didn't want to.

Still, the thought of ignoring my duty here made my mouth dry out and my blood run cold. So, I let instinct guide me where memory failed.

Whispering my prayers over the petals I'd dried last moon, I counted blessings and dropped them one by one into a wooden bowl on my window sill—to be kissed by the moon.

"May we be safe and secure. May the seeds of my duty reign so the roots of my neighbors' wealth will flourish. And may I have the strength to be weak, the courage to be timid, and the clarity to be nothing," I murmured.

The last word choked in my throat, but I paid it no attention as I plucked new petals free from the vase of roses at the altar and pressed them between crackling paper sheets.

Then, finally, I turned my attention to the Bargain Orb in

my hand. I stared at it for a long, long time. If I didn't shatter it now, I'd never find the courage to do so. But tonight, in all its foolishness, had shown me a life I'd never thought to imagine, and I couldn't let that life become nothing more than a memory.

So, before I did anything else, I wrote myself a note and stuck it to the mirror.

Bailey, do NOT chicken out.

Find another way.

Promise me.

Then, I placed the glass ball beneath the heel of my boot and shattered the cursed thing to smithereens.

CHAPTER 6

Sebastian

In the spirit of fairness and mercy, we offer your father's safety and health in spite of your transgressions. In exchange, these rules are to be followed on the other side of the water.
You will stay within the ribbons that enclose the circus grounds.
Your body will remain covered by tent or moonlight. Never shadow.
There is one gate available to end this Bargain, and a single key: freedom will be heralded by the arrival of a hidden fae. Find your father before that season ends, or have him slip through your fingers forevermore.
In magnanimity, we wait.

I LINGERED IN THE SHADOWS OF THE TENT LONG AFTER THE LAST audience member had left.

That wasn't anything new; I was a lurker and a scoundrel to anyone who bothered to give an opinion. The fact that my lurking behavior was purely because I couldn't leave my tent without meeting certain requirements was irrelevant. Lurker, scoundrel, cad. The usual unimaginative insults followed me like lost puppies.

But this time, I wasn't watching the crowd; this time, I was searching it. Searching for one human in particular—for her.

A task that was especially difficult when taking into consideration aforementioned restrictions.

Thanks to fae Bargains made during the folly of my youth, my choices of movement were hopping from moonbeam to moonbeam, like some kind of clown, or sticking to the tents. Generally, I preferred to linger in the tents and witness this strange human world from afar, as if its secrets might somehow arrive at my feet. For the first time in years, however, I was contemplating the clown option.

But then, after a few more minutes of searching from my shadowed corner, with my arms folded before me and my shoulder leant against the gilded rod that braced the entrance of the tent, I found her.

She hurried along the edge of the fairground with her older friend, the two of them exchanging fierce whispers as they made for the exit.

Good. They were clever then. They knew that the Lumière had ears everywhere. In the public spaces of the circus, there was no true privacy so long as you were within three meters of a tent.

The Lumière were always searching for a weakness— names, secrets, promises. Any way they could make a Bargain stick in a capacity that defied the very meaning of the word.

I watched, waiting for some hidden sign within her to reveal itself to me. To explain the strange magic I'd sensed as she'd breathed her name in that husky voice.

Could it possibly be the thing I thought it was?

After so many years, I didn't dare to hope. Because what

was stolen hope if not another kind of curse? But if there was any chance I was right, I couldn't let her walk away like this.

Just as they were almost through the gate, she looked my way. Her older friend tilted his head to catch her attention again, both of their faces lit up by the moonlight, but she didn't notice. She seemed to be searching the crowd for someone, although the furrow in her brow suggested she wasn't finding them.

As the moonlight caught her face, that now-familiar spark kindled low within me, and my heart leapt into my throat. I was right. There was magic within her.

Hidden fae magic.

The words of my Bargain hovered at the back of my memory: *freedom will be heralded by the arrival of a hidden fae.*

The words had been given begrudgingly, which was how I knew they were true. There were few rules that the fae had to abide by in our Bargains. But the one thing that was sacred was the gate—the key, or exit, that was written into the Bargain. It would be bound in a dozen loopholes of course. A dozen little tricks and lies but...

The gate itself was true, and it was the only way to break a Bargain without paying with your life.

For years now, I had searched for hidden magic within every human that crossed the borders of this circus. Not once had I ever found it, until now.

I smiled, watching her slip through our gates and run back to the human world. She would return; they always did. And this time, I'd be ready.

I'd trace that magic back to its source.

Something caught my attention, and my gaze flicked to a handful of ribbons that had broken free of their line designating the circus grounds. I froze. The ribbons had broken loose, which meant the boundary was broken.

Slowly, my gaze slid back to the forest, where Bailey had disappeared. My cursed Bargain bound me to the circus grounds, moreso even than the rest of the Lumière. But tonight, those grounds were not closed. I could follow her.

I could reach her tonight without ever breaking the rules. Whatever secrets she was hiding could be torn free and laid out, and I'd find the answer to my curse within them. My foot slid forward from the shadow of my tent, the intricate buckles of my boot glinting in the moonlight as I took one step out into the slanted silver beam that lit up the grounds.

An arm appeared before me, blocking my exit.

My expression closed off and I fought to hold back the sneer from my lips.

"Fynn," I said as neutrally as possible.

His gaze slid over me from top to bottom, glinting with cold cruelty. It was an expression he never dared show our human visitors when he invited them through the curtains to my tent. Not until the final night, at least.

Although, sometimes I had the strangest impression that he was still wearing a glamor then, even for me. That there was some secret about his face that I'd never truly witnessed.

"Going somewhere?" he inquired.

The faux politeness made my jaw clench.

"I thought a moonlit stroll might be pleasant," I said, baring my teeth in a semblance of a smile. "You look like you could use a little help enticing unwitting audience members to their doom—sorry, their entertainment."

His eyes flashed, and he took a look around the crowded circus grounds, one eyebrow raised as his gaze lingered on the queues lining up outside every tent. "Is that so?" he said lightly. "Feel like you could do better? By all means... perhaps we'll have to adjust your contract."

As if that were even possible.

"I'm sure you'd happily take my place, wouldn't you?" I said, smacking him on the shoulder and gripping tightly as the two of us grinned into each other's faces. "Bending into all those slippery positions to escape the Masters' punishment." I let my lips curve in a challenge. "You've had a lot of practice at that, haven't you?"

He threw off my hand with a sharp shrug and gripped the back of my neck, squeezing like a vice. "As much practice as you've had bending over for them," he snarled, all traces of civility forgotten.

A flare of heat ripped through my chest, but outwardly, I only laughed. With a steadying breath, I knocked his hand back; he barely resisted.

Fynn had never been a performer here. He lacked the muscles and strength required from those of us bound in contracts. Like shooting fish in a barrel, he was easy to smack away.

"Oh, sweetheart," I said, throwing him a wink. "Just admit you miss me and be done with it."

For a moment, something hot and raw burned in his gaze, something that nearly wiped the smile from my face, but it was gone again in a flash.

I glanced over the circus grounds, feigning disinterest so he'd hopefully go away. "Don't tell me you're looking for the pretty blonde girl?" Fynn drawled, shaking his head so the light glittered off his earring. "So predictable."

My heart kicked up its pace, but I was careful to keep my expression still. If Fynn sensed I had any interest in her, I was done for.

"What makes you think that?" I asked idly.

"The way you looked at her."

That nearly made me break my attempt at casual deception. The way I looked at her? I didn't think I'd looked at her in any particular way. Casting my mind back now, I considered the unexpected human woman with fresh eyes.

It had been a delight to spend those moments with her, and subtly stick it to her human friends—enemies?—with the performance. To see her laugh that inelegant little laugh. She was beautiful, certainly. And intriguing. Curling blonde hair with a hint of red that fell over her shoulders, and those mismatched eyes—one brown, one green. Gorgeous.

Not to mention the whiff I caught of secrets, held close to her chest. I did love a mystery. What was life without a little depth to challenge you?

But if I was perfectly honest, I found most people beautiful and intriguing. There was nothing special about her.

Besides, she looked like a woman who received more than her fair share of offers to warm her bed. She didn't need mine, too. I had no room for that in my life. No room, no time, no inclination. Even a night of fun would be more trouble than it was worth with a human.

Still, if Fynn thought that was what I was after, perhaps it would give me the freedom I needed to get what I really wanted.

"You don't think I have a chance?" I asked lightly.

His grin turned cruel. "I don't think it matters," he said, disgustingly confident. "Trust me, Sebastian, while you might be a deviant fuck, she isn't the type to push you down and ride you in a moonbeam for all of us to see." He angled his head. "She's the kind of woman who needs devotion, not a performance. And don't think for a second you'll be allowed to let her through the entrance to your tent to give her that either."

My lip curled at his deliberate crudeness. "Are those my only two options? Damn, what a choice." I pretended to mull it over, tapping my finger on my lip.

Fynn snarled—no longer pretending to be friendly at all as he leaned into my space.

"One wrong move. One broken rule," he reminded me, speaking slowly as his body pressed against mine. "And you lose your father forever."

Silence fell between us as we glared at one another. As if I could ever forget. With every move I made, every word I uttered, I remembered.

Judging by the curl of his lip, he knew that. He jabbed me in the chest, grin widening.

"So? What will it be? Risk it all for a girl?" Fynn hesitated, finger sliding down the middle of my chest. "Or be a good boy and get back in your box?"

He shoved me with one finger on my sternum, shunting me back through my tent's entrance.

I gritted my teeth, and even though I knew something he didn't—that Bailey might be the key to ending everything, rather than a distraction that put it all at risk—I hesitated. The old, familiar twist of guilt unfurled within me.

My father had always said I was too impulsive, too brash, and he was right. It was how we'd ended up here; how everything had been taken from me.

Movement caught my attention, and once more I glanced at the ribbons that flickered in the wind. My body grew still—calm—while my mind raced.

I might have been impulsive once, but I'd grown since then. I wasn't a foolish boy anymore. And while I might be guided by the fire within me, I also knew, now, how to play within their rules.

And that was what I would do.

"Oh, you know me," I said with a grin, grabbing his finger and shoving it roughly away. "My heart's as black as coal these days. Isn't that what you said?"

The words Fynn had hurled at me in a moment of rare abandon made him flinch. Didn't mean they weren't true, though. My heart was as dead as stone; I couldn't afford for it to be anything more. I had more important matters to deal with than love.

I took a step forward, moonlight streaming down upon my face. As soon as I was standing outside the tent, the tingle of magic caressed my skin. But without any shadow in it, it didn't hurt.

I pointed idly into the distance and waited until Fynn followed the direction.

The second he turned away from me, I twisted my other hand, making sure not to so much as glance down to check if the magic worked. I felt the note slip from my palm and flutter off into the distance—toward the human town.

"There's been a wind," I said casually, hands dropping to my side and slipping into the pockets of the loose pants I'd pulled over my tights. "And—would you look at that? The ribbons have blown into the distance. The boundaries are all messed up. It'll take all night to find and restore those markers."

I leant forward, scrubbing my hand through his hair and ruffling it until he hissed and smacked me away. Despite appearances, my breath caught in my chest as I waited for him to call me out. To shove me back through the entrance and seal the flap before I could put my freedom to the test.

Forcing my voice to remain light and easy, I said, "I think the bounds of the circus have gone all..." I wiggled my fingers. "Wobbly for the night. Gods." My grin widened. "I wonder how far they stretch." I backed away, lifting my arms in an elaborate shrug. "I guess I'll just have to enjoy a moonlit stroll and find out."

The expression on his face was pure fury, and I knew I'd have to be careful not to push him too far. But I had to push him a little. If he thought I was doing something stupid and risky tonight, then he wouldn't expect it tomorrow.

"You won't win," he said in a low voice.

For a moment, I almost stopped. Win what? It was such a strange way to word it. But I shook it off, deciding it didn't matter. *Fynn* didn't matter, despite how hard he tried to.

I had to stick to the plan, remain measured and sensible, and see how this unfolded. Then, I might finally be free.

My father might finally be free.

"She'll be home by now," Fynn called after me. "And none of the ribbons will have blown that far."

He was quite right, but the fact that he thought visiting Broodshire was my plan meant I'd already won. I bit my lower lip, turning the cocky grin into a challenge meant to anger him, instead of a triumph that would make him suspicious.

Because tonight, I wouldn't chase Bailey down. Tonight, I would be the poster boy for well behaved. But tomorrow...

The Lumière may have taken most things from me, binding my freedom up in their devastating rules, but there was one thing they hadn't quite bound, because it hadn't existed then. My magic.

Tonight, the ribbons had scattered by pure coincidence, breaking open the bounds of my cursed Bargain for a single night.

Stay within the ribbons.

Covered by tent or moonlight. Never shadow.

Tonight, it was a coincidence, but tomorrow, it was forecast for wind.

CHAPTER 7

Bailey

THE FIRST THING I DID WHEN I WOKE UP WAS LEAN OVER THE SIDE OF my bed and vomit all over the floorboards. The pitiful sound of retching filled the cottage, and I clutched the sweat-soaked sheets to my chest as I tried to make sense of the whirl of memories from last night.

What... was... *that*...?!

My Bargain had been supposed to give up my memories of Hayden—the pain I couldn't escape, which was infecting everything it touched. It wasn't supposed to give up my memories of my whole fucking life. There wasn't supposed to be anything to give!

And yet...

What I'd experienced last night was so completely different to anything I'd felt or done before... I couldn't deny the truth of it. The Bargain hadn't merely erased how I'd felt over the last six moons, after Hayden cruelly dumped me and I was left with nothing but guilt and heartbreak. It had erased how I'd felt since I'd been born.

And now, after only a handful of hours, that feeling of weightlessness, of joy, was gone.

A dull, familiar ache rang through my entire body. It set my teeth on edge, hummed in my joints, and dragged me down with a burden that was suddenly impossible to carry. How could it be that I'd never noticed this, when it had been present for as long as I could remember?

What would have happened if I'd shared it with Fynn, when he asked? Would I have found the words? Because I found them now. In the space between sleep and awake, where my mind still drifted in fog, I could no longer hide from myself.

From a distance, I heard my voice murmur the words I should have said, bitter and wild in a way I never let myself be:

"Oh, mysterious fae man, you want to know the wound I carry? It's nothing major. Only that, centuries ago, my village made their first deal with the fae—nothing fancy, just a trade of one child's life and happiness for all the others. One child to fail and be forgotten. To live as a mundane nothing while the rest flourished and brought prosperity back home. One child, for the entirety of their life, until the next generation was born.

Oh, and if the child ever forgot her place—like, say, accepted the marriage proposal of some arrogant pissbaby that the whole town loved and then didn't treat him right? Well. The Bargain Magic would make sure she didn't forget for long.

Would make sure the pissbaby came to his senses and order was restored.

Would make sure the child—now an adult—never, ever forgot her place again. Because if she did? Her village would burn in Hell.

So. Nothing big."

I began to laugh, the sound broken and far too loud. What was happening to me? I'd caught a glimpse of another life, and now I *wanted*.

The one thing that the Offering was not allowed to do.

I sat up abruptly, shoving the bedsheets away. There was

no point dwelling on what I'd had; it had already slipped through my fingers. Now, I had no choice but to take this pain and fucking swallow it. After all, I was the counterweight in the scales. I balanced the books so our village could succeed, and so we didn't crack the surface of Aelor and fall into Hell. Literally.

But in the privacy of my bedroom I finally confessed: I was so gods damned tired of playing that role.

I slid my weary feet free from the tangle of bedsheets and steadied myself on the ground. After a minute where I confirmed I wasn't going to vomit anymore, I walked to the bathroom. The headache was already fading. I wouldn't have to beg potions off Master Skylark to ease it—that was a relief.

I glanced at the time, noticed how late it was getting, and hurried through my preparations for the day. The world seemed to move almost sluggishly around me, as if I were ill or hungover, but I knew it wasn't that. Something had changed irrevocably last night, and I didn't have the words to describe what it was. I wasn't sure I even wanted them.

Acting out of self preservation rather than any actual desire to know, I opened the cupboard doors beside my bed. At the back, a familiar metal trinket box glinted in the lamplight; the box that I had given to the fae last night. I swallowed, and after a beat, carefully took the box down. The contents were still there, untouched. My Bargain had been returned intact, as if it were never made.

"Oh peaches," I murmured dryly, running my fingers over the tops of the contents. "At least that means no more fae are going to shoot arrows at my head, I suppose." My voice lowered in irritation. "Not that it will make any difference to a human who might fancy a shot."

Merelda dropped abruptly from the rafters, tumbled three times in the air, and mimed shooting a bow and arrow at my head. Cackling when I ducked, she flew out the open window and into the morning air.

I shook my head, calling after her, "If that's your way of telling me you're still pissed about the circus, it needs work! I didn't quite get the message."

A high-pitched, rude sound came from somewhere among my rose bushes.

"Real mature," I muttered, biting back my smile and returning to the letters.

I riffled through them and plucked one free at random. It was from my mother, the night after I'd achieved my Potions Honor by correspondence. I'd been granted a higher score than expected, and the school had sent an extra certificate congratulating me on my notable achievement.

The next day, three girls in my finishing school had come down with a rare case of measles. One hadn't survived.

Honey, I'm so sorry.

It's a rare burden you've been given, my darling. To uphold the strength and prosperity of our village on those shoulders. When you were little, I used to hold you close and cry at how tiny those shoulders were! So little, to bear such weight!

But we will bear it together, darling. I've written the Council, and told them how the examiners were only indulging you. How the exam questions were taken straight from your textbook, and by luck you had memorized those pages. They know you were not being greedy or indulgent, and in fact, your educated assistance to Master Skylark will do <u>so much</u> to serve our small town. It is a befitting position for the Offering, and they're glad to see you fill it.

They've agreed to let this unfortunate incident pass without comment. You returned the certificate, and the seasonal harvest produced a bounty, proving that the gods still favor our Bargain and are content with warnings rather than punition. The balance has been restored.

Andrie's sacrifice is to be taken as both a sober blessing and a reminder to remain vigilant.

The Council know that you will now be attentive for any other accidental achievements that could damn Broodshire to Hell, and they thank us for our diligence in upholding the Offering's sacred duty.

I've sent flowers to Andrie's mother on your behalf. However, it would be best if you avoided her for the next moon or so.

All my love,

Mother

My hands gripped the paper so hard it nearly shredded, and it took me several long seconds to get my breathing under control.

That was the thing about the Offering. Apart from a daily ritual of prayer and the coronet I wore at the yearly Compact Festival, most of the time it was passive. I had rules to follow, but they were just a part of everyday life: don't take more than anyone else, stay humble, serve your neighbors, and if the necklace of the Offering ever warms, stop whatever you're doing at once because it is forbidden.

But when the Offering's Bargain Magic became active, like when a blessing I didn't deserve slipped through and the necklace didn't warn me fast enough... then it was *really* active. I had to act quickly to rectify it, and if I didn't, the Bargain Magic would do it for me.

At first, it would only be a warning or two. Spoiled milk. A flat tire on my bicycle. But if I ignored those warnings, life would begin to get a little crazy. People would scream at me on the street, and then have no memory of doing so. Hateful letters with no return address would appear in my mailbox, full of scathing commentary on secrets I'd never shared.

When Hayden left me at the altar, it was deemed part of that craziness. A moment of wild rebellion, as the Bargain Magic desperately tried to re-balance the scales.

And when they found out that the necklace had been burning for moons, and I'd ignored it... whatever sympathy I might have been given burned, too. Especially when the fire took the school, and everyone realized just how close we'd come to destruction.

Only one warning of that magnitude was given—a death, a fire, a quake. Some form of disaster would appear as the final effort of the magic to save us. If it was still ignored, then the Bargain was considered broken, the pit to Hell would open, and the daemons would come.

Hayden might have been an arrogant pissbaby, but the rest was all my fault.

I blinked, returning the blurred words of the letter clutched in my hand into focus. Clearly, I needed the reminder—again— before someone else died from measles. Or another fire took the school. I'd pin the letter to my bedside if I had to. With luck, the strange experience of the circus would be forgotten soon enough, and I could go back to my normal life.

Queasiness churned in my gut again, and once more, I gritted my teeth and ignored it.

Moving carefully now, I bent to clean the vomit and pick up the broken shards of glass from the orb I'd shattered last night, still littered across the floor. Without examining them, I dropped them into the trinket box one by one. However, as I collected the final shard, I noticed something odd.

Frowning, I held it closer. It twinkled in the light, and in the reflection of its splintered face I saw a dozen memories. Mine, and ones I didn't recognize. Something plucked at my memory, a forgotten piece of information: something about glass and dreams. There was a link there, magically speaking, I just couldn't remember what it was.

Perhaps these were some of the other offered memories from the pool of Bargains the orb had joined so briefly—remnants of the magic it had touched for a single evening.

Whatever they were, they had nothing to do with me, and I had nothing to gain by examining them. I dropped the shard into the box.

It didn't fall.

As if drawn to me, the broken shard rose and floated closer, circling me like a curious bird.

No. Absolutely not.

With a hitch of my breath, I snatched the shard and threw it into the box, slamming the lid shut and storing it back in the cupboard before the Bargain could somehow reignite. What-ever leftover magic it had could stay at the back of my cupboard until it faded. I wanted nothing to do with the fae anymore.

Hurrying back into my room, I glanced at the mirror to check my hair briefly and then froze. There was a note stuck to the mirror. A note I had written myself.

Do NOT chicken out. Find another way.

Promise me.

A thick layer of shame curled low in my stomach. Huh. I knew myself well, apparently. But whatever half-drugged, euphoric dreams I'd come up with last night simply didn't hold in the cold light of day. There was no other way, no matter what Fynn said. It wasn't about chickening out; it was about doing what was right. I had my sacred duty, and no amount of fae promises would change that.

Seconds passed. Minutes. I kept staring at the note, unable to turn aside and go about my day.

There was no other way... but what if there was?

Something caught my attention—an odd shape that shouldn't be there. I tilted my head, eyes landing on a corner of paper that didn't match up. There was a second note tucked behind mine.

An odd sort of hysteria rose inside me: half of me wanted to laugh while the other wanted to shrink and hide. First, my shattered orb still had magic, and now this. Would Criera keep throwing magical signs at me until I stopped ignoring it? Would I end up with an entire trinket box full of shattered Bargains and hidden notes before this world finally gave up trying to ensnare me?

Or would it never give up?

My body froze, tingles rushing through me, and for half a second, I was back in that tent with the spotlight on me and the dove flying free. My bedroom felt charged with magic, and whatever energy fueled these coincidences, it gave the same impression as the craziness that would ignite when the Bargain Magic tried to guide the Offering back to her path. Only, this time it wasn't trying to guide me back. It was trying to lead me astray.

My eyes slid back to my own message, written in big, bold handwriting. *Don't chicken out.* A secret note, delivered invisibly, promised many things, and none that I should be allowed to have. I was risking measles, mumps—the plague!—by even reading it.

But last night, I had learned how it felt to want freely... and that wasn't something that was easy to forget.

I stepped forward and ripped the note free from behind my own. It didn't take long to scan the words.

Meet me by the lake on the east side of the fairground, tonight, just after opening.

There's something fae hidden within you.
I can sense it.

Seb

After a minute, I realized my breathing had grown ragged, and yet I still hadn't put the note down and walked away. I knew what Sebastian was sensing: the Open Bargain with Fynn. But just as Fynn had promised, Sebastian could not tell what it was.

He thought this strange human had a secret, a secret that perhaps even she was not aware of. If I was reading the intention of this note correctly, he thought I might be half fae, and there was magic hidden inside me.

I couldn't go, of course. It would serve no purpose at all, and might expose everything in the process. But for just a few seconds I imagined that I did. I imagined that the Offering stopped hiding in the shadows and letting everyone else go first. That the Offering seized something—just for her—and damned the consequences.

If only I did have hidden fae magic inside me. That would mean I never belonged here, and there would be no reason to stay.

I tucked the note behind my own again, ignoring the words I'd written on there only hours ago, and left.

☽

The morning passed in chaos. Master Skylark was in one of her frequent moods, and after she'd made several circuits of the workshop, nothing was where it should be. I silently thanked the gods that the shop front wasn't open on mid-seven mornings.

Typically, it was so that the Master could brew and restock the shelves. And so that I, as the assistant, could scurry around and clean, or forage for any missing ingredients. Sometimes, I'd even borrow the horse and cart to ride up to the post stop a couple of miles north. Master Skylark had standing orders that were sent in from the city, but that was as far as the delivery wagons came.

It would have been better if it was one of those mornings, since then I could get out of her way. But such was my luck.

I ducked as she sent another soiled rag, stinking of wormwood, over my head toward the overfull laundry basket.

"When are you going to wash them, girl?" she snapped at me.

I fought down the instinct to sneer.

Maybe when you stop dumping new dishes into the sink every time I empty the water, so I have to start again, I can move on to the laundry, I thought but didn't say.

Smoothing my expression, I said serenely, "The water's just heating up, Master. It won't take long."

"See that it doesn't," she snapped. Then, she paused in the middle of her pacing and glared at me, eyes narrowed. "Can't believe you went to the circus last night," she muttered, stalking off.

She'd said it at least four times to me already. It was getting tiresome.

"I saw a number of people from the village there," I said in a casual drawl, as if I were commenting on the weather.

"Fools, the lot of them," she snapped before returning to her bubbling glass instruments.

A rush of rose scent drifted through the room as she tweaked a dial and spun a wheel.

"And you, most of all. Your luck can't afford what they'll do to you."

I glanced at her. It was the first time she'd said that.

"But they're the fae," I said, my voice still neutral, my expression as serene as a still pool of water. "The Bargains we trade with them are fair." I gestured out the window. The cool metal of my necklace weighed against my collarbone. "Our village would have nothing if not for them."

She slammed a wooden bowl down so hard I jumped. "Are you talking back to me?" she asked, incredulous.

I clamped my mouth shut, realizing that—shit—I was. I shouldn't be saying these things. A flurry of emotion twisted in my stomach. For a moment, I'd felt like I had last night—as though I could say what I really thought, and danger was only a dream.

Mutely, I shook my head. Master Skylark grunted something and turned away.

"It's not those fae we Bargain with," she said through gritted teeth. "The Lumière are different, child. There is far more out there than what those charlatans would show you." She huffed a laugh, the sound as bitter and twisted as the taste of her potions. "The Lumière would as soon find a way to undo your oath and make the rest of us suffer just to laugh."

A sharp jolt coursed through me. I grit my teeth and let my gaze fall on the pretty bluebirds at the window, dancing along the sill. So that was why she didn't want me going there. Not because I might be in danger, but because the town might be, if the Lumière were to take a fancy to my oath and find it amusing to undo it. I watched the birds peck at grubs in the planter until I felt steady enough to speak.

"You'll be glad to know that I stuck to the shadows," I lied, and then muttered, too low for her to hear: "Just call me leader of the mice. Squeak squeak."

"As it should be." She squinted at me again. "You know that tanner's boy's been giving you the eye?"

A tiny flash of fear rippled through me before I placed who she was talking about. Oh, Luke Tanner.

Yes, of course. He would be a fitting match for the Offering. The moron who'd traded his memories for seeds, or for the love of a girl who had probably threatened to skin him alive at least once. Most girls had.

Master Skylark sniffed "Would do you good to look after a man like that."

"I'm sure it would," I answered serenely.

She glanced at me, eyes narrowed, but couldn't seem to find fault in what I'd said.

"Consider it," she said, chopping an ingredient brutally with a butcher's knife. "Next time he comes around, listen to what he has to say."

Thankfully, before I could respond and ruin her last scrap of good will by mentioning the skinning alive dilemma, a knock on the door interrupted us. I looked up as it swung inward and a cloud of steam escaped.

"Shut the door! Shut the door!" Master Skylark hissed at the newcomer with a yelp.

Galdren shut the door and hobbled over, his cane clicking on the ground. "I know you're not open, Mistress," he said sharply, wincing a little as he spoke. "But the cat jumped up and knocked off the last of my pain potion, and I'm desperate. If you've got anything, I'll pay double. I'll need a large dose, too."

Master Skylark waved at me. "Go on, take him out the front. You know where they are."

I set the soapy dishes down and wiped my hands on my apron, but as I turned to go through the door connecting to the shop front, Galdren cleared his throat.

"I'd prefer if it was you, Mistress, if it's all the same."

I stopped, and a weight like lead sunk to the base of my abdomen. The sensations I'd been trying to ignore all morning shot through me. My position had never bothered me like this. I knew that the Offering's role was to be bad luck—to suffer so others would succeed. Before the circus, it had never bothered me that this promise of bad luck meant I was occasionally shunned by people who didn't want to risk that misfortune rubbing off onto them. Even though the whole point of it, of course, was that they would have good luck in return.

I used to point that logical flaw out as a child, but I stopped once I grew up. Enough canes over the knuckles would do that to you, especially when your friends were giggling in appreciation off to the side.

"Of course." I nodded to him as I moved back to my station, but I wasn't quick enough to miss the sneer of repulsion on his face.

Another jolt.

Ah, so that's what this was. Another person who'd heard the sordid details of the wedding, and all that I'd done to their precious golden boy.

"Run along, then," Master Skylark grunted at me, and it was obscene just how unbothered she was when she should have gone for the jugular over Galdren's interruption.

But no, it was right and fair that he didn't want the Offering to serve him. What if the potion I touched soiled? What if I spilled another bottle, or broke it like his cat?

What if the gods weren't done punishing me for Hayden,

and they decided to smite me where I stood and damn the collateral?

"I'll have to do some re-bottling out here," Master Skylark continued. "We've only got the small sizes, otherwise. It's best if you're not in the room."

I nodded, moving toward the tiny servants' corridor at the back that would lead downstairs to the storage and prep rooms. She called after me as I left. "Bring me those notes on belladonna, would you? We're getting low, and I'm trying a new recipe for warts."

"On it," I called back, giving an exaggerated curtsey when she wasn't looking, and then disappeared into the encompassing darkness of the basement.

By the time I reached the back room where the reference tomes were stored, I was shaking with anger. I clenched my fists, standing in the doorway and taking a few slow breaths as I tried to recenter myself.

On the days when everything felt like too much, when my mind screamed against the suffocating fairness of my oath, I had always been able to come back to myself by finding the beauty. I would count slowly to ten, remembering that a life of mediocrity for one person was a small price to pay, and that I would gladly pay it. Because there was so much to be proud of in Broodshire. So many lives flourishing, so many children with full bellies and open hearts. So many endless possibilities opening up around every corner.

But I couldn't find that stillness now, and there was no beauty in sight. As I stood there, my breathing grew more rapid, my teeth grinding together involuntarily, until it was only the sound of bone crunching that snapped me out of it.

I cursed, striding into the room and plucking the first book I saw free from the shelf.

"Belladonna," I muttered to myself, hoping the work would

focus me. "Belladonna. Properties. She wants to redo the recipe for the wart tinctures. Think, Bailey, what does she need? *Help her.*"

I talked to myself until it became an anchor, flicking through pages in almanacs and long-winded forager accounts—things that had gone wrong, things that had gone right. And all the while, my blood bubbled beneath my skin.

A tap-tap-tapping at the window jolted me out of a fury so bright my vision felt like it was clouding over. I snapped my head up and saw Merelda hovering at the window; that produced a smile at least.

I crossed the room and pushed the window open so she could flutter in. And as she did, I caught sight of a title that I hadn't read before. It had never been relevant. My apprenticeship had only covered the basics—what was necessary to support a Master Apothecary, considering I could never become one myself.

But this was a book of legends. A book of first-hand accounts recalling the time when the fae had first crossed the water and come here. It was a book of magic.

Before I knew it, I had pulled the book free, blown the dust off the cover, and cracked the spine. Merelda chattered away, glancing curiously at the open pages. Whether she could read them or not, I had no idea. Instead, she skipped over the desk, sticking her feet into the ink pot and walking pretty circles onto a scrap piece of paper I laid out for her. Every time she made a new layer, she spun and giggled, lost in her own joy. Normally I envied her, but now I couldn't look away from the book.

When the fae are interested in you, play along until they get bored, the book cautioned.

I thought instantly of the note tucked on my mirror. Perhaps the book was right. If I avoided Sebastian, would that not ignite his curiosity more? What lengths would he go to in order to uncover this mysterious magic, and what would happen to me if he somehow did? Frowning, I turned the page, reading more.

They weren't merely factual accounts. This book was full of advice from the first humans who had crossed paths with the fae. The things they had learnt, the things they had died for.

And then I found the first mention of the Lumière.

The tone of the book up until now had been cautious but welcoming. Keep your wits about you, don't be rude—the standard advice. But now I could sense the darkness creeping in.

Never forget how they lie, the book cautioned. *And the Lumière are the worst of all. Brought together by their Master, Heillon, an immortal who has seen many centuries and has perfected the art of Bargains and power.*

I turned the page, revealing a brilliant illustration of a gated castle—wrapped in vines, surrounded by orchards, and topped with a hazy bubble.

Their castle is one of the most heavily warded and intoxicating places of hedonistic power within the fae world of Criera. And they owe this strength of power to the performances they inflict on unsuspecting humans.

I sucked in a breath. What?

I scanned the words, skimming quickly now, but beyond reference to something called Bargain Night on the seventh night of the circus, the book did not explain what, precisely, was so dangerous. I returned to one line, reading it over and over.

No human can recall what happens on the Bargain Night, and none of the Lumière have ever shared.

A Bargain Night... It sounded like our Compact Fairs, except more dangerous.

Well, that was simple enough to avoid—I wouldn't go if it was so dangerous. Six nights was enough. Hell, one night was enough. I didn't see any reason I should return and risk it again.

But then... I chewed my lip. I owed Fynn. I still had to pay him for his Bargain, which meant returning at least once.

And there was that feeling, the sensation that had haunted me ever since I awoke and vomited my guts over my bedroom floor. I'd tried to ignore it, but the niggling voice at the back of my mind was only getting louder.

I knew what it was like now to live without pain. And as that thought echoed through my mind, and I flicked idly through the pages in search of a faerie story that didn't threaten all I held dear, I landed on a simple anecdote.

It was a few scant sentences—rumors of humans who had run away to join the fae. People who procured a special ticket from the Lumière, and risked the danger of that ticket for the chance of a new life on the other side of the water.

My heart beat so heavily in my throat I could practically taste it.

The Offering was bound by the Oath until she was killed or lost, after which the next generation replaced her. I'd always assumed that being lost must mean kidnapped, but Bargains were all about the wording—what was the wording?

I closed my eyes, wracking my memory to recall the paintings of past Offerings that were displayed in the town hall. There was one that had terrified me as a child, where a woman had been stolen in a faerie hunt and taken back to Criera to endure unknown horrors. The town had honored her sacrifice deeply, knowing that it was only through her duty as the Offering that no one else had been taken.

For half a dozen moons, I'd dreamed of the bright eyes and sharpened teeth belonging to the faeries in that painting. But now, I fought to remember the words written below—words that had burned themselves into my brain.

Taken from her home by those who live across the water, leaving no ties behind to bind her, the Offering was lost, and her oath complete.

Taken by those across the water, leaving no ties behind her... Slowly, I opened my eyes and stared at the etching of two humans clutching a ticket as they crossed the bridge.

It was safe.

The oath didn't say the fae had to hunt me, or steal me away in danger... They just had to take me. Carry me from one side to the other. Like with a ticket.

A dull, static sound echoed around my skull. I stared at the book and then at Merelda, still happily skipping over her artwork. At the back of my mind, a part of me screamed: *don't do it.*

Surely, it was too dangerous? Master Skylark had already told me what she would do if I risked the village, not that I needed her to remind me of the consequences.

But this wouldn't have consequences. I'd be taken by the fae. Lost—Oath fulfilled. It didn't have anything to do with the village. It wasn't about them.

For once it was about me.

Don't be a coward, Bailey. Don't chicken out.

Nervous and fidgety, I turned the page to avoid answering the burning question that now loomed before me, and landed on a new legend: one of a hideous daemon called a soul eater. I stared in abject horror at its face, my blood turning cold.

My attention caught on a symbol at the top of the page. It was familiar, although I couldn't put my finger on why.

Abruptly, Merelda kicked over the bottle of ink and rose into the air, hissing as she stared at the etching of the daemon. I startled forward, correcting the bottle; it was the jolt back into reality that I needed.

"What would you do if you were me?" I asked Merelda.

She didn't answer, too busy flying loops around the lamp, far away from drawings of terrible monsters. But I didn't need her to answer, because I already knew. I'd seen too much, *touched* too much, to let go of hope so easily.

There was no going back to who I'd been.

Gods above, I was going to do it.

I slammed the book shut and tucked it away in my satchel, ready to take home and study at leisure. To do this, I would need to learn everything I could about fae magic, in a shorter length of time than even our brightest academics could manage. I'd have to uncover as many Lumière secrets as I could, especially about that final night: the one no one remembered.

It was an impossible task by all accounts...

But even the brightest academic of Broodshire didn't have two fae men on hand to ask their questions. Between Fynn and Sebastian, I could surely find the answers I needed.

Fynn had told me to find another way, and I had.

Master Skylark's voice echoed from the front, creaky and agitated.

I threw my bag over my shoulder and brought it with me as I returned to the workshop. "Yes, Mistress?"

"We need another basket of thistle roots," she said, shaking an empty and faintly dirty basket in my face. "Galdren says there're signs of stomach flu spreading through the kindergarten, and we'll need to be on hand for treatment. Go find them."

"I'm on it," I assured her, taking the basket and slipping out the door.

She didn't notice the bag hooked over my shoulder, but before the door could slip shut, she called after me once again. "Did you put all the books away?"

I turned to her. "Of course."

"Every last one?" she pushed, as if she weren't currently standing in the midst of a chaotic whirlwind of mess.

My heart fluttered. Did she know? I didn't think so. This was just her typical demeanor, bossing me around. Making sure that every trace of me that could be left behind—anything that I might have done, anything that I might have touched, anything that I might have left an imprint on—was gone. Ensuring that it was returned to a pristine condition as though I'd never been there.

"I put all the books away, back where they belong," I lied, my face as calm and serene as ever.

She sneered at me. "Good. And would it kill you to smile once in a while?" She shook her head, turning away. "You give me the creeps, you do. Like you're made of damned porcelain."

My shoulders tightened, and I turned, letting the door slam shut a second after Merelda scooted out after me. Then I left, first to collect the thistle roots, and later to meet Sebastian.

And at the thought of what was to come, I smiled so sweetly, Master Skylark would have been horrified.

CHAPTER 8

Bailey

THERE WERE NO USHERS AT THE ENTRANCE TONIGHT, BECAUSE THEY weren't needed. The magic did it all.

I waited in the shadows until most of the crowd had entered the gates. A few stragglers trailed behind: people who hadn't bought entry the first night and still thought to test their luck entering on day two. They egged each other on, slapping each other's backs and laughing, until one at a time they charged at the magical barrier enclosing the grounds—and were inevitably thrown three meters backward.

When I'd decided they were suitably distracted, I slipped onto the path that led back to the lake, where the fae had first appeared.

It didn't take long for the paperbarks and willows to thicken, and the path to become little more than a narrow dirt line that wrapped along the shore. A wind must have blown through, because some of the ribbons that marked the circus grounds had blown free and wrapped around the branches, and the effect was like a dozen creepy hands brushing against my face when I least expected it.

Soon, the lack of light became suffocating, the shadows

stretching across every surface. Even the sound had cut out, little rustles and whispers setting my skin on edge and the hairs at the back of my neck rising. In the distance, I could hear the muffled sounds of the circus, but it was faint enough to ignore. Out here, I was truly alone.

Even without the dangers of the Lumière, we didn't often enter this forest, and certainly not at night. It was too thick. Too overrun with wild animals. But Sebastian had been clear about the meeting point—the eastern side, away from the entrance to the circus grounds. That, coupled with the way he'd made this note appear so secretively, told me he didn't want any of the other fae following us.

That could be a really good sign for me... or a really bad one.

I brushed my fingers over the list of questions tucked in my pocket. They smelled faintly of the rose petals from my prayers tonight, and as the scent folded around me, I drew myself up taller. He wanted something from me? Fine—I wanted something from him, too, and I wouldn't leave without it.

With his help, safely Bargained for, I'd learn the truth behind those rumors. Had humans really stowed away, over the centuries? More importantly, once they reached the other side, had they survived?

What would it take for me to do the same?

After a handful of minutes, I reached a clearing, and the space before me opened up into a silvery, moonlit path. Most of the lake was bathed in light, and I saw that not only had the ribbons surrounding the fairgrounds shifted, but the grand curtains sealing the circus from people trying to see in the back had also blown free. So much so that the eastern side of the performance tents butted up almost to the lake's edge. The entire path, from fabric wall to the water, was lit with moonlight.

Feeling oddly exposed, I stepped free of the shadows, my

feet crunching over the tiny stones. I looked around, searching for any sign of monsters. When the fae crossed the bridge, the pathways were briefly open; there was always a chance something nasty had crossed over with them. But the lake remained silent, and after a few cautious breaths, I decided I was alone.

The minutes passed, and my agitation faded into boredom. Where was he? I checked my watch several times—first at two minutes to eight, second, right on the dot, and then again five minutes later. I let out another sigh, eyes roaming the shore.

My breath caught. Was that—

I leaned forward, and for a moment I swore there was a figure standing on the other side of the water, wearing a hint of green, like the outfits Fynn and the other ushers were clothed in. But then the shadows chased over the shape, rustling like leaves, and when they disappeared, there was nothing there.

Movement sounded behind me, and I turned with my fists raised, ready to go down fighting. But it was only Sebastian, emerging from between the sagging curtains.

I let out a slow, deliberate breath, willing my nerves to calm. My mind might have been made up about running away, but my body had a few more protests to make. With that in mind, I smoothed my expression into a familiar mask of calm serenity, letting the corner of my mouth tick up into a faint, knowing smile.

Something about the slightly amused, confident expression reminded me of who I'd been on that first night here—how I'd felt. I liked that.

As Sebastian strolled up the path, the moonlit bathed his features in light, caressing every sharp angle in his jaw. It brushed the soft waves of his slightly longer than normal, auburn hair, and the lithe twists of his sculpted muscles, even beneath the sleeves of his tight shirt.

One thing could be said without hesitation: Sebastian was

gorgeous. Fortunately, I'd come to my senses and was once more immune to such things. But like any good tourist, I could appreciate the view.

As he came closer, something in his gaze flickered—an unexpected warmth and amusement. I realized he was close enough to see that I was admiring him, and a faint curl of heat sunk low in my abdomen. He came to a stop before me, hands slipping into the pockets of his loose trousers. Even those managed to hug his figure, as the gentle breeze molded his clothing to his body and showed off just how thin the fabric was.

I swallowed thickly, forcing my eyes up to meet his, only to find he was giving me the same attention.

Suddenly self-conscious, I smoothed my hands over my woolen coat. It was enough to snap me out of the moment. To remind me that, while I could certainly look at pretty men without falling for their traps, they were looking at me too. And, historically speaking, I knew exactly what they would find— what they *should* find.

Nothing special.

Whatever budding attraction I was toying with fled my mind, replaced instantly with familiar calm. Everything was as it should be. Sebastian was a way out of here for me, nothing more.

I cleared my throat and held out the slip of paper to him. "You said to meet you here."

"I did," he replied easily. Once more, I noticed the lyrical quality to his voice, and even though he said the words quietly —aiming, I presumed, to make sure we weren't overheard— there was still a performance-like quality to the way he spoke. Like he was working a crowd, even now.

This was a man who was used to being watched from every angle. Who was always, always aware of it.

"And here you are," he added when I didn't say anything else, humor flickering once more in his gaze.

Since he made no move to take the note back, I slipped it into the front pocket of my coat instead and waited. He seemed in no hurry to explain what we were doing here, instead studying me like I was a mathematical problem he was trying to solve, rather than a person holding a conversation. It was bewildering, and kind of offensive.

I wondered if this was a test, and he was waiting for me to grow impatient. He'd picked the wrong girl if that was his game. I was used to people not speaking to me.

"So, there's hidden fae magic in you, it seems," he finally said, his attention returning to my face.

Just as it had when I read the words in the note, my heart skipped a beat. Did he already know about the deal? Was he about to demand a favor I couldn't say no to?

I forced my heartbeat to slow and unwound my clenched fingers, letting them rest casually at my sides. Fynn had promised me no one would be able to guess the truth. As long as I didn't confess, everything would be fine.

"What does that even mean?" I asked, relieved that my voice came out steady and slightly skeptical.

In answer, he pulled a face, as if mulling it over. "Could mean a number of things, but until we know what kind of magic it is, we can't be certain." The furrow in his brow deepened, reminding me abruptly of how serious he'd looked when crossing the bridge. Strange; there'd been no sign of that early darkness until now. "So, first, I have to make sure this isn't a trick."

I waited for him to say more, but he'd fallen oddly silent.

"Oh?" A tinge of nervousness made its way into my voice. Fynn hadn't said anything about someone testing the magic. What if Sebastian's magic was stronger than the Bargain?

"Well, if it's a trick, it's certainly not mine..." I laughed faintly. He didn't respond, so I babbled on. "I'm terrible at practical jokes. Want me to prove it?"

Gods, what if he interrogated me and the truth slipped out?

Sebastian shook his head suddenly, as if emerging from underwater, and I realized he hadn't simply been quiet; he'd been thinking, his mind far away from here.

"No need to prove anything," he said softly, sounding completely unlike the amused, slightly dramatic faerie I'd known so far. Then, the charming grin reappeared on his face and he gestured toward the lake's edge. "I only need to cast a spell or two. It helps if we're close to water, since that one's the hardest for me to conjure. Although I hope we'll reveal it before we get to that."

My eyes widened in alarm as I followed him toward the shore. "Get to what? You're not dunking me in that, are you?"

He laughed, the sound low and rough. "Of course not. I wouldn't do that to you. Besides..." He shrugged, glancing over his shoulder at me as he came to a halt by the lake's edge. "You look like the kind of girl who'd stop me before I did."

My stomach twisted with something dangerous, and I swallowed down the instinctive need to correct him. He'd seen me last night, when I pushed back and fought for myself. He didn't know who I really was.

When I didn't answer, he gave me an odd look, but thankfully he didn't question it further.

As Sebastian reached the shore, I came to rest beside him, the toes of my cherry red boots dipping into the water. I realized my arms were still folded before me, and instead of giving the appearance of nonchalance, it looked like a defense.

I slowly lowered my shoulders from around my ears and let my fingers rest lightly on my biceps. Despite how I knew it looked, I couldn't quite bring myself to drop my arms altogether. It was defensive because I needed to defend myself. And one plus one made two.

"Okay then," I lifted one eyebrow, tilting my chin a little to bridge the gap in our heights. "What now?"

"Well," he slipped his hands free from his pockets and held them up on either side of his face, as if feeling the moonlight caress his fingertips. His eyes fluttered closed, and I watched his breath visibly slow.

Before I knew it, I was matching mine to his, inhale for inhale. A steady wave of calm washed over me.

"Now, we call to the elements and see which one draws forth your magic," he said quietly.

"Gods above," I murmured under my breath. What on earth was he going to do when nothing happened? "Right to it, then."

One eye snapped open, its dark depths filled with amusement. "Would you like to chat first?"

His amusement held just enough of a hint that it was *at* me rather than *with* me that my fear faded a little more. Suddenly, I felt closer to how I'd been last night than ever before. My arms fell to my sides, and I propped one hand on my hips.

"We don't need to *chat*," I said dryly. "But clearly you've never heard of warming a girl up."

The other eye snapped open, eyebrows immediately lifting in unbridled delight as my cheeks burned in a fiery blush.

"I believe the word you're looking for is forepl—" he began, but I cut him off.

Unfortunately, the way I chose to do that was by slamming my palm over his mouth.

The heat from his body bled into my skin, fiercely hot on this cool autumn night. My fingers burned, both with the need to pull back and to keep touching.

It had been so long since I was with someone, that was all.

So long since I'd felt the warm press of a friendly body against mine.

So long, and so infrequent.

"Don't you dare," I said as slowly and steadily as I could. Then I let my hand drop.

His eyebrows were no longer lifted in wicked amusement, but there was a gleam of something new in his gaze. Blessedly, he didn't say anything. And when he returned to his previous position, hands lifted and eyelids fluttering closed, I didn't interrupt him.

"First, we call upon the earth," he said quietly.

His voice was different. Deeper—darker. It sounded like caves and gravel. Like underground streams, and places that had never seen sunlight. And when his eyes snapped open again, this time, they were pitch black.

I sucked in a breath, stumbling backward, but there was nowhere to go because the earth at our feet had risen, capturing us in a tunnel. There was no moonlight in here. It was nothing but shadows. Shadows and—

No, that wasn't true.

There was one small gap. One tiny stream, no more than a centimeter wide, of light beamed down. It didn't illuminate me, but it did land on Sebastian, casting his features into something frightening and new. Those coal-black eyes burned into me.

"What am I meant to do?" I asked, no longer bothering to keep the tremble from my voice. I'd be a fool not to be frightened now.

But Sebastian was already shaking his head, and by the time he let his hands fall, the earth had settled around us and his eyes had returned to normal.

They were slightly golden, I realized, in comparison to the black depths from before.

"It's all right," he said, and this time, the corner of his

mouth that curled up into a smile had nothing to do with humor. It radiated calm reassurance—exactly what I needed. "You don't need to do anything apart from stand there. The magic will call to you and your own magic will call back. Now, this next one," he cautioned me, voice lowering, "is fire. It won't hurt you, I promise, but—" He pulled a distracted face. "I have been told my fire illusions are..." He trailed off. "Well, let's just say there's a reason I'm not one of the fire-twirlers."

Before I could even begin to wonder what he meant by that, he lifted only one hand in the air, fingers crossed in a gesture I didn't recognize, and then suddenly—flames.

But they didn't whirl around us like the earth had, and thank the gods for that. Because these flames... oh... they filled every breath of air between us, around us. They caressed the trees, flickered across the surface of the water...

They were searching for something.

My eyes widened, but instead of fear rising within me, it was recognition. My eyes met Sebastian's, and they didn't burn like coal this time. They were pure flame, a brilliant golden orange blazing from deep within his soul.

I knew this face.

I'd never met him before, never had anything to do with him, but I knew him—because looking at him was like looking in a mirror. Only this mirror didn't lie. This mirror was nothing but the fierce, raw, terrifying truth.

There was a fire in him. It was raw, blazing, powerful... and it burned with the same heat as something unknown within me that I'd long since hidden away.

This fire *wanted*.

No sooner had that thought appeared than the flame died out. To my shock, it didn't leave charcoal behind. There were no tree corpses, smoking as they withered to ash, and the surface of a lake didn't bubble with fire.

But there was nothing magical appearing within me either, which meant this, too, had failed.

Of course it had; that was no surprise. What was a surprise, however, was the fierce determination that etched itself onto Sebastian's face. He was utterly convinced I had hidden fae magic—unyielding in his belief, despite the odds.

We had two trials left before he had to concede defeat. What would he do when he realized the magic hidden inside me wasn't something he could call free? Okay, so he wouldn't be able to guess its true source, but that didn't mean he'd just walk away and stop trying.

A hint of unease uncoiled within me. I'd been so intent on surviving this encounter with my secrets intact that I hadn't thought about what he would do when he was proven wrong.

Without announcing anything this time, Sebastian lifted his right hand, fingers twisting in a different gesture, and suddenly we were at the center of a hurricane.

Wind buffeted us, rocking us back and forth, and before I could lose my feet, he reached out with his left arm, curling it around my waist and holding me against him.

He was like a rock—an anchor in this strange world. A tree with roots so deep, he was part of the earth. One with it. And as I stared into his eyes, it occurred to me: I'd never really asked what the fae were.

What it would mean to be part of that other world.

To stand on that earth.

For the space of a heartbeat, I dared to imagine. I dared to believe my life was like it had been last night—carefree and full of possibility. I dared to believe that magic and all it held—joy, wonder, love—could be mine.

The wind howled, and a horrible realization slammed into me, as strong as the storm around us. There was nothing in me answering this call, but for the briefest moment, even knowing what the hidden magic was and that Sebastian would never find it like this, I had believed him.

I had believed there might be something wonderful hidden in me, simply because his own faith had been so true.

Feeling sick, I leaned backward, away from temptation. My hand flew to my neck, searching for the cool metal of the Offering necklace beneath my fingertips, and when I found it my eyes fluttered closed in relief. The metal didn't burn. This night was still safe, no matter what I'd nearly believed.

There was one trial left, and if I wanted to survive it, I had to get myself together. I remembered my plan and the list of questions in my pocket. The fire of want that burned deep within me, inextinguishable no matter how much I'd lost.

I held onto those truths and drew myself up tall within the steadying embrace of his arms, ready to step free the second the wind stopped.

Sebastian tilted his head as if he could hear my thoughts, his eyes burning pale white, like the ice of a frosty wind in winter. Of a gale hammering against bare skin. They cut right through me. Without a pupil, I couldn't see where he was looking, but I knew his gaze was fixed to mine.

My hands curled into claws as I fought to keep myself upright against the onslaught of magic. He didn't so much as stumble.

He was as alien to me as I was to the ants at my feet.

The hurricane vanished, and in the shock of its absence I fell, held upright only by his arm at my waist. And while the position was intimate in every way, there was nothing heat-filled about the look passing between the two of us. There was only fear. Uncertainty.

Because he knew as well as I did, now; it wasn't working, and there was only one trial left.

Slowly, almost reluctantly, his hands fell from my sides, his fingers lingering a beat longer than the rest.

"Water it is then," he said, clearly trying and failing to mask the uncertainty in his voice.

I couldn't help it; I laughed, all my brittle edges coming out in full force. This night was too much. I'd been swallowed by the earth, burned in a wildfire, and then caught in the heart of a hurricane—steadied only by the terrifyingly alien male before me.

There was no serene mask left to hold on to, no armor left to protect me. All I had was the raw, vulnerable truth—my anger.

I was angry at him. Angry that he was confusing me, making me believe something I *knew* was a lie.

Angry at myself for being so stupid. For not thinking up a convincing excuse and going straight to Fynn with my questions.

"Stop lying to yourself," I said, my words a painful rasp as I took a step backward.

Sebastian's eyes widened, and he reached out, snagging my palm in his. He still burned so hot, but I could feel that, against him, I was ice cold. Like a sculpture of a human instead of a living, breathing person.

"Just admit it," I insisted.

A voice inside me was screaming to leave. Now. It was telling me I wouldn't survive this final test.

His eyes, startlingly gold once more, flared with an emotion that reminded me of that brilliant orange flame, even though there was no magic in sight. I found it strangely compelling— almost soothing. My heartbeat steadied, and I told myself I could bear a few minutes more. Just long enough to end this farce. To convince Sebastian he was wasting his time before his curiosity drew attention to me.

Shouldn't be hard, I thought.

He didn't lift his hands this time, but rather spread his fingers out at his side, hands pointed down like arrows into the earth. Beside us, the lake rose.

Not a part of it; not a tornado of air or a whirlwind of earth; not even a wildfire burning across the trees... but rather, the whole of the lake.

It rose, and in its center I could see fish swimming, their bulbous eyes failing to comprehend the change in scenery as they stared through the glassy depths at a sight they had never seen before. A funnel emerged from the center, stretching to whirl above our heads, as though we were standing at the base of a whirlpool and staring up.

My perspective shifted, transforming into something utterly new, and I knew I would never be the same again. I swore, in that moment, that something was calling to me. That Sebastian had been right all along. What he sensed in me—it wasn't the open Bargain with Fynn, but something older. Deeper. Something that was mine and mine alone.

I knew it in my heart, in my bones.

And then, just as my held breath reached the point of gasping, the water collapsed. My mouth dropped open, air and water sucking in together so that I doubled over in a coughing fit, retching up lake water as the giant mass settled back into its muddy confines.

I knelt against the soaked, sludgy ground—utterly, painfully human.

A muttered curse sounded from above me, and then Sebastian was kneeling, hands clasping my shoulders and drawing soothing circles across my back as I coughed up the lake water. I couldn't look at him. Couldn't bear to face that failure again—failure I should never have even questioned because I knew there was no magic in me. I knew it.

No wonder the necklace wasn't burning; it didn't need to.

Who needed tormenting warnings when you were ruining your own life just fine?

"It didn't work, I take it?" I muttered, voice rasping in my throat.

A long pause greeted my question, and to my surprise, I found within myself a final kernel of bravery. With that kernel, I braced my hands on my knees, mud digging into my nails and breeches, and tilted my head up.

I nearly reeled back at the expression on his face. I'd expected disappointment. Maybe even devastation.

I hadn't expected anger.

"Who put you up to this?" Sebastian asked, his voice ominously low and quiet.

"Excuse me?" I snapped, shocked into harshness.

"Was it Fynn?" he insisted, ignoring me.

"Fynn has nothing to do with this!" I lied, throwing all my indignation into the words and only realizing my mistake at the last second.

Sebastian grew very still. "So, you know each other, then."

I gaped at him, my words vanishing. What should I say? If I said anything at all, I might risk confessing the truth about the open Bargain. Anything to wipe that look from his face.

That look of hatred.

A strange, new feeling in the pit of my stomach grew, twisting violently. I shoved myself to my feet.

"Sebastian, it's—"

"No," he said sharply, rising to his feet with inhuman grace. "It appears I owe you an apology." He swept an elaborate bow. "My first assessment was correct, and I merely became swept up in an illusion."

For the briefest moment, hope rose. Perhaps not everything was ruined.

But then he shattered it by straightening, a savage smile on his face, and saying, "You are, indeed, nobody important after all."

The world stopped, his words ringing in my ears.

My first assessment was correct.

It shouldn't have been a surprise; it shouldn't even have hurt. I was used to it, and it wasn't like it mattered. This was my role in life. An important role, ironically enough. A *vital* role, to be so worthless.

And yet, the way he said it—the way he looked at me, with a slight curl of disgust to his mouth... Like I'd disappointed him. Like I could have been something more, and this inability to measure up was my own fault, instead of an unwanted destiny I couldn't escape.

My stomach churned with shame. How many more times did fate have to remind me?

It was time to leave. Time to return to the shadows, to stop trying to reach out for something better. To remember, finally, the role I played and what it required of me.

I didn't move.

It was as though I had become rooted to the spot, and, through the rapid drag of my own breath, I began to feel something different. Something just as strange and new as the pain my foolish Bargain had revealed—but I liked it much more.

This was fire.

This was the fire I'd felt last night, standing beneath that spotlight, taking Sebastian's hand while the woman beside me fumed. This was the fire I'd seen in Sebastian's eyes only minutes earlier. The one that wanted. The one that took.

My memories whirled, still unsettled from the night before, still churned up and wild. In my mind, I was thrown back to that white altar, back to when I saw the look on the priest's face as he stared at my solitary figure waiting and waiting in the alcove behind the tent. I saw the looks on the faces of the guests in the audience as the man I loved was out there fucking my sister, leaving me standing there alone.

I saw their relief that everything was back to the way it should be—that the darling of their village was no longer marrying the hag.

I saw it all, remembered it all, and I thought—how was any of this my fault? I wasn't the one to leave some poor woman standing there. So what if I had dared to believe that such a beautiful life could be mine? So what if I had convinced myself that the warning that burned from the Offering's necklace was no warning at all?

Could you blame me?

And yet, these men... They somehow made it my shame. My fault.

I knew I should walk away; instead, I took hold of that kernel of bravery and seized it. Then, I lifted my palm and slapped it across Sebastian's face, wiping his expression clean.

He staggered back, his palm coming up as if he couldn't quite believe the touch had been real.

"How dare you?" I hissed.

He stared up at me as I straightened and backed away. Utter shock had spread across his features. It was almost comical.

"How dare you turn this around on me?" My voice rose, and I had to choke back what felt like a thousand words catching in my throat. I didn't even know what they were, or why I was so angry. "You asked me here, you made all these assumptions, and then *you* were the one who was wrong. Don't you dare act like I'm the problem."

I took a step back, and then another, waiting for more words to spill out, but there were too many. I couldn't see them all. Didn't want to see them all. There was so much anger, so much hurt, and I didn't know how to hold it.

All through my little speech, Sebastian remained silent, his eyes wide and incredulous. A pink mark was already coming up on his cheek. He opened his mouth, but I'd had enough.

Before he could utter a single word, I turned on my heel and left. Not toward the path that led back to town, but deeper into the forest, where I could be alone with my thoughts.

He called after me, but I didn't bother to acknowledge it. Besides, my mind was screaming too loudly to hear anything beyond my name.

With my pace steady and my back straight, I left the clearing with Sebastian standing behind me in the mud.

CHAPTER 9

Bailey

I REGRETTED MY DECISION INSTANTLY.

The night swallowed me whole, trees surrounding me on all sides, until I couldn't forge a path, let alone find one. I slowed to a halt, looking around and listening intently, but I couldn't even hear Sebastian's voice calling anymore.

All I could hear were the night sounds—creatures rustling, animals calling. They were sounds that I had grown up around my whole life, albeit distantly, and yet here, they didn't sound quite right. I didn't recognize them, and I remembered once more how other things could cross over the bridge while the pathways were open.

"Precisely how much of an idiot do you want to be tonight, Bailey?" I muttered under my breath, instinctively seeking any form of company, even if it was just my own. "Will we take the shadowed path into the vines of despair, or the hidden trail toward the pit of doom?"

I swallowed, the sound far too loud, and took another careful step forward.

Despite the racing of my heart, I forced my rational brain back in charge. If I could just find a clearing, then I'd be able to see the stars. I hadn't run so far that I'd left the fairground entirely, which meant my town was north west. Find the Knight and Sword, count three stars down until you see one that glows almost blue if you look closely; that way's north.

I could do the rest from there.

Easing my way toward a stream of moonlight that had broken the thick canopy above, I crossed my fingers that the clearing would be wide enough to see the sky.

It was. I let out a rush of air; thank the gods for that.

From there, it didn't take me long to locate the Knight and Sword—four circular stars next to a big line—and then three down. There it was: north.

"That way, then," I muttered, and just the thought of knowing something had me standing a little taller, my spine a little straighter.

I'd so rarely been given the opportunity to use what I had learned from all those books, growing up. To lead without being immediately shunted to the rear, where I could only follow. The feeling was intoxicating; I wanted more.

I took a step to the west and then froze; something else had taken a step, too.

My heart began to pound. Whatever it was, it sounded large. Were there any large nocturnal prey animals in this forest? I didn't think so. But there were many, *many* large creatures that lived in Criera.

But maybe it had been the echo of my own footstep. I stepped again, carefully, testing the noise. Nothing. One more time—nothing still.

But then, I didn't move at all, and yet the sound returned. Sticks broke with a snap, leaves rustling. The thing was large. Very large.

Two eyes gleamed in the darkness, hovering at the same height as my own.

"Sweet gods below," I hissed.

To the accompaniment of a low snarl, I ran. Trees slashed my face, branches whipping back and tangling in my hair until all manner of leaves and sticks were caught in it. I didn't care. I thrashed through the undergrowth, briefly thankful that it seemed this creature didn't belong in this forest, since it was having as much trouble fitting among the trees as I was.

But that was poor comfort, because if it didn't belong here, that meant it came from *there*.

What manner of fae creature had I stumbled upon?

I ran, keeping as close to a western direction as I could, but not really caring at this point. If I could only reach the edge of the forest, surely the creature wouldn't risk open ground in a foreign land.

No sooner had I thought that, than I slammed into something hard.

"Oh no," I hissed, leaning forward and feeling vine-covered rock as far as I could reach.

I'd run into some kind of boulder, or perhaps the side of a hill. I didn't know how far it spanned, but I couldn't even push through the forest here to find out. It was too overgrown with vines.

I turned my back to the rock and vowed that I would at least face this creature as it took me down.

Those two glowing eyes appeared once more, and the shadows peeled back to reveal long, dripping teeth below a scaled snout. A huff of warm air brushed my face, tinged with the scent of rot.

And then a man stepped in front of me.

My heart leapt into my throat as he hissed a series of complicated syllables at the creature, and against all odds, the thing fled. The air in my lungs burst free in rough pants as he turned to face me. For some wild reason, I expected to see Sebastian. But it wasn't.

I blinked, my brow furrowing and my heart pounding too loudly for me to think.

"Fynn." His name came out in a breathless rush of air as my straining mind finally accepted I was safe. "Thank you," I whispered.

Fynn's eyes glinted as he stepped forward, reminding me of the moment only minutes earlier, by the lake, when I'd realized how alien the fae really were. But as the moonlight caught his face, I found the smile on his face was pleasant—concerned, even.

He reached out a hand to help me free from the encroaching vines. "Are you all right?" he asked.

His voice was low and gentle, filled with a kindness I didn't expect. Still, with that creature so nearby and my own flight through the forest still pounding in my veins, I couldn't help the hairs on the back of my neck from rising. I hesitated, unwilling to take his hand.

His gaze flicked down to my palm, poised halfway between us in the air, and his brow furrowed. Shaking my head, I forced my hesitations away, took his hand, and stepped down toward him.

"What was that thing?" I breathed.

His expression turned grim. "Lora beast," he muttered. "Nasty things. One or two usually follow us over the bridge, but they don't last long out here. They slink back over the bridge as soon as the next crescent moon rises."

"How come I've never seen one before?" I asked, eyes wide. "It clearly eats humans."

His eyes glinted again. "That it does. But it can't survive away from the trees. It draws its energy from them like any other plant."

I scoff. "That thing was not a plant."

To my surprise, Fynn—who I realized abruptly was still holding my hand—gnashed his teeth with an amused smile. "Have you never seen a carnivorous plant before?"

I stared at him, lips parted, incredulous. Before I knew it, I began to laugh. "You can't be serious," I said.

After several moments of dazed, hysterical laughter, Fynn's smile had grown wider, amusement caressing his features. It was a pleasant smile, although I couldn't quite shake that feeling of unease. Like my body sensed danger that my brain hadn't yet noticed.

"I am joking," he confessed, finally letting my hand go and turning back toward the shadows. "It leeches energy from plants, which is why it stays in the forest, but it is not a plant. It's a kind of lizard-lion hybrid." He shrugged one shoulder. "That's the closest I can get to a comparison with your creatures." He turned back to me, one eyebrow raised. "Did my distraction work?"

It took me a second. My eyes widened as I realized my heart no longer raced, and my breathing was almost normal again. He'd said all that stuff about plant-animal hybrids to distract me. To bring me out of the fear and into benign confusion.

And it had worked.

"Yes," I breathed, still stunned.

This time, his smile was brilliant—blinding. "Then," he said with a charming half bow as he offered me his elbow, "allow me to escort you back to the path."

I didn't hesitate this time. I hooked my arm through his and watched as the trees seemed to part before us. This time, nothing whipped through my hair or smacked me in the face, and our pathway back to the moonlit trail passed in seconds.

I let go of his arm, stepping away. "That was..." I let out a breath, shaking my head. I didn't bother to hide the trembling from my hands, not after that. "I can't believe that had... That *thing* had... Well—" I began to say thank you and then stopped, eyes wide.

Never say thank you to a fae. But I already had, hadn't I?

The moonlight caught in the dark depths of his eyes, and I couldn't read the expression there. The world was all a blur. This was the danger my body had sensed, my mind still too shaken to realize what I'd done.

Then the moment passed and he leaned forward, apparently taking pity on me as he said, "You did say 'thank you', but I'll make it easy for you."

He held out his hand. Slowly, carefully, I put mine into it. He lifted it to his face, eyes never breaking contact with mine, and brushed a kiss over the back of my hand.

"A kiss," he said. "The simplest and most traditional payment of them all. Go, and be blessed."

I felt the magic settle around us, the words of a Bargain given and then taken away, just like that.

The pounding of my heart eased and I wondered if maybe I'd made the right choice for once. Fynn offered me safety and aid, where Sebastian had only torn me down. Perhaps I knew the right man to trust after all.

"Well," I said slowly. "That was an adventure."

He burst into laughter, standing up straight. He was nearly a head taller than me: something I hadn't noticed until now. And while he wasn't muscled like Sebastian, there was a lithe elegance to him that held me more than a little spellbound. Even his walk was beautiful, as he moved with a feline grace that matched the sharp edges of his eyes and lips—and his personality.

Sebastian was gorgeous, but Fynn was deadly.

He shrugged one shoulder, turning back to the circus for a moment. Beyond its boundaries, marked by ribbon and velvet drapes, laughter and music spilled out. A different sort of adventure lay within those walls, and despite all that had happened tonight, I realized that nothing had changed.

I still intended to find a way to leave Aelor with them.

"Have you thought about what I said?" Fynn asked, still gazing thoughtfully at the distant tents.

I didn't have to ask what he meant.

"Yes," I breathed. "You were right—there is another way."

He waited, neither pushing me nor trying to squeeze out whichever answer he wanted.

"I found... rumors." I mulled over the words, choosing them with care. "Humans who've crossed over with you while the borders were open."

Fynn's eyebrow lifted. "Looking for a life of daring acrobatics? Not what I expected, but perhaps that's my fault for making assumptions."

My lip twitched. I slipped my hands in my pockets, rolling back on one heel as I trailed my toe absently through the leaf litter. "I don't want to stay with the circus. But if I can get over there, do you think I could survive?"

I finally turned to face him. He was studying me carefully, expression unreadable.

After a long pause, he said, "It depends."

"On?"

"On how you respond to our magic."

My lip wrinkled. I'd just become intimately acquainted with their magic; it hadn't gone well.

Fynn leaned one hand against a tree and drummed his fingers thoughtfully. The blue of his eyes glinted in the night. "We could train you, I suppose."

The air seemed to still, as if waiting for something. Or maybe that was just me, caught in anticipation. I'd hoped to stumble on instructions, maybe a book or two, but training? I hadn't dared hope someone would actually help me.

As soon as I thought it, the giddy feeling faded away, replaced by the far more familiar suspicion. *Why* was he helping me? Surely he realized by now who I was. I'd shattered the orb; all my memories had returned.

The fae shouldn't help the Offering escape her oath.

"What would training do?" I asked all the same.

He lifted one shoulder. "Teach you to take on creatures like the lora beast, for one." He spoke slowly, as if feeling out the answer for the first time. "Expose your body to our magic carefully enough that your human nature doesn't reject it, even if it's inclined to. You could learn how to protect yourself with the forest's abundance—various plant concoctions can provide basic shielding, even simple offensive spells if you brew them correctly." He flashed me a grin. "Or eat the correct part."

Piece by piece, with each word Fynn spoke, my world opened up. He would have resources to share, books and things that he must be offering to lend me in the time before the circus left. A training program, as opposed to me selecting random titles with increasing desperation while the clock ticked down.

I could read about their world and learn how to survive it.

The fire I'd felt by the lake returned in full force, and I felt abruptly as I had last night: changed. Raw. Brimming with possibility. If I succeeded at this, I would become a new person in Criera. One who was not bound by the oath I'd never chosen, and who could instead live as freely as I had when my memories were lost.

And I *could* succeed. It would be difficult but not impossible —while living here was both.

"Tell me how," I said abruptly, accidentally interrupting him mid sentence.

He regarded me. After a beat, he said, "Traditionally

humans are not allowed to linger, but there are ways. You'll need a ticket, and the ticket will require payment. But you have time. It isn't like a Bargain; no one will intervene, or even sense the ticket is with you." With a twist of his hand, he produced a slip of crimson paper, its edges trimmed in gold, and held it before him. "The ticket is useless until paid for, mind. You'll need to secure its magic before the final night."

"I'm not obligated to follow through with anything if I take this from you?" I asked, eyes narrowed.

Fynn smiled. "No one will force you to pay, or extract any other obligation from you. You either pay, or you change your mind and you don't. Simple."

"And I'll get safely to the other side?"

He bowed. "I will personally see you safely to the other side, whole and unharmed."

Five more nights. I had five nights to learn their magic, study their world, and pay for my ticket. And then I could leave, simple as that. It was practically a dream offer, given how tangled trading with the fae usually was.

Which meant there must be a catch. Not to mention that I still didn't understand why he was helping me at all. What did he get out of this that was worth helping the Offering escape her duties? What was I missing?

Fynn stepped closer, the ticket held lightly between his middle and forefinger. "Once you cross the bridge, you won't have the easy life you do here. There will be no friends to help you, or lovers to soothe you on the cold, dangerous nights." He paused, something darkening in his gaze. "Well, no human lovers."

I swallowed.

He kept speaking. "You will have to say goodbye to everyone you've known, everyone who's ever loved and supported you. Can you do it?"

Something in me grew still. Of course: he didn't know. He didn't know I was unwanted. Didn't know I was the Offering. Sebastian hadn't seemed to realize either, for all that he had stared into my multi-colored eyes for an age.

I couldn't tell him. Not only would it risk him withdrawing his help, or twisting my oath against me and my village, but... I couldn't bear it.

I couldn't bear Fynn looking at me the way the rest of them did. Like I was worthless.

"I'll do it," I said in a rush. "I'll run away with you. With the circus, I mean," I amended quickly, heat rising on my cheeks. "Not you, specifically."

Amusement danced in his eyes. When he spoke, his voice was quieter than before. "Why would you want to leave your home? Surely you have a life here that would miss you."

I scoffed, a dozen words suddenly choking in my throat. For a moment, they almost came pouring out, spilling all of my secrets. But finally, I managed a simple, bitter, "You'd think, wouldn't you?"

For a long while, there was silence, until finally, Fynn said, "In that case, if you want it, it's yours."

My hand fluttered to my throat, to the necklace hidden there, and I waited for it to burn. For the binding oath of my destiny to ruin even this—my one small chance of escape.

It didn't. The metal remained cool to the touch, and for the first time in twenty-eight long years, true hope surged within me. The woman I'd become last night didn't have to remain a memory; I could become her right now. Forever.

I hesitated for only a moment, then I reached out, fingers lightly clasping the thin paper. As I plucked it from his hand, I stared at it, reading the words.

Admit one: Disguise Included.

And then, at the bottom in fine print: *do not tear, break, or bend*

Disguise included? I supposed that was how the 'no humans after midnight' rule was bypassed. But what kind of disguise did it mean?

After a minute, I decided it didn't matter. Finally, everything I wanted was in the palm of my hand. And if there was a catch, I had five days to find it and no obligation to follow through.

I looked up, not knowing what to say when the words 'thank you' were both too little and too dangerous. The look in Fynn's eyes made me wonder if he knew exactly what I was thinking, anyway.

Which brought up another question: "How did you find me tonight?"

A slow smile spread across his face. "I offer to you seven nights entry to the circus of the Lumière, and safe passage home as many times as you will," he intoned, reading the words of our Bargain back to me.

Safe passage home.

I gaped at him. Had he really been bound by the Bargain to save me?

But before I could ask anything further, the moon slid behind a cloud, shrouding us in darkness. By the time it emerged, Fynn was gone.

CHAPTER 10

Bailey

THE DUSTY QUIET OF THE LIBRARY FOLDED AROUND ME AS I TRACED MY finger over the spines. Merelda hopped along the shelf to my left, jumping from book to book and kicking up tiny dust plumes wherever she stepped. I'd had to hide her from the librarian when we came in; while the village may have tolerated Merelda's presence among them out there, they didn't like it when an imp had access to their own spaces, especially not with me.

She'll start a fire, I'd been told once or twice. *She'll chew the furniture like a dog*—more than twice. If I was honest, they probably weren't wrong about the chewing part. I glanced over at her, and she bared her teeth in a sharp grin.

I bit down a laugh that would give us away in the silence and resumed my search.

Master Skylark had sent us for more volumes on her belladonna project, and I welcomed the chance to get out of the workshop. For one thing, it meant I didn't have to deal with the cold discomfort that was now a permanent companion whenever I was in the village, away from the solace of my home or the intoxicating danger of the circus. And secondly, it meant that Merelda couldn't hurl expletives at me in a language I didn't understand—something she had been doing all morning until I distracted her with the library playground.

Without mentioning the ticket or my ultimate plan, I had tried to tell her that I knew the danger of returning to the Lumière night after night. That I was being cautious, and the fae hadn't ensnared me in their dangerous tricks. But she didn't listen, or she didn't understand.

Maybe when she finished playing hopscotch on the atlases, I'd try again. I'd draw a big picture of Sebastian's face and put a cross through it, showing that I wasn't falling prey to a pretty face and a gorgeous smile anymore. Even if it was an exceptionally gorgeous smile.

Maybe I'd put a cross through that too. Or use it as a dartboard.

I turned the corner and froze. Ahead of me was a familiar, hulking figure. Luke: the very man who the Fates had deemed an acceptable match for the Offering. Largely because nobody else wanted him.

I ducked back behind the shelf. He was a cruel man, prone to fits of rage where he smashed up the windows and doors of his house. But he needed someone, they said. Someone to help him grow and reach his potential. And what a perfect duty for the Offering to perform—a humble, supportive wife, who talked him down from his self-sabotaging fits.

"Absolutely not," I whispered to myself, ducking around a corner and down a small, winding section of the library that held the least popular books. "You want support? Buy some suspenders."

I'd wait down here until he was gone. It wasn't as though Master Skylark was in a hurry to have me back. Every time she looked at me, she rolled her eyes as if she could smell the circus lingering on my clothes.

Speaking of the circus...

I tilted my head, glancing at the shelves with fresh eyes as Merelda fluttered over and perched on the top row.

This was where they kept the fae records. Not the interesting ones—the magical books that were stored in the city—but the boring archives of our village's past. I traced my finger along the spines. The book I'd taken from Master Skylark hadn't offered anything useful beyond what I'd already read, but these could hold an entirely different perspective.

Last night hadn't gone well, by any measure, and although I'd managed to obtain the ticket I hoped for, I was even further away from getting the answers I needed to survive it. Sebastian was no longer an option, and while Fynn had only ever helped me, he also made me uneasy.

I owed him twice now. Two Bargains, or trades at least, loomed over my head and threatened untold consequences. If I also relied on him for all my knowledge about Criera, and how the fae lived over the water, then I would be submitting to him completely.

I may as well marry Luke and be done with it.

And... there was the way Fynn looked at me sometimes, when he thought I wasn't watching. A haunted, hungry look. It sent a shiver through my entire body, every time I caught it—a not entirely unwelcome one.

But so long as I held on tight to that initial feeling of unease, I could ensure I didn't fall for any tricks there, either. Suspicion was healthy, when dealing with the fae. I had to trust my instincts.

A tiny kernel of remembered fire flickered inside me. My instincts were *good*, gods damn it. I was allowed to have this, and soon, everything would change. My shoulders eased, back straightening, and I arched a brow as I faced the shelves and selected my first book.

However, as the minutes turned into hours, while I hid in the darkest corner of the library and skimmed through their pages, I quickly found that these books weren't very helpful at all. Whatever history they were recording, it was as though there were pieces missing—deliberately scratched from the annals of record. I shut the last book a little too forcefully, sending up a cloud of dust that did nothing to improve my irritation. I coughed, trying to muffle the sound, and then sneezed three times in a row.

From across the rows came an idle 'bless you', and I had to choke back the instinctive 'thank you' that caught in my throat. I knew that voice. He began to speak again, chatting away to the librarian.

Against my better instincts and Merelda's fierce glare, I crept along the shelving and peered through a gap at eye level, toward the front of the library.

Hayden looked well. Better than he had any right to.

I cut that thought off immediately; he had every right to. Just because I didn't like it didn't mean it wasn't fair. Hayden was the heir of the village's founding family, and the elders had seen him grow from a bouncing golden boy into a laughing, carefree, charismatic man. Our romance had been a pathetic blip on his life from the beginning, an ill-fated tryst where it became quickly obvious that I wouldn't be the humble, supportive girlfriend he needed from me. It should have ended long before it did.

If I'd only listened to the warnings screaming at me, instead of clinging to what wasn't mine, it would have. But I hadn't—I couldn't. I wanted too much.

A rough, choked sound rose in the back of my throat; I cut it off before it could escape. For the briefest of moments, I wished Fynn hadn't given my Bargain back. Whatever the fae did to use my forgotten memories against me, it couldn't be worse than keeping them.

I realized I'd squeezed my eyes tightly shut when small fists began pounding on them. Flinching, I pulled back and glared at Merelda as she stuck her tongue out at me.

"That was rude," I mouthed at her, wincing and fighting back the urge to scrub at my eyes. She'd barely hurt them in truth, but it was damned uncomfortable.

She cocked her head and eyed me shrewdly, sending an unexpected tingle of awareness racing through me. I paused, studying her.

Half the time, Merelda acted like some kind of mix between a happy pet and a small child. But then there were these moments when I got the impression she was studying me so carefully, so fiercely... and there was nothing childlike about her at all. Almost as if the rest was an act to avoid people looking at her too closely.

I shook my head and turned back to the front. Hayden was still there.

"Oh, it's lovely this time of year," the librarian agreed, leaning forward on the bench and smiling up at Hayden with a besotted expression. "You'll have such a wonderful time, the two of you."

My body stiffened. Hayden laughed, the sound echoing over the library.

"To be sure," he agreed, giving her a wink. "Though I imagine I'll come home with my purses a fair bit lighter than they began."

She waved her hand, still smiling. "All worth it for a beautiful woman."

Her lips pressed together for a minute, and she flicked her gaze over at the stacks where I had been before I ran from Luke.

"The scales are balanced once again," she said in a lower voice. "Surely any price is worth that."

A cold sensation slid down my throat, landing heavy in my gut and dragging me lower with every passing second. Of course. Hayden was golden and glowing, poised on the advent of a holiday with my sister. A holiday of fortune and prosperity. And it was all his because he had done the right thing and left the Offering at the altar.

A crashing sound snapped me out of a rapidly descending fog of rage. I blinked, alarmed at the change that had come over me. I'd never felt anything like that before. Even the pain I'd tried to Bargain away to the Lumière hadn't been anger; why would it be? Anger was about injustice. Things that weren't fair.

Everything was fair about this. I didn't have to like it, but I couldn't argue that it wasn't just. One child for the rest of them, and my village had prospered. Sickness, pain, disaster... they never visited, and all it cost was for me to remain in the shadows. I could still have a good life, still have a quiet, mediocre life of servitude and comfort. There was nothing wrong with that— it was noble, even—but as I strained my neck to see what the crashing sound had been, I realized that someone, at least, disagreed.

I gaped at Merelda, reaching out to stop her as she hurled another candlestick into the far corner of the room. Hayden and the librarian whipped around to peer into the shadows, the confusion on their faces deepening.

"Stop it!" I hissed, snatching for her again.

She buzzed out of reach. Then, locking eyes with me in a clear challenge, she picked up a strass beetle that had wandered onto the shelf, minding its own business, and hurled it straight at Hayden's head. With an angry buzz, it connected.

I stared open-mouthed as he rubbed the back of his head,

spinning around in confusion. The strass beetle flew, irritated but unharmed, onto the desk between them.

"Man, that hurt!" he muttered, looking over the library.

I ducked out of sight before he saw me. Then, through the gaps near the floor, I watched as he noticed the beetle. His face relaxed in understanding.

"The damned thing's drunk," he said with a laugh. "I thought it lost its cuticle for a minute there."

They relaxed, and I took the opportunity to glare up at Merelda. "You'll get us caught," I hissed.

Subdued, she fluttered down beside me to perch on my shoulder. Something rolled near my feet, and I glanced down to see a tiny glass orb. Huh, Hayden was right. The strass beetle had lost its cuticle, although by now it would have grown a new one.

That was the distinctive feature of those beetles. The hard exoskeleton that surrounded them resembled the same Bargains that we wrought with the fae—and contained a drop of the same magic.

I picked it up and studied it, turning it slowly in my fingers. There was an iridescence to it that marked it as a Strass Bargain, rather than a true one, but that only meant the magic wasn't quite as strong.

As children, we would hunt strass beetles by the river, plucking them from the air, where—in self defense, like a lizard dropping its tail—they would drop the orb-like feature from their backs and then fly on, already growing another. We would whisper our wishes into the orbs, promising to trade things with each other in return for magnificent fortune. Whether the strass beetle's existence was some joke of the fae, or one of nature's magical creations, a tiny amount of Bargain Magic did exist within them. And if our wishes were accepted, the glittering orange at the center would ignite into blue flame, just as it did with true Bargains.

I'd only made one successful Strass Bargain in my life with my sister, and as I stared at the orb in my fingertips, I realized abruptly that I couldn't remember what it was. I frowned, turning it over and over. I remembered the orb, and I remembered the blue flame inside, but I couldn't remember the words of the Bargain at all—even though I knew they had held for so long.

Until something shattered it.

At the thought, I accidentally squeezed too hard on the cuticle, and the entire thing collapsed with a quiet fizz.

"Shit," I muttered under my breath.

"Is someone else here?" Hayden asked, and I froze where I was.

But either the librarian had pity for me or she thought she was somehow helping the golden boy by not admitting it. She said 'no' in a breezy voice, and within the next minute I heard him pack up his things and leave.

I let out a slow exhale of relief and rose to my feet. I would have to wait a little while longer before leaving, in case he lingered out the front. Besides, I couldn't face the librarian just yet.

But when I stepped around the shelf toward the center of the library, where the study tables were, I saw a familiar face. It was not one of the two who had been talking.

"Katerina," I breathed.

My sister studied me, the corner of her lip twitching into a familiar smile. I used to think that smile was so magnificent. So calm and poised. But now when I saw it, I only thought she looked cruel. Had it always been that way?

She took a step toward me and lowered her voice.

"Bailey," she said, "it's so good to see you."

Before I could stop her, she'd pulled me into an embrace. My body stiffened in horror and rejection. I should have pushed her away. Should have screamed in her face, but who would stand by me if I did? The librarian would shun me, and by evening the entire village would know how the Offering had selfishly shoved her sister aside, instead of wishing her good fortune.

As I stepped back and regarded her, a tiny part of me was forced to admit that self preservation wasn't the only reason I hugged her back.

"You look well," I said, unable to keep from my voice the hint of hope that she might return the compliment.

"I feel it," she agreed.

She tilted her head, scanning my face as if trying to read the expression there, as too many people before her had given up trying to do.

"Gosh, Bailey, you're as much of a closed book as ever." She shook her head. "Would it kill you to smile?"

Probably, I thought, but outwardly I merely attempted to do as she said. A huff of laughter escaped her, even while she clapped her hand over her mouth and tried to stop it.

Fire. It swelled within me, reminding me of all that I had decided last night. I dropped the smile, lifted one brow, and leaned back against the shelves with my arms folded before me.

Katerina blinked, quickly smoothing it into a breathy laugh. "Never mind," she said. "Look, I do hope there are no hard feelings by now. It wasn't how I wished it would happen, but—" She gave a shrug. "Hayden didn't want to hurt you, so he kept waiting until the last minute to tell you what we'd decided."

The last minute. Right, of course.

A beautiful smile graced her expression, almost sheepish in the way she lowered her eyelashes and flushed. "And if it weren't for the Offering's magic lashing out, we all would have been much more sensible, wouldn't we? It's such a wild thing when it's ignored! Do you remember the crack in the town square?" She burst into laughter.

Merelda was nowhere to be seen, and it was a small mercy, because if she was here, I was certain she would gouge my sister's eyes out.

The crack in the town square had emerged when I was learning Criari. I hadn't realized... hadn't guessed that my success with the strange language would be forbidden. But Katerina had been failing her classes at the time, and so, the scales were imbalanced.

That was the first time Mother had tried to make me renew my oath, wheedling and cajoling until I couldn't bear to even hear the word 'oath'. I refused, hiding away whenever she came for me.

When the earth had split, and the daemon-stench of sulfur rose in the air, I'd been so terrified that I hurled my favorite fairytale book into it. The one with all the trickiest Criari words. I told them it was a book of herbs.

The stench had vanished, and Katerina passed her classes the next day.

I'd been sure to practice slowly from then on, and never to speak it out loud.

"Such a wild thing," I told her. "There are no hard feelings."

It was strange, but the words even sounded true. What was the point in blaming anyone? It was easier to look for the beauty, to find the layers that hid like treasure inside all the ugly decisions people made. My sister had hugged me close for a seven-day after I destroyed the faerie book, and when she accepted her achievement award, mine was the first name she thanked.

There was always beauty; you just had to look.

Her expression flickered, and for a moment she looked at me with something close to pity.

She stepped in close. "You know," she said, her voice a low murmur, "Hayden told me about Michel."

Through the thick silence of the library, I heard the ticking of the clock. The rustling of pages as the librarian breezed through a romance novel at the front desk.

"What about him?" I asked serenely.

Her expression wavered, unreadable. "Only that he kept visiting... to see you."

It had been the beginning of the end, when Michel showed up. Here was another man who saw the Offering as a challenge to defeat, and who cared more about the notches on his bedpost than the feelings of another human being.

And because I always fell for pretty faces and words, I had smiled at him. Enjoyed his company. Laughed at his jokes and preened at his unsubtle attention.

Maybe I even flirted, I don't know. It hadn't meant a thing, because I was happy with Hayden. I'd thought I had it all.

I'd thought that people were starting to see past the Offering's Bargain to discover who I was outside of it.

But Hayden's true face had appeared when he'd seen the look in his friend's eye. Our first fight had been about Michel, and while I thought it was resolved within a day, Hayden had merely waited with cruel calculation to deliver the final blow.

The Offering's Bargain Magic was a wild thing indeed...

"I didn't realize my social calendar was so interesting," I drawled. The words just spilled out of me, where before they would have remained in the privacy of my mind. "I can send you copies if you like? Highlight the points of interest in red?"

Her lips parted in wordless surprise, and then she laughed. The sound tinkled like bells. "Never bother. Hayden has shared the story around, now, so we can all be on the lookout for discrepancies in your *social calendar*." Her gaze flicked to my necklace. "If you're so used to that thing by now that you don't notice its warnings, we should all be vigilant, to help you. Right?"

My expression was the cool, granite rock-face of an ancient cliff. It didn't move. I remembered the nights my sister had sung me to sleep through the nightmares. I held onto them so tightly I left claw marks in the side.

"How kind of you," I murmured, my voice husky—almost cruel, "to be so diligent."

For half a second, I swore unease flickered in her features. Then she lowered her gaze and said demurely, "It is our burden to share."

From behind her back, she produced something and held it out to me. It took me several seconds to make sense of it. A rose, with pretty pink petals on the cusp of falling. Ready to be pressed and dried.

"I brought you a rose for your prayers," she said. "I was going to bring it by your house, but I needn't now." Before I could think of responding, her next words wiped any answer from my mind. "Mother sent it."

Memories of strass beetle shells swam through my mind, glittering with magic. In their glass reflection, the faces of two sisters appeared, side by side. I'd have given anything to remember what secrets they held.

After a long, uncomfortable pause, she set the rose on the shelf between us.

"Well, until next time," she said brightly, backing away. "I'm sure I'll be seeing you."

I didn't reply.

CHAPTER 11

Bailey

"Where to first?" Stefan asked me, blowing on a steaming paper cup of spiced chocolate before taking a tentative sip.

When he'd met me at my front gate, despite neither of us going to the circus on the second night, I hadn't known what to think. He was only going to keep me company, but I couldn't understand it. No one had ever done that for me before. I knew, of course, that it was because he hadn't grown up in our town. He didn't have that instinctive understanding of what the Offering was and what she deserved.

But that didn't change how nice it felt—to be so simply, casually, supported.

"Well, we've seen the contortionist," I said, pleased when the words managed to come out with casual indifference. "So no need to see him again."

Stefan tilted his head from side to side, mulling my answer over. "They do change their acts as each night goes on," he admitted with some reluctance. "If you enjoyed his show, it could be worth seeing again."

He glanced at me sideways. I hid my smile behind my own steaming paper mug. "Are you fishing for gossip, old man?"

He broke into laughter, slapping me gently on the arm. "I heard your knees crack when you stood up, girlie. Don't go naming what you can't face."

I laughed, the sound catching in a snort, and we linked arms to stroll away from the contortionist tent.

"So," he said, side-eyeing me again. "*Is* there gossip?"

"There is not," I said firmly. "I am immune to any and all pretty fae men who would dazzle me with their impeccable jawlines and trap me inside the... I don't know... the veins of an oak leaf."

He pulled a face. "Creative."

"Thank you. Years of being alone will do that to you."

Stefan's expression softened, and I regretted the glib comment, even as that new, bold part of me found the honesty thrilling. I never said these things out loud, where people could hear them.

Still, it wasn't fair, drawing attention to my lonely little life when it was perfectly fine. Stefan had never accepted or understood the Offering's duties; he didn't like me speaking about them so casually.

For once, though, he didn't comment. Merely took another sip of his hot chocolate and said idly, "I'm not sure that particular *pretty fae man* would do that to you, actually."

My head whipped sharply toward him. "Why not?"

Stefan shrugged. "Instincts, I suppose. Not quite sure."

An uncomfortable feeling settled low in my stomach. Would you look at that? Even Stefan wasn't immune to fae manipulation.

"Come on then," I said, distracting him. "Where shall we go first?"

Taking the redirection begrudgingly, he led me to the outskirts of the fairground, where we strolled aimlessly for a while. As we rounded one corner, I saw Sebastian standing in a pool of moonlight. He leaned against a pillar, body angled toward a group of swooning women. Even from here, I felt the heat from his smile—the seduction of it. I shivered.

"What about the fire-twirlers?" I said after we'd done another circuit, slowly meandering among the illusions and games.

Stefan's eyebrows shot up. "At least we'll be warm," he conceded. "Onwards!"

We walked across the other side of the fairground. Before the night was through, I intended to scout out an avenue or two where I might learn more about the fae and their magic. Perhaps a storyteller, or even just a group of performers spinning tales by the bar. Anything to give me leverage for the final night, when I paid for my ticket and crossed over with them. And of course, I had to track down Fynn and ask him for the training resources he'd offered.

But there was no rush. Without my ridiculous Bargain, I was as safe as any other human tonight, and so I figured I may as well enjoy the sights while I could. They were beautiful, after all.

This time, my head wasn't giddy with magic, my lost memories leaving me almost drugged in their absence. This time, I saw everything clearly and calmly.

Illusions floated past my head, tiny butterflies of light dancing on the wind. When I turned, I saw they were blown like bubbles through a golden hoop by a fae dressed in brilliant colors. Two booths down from her, there was a man who sang to ropes like Sebastian had, calling them free like snakes from a basket. They writhed, wrapping around him in soothing caresses before reaching out to touch the audience, who gasped and jumped back every time.

Except for one girl, I noticed. The corner of my mouth twitched, and I had to bite back a laugh as I watched her eyes darken with heat every time the rope snared around her wrist.

I couldn't blame her. I'd had my fair share of those moments with not one but two fae, by now. Apparently even knowing it would come to nothing didn't stop me going back for more.

Except with Sebastian. I'd learned my lesson there.

We passed by various warm-up acts, designed to ensnare us into the bigger performances within the tents, and landed upon a sandy square drawn out in chalk. In the center stood a long, dark-haired fae with pointy ears, holding batons high above his head. Their ends were alight with blue flame.

As we came to a stop, the pounding of a drum began, and he started twirling the batons. Pulling them over his head at first and then spinning them all around until he was encased in a wall of flame.

A familiar face turned toward me—one of the farmers from the village—and, seeing who I was, stepped in front to claim the better view.

I sighed, shuffling an inch to the right so I could see better just as the fire-twirler spun to face us. In an instant, the entire audience was spellbound, and as he danced with the flame, not a single sound emerged. The element moved like it was alive, a creature of light and heat just as the fae was a creature of magic and danger. Among the crowd, lips parted in awe, eyes widening, while beneath that blazing inferno, the only glimpse we caught was the occasional flash of dark eyes, pointed ears, and long black hair.

My heart was in my throat, and not entirely because of the performance. That wall of fire made me think of the magic I'd seen last night—and how the night had ended.

Why had Sebastian turned on me like that?

More importantly: why did it bother me so much? It wasn't like his opinion mattered, and it wasn't like he was saying anything I didn't already know. It was my own stupid fault that I'd become swept up in his conviction, even knowing he was wrong.

"Urgh," I muttered under my breath, taking another sip of my spiced chocolate. It left tingles through my body, matching the kiss of heat from the flames outside.

I stopped trying to fight it.

My eyes unfocused, so the fire stopped being individual flames and instead became a wall of magic. It really was beautiful, just like it had been last night, when Sebastian had tried to call out the magic inside me.

I'd sworn then that I felt something answer his call. An echo of this wondrous illusion, crying out from within me. It had all been in my head of course, but now, in the safety of the anonymous crowd, for a brief handful of seconds, I allowed myself to pretend once again.

The heat washed over me, the magic singing as it kissed my skin. My body sung back.

What would it be like to have this for real? To not be relegated to the shadows, but to live in the light?

Dangerous thoughts.

Reluctantly, I opened my eyes and mentally distanced myself from the spectacle. I was just a human enjoying the show, nothing more. By my bedside lay a coronet of half-threaded rose petals soaked in prayer, to prove it.

The fire-twirler left two of the batons in midair, spinning on their own, and produced another—this one a flaming ball. It hovered two inches above his hands as he spun it, throwing it back and forth.

I rested my hand on Stefan's arm, squeezing tightly to ground myself. Just a human.

Gods, but I wanted more.

To my surprise, I blinked away a tear, and then dashed it

furiously aside with my thumb. But in that moment of blurred vision, the fire-twirler's face changed.

I gasped, rearing back in horror. As if in slow motion, the fire-twirler turned to see me, his eyes holding mine. My heartbeat quickened, but it didn't appear as though he was chasing me, like they all had on that first night. He didn't seem drawn to me at all; this moment was more of a recognition. An "I see you, and I know you see me". As I stared at him, he winked one coal-black eye and returned to the crowd.

I swallowed thickly, realizing what was happening.

It was as they said—as the circus nights wore on, the fae's true faces revealed themselves. Their magic was climbing. As the waxing gibbous passed, becoming closer to full, the fae's magic grew stronger.

Last night, I'd touched that magic, and then I'd accepted a ticket to cross the bridge with them. I might be as human as the rest of the crowd, but it slowly dawned on me that I was *not* like them. Not at all.

Piece by piece, the circus was claiming me.

Perhaps it was time to get that information. I had four and half nights left to learn what I could, and suddenly that didn't feel like long enough. My fingers tightened on Stefan's arm, and he turned to look at me, brow furrowed.

"I think we should leave," I whispered.

I could still feel the fire-twirler's eyes bearing into me—two blazing pits. What else would change as the moon grew fuller?

Stefan must have seen something in my face, because he didn't hesitate. Merely steered the two of us away from the awestruck crowd, their numbers quickly swelling and filling the gap we left behind.

As I took in the vibrant fairground, I noticed that something had indeed shifted. Nothing wild or terrifying, like that first night. No one was hunting me, and no one looked at me like I was at the top of the menu. But the fae... Oh, they had changed.

Teeth seemed sharper, longer. Their eyes glinted in the light, alien and unknown.

"Can you feel it?" I asked Stefan.

He looked around, brow deepening. "Feel what?"

So he couldn't sense it either. It really was the ticket in my pocket, and perhaps a little of Sebastian's magic still lingering.

A thrill ran through me, surprising me into silence. I wasn't scared, I realized. I was *delighted*.

Maybe the Council had been right to chastise me for bringing home that Talking Mirror set, and welcoming an imp into my home. At my first taste of real magic, I was hooked.

"It's all right," I said, soothing him with a gentle pat on his arm. "Let's find a storyteller. I could do with another hot drink and somewhere to put my feet up."

We wandered past a giant tank filled with water. The fae inside it, her tail twisted around like a glimmering fish, turned to watch us, waving long, taloned fingers in a coy greeting as we passed. Her eyes blazed with power like the others. Without overthinking it, I waved back, a tiny smile curving onto my lips that only grew larger as she cackled in clear delight. Bubbles rose from her open mouth, revealing shark-like teeth when they lifted away.

Everywhere I looked, the glamors were shifting. Not enough to reveal the truth of their intentions, not yet, but soon. And each step I took brought me closer to becoming part of this world. To dancing among these creatures of fire and magic, teeth and talons.

I bit down on another smile, lowering beside Stefan to join the seated crowd gathered beneath the sweeping branches of a willow.

"*But the boy was lost,*" the woman at the center of the circle intoned, her voice like sand falling through glass. As she spoke, the pool of water by her feet flickered and changed, sending shapes rising to the surface. Images from a time long ago. *"And his only way free was to Bargain..."* She tapped one long fingernail on her cheek bones, beneath her eyes. *"One for each,* she whispered. The crowd was so quiet, I could hear her easily. *"One for servitude, and one for freedom."*

"He traded his *eyes*?!" A drunk girl at the back of the group yelped, catching on a little slow.

A shiver rippled through the crowd as the fae laughed. "Wouldn't you? If it was all you had to offer?"

The bubble of rising joy wobbled as my stomach turned, reminding me viscerally of what I was walking into on the other side of the water. It wasn't all magic and wonder. The Bargains I knew were nothing, compared to what could be offered. Stefan and I shared a glance, his expression as unsettled as I felt, although he didn't know quite how much I was hanging on the fae's every word.

Still, that was what these remaining nights were for, wasn't it? Uncovering as many secrets as I could, so that I didn't end up trading away my eyes, or worse. I just had to be sensible about it. Smart—well, as smart as I could be. And if there was ever someone who knew how to keep a life balanced in fair trade, it was me.

Absently, I touched the necklace at my throat, feeling its cool, watchful presence. My resolve hardened, and the wicked thrill of magic took over once more.

"I'd have to be beyond desperate to give my eyes over to the fae," Stefan murmured to me as the storyteller continued. "Who knows what magic they could weave with them."

"'Beyond desperate' is just how the Lumière like you, didn't you know?" another voice answered from my right, far too breezily for the topic at hand.

I jumped, spinning to find Fynn lounging against a tree. He grinned at me, blue eyes glinting in the firelight.

"You never know what you'll trade until that icy grip of hopelessness squeezes around your heart," he finished idly.

"You could be a storyteller yourself, with poetry like that," I commented, lifting a brow.

An odd expression crossed his face as his lips parted, as though I'd surprised him into a genuine smile. Just as quickly as it had appeared, it faded.

"Perhaps I'll weave you a tale before the season is over," he suggested, ignoring Stefan's threatening glare.

I laid a hand on Stefan's arm, silently communicating that it was fine. He shot me a suspicious look but said nothing.

Fynn leaned in casually, as if commenting on the story, although his voice was pitched low enough that no one else could hear. "You might want to lie low for an hour or so."

My heart thudded. "Oh?"

"Mmm. Heillon is making rounds early."

Heillon—that was the name the fae had spoken at the archery show, when they'd tried to make me bleed. They'd spoken about him as if he were some sort of leader.

I tried to subtly catch Fynn's eye, but he was giving a far too convincing impression of being enthralled by the story.

"Why don't I want to meet Heillon?" A spike of fear stabbed me in the chest. "Will he be able to sense the..." I trailed off, not wanting to say it.

Fynn shook his head, gaze softening. "No. No one can. But he won't like seeing something he can't understand. You don't want his attention, that's all."

Noted.

His message delivered, Fynn slipped away into the night.

"Curse it," I muttered. I'd wanted him to describe Heillon,

so I knew who I was avoiding. But in lieu of that, I supposed it was better to simply get out of sight for a bit.

Lifting one hand, ready to haul myself up, I paused. A number of possible scenarios raced through my mind, but I'd already decided I had to follow my instincts here, if I wanted to survive. And unfortunately, there was only one performance tent where I felt safe enough to lie low.

Sebastian might have wounded my pride, but he hadn't hurt me. By contrast, the mermaid in the tank had thrilled me, but I had no guarantees she wouldn't step over her own grandma to sell me out. My read on Sebastian was that he had his own secrets, ones he guarded as fiercely as I guarded mine. And although I hadn't liked it, when he had a problem with me, he was fire and fury. Confrontation. Not treachery or hidden games.

"You know," I whispered to Stefan, "I think I would like to see the contortionist again, actually."

Stefan agreed readily, and we turned to leave.

As we did, though, I caught sight of a fae on the other side of the circle. He was tall, with broad shoulders and straps of leather braced across his chest. His long red hair fell in three braids down his back, and his eyes...

They were like the night.

"Shit," I muttered under my breath, my body coming to a sudden halt all of its own. No need to get that description after all; I'd bet good money that this was Heillon.

As if he heard me, the fae tilted his head, ear cocked in my direction, and turned. My heart kicked up like a rabbit, and I didn't stick around to see if he looked my way. Grabbing Stefan's hand, I all but ran from the circle, dragging him straight to the other side of the fairground.

Had he seen me? Had he noticed the strange aura of magic, just as Sebastian had?

Shit, shit shit.

Stefan cast me a worried glance, and I forced my movements to calm, locking away the worried thoughts behind a thick, impenetrable door in my mind. Only then did I step through the entrance to Sebastian's tent.

Inside, it was dark. On the first night, there'd been ordinary lanterns and faelights placed throughout, but tonight, it was decked out with a thousand tiny pinpricks of light, each suspended in the air. Most hovered so far up toward the ceiling of the tent that they barely illuminated anything. Instead, it gave the effect of some kind of cosmos, as though I had stepped beneath a blanket of stars that shone brighter and fiercer than the real one outside.

An odd, expectant stillness filled the space, and we took our seats. This time, I chose a position up the back and toward the center of a row, so that I couldn't be selected again. Stefan gave me a sideways glance as I chose our places, but otherwise said nothing.

But then, the soft glow of hidden lights illuminated the tent, and music began once more, this time just the cello—a low, aching, sorrowful tune. The pinprick stars above our heads began to glow brighter until a whole galaxy blazed across the velvet sky.

Starlight graced Sebastian's face as he stepped into the center of the ring, moving fluidly, undulating with every soft bow of the cello. It kissed his face like moonlight, and under that touch, I thought there was something a touch sorrowful about his expression as he let the light caress his skin. As if there could ever be anything sad about the moon.

In that moment I was so, so glad I'd chosen to sit where he couldn't reach me, because I knew if he turned to me and held out his hand I would take it. I would take it just for the chance that he might say sorry—it had been a misunderstanding. He hadn't meant to hurt me.

Sometimes, in my darkest moments, I thought Merelda was right: forgiveness came too easily to me.

I sunk back into my seat, the fabric folding over my shoulders as I tried to ensure he couldn't see me. Stefan didn't notice. He sat, entranced, fixated on the sorrowful tale that Sebastian was weaving; because tonight, it was a story.

Like a ballet unfolding upon the stage, he twisted and writhed, sending illusions dancing in light both above and below him, and I realized he was telling a story of lost love.

No, not love—but something was lost. Something had gone missing and withered and become frozen in time, and my heart ached at the thought of it.

I could feel something in me shifting, changing, and the terrible, rising unease that came with it told me what it was.

I had a bad habit of falling for the wrong men. Men I could never have; men who would never have me. I'd watch the world quietly, from the shadows, and feel my heart move as I came to understand their sorrow and their joy. The flawed choices they made, and the ways they struggled and fought to keep to the light.

Forgetting, always, that these same people would never bother to watch or understand me.

I'd forget my place, my destiny, and I'd look at that beautiful face, and I'd *want*. I'd want so badly that I listened to their lies and believed them when they led me down roads that served them and no other.

If I sat here and watched Sebastian weave this tale of heartache and loss, looking as beautiful as he did, I was going to fall for him, too.

I stood.

The shadows concealed me, and I mumbled my apologies to

Stefan and then to the people beside me as I shuffled quickly toward the exit. I had to leave. There was nowhere safe for me here, and I vowed instead to demand those resources from Fynn and spend the rest of the season at home, reading them.

The cello screeched. I jumped, turning on whiplash reflex to see Sebastian frozen, entwined in a number of hoops at the center of the ring, his eyes fixed to mine.

To the audience, he no doubt appeared to be transitioning between one act and the other, loss and grief transforming into wide-eyed wonder, but I knew it was because he had seen me.

I froze on the path leading out of the tent as Sebastian began to move again, and with every discordant note of the cello in this new act, with every twisted illusion, I held his gaze as he held mine. Because in it, there was hope.

He looked how I felt, and there was no power in me, no lessons learned, no strength won, no ruthless willpower that could make me turn away from that.

The music crescendoed and then screeched once more and—

There was a weight in my palm.

Moving slowly, I lifted my hand to my face and saw a flower in it, and when I looked up, I wasn't standing halfway up the path toward the exit anymore. In my trance, I'd walked to the front and was now leaning against the barrier around the ring.

Oh gods, everyone was watching me. Had I not had enough mortification in my life by now?

I stared down at the rose, hoping desperately that it looked as though I'd been drawn up for participation again, rather than just standing here like a ninny of my own free will. And then I saw there was a note nestled amongst the petals.

I am so sorry for hurting you, it read in that now-familiar hand.

My breath hitched.

Please allow me to even the field.

A furrow appeared between my brows. Even the field; what did he mean?

Drums began to pound. I looked up, and where before Sebastian had been entwined through a number of hoops, now the silver hoops had vanished and become thorns. Thorns that reached out toward the rose I held in my hands.

The audience gasped. At the same time, I noticed the thorns were poised, hovering above the palms of his open hands, and I realized in that moment what he was about to do.

It was meaningless, truthfully. An eye for an eye, but in a way that achieved nothing. It was dramatic, sensationalized, performative...

And yet, when I looked in his eyes, I saw an earnestness that threw all of that away.

He was clearly waiting for some kind of answer from me, either approval or rejection, but I couldn't bring myself to respond one way or another. My thoughts were a raving mess. I bit down on my lip so hard the sharp, metallic taste of blood filled my senses—just as the music broke and the thorns plunged, leaving crimson droplets to pool in Sebastian's open palms. Unlike his pictures of light, those droplets were no illusion.

The crowd gasped, but he wasn't finished; he spun, those same droplets forming a circle around him in the sand, and I realized this was fae magic.

More specifically, this was the darker side of fae magic, and it should have sent me running, just like the rest of the crowd who'd moved abruptly from awe to fear. A low murmur rippled through the audience. They were remembering what I had already discovered—that the danger mounted here as the nights progressed.

My heart skipped a beat, pulse racing, but just like with the mermaid in the tank, I felt only delight. Exhilaration. The Offering would be in danger, prostrated before the Lumière to pay the price of her village's safety. But I was shedding the Offering's skin. By the full moon, she would be gone.

Sebastian caught my gaze again as the circle closed with him in the center and...

A pathway opened.

There was no other way to explain it. I didn't know what the rest of the audience saw, but for me there was a shimmering cord of light that led from my rose to his circle of blood—of reparation. It was a pathway leading somewhere unknown, but Sebastian's earnest gaze was begging me to accept this offering, and to follow him through the portal where, presumably, we could talk alone.

I should have turned away. It was in every lesson I had learned, every hurt I had wielded like a shield since Hayden left me and I finally accepted what the world had told me from the beginning.

Instead, I nodded.

Lifting the rose to my face, I moved on instinct, trusting the look in Sebastian's eyes in a way I shouldn't have trusted anything. I breathed in the scent of the rose.

The noise of the crowd immediately dulled.

I turned, intending to catch Stefan's eye so I could assure him not to worry. But instead, I saw Fynn, standing by the doorway. It was strange, but his face reminded me of the fire-twirler's: something in it had changed beyond recognition, as if overcome by a seed of power. But he was standing in the darkness, and I couldn't tell what was different.

Then the tent vanished, and I reappeared alone before Sebastian.

CHAPTER 12

Bailey

COMPARED TO THE THUNDERING APPLAUSE OF THE PERFORMANCE TENT we'd just exited, the silence in this space was deafening. It took me a moment to adjust, to see beyond the dim orange warmth of the lanterns and work out where we were.

When I did, my heart began to pound.

It was a simple enough tent, furnished with a low writing desk, a table in the center, where I assumed meals were eaten, and, on the far side, a bed.

My gaze slid back to Sebastian standing before me. His eyes widened as he took in where my attention had landed.

He cleared his throat. "I didn't bring you here for anything untoward, I promise," he said, holding up his hands in a slow, careful defense.

My eyes darted to the doorway. It was a simple flap of fabric that I could push through and be out under the stars again in seconds. He noted that, too.

I took a step back, not making any decisions, just trying to keep my options open.

Still in that same low, careful voice, Sebastian said, "You can leave if you want. I won't chase you."

My heartbeat stuttered, and the hot slide of disappointment thickened in my throat. Why was I here, then, if my presence meant so little?

But then he continued. "But you should know that it isn't because I don't want to. It's because I can't."

Huh?

My brow furrowed, head tilting to the side. "What do you mean you can't?" I asked, taking another step toward the exit.

An odd look crossed his features. It looked like disappointment mixed with resignation, and all of it tainted by a deep sadness that felt all too familiar. I hesitated, one foot poised above the ground.

"I mean that I'm cursed to serve in this circus until..." He trailed off. "Well, I can tell you the details if you decide to stay. But in the interest of urgency, I can't step free of these tents in the human world unless the path is bathed in moonlight. And there are too many shadows out there for that to work in my favor.

"So you're in no danger from me chasing you. I wouldn't be able to. You would only need to stand in the nearest shadow." He let out a self-deprecating laugh. "And you would be beyond my reach." His voice lowered. "But if it were up to me, I would ask you to stay, so that I could tell you how very sorry I am for what I said last night, and explain that it had nothing to do with you."

Slowly he lowered his hands to his side, and I realized then how still he was keeping. How careful he was not to bridge the gap between him and me until I told him to. Until I gave him permission.

Having someone listen to my desires instead of their own felt strange.

Slowly, I lowered my foot to the ground but didn't take the step. "Okay then," I said. The pounding of my heart hadn't ceased, but this time, it wasn't pounding out of danger.

I ignored it.

Glancing once more at the table in the center, I spied the two elaborately embroidered cushions stacked beside it and jerked my chin. "Shall I take a seat, and we can treat each other like civilized..."—I paused before the word 'humans'—"people."

The corner of his mouth twitched as he noticed my deliberate word choice.

"Or is that not dramatic enough for you?" I prompted, thinking of the thorns.

The hint of that smile widened, blooming into something bright. "I can always flip a chair if it's getting too peaceful." He gestured to the table. "Please, hear me out."

As I knelt on one side, he leaned forward, snagging the top cushion from the pile and handing it to me. For some reason that act seemed unfamiliar to him, and I wondered how many guests a cursed fae would get in their tent.

That second cushion now seemed oddly hopeful.

I settled myself comfortably and propped my elbows on the table, clasping my hands before me. My gaze fell on a mirror behind where we'd entered the tent. I blinked.

"I have one of those."

Sebastian glanced over his shoulder, lip quirking into a faint smile. "A Talking Mirror? It's one of the Lumière's little jokes, I'm afraid." He folded gracefully into a cross-legged position opposite me. "That one doesn't have a partner. A fun reminder that I am their lonely little pet." His teeth flashed white as he grinned.

"Oh..." My brow furrowed. That was so... unnecessarily cruel.

He waved a hand. "Perhaps one day I'll play with it, see if I can break whatever curse they put on it and find a new partner." The grin widened. "Get myself a pen pal of sorts."

I raised an eyebrow. "Are you stalling?"

"You started it," he pointed out, his face the picture of innocence.

My first instinct was to submit to the accusation, no matter how jokingly delivered. To accept the blame that was my due, since ill luck or selfish behavior always came back to the Offering. But I let the words die on my tongue. This was my new life, my fresh start.

I didn't have to be that Bailey anymore.

"Fine," I said, biting down on the urge to smile. The word sent a delicious thrill running through me. Not just the word, but the confidence with which I was allowed to say it, between these walls, with this person who hadn't recognized what the different colors of my eyes must mean. "I'll start the rest too, then. Spill. The number of backbends I've seen you twist into, you seemed like the kind of fae who could twist his way out of any situation. So what could have someone like you trapped?"

He huffed a quiet laugh, almost as if he were surprised. Meanwhile, his eyes burned into me, soaking in every drop. No doubt reading things in my expression that a mere human could never hope to. I studied his face in return; it was a beautiful face, and I'd looked at it many times on that first night, noticing the gentleness and the calm, deliberate way in which he'd seemingly tried to put me at ease.

Now, I saw something different. I saw jagged edges and darkness, something much closer to the man I'd spied on the bridge, and the man who had accused and insulted me last night.

My nails dug into my palms as I waited for his answer, recalling the words he had hurled at me last night. For all that he seemed primed to apologize, he still thought I was nothing special. I had to remember that.

He folded his arms before him on the table, leaning forward. The deep brown of his gaze was arresting, and although I tried to resist, it quickly held me captive.

"I can see this is going to be a more complex issue than mere words could resolve." He rolled the syllables with deliberate enunciation, delivering his half-formed thoughts like a monologue on a stage. "I offer you an answer, you question my motives, I accuse you of concealing half truths... We could go on forever. Or..." He lifted a brow. "If we are to be sharing truths tonight, perhaps we could step boldly forward and claim them."

"Is that what we're doing?" I countered, understanding only half of what he was saying. "Sharing truths."

Sebastian smiled like I'd just proven his point.

There was very little space between us, a scant few inches separating my lips from his. If I were anyone else, it would be considered intimate. I appreciated the fantasy, but I wasn't going to fall for it.

"We can make a Bargain out of it," Sebastian suggested, trailing his finger over the wood grain. "If you aren't going to believe me, that is."

My breath caught. "So that's your game." I pulled back. "You're not here to share truths out of the goodness of your heart, or to apologize like you want me to believe. You want something from me."

Agitation flashed across his face, the corner of his lip curling —not in a smile this time, but in a hint of a snarl.

"I think we're getting off on the wrong foot again," he suggested flatly. "I'm only offering a way that you can trust me."

My eyebrows shot up. "Trust you? You want me to enter a

Bargain with you in order to trust you? You really don't know what humans think of fae, do you?"

"No," he said simply, and the honesty in that one word struck me silent. "I have no idea what humans think of fae," he went on slowly. "But I know what I think of fae, and I think our word is never to be trusted. But I offer you this Bargain, with wording that is clear enough that you can see for yourself there is no subterfuge hidden within it. I will offer you the truth of your questions. And as payment—simple payment—you will offer me the truth of mine. Or you may keep silent about anything you wish to keep for yourself."

Leaning on one elbow now, he stretched his hand across the table toward me. "Do we have a deal?"

My heart fluttered, and my mind was caught on that one phrase—simple payment.

I remembered Fynn from last night, and the brush of his lips against my hand. The two of them had very different ideas about what constituted simple, honest payment within a Bargain between fae. And in a strange way, I couldn't pick which one I preferred.

Both seemed so true to them, at least in as much as I knew these strangers.

But in this moment, here, now, I could see the value of what Sebastian was offering. To know that what I asked him would be answered in truth, and to know that I could keep my secrets if I wanted. The forced honesty of any words I did choose to speak would be all the payment required.

It was a good Bargain, no matter which angle I looked at it.

Carefully I stretched my hand across the table, resting it within his. His clasp was surprisingly firm when I returned it in kind, unable to help comparing his touch to Fynn's as he murmured the Bargain phrases and waited for my reply. Then we slid free, and he leant back.

"Ask your questions," he said.

"Why did you insult me last night?" The words were out before I could stop them.

Sebastian's eyebrows flew upward, his expression twisting into regret. "I didn't mean to, Bailey," he said earnestly, then winced, digging his fingers into his temple as if it pained him. "Actually, that's not quite true. I lost my senses when you let slip that you knew Fynn. I was convinced you were working together to take me down a peg, as he so loves to do, and then —and I am truly sorry for this—I tried to hurt you with my words." He swallowed. "As you had hurt me. Or so I thought."

I stared at him. Such a simple explanation. Not one I entirely understood, since I don't think I'd ever tried to hurt someone like that in my life, but... it did make sense. And because of our Bargain, I knew it to be the truth.

Which presented an entirely different problem.

"What do you mean Fynn tries to take you down a peg?" I asked, forcing the words past a mouth that didn't want to speak.

Sebastian pulled a face, reclining against the leg of the writing desk behind him and brushing his hair free from his face as he thought.

"It takes a bit to explain," he said finally. "But first you have to understand that it's like I told you. I'm trapped here because, when I was a young idiot, I disobeyed their rules. My father and I used to work for this circus voluntarily. He was an acrobat, and I was training to be..." He gestured vaguely toward the other tent. "Everything you see now."

Briefly, I was astonished at how easily he dismissed what he did. The grace of it. The magic. Did he not know how beautiful his act was?

"We were meant to follow the rules, just like the humans. No disappearing off the grounds after midnight, no cavorting.

But..." A reluctant grin appeared on his face. "I was entranced by you all. I wanted to see the humans for myself, and I slipped free. Ran down to the nearest town and watched you. I didn't come back until well after dawn. Then they caught me."

His expression turned shadowed.

"They caught me, but, in typical Lumière trickery, it was my father who paid the price. He was torn from me, no matter how much I begged. Fae love it when you beg." His eyes flashed. "They took him from me and chained him up somewhere. Gods know where. And in order to keep him safe..." He sighed. "I have to follow their rules. That was the Bargain. From the moment that we cross the bridge, I cannot leave these tents unless I'm bathed in moonlight. And even then, I cannot go beyond the circus bounds."

My breath caught, and I remembered how those boundaries had extended to the lake last night. They'd given him a simple moment of freedom, if it could be called that.

"How long do you have to follow their rules?"

"Until I find him." His voice was so fierce, so determined, that shivers raced down my spine.

"But how can you find him if you can't leave the circus?" I shook my head. "I assume that's where the trickery is. That he's hidden here in the human realm somewhere."

The thought of some fae trapped below the ground, bound in chains beneath my very feet made me shudder in horror.

He gave me a rueful smile. "You're smart," he said. "You know fae Bargains even without falling for them."

Huh. I almost laughed out loud; I wasn't smart, and the proof of that was in every conversation I'd ever had with Fynn, if what Sebastian was telling me was true. Why would Fynn hurt someone who was already trapped like this?

"Yes, my father is here," Sebastian continued, unaware of the direction my thoughts were running in. "Somewhere I cannot find him. But there is always an exit clause in a fae Bargain, a gate that will appear under the right conditions, and this one is simple. The night that a hidden fae, filled with secret, trapped magic, entered the circus... that would be the season that I could find him." He shook his head slowly, staring down at his hands. "And if I didn't, he would slip through my fingers forever."

Silence fell, and the horrible truth of his words ricocheted through me. That was why he'd been so disappointed when I didn't show any magic. He thought I was the hidden fae.

Everything he'd worked for. Everything he'd tried to fix from his youthful mistakes. It had all come to nothing the second my hidden magic hadn't shown.

"Does that mean he's lost to you for good?" I asked, my voice barely above a whisper. "Was the gate a lie?"

Sebastian gave a wry, bitter smile. "The gate is never a lie. But I do think they've designed it to trick me." He took a careful, measured breath. "I think this is still the season I have to find him." The hope in his words tore me apart. "It would be just like the Lumière to make me think I'd read the signs wrong, give up, and lose him forever. So..." He shrugged. "I've begun the search. The fact that you were not secretly holding fae magic doesn't mean you weren't the herald of my Bargain's gate. It's too great a coincidence to ignore." His voice grew firmer, stronger. "I will find him."

Urgency overcame me, filling my mind with one single thought: I should tell him. I should tell him about the Open Bargain with Fynn, so he knew what it was that he'd sensed. It might give him the information he needed to find his father.

But...

It would damn me in the process, putting me at the mercy of a fae I'd only just met. I couldn't trust him, no matter how much I wanted to. And besides, what difference could it truly make? He was already searching.

I realized abruptly that I was holding my breath, and I let it out in a slow, shaky sigh.

"I see," I said.

My voice rang soft with forgiveness. Sebastian's head whipped up, startled, and I realized then that he hadn't expected me to forgive him.

Gods, what pieces of shit must he be surrounded by if he thought I wouldn't listen to his story?

"And Fynn?" I prompted, ignoring the sick twist of fear in my gut. I didn't want to hear the rest, but I had to.

"Fynn..." Sebastian exhaled his name in a sigh. "Fynn has always had it out for me. If there's a way to make me pay, he will." He chewed on his lower lip, as if debating something, and I realized with a jolt that there was a part of this question he didn't want to answer.

"You don't have to—" I began, no longer needing his absolute truth to trust him. He'd given me enough, and we were all entitled to our privacy. But I was too slow.

"Fynn and I were once lovers."

My mouth fell open. "You were—" I broke off, flushing. "Oh, I see. I'm sorry. I didn't know."

The bitter twist to Sebastian's mouth softened into reluctant amusement. "How would you?" The amusement faded. "Listen, I don't know what your deal is with him, or how you know him, but... be careful. He used to be more honorable than anyone I knew, but when he turned..." A note of something raw entered his voice. He cleared his throat. "I don't know what happened, what I did to make him hate me, but it changed everything. Either that, or I never really knew him at all. Maybe he won't take delight in hurting you like he does with me, but..." He shrugged. "Maybe he will."

My stomach twisted, although I couldn't say I was really surprised. This was nothing new. Nothing I hadn't seen coming. I already knew not to trust them—any of them. This was merely confirmation.

"Again, Bailey, I'm so sorry," Sebastian said, reaching across the low table to take my hand. His words were so earnest that even without the Bargain, I'd have believed him.

But for the first time, that didn't feel like a failing.

"The way that you spoke, telling me to stop lying to myself..." Sebastian continued, his thumb stroking the back of my hand almost absently, as if he didn't realize. "It sounded like the fae. I thought that you were working with Fynn, or even one of the others, and this was another one of their cruel games." He dropped his head into his free hand, clenching it in a way that looked almost painful. "They've played so many over the years. I thought this was just one more, and you'd been used against me. But I should have given you the benefit of the doubt. I should have asked first, and then actually listened to you."

"Why did you?"

He looked up, frowning. "But I didn't."

I shook my head. "Not then—but now. How did you work out you were wrong?"

An expression crossed his face, one I couldn't quite read. He sat up slowly, settling his free hand on the table, palm pressed down. "I saw how hurt you were," he said, his tone and manner radiating discomfort. "If you'd been out to taunt me, nothing I said would have upset you." He huffed a strange little laugh. "It's been an unconscionably long time since I managed to hurt someone with my words."

My eyebrows lifted, but I didn't question him. I supposed when one was living with the Lumière, the world was different. Crueler, by the sound of it. And Sebastian was naturally a charmer, I could see that much. The people he spoke to were likely easily persuaded into enjoying his company. Or, they were manipulating him for their own pleasure. It sounded like there was no in between.

Still... he'd managed to remind me now of exactly what he'd said, when he wanted to hurt me.

My initial assessment was correct. You are, indeed, nobody important after all.

He regretted saying it, but had it been a lie? Simply a harsh dismissal, designed to slip between my ribs like a knife?

Or had it been the truth?

Carefully, I withdrew my hand from his and studied him. It would be so easy to forgive him. I did, in fact. He had tried to hurt me because he thought I was the enemy, and he'd given me more than enough reason to accept his apology.

And whether his insult had been honest or not, that didn't matter. He didn't owe me his interest, and he'd hardly be the first to find me lacking; it was by design.

But I appreciated the reminder not to fall head over heels all the same. I also appreciated that it forced me to pause long enough to think...

I could tell Sebastian the truth: that I forgave him. Or, since I meant nothing to any of these people and was merely a passing fancy for four more nights, I could think like the fae and ask for something in return.

"Consider it water under the bridge," I said neutrally. He straightened at my tone, eyes sharp. "But I'd like to ask a favor as an apology."

He nodded immediately. "Of course. Anything."

I paused, chewing my lip to keep from laughing. "You know, for a fae, you're awfully unguarded around Bargains."

The contrition flickered, revealing a little more of that real personality beneath. Something I was discovering was quite mischievous, when he allowed himself to be. "You haven't offered me a Bargain, only a request."

"And you've already said yes," I pointed out.

"You think you can outsmart me?" he asked, propping his chin on his fist.

I blinked, not because of what he'd said, but the way he'd said it. As though he thought I *could* outsmart him. I looked away, my laughter a bit too loud as I dismissed the joke.

"Well you only said yes to hearing the request, technically." I brushed my hair behind my ear. Sebastian's gaze followed the movement. "I wondered if you knew of any resources here that might tell me more about your world. How to survive there, specifically. Maybe a small archive, or a traveling library of folk tales."

Only Sebastian's eyes moved, flicking from my ear, where they'd been fixed to the hair I'd just moved, back to my face. After a moment, he answered.

"There is a small archive. It contains ephemera related to the circus, mostly, but also some history and tales."

My heart beat faster. "Where is it?"

Again, he didn't answer for several long seconds. Then he shifted, his position more casual now.

"It's hidden within our network of alleys," he said, "which humans can't see. But before we continue, I must ask that we conclude our Bargain." When he smiled, it didn't reach his eyes. "If I were to reveal any true secrets, they would kill me."

Cold dread slid down my throat, and I hastened to nod. The Bargain would conclude once he'd asked me his questions, and I'd either answered truthfully or chosen to stay silent. "Of course. Ask away."

Sebastian leaned back, his body taking on a curious tilt as he studied me. Before he could open his mouth, I knew what he was going to ask. It would be the same thing that Fynn had asked. The same baring of my soul, demanded in exchange for the suggestion that he cared.

Tell me about it.

Tell me about your pain.

But I barely had time to wonder whether I would share the truth with Sebastian when he asked something different.

"Why the circus?"

I frowned. "What do you mean?"

"Well..." He mulled the words over. "People have reasons for coming here. Especially if they come more than one night in a row. I can tell you have secrets, and I won't ask for them. But I just want to know, why do you think it's the circus that will bring you answers? There are a thousand magical places in this world, even in the human realm. And yet it's here that you've chosen." He lifted a shoulder in a shrug. "I'm not asking you to spill your innermost desires to me, just... why here?"

I blinked at him.

There was so much room within that question. So much space to answer. I could share a dozen truths in response and never once reveal my secrets. He didn't even realize he was also asking why I'd chosen to run away with them, and with the way he'd asked, I never had to tell him.

Why the circus?

Because it was unknown.

Because it was close.

Because, like all magic I wasn't supposed to want, it had enchanted me since I was a child.

Because I was sick to death of humans and the ways that we stabbed each other in the back.

"The fae might have their Bargains," I said in a low voice, speaking as if in a trance, "but you know the danger of those. There are rules within them. Even with your Bargain, there's an exit clause. An unbreakable truth. If someone is going to hurt me, I want to see it coming."

Sebastian's brow furrowed. "Someone has hurt you." It wasn't quite a question.

I couldn't stop the bitter laugh. "No more than I deserved," I pointed out, but it didn't get the reaction it would have at home. If anything, his frown deepened.

"Look, it's more complicated than that." But then I paused.

Just like with Fynn, I didn't want to tell Sebastian about the Offering. I didn't want to tell him that the gods had taken all the measly, weak, pathetic bits that made up a human and put them into me, and if he'd thought something different about me for a minute, then all it meant was that I'd managed to fool him.

And besides, Hayden *had* hurt me. He'd hurt me... gods... so fucking much.

I took a deep breath, forcing my lips to stay shut this time, but the pain ripped through me and I couldn't quite stop a small, wretched sound from emerging.

Something sparked in Sebastian's eyes, and all of a sudden the air between us was charged. Thick with anticipation.

"I have another question," he said, and although his tone hadn't changed, still slow and gentle, there was steel behind the words.

I shivered.

"And I think you know what I'm going to ask, so I'm going to give you a choice. Do you want me to ask it?"

I could barely breathe. I'd never seen a look like that in someone's eyes before.

Well, no, that wasn't true—I'd seen such anger directed at me. I'd seen it in the expressions of every one of Hayden's ex girlfriends, when they heard he was marrying me. I'd seen it on my friends' faces when I told them I'd completed the academic component for my apprenticeship by correspondence, after the elders wouldn't let me travel for school. Once, even, when I'd quietly, humbly revealed to my sister just how much I'd learned and never expressed from all the books I'd read in my solitary childhood.

I'd seen it directed at me many times; I'd never seen it *for* me.

"Ask me," I whispered.

"What did he do to you?" Sebastian asked, his voice deceptively calm.

Again, there were a thousand answers I could give. So many ways I could interpret that question and not reveal my biggest secrets. But there was only one truth. I had promised the truth.

And I was sick of staying silent.

"He left me," I said slowly, the words halting, "at the altar..." Fury flashed in his eyes. I felt sick, forcing the next words past numb lips, "for my sister."

Flame erupted from the lanterns. A pillar of fire three feet tall.

I yelled, startling back from the table, my hands slamming down on the wood, but Sebastian didn't move. His control was so good that, to look at him, you would think he had nothing to do with the flame. Apart from the glint of rage in his eye, he looked almost bored. Sleepy.

After an age, he slowly closed his eyes, seeming to force himself under control, and the flames returned to normal.

It was only because he didn't know about me that he felt so indignant. If he knew the truth, he'd understand that it was a fair trade. That I'd risked everything by trying to take what wasn't mine.

Hayden was never meant to marry me; he'd been fated for something better long before his eyes ever strayed in my direction. Long before his curiosity and sense of charity got the better of him. And my sister was the perfect match. They were the two golden children, successes of our village. If I'd been humble about it and kept to his shadow, perhaps I could have kept him, but I hadn't been.

Anyone who got close enough to me knew I was greedy. If someone smiled at me, I leaned in closer. Wanted more, always more. When my necklace had warmed in danger, I convinced myself it was nothing, even knowing what being wrong would cost.

When Michel had looked at me with the same curiosity that Hayden had, I'd let him look. He'd wanted me, however briefly, and I'd enjoyed it.

Not long after, the house of cards had collapsed, as it should have long before.

But Sebastian didn't know any of that, and the anger he felt for me was so rare, so intense, I almost couldn't bear it.

I never wanted it to end.

"Have you asked all your questions?" I forced out, unable to look at him.

After a moment, he answered quietly, "Yes."

I felt the magic of our deal fade away, and I should have felt relieved, but in its absence I only felt hollow.

With his eyes still closed, he said, "the archives are only accessible by the fae. I can't steal anything for you—I won't— but I can take you to the key, and what you do from there is up to you."

"Won't you still be in danger?" I asked, trailing my fingers over the grain in the wood. I felt him watching me, his eyes open once more. "They'll know someone had to take me there, and they'll know I was with you."

The flash of his grin shone white in the corner of my eye. I looked up in surprise.

"They have to see me break the rules for it to violate my

Bargain; they can't guess. I'll give you something that will allow you to travel there alone," he said. "And if you're caught, you'll tell them that you stole it. As for traveling there now..." His eyes glinted. "I'll have to pretend I've enthralled you, and we're stealing off for a little fun together."

My breath caught. I couldn't look away from the intensity of his gaze.

"Can you handle that?" he asked quietly.

I'd seen Sebastian with those other women. The way they giggled and fawned. The pleasure on their faces at the simplest touch from him. It was only a farce, but he was offering that same pleasure to me now.

All I'd ever have was a farce, so, yes, I could handle that.

"Lead the way."

CHAPTER 13

Bailey

HE DIDN'T LEAD ME OUT THE FRONT OPENING OF HIS TENT, BUT neither did he open up a portal from his blood like before. This time, Sebastian crossed the tiny space to what I had assumed to be a shadow at the back of the tent. But when he folded his fingers beneath it, like fabric, I realized it wasn't a shadow at all.

He peeled back the darkness, and behind it was a corridor. I leant around him and peered down the length of the hallway. Every few feet, a wrought-iron wall sconce was mounted at head height, complete with a ball of golden faelight dancing in its center.

I reached out, smoothing my hand over the surface. It wasn't quite fabric, but it wasn't stone either. It was something in between.

"It's made from ether," Sebastian explained, holding the shadow further back so I could slip through.

Hesitating for only a moment, I stepped past him and into the darkness. He followed, the shadow falling like a curtain to seal us off.

"This place exists outside of time and space," he

explained, keeping his voice low so it didn't echo down the corridor. "It's how all the tents are connected, and how we move among you without wasting our energy on light-walking."

"Light-walking?" I asked with a frown, falling into step beside him as he set off cautiously down the corridor.

He hummed in agreement. "Perhaps I'll show you one day."

Then he looked over his shoulder at me and winked.

I felt a blush creep up over my neck and cheeks, and kept my gaze fixed resolutely forward. We continued on in silence, and I saw immediately what he meant about this place being excluded from time and space.

It wound around itself in a way that made no sense, considering the fairground it should have been a part of. These passageways couldn't possibly fit among the dozens of tents dotted through the field back there. And leading off from the passageways were so many doors and alcoves, it was a veritable maze.

"Am I really expected to find my way through here alone?" I asked him quietly, staring with trepidation down a long passageway that appeared to be decorated with spikes of bone.

"You're expected to do no such thing," he reminded me, arching a brow. He must have caught sight of the fear in my expression though, because his gaze softened, and he reached out to pluck something from the air beside me.

I stumbled to a halt, watching with wide eyes as his clever fingers transformed a cobweb into a shimmering, gossamer wing. The butterfly stretched, wavered, and took flight, practically dancing on invisible air drifts down the corridor. A soft laugh of wonder escaped me.

When I looked up, Sebastian's eyes shone with a strange light. I felt my smile falter. He was going to do what they always did. Tell me to smile more. Tell me to show some affection.

But instead, he simply said, "You don't laugh very often, do you?"

An observation, not a judgment.

"No," I said.

He gave me a wry smile. "It's a shame, isn't it?"

My heart fluttered. Oh, that explained the strangeness of our first meeting. That incongruent mix of darkness and joy that I had sensed in him. He gave the impression of being all darkness—too serious, too stoic—but that wasn't who he'd always been, clearly. The hints of drama and showmanship he kept letting free proved that easily enough.

And yet, he knew how it felt to have your laughter smothered. For the smile to become an ill-fitting mask, no matter how real it was.

Sebastian cleared his throat and kept walking.

"I'll show you another entrance," he said when I caught up. "That way you won't have to go far on your own, so you needn't worry about remembering the path from here."

I gave a quiet laugh. "Ah, so I become dependent on you, and you can ensnare me in your trap, oh fae one. I'm onto your twisted games."

The corner of his mouth twitched. There was nothing wry about it this time. "It's not a very good trap if you've already uncovered it," he pointed out.

"Well, that's on you."

To my surprise, I felt something shifting in my expression—a smile that was more than a twitch. More than a serene image upon my face to appease anyone watching. It felt genuine.

There was an answering warmth in Sebastian's face as he regarded me, but then movement came from the other end of the corridor, and he switched immediately into alertness.

"This way," he said, ducking to his left.

The room behind this particular shadowy curtain was eerie. Every inch of the visible walls was lined with masks.

"Gods," I murmured. "What is this cursed place?"

Sebastian blinked, looking around as if only just noticing where we were.

"Oh," he laughed. "It's not what you think." He ran his hand through his hair, curls falling across his face. "It's actually just a dressing room—nothing exciting at all."

"Oh," I breathed, leaning close to one of the horned masks as we passed by. I swore some of them were rustling. "You mean for your performances? But why so many? I haven't seen anyone wearing these yet."

"Well." He pulled a face. "It's not quite for the performances." He cast a glance over his shoulder at me. "Do you know anything about Bargain Night?"

My heart stuttered. Bargain Night? This was what the book had warned me about. The source of untold magic for the Lumière. Reality slammed back into me: Sebastian was Lumière. He might be their prisoner, but something had drawn him here once.

Did he profit from this night, too?

"Not really," I confessed. "Can you tell me?"

I waited for him to do his lying tricks, to talk around it as the fae always did. But to my surprise, his mouth twisted in genuine reluctance.

"Actually, I can't. It's forbidden, in the magical sense."

"Oh," I breathed.

"What I will say is this, though." He seemed to choose his next words carefully, as though there were few available to him. "On that final night, don't dawdle, and do not speak with anyone you do not trust."

I stared at him, transfixed by the sudden change of tone. "Okay," I agreed. "If you say so."

It hit me that this implied I trusted him. I turned away quickly.

As we reached the end of the mask room and the door on the other side, Sebastian paused, listening with one ear tilted toward the shadow.

"Hmm, not yet," he said. "There's movement out there. We'll have to stay here."

My nerves, already fraught with tension, buzzed. Tuning into the sensation for the first time since I'd entered this strange place, I was shocked to find just how on edge I really was. I wondered briefly if it was possible to vomit from fear.

"Okay," I breathed.

He turned back to me sharply, eyes roaming my face, and then, in another abrupt change of pace, spun to face the wall, and plucked a mask free.

"Here," he said, throwing it at me. "Go on."

I glanced down, but he immediately stopped me with a finger under my chin.

"Nope—no looking at it first." The smile he had toyed with ever since we entered here became, for the first time, a full-blown grin.

My resolve wavered. This was the charming smile I'd seen him turn on the other women. This was a seducer's smile.

Already, I could feel my mind fooling myself into believing that the smile he was giving me was unique—real—in a way that the others had not been. An irritated huff escaped me. He'd already told me what his first impressions were; there was no reason to think they had changed.

Flushed with my own naivety, I lifted the mask to my face and turned to him. He broke into quiet laughter, waving his fingers in a deaf man's applause.

"Simply stunning," he said in a low drawl.

His words were just the right amount of tease mixed with

torment that my fear faded. I whirled on one foot, searching for the mirror we'd passed not long ago, and saw a chicken.

I hissed, eyes wide beneath the gaudy, elaborate mask that was, without a doubt, a rooster.

"It seemed fitting," he said, closer than I'd realized.

His breath brushed my cheek as he leant in to keep our conversation quiet. I fought not to jump.

"Well then," I murmured. "I suppose we'd better find the perfect mask for you."

Sebastian's eyes glinted in delight, but outwardly he only raised one eyebrow. I dropped the hand holding the chicken mask to my side and scanned the walls, searching for the right one—there.

I snatched the mask from the wall, spun, and held it up to his face before he could see it.

"Huh." Lifting my chin, I made a show of exaggerated satisfaction. "It's like there's two of you."

With his grin now stretching across his face, Sebastian held the mask in place, adjusted the flow of his shirt as only a performer could do, and strode to the mirror. When he saw his reflection, he burst into quiet laughter.

"A snake in the grass, you think?" he said, rounding on me without dropping the silvery mask.

I realized my mistake too slowly. While the mask was undeniably serpentine—the perfect insult for a man who could twist as he could, and who had so swiftly stabbed me in the back with the chicken mask—it was also... beautiful.

Where my rooster mask was gaudy and elaborate, his snake mask was entrancing. Hypnotic. Jewels glittered along the cheeks, and the placement of bright yellow metal around the eye holes, giving the impression of big yellow eyes, was frankly hypnotizing.

Sebastian clearly knew it. He leaned in close, striding

toward me. I took a step back, and another, but my feet butted up against a wooden chest within seconds. I was already trapped, and he did nothing to stop it as he braced one hand beside my head and his body caged mine.

"And so, tell me, Bailey," he whispered, enunciating the susurration of the 's'. "What would a snake do once they have caught their prey?"

I couldn't tell if it was my imagination, but I swore he flicked his tongue at the last second, and that same illusory magic that had created the butterfly now produced a long, forked strip of light.

I shivered. "Well..." I tried to think of an answer that wasn't 'bite them'. "Perhaps—"

Sebastian froze, and all of a sudden, a change came across him.

Earlier, I had foolishly hoped there was a difference between the way he was seducing me and the way he had seduced those other women. Now, bizarrely, I was certain there was, because the expression that crossed his face here was, without a doubt, fake.

No sooner had I formed that thought than the shadows separating us from the corridor outside shimmered, lifted, and vanished. Two fae stepped through, just as Sebastian grasped my hand by the wrist and lifted it so the mask was back in position, hiding my face.

At the same time, his other hand trailed low, marking a line from my collar down to my waist, his fingers hovering an inch over my skin. When I looked up at him, my eyes no doubt bright with fear, his mouth was curved into an arrogant smile.

"Well, well, well," the newcomer said, glancing at his companion and smirking. "What have we here? Sebastian's caught a fly."

"Back off, boys," Sebastian crooned. "I'm having fun, and I don't want to be interrupted."

Shockingly, they did not back off. The two fae approached, and I realized at the last second that I was meant to be enthralled—and so, to play along, I couldn't look at them. I couldn't assess the danger for myself.

It was terrifying, knowing I had to keep my eyes fixed on Sebastian's and trust that he would protect me.

The cold material of the wall seeped through my shirt, threatening to make me shiver. I bit my lip, softening my shoulders and fists inch by inch. Finally, I let my eyes unfocus, and plastered a drunk, happy smile on my face. A face that, historically, had done no such thing.

Sebastian's smile twitched, and he lifted the hand from my wrist and smoothed his thumb over the corner of my mouth. "A little wider, sweetheart," he murmured, and I had the impression that instruction was just for me.

I did as he said, hopefully looking like nothing more than a silly, enthralled human.

The two fae leaned against the wall beside me. One reached out, his hands brushing over my hair. With a sharp flick of his wrist, Sebastian smacked his hand away.

"I'm not sharing tonight," he drawled, straightening just enough to glare the fae down.

"Are you sure about that?" The second one laughed nastily. "We could just ask the Masters."

"Yeah," the other agreed. "As far as I know, you're not allowed to keep things like this from us, are you?"

Sebastian huffed a soft, deadly laugh. "To keep her, you mean? To hold a girl secret from you, locked away in my tent? Just the two of us for hours on end?"

Despite the fear, despite everything, my body shivered at the thought, a pulse of desire kicking up within me.

"No," he agreed, voice a low purr. "I can't do any of that, but does that look like what I'm doing, gentlemen? Or does it look like I've caught a few sorry minutes to myself and a lady who"—he turned back to me, smile widening—"won't remember a thing?"

I had no idea how this would get them to leave us alone, instead of pushing back further, but to my surprise, the guard by my ear barked a laugh and pushed off the wall.

"Oh, he's bold tonight, isn't he? Go on, then. Poor lad's only got about three minutes before he's done. We should let him have it."

The two of them burst into cackling laughter. Sebastian's smile clenched into something more like a grimace.

"What about when you're done, though?" the second insisted.

He had spoken in Criari this time, and it took everything in me to keep from showing that I understood. A frisson of fear slithered, ice cold, down my spine.

But the low, animalistic rumble at the back of Sebastian's throat cut that offer off instantly. Finally, the two intruders backed up a step, the atmosphere shifting into something a touch darker.

"At least give her a kiss from us now," the first added, the humor gone from a voice that was now marked by vicious greed.

It was a challenge, a refusal to accept Sebastian's power even though they were clearly scared of it.

Confusingly, a wave of desire overcame me, mixing in with my fear and piercing me so abruptly it made my breath hitch. I wouldn't mind that at all. So long as those two kept their hands off me, Sebastian could put his wherever he wanted.

It had been so long, and this was all I could get, after all.

Sebastian's smile turned cold. Cruel. He leaned one arm by my head and turned to face them.

"I spend all night performing for you bastards," he murmured, his low drawl sounding completely bored. "And you still have the gall to demand it of me. But fine."

He turned back and leaned in. I held my breath, and it was only at the last second that I remembered to appear enthralled. I let my eyes flutter closed, waiting for his touch.

But nothing happened. And when I opened my eyes again, just a little, I realized—he was using magic.

Sebastian had twisted the light around our faces somehow, and even though he was angled toward me, and his hands had twisted into my hair to pull my head back and my face up to his, we weren't actually touching at all.

It took a mountain of self control not to meet his gaze, because I knew if I did, my composure would break. His breath brushed my lips, his fingers oddly gently in my hair even as he grasped a fistful of my curls and pulled. We were poised there, sharing breath, caught in a fragile moment of treachery and deceit. I kept my attention fixed on his lips as long as I could, but all the while, I felt his eyes burning into me.

At the last second, I broke, and when I looked up, the hunger I found there shattered me.

The intruding fae cackled once more, shoving each other roughly, and then with a final clap on Sebastian's shoulder, they strolled out the other end of the room.

I collapsed against the wall, my heart beating violently in my chest, as Sebastian pushed away from me and turned. For a long while, he just stood there, hand clenched in his hair, the serpentine mask thrown off in disgust.

"Sebastian?" I asked cautiously.

"That was close," he said after a beat, finally lifting his head.

"Let's find that key and get out of here. It's actually just through here."

He pushed through the shadow that the other fae had come from without another word, leaving me to follow quickly before I lost him.

He wasn't lying. There were only two more doors to pass through: one holding chests for storage, and one storing several bottles of a smoking substance. And then we reached a simple mud room.

Coats and boots hung around the place, along with a few weapons stored haphazardly enough to tell me they weren't special in any way—likely just for hunting. Finally, there were hooks with keys.

It was almost underwhelming, and yet I felt like I'd just run a loop around the entire forest.

"Wow," I breathed. "So which one is it?"

Sebastian brushed his finger over an ornate iron key, its design clearly recognizable, and then he leaned out the doorway and pointed to the far end of the corridor. "That door leads to the archives," he said. "And this mud room exits just on the other side of the archers." He grinned. "Filthy bastards, always coming in covered in muck."

I forced a laugh. The memory of his fingers in my hair still tingled; it was hard to focus on anything else. Sebastian's brow furrowed, but he didn't question my strange mood.

"I suppose that's it then," he said when I remained silent.

"I guess." All of a sudden I found I couldn't look at him. I twisted my fingers together, looping a loose thread from my shirt around and around. "Well," I said to my feet, "you know what I would say, but—" A nervous laugh escaped me. "Fae and all."

"I understand," he said quietly.

When I looked up, he still had that strange expression on his face.

"Why do you look so disappointed?" he asked me.

The sheer gall of the question shocked me so much I nearly answered. I bit my lip, fighting to keep the words where they belonged. I didn't deserve this, hadn't earned this, couldn't have this.

But then I remembered the other fae. They had told Sebastian he wasn't allowed this either. Specifically, that he couldn't keep it—just like me.

What if, through some wild trick of fate, this was one of the things I could have?

"You're not allowed to keep anything, are you?" I asked.

I'd meant the words to sound casual, but there was an undercurrent of intent in them that I couldn't disguise. A promise—a hope.

Sebastian's eyebrow raised as he tilted his head. The shadow of the faelight fell across his face.

"Keep? No," he murmured in a low, thoughtful voice. "But I am allowed to play. Is that what you're really asking me, Bailey?"

A flicker of heat surged within me. He didn't look away, and the air slowly shifted between us.

Sebastian couldn't keep anything. He could only play.

A wave of hot desire overwhelmed me, setting an aching pulse between my legs. He was safe. I wasn't allowed to keep something that could go to another, and he wasn't allowed to keep anything at all.

But he could play, and, so long as it didn't infringe on someone else's joy—so long as it wasn't selfish—I was allowed that much.

He was safe, and I was hungry.

"Why do you look so disappointed?" Sebastian asked again, in a very different tone of voice to before.

"Because I thought you were really going to kiss me."

He took a step forward, and then another. And suddenly I was caged against the wall once more, only this time there were no masks between us.

Sebastian leaned closer; his voice had dropped so low, it was only a faint timbre echoing in the velvet passageway. I could hear the wind racing outside, hear the thudding of my own heartbeat.

"Just to be clear," Sebastian said, his breath once more brushing my lips, "you know nothing can come of this, right? Even if I were allowed to, I have no room for romance in my life, and I'm not the kind of man you'd want it from anyway. Trust me. But..." His mouth curved into a wicked grin. "If you're not looking for romance—if you're looking to wipe that prick from your mind and remember how it feels to be wanted. Then, sweetheart, yes—I can give you that."

Remember how it feels to be wanted—like that was something I'd ever known in the first place.

I shivered. "I know." I told him. "I'm counting on it."

One eyebrow raised at that, but he didn't ask anything further. For a moment, his eyes fluttered shut, and he appeared to be holding his breath. But then, they snapped back open, and they were filled with heat. With fire.

"Then it seems I owe you another apology, Bailey," he said. His lips brushed mine in a chaste kiss that left me aching for more. "I didn't realize, but I had promised you a wild and wicked memory to take home with you tonight, and a man should always be as good as his word."

Then, his hand fell to the back of my neck, his lips crashing into mine, and we were moving in an achingly slow rise of temptation. His fingers threaded through my hair again, only this time it did hurt. This time, it was not a calculated performance; he barely seemed to notice what he was doing.

With a low moan, he dropped his hands to cradle my thighs and hoisted me up, the wooden pillar creaking roughly as he encouraged me to wrap my legs around him—still kissing me, never leaving me.

It was everything he had promised.

Every bit of romance and desire that had been taken from me, robbed from me these last six moons—and while I was being honest, for far longer.

Every moment that I'd been told I wasn't worth anything. I wasn't worth desiring, wasn't worth loving.

In those seconds, Sebastian stripped it all away. He kissed me like we were on fire, like we were those same pillars of flame soaring towards the tent's ceiling.

I knew somewhere in the back of my mind that he had only promised me this and nothing more. That he was trapped within the confines of his curse, bound to free his father from his own sins, with no space to care for anything else.

And I knew that I couldn't give him anything either. If I took something as wild and wonderful as Sebastian for myself, the scales would shatter, and my village would fall to Hell before I even made it to the other side of the water. I would become an oath-breaker; I wouldn't do it.

Besides, I couldn't give myself to a man again—*any* man. Couldn't bring myself to trust him with my heart, not when I knew how the Fates would make it end.

Worthless. Boring. Nothing special.

But in those moments, in that brief second of a promise fulfilled, I could trust in this.

We broke apart. Sebastian's breathing came out ragged, his brown eyes hidden by the dark eclipse of his pupil. His gaze fell to my lips, and he kissed me once more, lingering—and then again, sucking my bottom lip between his teeth with just a hint of pressure. A hint of the wilder, unchainable man that he was keeping hidden inside while he fought to toe the line these cruel fae had bound him to.

The pink flush rising along my neck burned so hot that the contrast of my ice cold necklace almost hurt. But the meaning behind that coolness left me dizzy: there was no resistance from the Offering's Oath here. No signs telling me to turn away from this small moment of pleasure, so I wouldn't.

For the next four days, I would take everything I could, soaking in the life I'd never been allowed. Because it didn't matter. I wasn't keeping any of it, and once it was over, I would never be the Offering again.

For the length of these last, lingering days, this was *mine*.

Still with his fingers digging into my thighs, Sebastian adjusted his position, and all of a sudden I could feel the hard length of him pressing into me. I fought the urge to grind my hips down into him, but I was desperate to feel more than just this moment. Desperate to take everything he offered, no matter the danger that could walk in at any moment.

Sebastian made a low, aching sound at the back of his throat, hips thrusting minutely forward as he appeared to struggle with the same decision I was. Then, reluctantly, he lifted me from his waist and set me back down on the ground.

Before moving away, however, he gave me a wicked grin and said, "You'll need something from me to enter these alleys alone." He took my hand and guided it into his hair, wrapped my fingers around several strands.

I gaped at him. His grin widened.

"Go on. Make it hurt, love."

Heat rushed through me, and before I could question it, I tugged the strands of dark hair free. Sebastian made a soft, rough sound as I did, and slammed his lips back into mine, kissing me deeply, thoroughly, as my hand fell back to my side.

"That's better," he murmured against my mouth.

Something about the violence of it struck me—this was real. The danger was real. Silently, I vowed not to take this gift lightly. I wouldn't get him caught, not when his freedom was already so scarce.

He shook his head as if emerging from underwater. "Well then." He gave a shaky laugh, stepping away. "You should probably go and find your friend before he picks a fight he can't win."

My eyes widened in shock, and I pushed away from the wall. "You're right."

A lingering, rhythmic pulse thudded in my throat, and the pleasant heat left behind from his touch didn't stop at my cheeks. I ran my hand through my hair, still dazed. I hadn't been kissed like that in...

I'd never been kissed like that.

Wetting my lips, I started to turn away, suddenly eager for the cool breeze that awaited me outside.

"Before you go..." Sebastian frowned, taking a step toward me as I moved toward the exit. "I know I don't know all your secrets, and you don't need to share them, but this thing with Fynn... are you safe?"

I hesitated, my hand lingering before the doorway. I couldn't tell him about the open Bargain, but... maybe I could show him the ticket and let him think that was what he'd sensed from me. It was only a half lie.

Besides, I had so little time to wrap my head around this dangerous world, and so many ways it could go wrong. After tonight, I almost trusted Sebastian again—as much as I trusted anyone, that was.

It couldn't hurt to see what he thought.

So I plucked it from my pocket and held it out. "I want to cross the bridge with you when you leave," I said. "Only as far as Criera. Then I'll find my own way."

Shock cut across his face, but he didn't demand I change my mind. After a moment, he nodded slowly.

"Will this do it?" I pressed. "Will it work?"

He took the ticket, frowning. "Fynn gave this to you?" he said, his voice low and dangerous.

I didn't see any point in lying. "Yes. Can I trust it? I haven't paid for it yet, so there's time to refuse."

His eyes flashed darkly, and he turned the ticket over, examining it. After a while, he admitted reluctantly, "I can't see anything wrong with it. But..." He threaded his fingers through his hair, choosing his words carefully. "I trusted him once. He was the person I called when I had no one else, and he would answer every time. In fairness to him—which he likely doesn't deserve—he has saved me over a dozen times from death, and worse."

My breath caught; that was a resounding recommendation.

"But," Sebastian went on quickly. "He plays games that no one else understands. By the time you realize what he was doing, it's already done." He handed the ticket back, voice low with warning. "Beware Bargain Night, Bailey, and beware what payment he might demand from you. You can do as you like. It's your life. But please don't use that ticket without deep consideration. Let me think about it, and I might be able to find another way for you to cross the water."

I lifted an eyebrow. "Even though you can't leave your tent?"

He flashed me another of those brilliant grins. "I'll hop from moonbeam to moonbeam and pretend I'm a clown," he said, plucking two keys from the wall and juggling them. They caught the lamplight, flashing across his face before he let his hands grow still. "I'll think of something. Find me before the final night, and we'll search together. At least that way you'll have options."

I hesitated, my chest tightening. "Why are you helping me?" I blurted out.

Everything he said, everything he did, felt real. I trusted it. But it made no sense.

Sebastian's eyebrow raised, and for a minute he didn't answer. Finally, he said, "You're a mystery, Bailey. I do love a mystery."

I wasn't sure how I felt about that. I'd been a mystery to people before—the strange, silent Offering, who rarely spoke and never smiled. But Sebastian seemed genuine, and so I nodded, accepting his answer at face value.

With that, I slipped free into the night. When I made it back home, I tucked his hair into a small pouch I could wear under my clothes, and vowed to sneak into the archives tomorrow, when the fae were distracted with their performances. Then, after I whispered my prayers and threaded several new petals onto the woven coronet of thread hooked above the altar, I curled up in bed.

As I fell asleep, already dreaming of Sebastian's kiss, I felt Merelda curl up on the pillow beside me—the first time I'd seen her since the library—her tiny hand clutching my hair in apology.

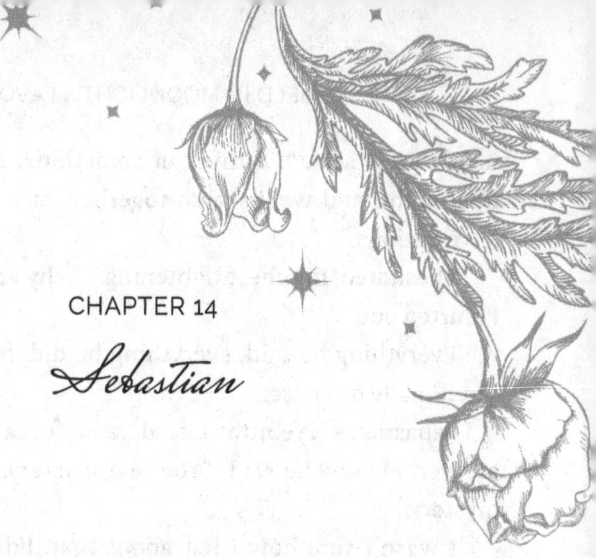

CHAPTER 14

Sebastian

I WAITED UNTIL THE LAST FAE HAD MADE THEIR WAY, LAUGHING AND howling, to bed before I finally allowed the true mask on my face to drop. Gods, what had come over me tonight?

I hadn't risked so much in...

Well, I never had. Not since the Bargain had taken hold and I'd finally understood what consequences were.

I shouldn't have taken her to the archives tonight. I definitely shouldn't have kissed her.

The gentle breeze stirred my hair, almost curious. I ran my palm over my face, pausing to squeeze my jaw and stare, wide-eyed, out into the night. The moon was at its highest, the shadows as short as possible. A few minutes longer to make sure the lingering nasties were gone, and then I could leave.

My thoughts returned to Bailey.

I couldn't keep her. I couldn't keep anything in this gods forsaken place—not without destroying it.

And yet, no amount of looming consequences could make me regret that kiss, or even dream of taking it back. The memory of her lips pressed against mine still haunted me, the ghost of her touch overwhelming my senses.

I was no romantic fool. There was no reason for me to act like a teenager smitten by their first hint of a crush. But could I call this romance? Because it wasn't truly the kiss that captivated me, nor was it the careful way Bailey accepted every step of danger I drew her into.

Although that, in itself, had been delicious to watch. She was brave and she didn't even know it. I liked that. Admired it, and I wanted to be there when she claimed it.

But no, it wasn't that which had our brief interaction echoing through my mind; it was the look on her face when that pretty, serene expression—the mysterious one that had so drawn me in, no doubt like every other idiot in her life—had broken into a smile. Gods, her smile was beautiful. And the true terror of it was, as I kept imagining that smile over and over, I wondered if there was anything I wouldn't do to see it.

Was that romance? Surely not. Falling for someone's smile was merely the basics. The opening night on a grand show. I didn't have to turn up for the rest of the season, and Bailey had made it more than clear that she wouldn't thank me if I did. I had nothing to be concerned about.

Still. It was one hell of a kiss.

When the last of the chatter faded, I stepped casually out of the tent and glanced over the fairground to make sure it was empty behind me as well. There wasn't even a flutter of movement, and the moon rose high, bathing the paths in light.

I stepped free, running my fingers through my hair and giving my shoulders a restless shake. It might be roomy in my tent, but it felt as cramped as a cupboard.

The sounds of the night washed over me as I strolled along the paths, enjoying the rare freedom. Foreign birds called, and the rustling sound of creatures moving among the trees followed me. I wondered what human creatures looked like; were they like our fae ones across the water in Criera? Were they as eerie and terrifying as ours? Or were they as stoic and fascinating as the humans themselves?

Part of me longed to find out—the same part of me that had snuck free from the circus over a decade ago and lost everything. I gritted my teeth and strode toward the far side of the circus. There, a hint of movement did flicker in the light, but I didn't flinch. I lifted a hand in greeting.

The movement waved back. As I stopped at the very edge of the moonlight, a hint of shadow lapping my toes, two eyes appeared in the darkness behind a tree.

"Sebastian," he greeted.

I squinted, but Alfrich had picked his location well. I could barely see the long, tattered ears lined with piercings, or the sharpened jaw above elongated arms and fingers. The suggestion of scales to his skin was the only glint in the moonlight that hinted this hidden person was not human.

Trolls had migrated across the water centuries ago, although the humans hadn't realized it. Bless them.

"It might be time," I told him.

Alfrich nodded, his hooked nose carving a path through the darkness. "I received your bird," he murmured, his voice grating like stone. "Hoped it was true but didn't dare to believe."

A wry smile twitched on my lips; I knew the feeling. "It could be nothing," I said, more to quell my own rising hope than his. "But there was a sign. A sign that—"

I swallowed down the guilt that rose in me as I remembered what I had done to Bailey. The assumptions I had made about her and the way I had let those assumptions turn me cruel. No better than any other Lumière.

"It came to nothing," I went on, pasting a wider grin on my face. "A flash in the pan, darling. Not worth thinking about." I clenched my fists. For so long, I'd hoped that the secret fae who heralded the arrival of my gate would possess powers that could help me find my father. Clearly, that wasn't to be. "But even still, I'm almost certain that the sign failing means the gate is working exactly as intended. I think Heillon wanted me to give up after the magic revealed nothing, and to assume I'd read the signs incorrectly while the gate passed me by."

As I said the words out loud, they felt even truer than before. Whether Bailey had hidden fae magic inside her or not, it didn't matter. That first glimpse of power was the signal that opened the gate, and I would not let this opportunity pass me by. I'd waited ten years for it.

"Search for..." I paused, thinking through the list I'd spent the last two days compiling. "Signs of chains," I settled on. "The Lumière know how much my father hated being restrained." My voice choked, but I forced the words out. "How much he loved the freedom of the open road. He'll be in some form of cage, and since we are talking about Heillon, its craftsmanship will be nothing short of the best. Check for unusual trade deals in carbon steel. Or gold—they might choose jeweled shackles to drive in the pain of his torture."

I looked up and saw Alfrich's eyes glinting with understanding. The compassion in them nearly undid me.

"Anything else I should know?" he asked.

"If they've allowed him a modicum of freedom," I said carefully, driving the words through gritted teeth, "he loves lavender. He'll plant fields of it if he can, even if it forms part of his own torture. If they haven't allowed him freedom..." I swallowed. "Listen for screams. They'd love to make him howl where no one could find him. And he'll be near water," I added on a whim. "It wouldn't be right if he wasn't just out of reach. If he couldn't see his own escape and have it torture him day after day."

Alfrich nodded.

I fell silent. There were no further instructions to impart

and nothing I could offer to help him. Sometimes, it seemed that was the cruelest part of this entire venture. I had to rely on my friends to find my father, because my role was simple—the only scripted character in this haunting tragedy.

I had to follow the rules. Every single one.

"The moon is too high for me to come forward, since I can't risk being seen by all those hidden eyes," Alfrich said, glancing toward the tents. "And am I to assume you won't risk stepping into the shadows for a hug?"

I couldn't help flinching. More than anything, I wanted to step into the shadow of that tree and hug my old friend. To thank him wordlessly for the danger he was putting himself in —going up against Heillon and the lower Lumière Masters, all to find my father and correct the wrongs I'd made in my foolish youth.

"I can't," I whispered, shaking my head. "But it's so good to hear your voice, old friend."

Alfrich nodded and took a step backward into the darkness, as if knowing the temptation was almost too much for me.

"I'll send word by raven," he murmured.

Then he was gone.

I stayed there, staring into the darkness for an age, almost wishing someone would find me and demand answers. That way I could shove it in their face: I haven't broken any of your fucking rules.

For ten long years, they'd waited for me to break, pushing me toward it. Fynn, most of all. Not a day passed that he didn't taunt me, dare me. But I wouldn't do it.

I knew what mattered above all else.

Finally, I turned from the darkness and back to the moonlight. As I strode toward my tent, lost in my thoughts, the memory of Bailey's lips on mine returned once more.

My brow furrowed. It was an odd feeling, being haunted by a girl. I hadn't kissed anyone I cared about in years. Not since—

I broke that thought off before it could form.

But I was forced to admit one truth to myself as I slipped back into my tent. Romance or not, seeing that smile upon her face and knowing from her accompanying shock that it was rare, I had felt a flicker of something. An emotion rising from deep in my chest, where everything I had once cared for lay buried. I suspected before the season was over, I would have to sneak another kiss or two with her, just to feel that again. Just to see that rare, beautiful smile.

I'd give her a proper goodbye, maybe, before we parted forever.

I knew my purpose, here. I knew what mattered, and I wouldn't deviate from it. But it was nice to have the reminder. To think that perhaps there was something I could care about after all this was over.

Perhaps Fynn was wrong and my heart wasn't quite so blackened after all.

CHAPTER 15

Bailey

I STARED DOWN AT THE TICKET IN MY HANDS, WAVING IT GENTLY BACK and forth in the air as I thought. It was oddly mesmerizing, watching the little slip of paper bend and sway. Every now and then, a little spark would pop up, timed perfectly for when Merelda completed her circuit of the room and landed above my head.

"It recognizes you," I cautioned her in a sing-song voice. "Better watch out. You might get fae cooties."

Merelda hooked her legs over the lampshade, swung down until her little face was level with mine, and hissed at me.

"Yeah, yeah." I waved her off.

The ticket sparked even more, a tiny ember gliding off and hitting my finger. I gasped and dropped it onto the counter.

"That hurt," I said, narrowing my eyes at Merelda. "Do you think you could help me here, or are you determined to cause chaos?"

The upside-down hiss became a big grin.

I sighed as she fluttered upward and continued her circuit of the room. No help from that corner then.

The apothecary walls reflected the early morning sun back at me with their shimmering illusions of magic: rows upon rows of colored glass bottles filled with all number of concoctions dancing in the sunlight. I had a rare morning on my own, today, where I could open the shop without Master Skylark breathing down my neck. She was busy brewing in her home workshop, to keep up with demand. The stomach flu had indeed become an outbreak, and tinctures were needed all through the kindergarten.

I'd felt a faint twinge of unease when I heard the news, but no one had accused me of anything, and my necklace had been as cold as ice for moons. A pile of roses lay at the end of the counter, ready for me to take home for drying tonight. I ran my fingers over the soft pink petals, letting the comfort of that prayer soothe me. Everything was fine.

Shaking off the unpleasant thoughts, I turned to the shelves, admiring the way the blue glass of the largest bottles turned seaweed green with the light of the sun. Such a small thing, but so beautiful.

Mornings like this reminded me why I'd completed my Journeyman, even though I knew nothing could ever come of it. As the Offering, I'd never be allowed to have my own shop, or to turn a profit that threatened the livelihoods of my neighbors. Still, on mornings like these, I used to dream it was mine.

Apothecaries were a source of healing completely removed from magic—fae or human. They didn't rely on Bargains or trades, the ever-present weight of the scales balancing so carefully each for each. These tinctures were created from centuries-old wisdom, passed down from the people who had come before me, for the price of a few simple coins.

They weren't true magic. They didn't use anything from across the water. They didn't even tap into the earthbound magic that the Spell Masters used. They couldn't create witch-light. They couldn't spin illusions from thin air.

But they could heal a sore stomach. They could help blood flow. They could ease a pounding headache.

And okay, sure, I hadn't created these ones—Master Skylark wouldn't let me, for obvious reasons. The risk was too great. But selling them was enough, knowing they were treating my friends and neighbors. Helping them, just as I helped them by existing and balancing their scales of good fortune.

This morning, however, something was different. The shimmering magic of those bottles only made me think of the real magic from the night before. Of the dark and dangerous shadow of a ring drawn in blood, next to the beauty and wonder of a rose that would become a doorway.

I was playing with fire here, and I knew it.

I craved it.

A smile crept onto the corner of my mouth. The Offering wasn't meant to want or have things like this. This spoke of adventure, and every secret dream I'd had as a child. The kind of dreams I'd shared only to my pillow late at night, or to the books I poured over, soaking up every word, every story, and begging for a Bargain that would end my curse. Of course, nothing on this side of the water could end it. When I'd forgotten that, the world had reminded me in crystal, brutal clarity.

But in four more nights, I wouldn't be on this side of the water.

I wouldn't be the Offering anymore.

My fingers, wrapped once more around the ticket, twitched, and I drew in a shaky breath. What kind of life would I find over there? Sebastian had given me a taste of desire that didn't come with pain. The kind of pleasure that I might be able to find in Criera, if I wanted.

I'd thought running away would be the end of my story, and the village would happily move on without me. But if the other side of the water promised *good* things, not just an escape... what did that mean?

A soft hissing sound had me looking up, wondering what on earth Merelda had her nose out of joint about this time.

I gasped; it wasn't Merelda at all. The low, snarling, growling sound was Merelda, but the hiss had been the sound of air displacing as a body appeared where there hadn't been one before.

The sound of, to put it mildly, Fynn appearing in my apothecary.

"What in the gods' name are you doing here?" I said, eyes wide.

I glanced down at the ticket, half wondering whether I had summoned him myself. Not really sure why, I slid the ticket subtly behind the cash register, out of sight.

Finn gave me a little half smile, glancing curiously about the place as he gave an elaborate bow. Flicking his blonde hair out of his face, he regarded me curiously.

"I'm sightseeing," he said in a tone of surprised innocence.

I bit back a laugh.

There was something sharp about his gaze, as always. And yet, the way he carried himself was so loose and relaxed. The gentle tilt of his head as he admired the bottles with a curious eye didn't set my teeth on edge. He was giving only green flags.

Was he really as dangerous as Sebastian thought? Or was it just because of their history? For all I knew, Sebastian might have been as cruel as Fynn in return. Most people were vicious when it came to exes, after all.

"You're sightseeing," I repeated, leaning my hip on the counter and folding my arms. "And so, pray tell, what sights are you seeing in my dingy little shop..." I made a show of glancing around the room. "...that has absolutely no useful wares to you."

A delighted look crossed his face for half a second before he widened his eyes in mock indignation, hovering his hand over his chest and strolling casually toward me.

"So judgmental of the little human," he said. "Do you think the fae do not get sick? That we do not suffer from..."

He reached out on his way past a random shelf, plucked a bottle free, and examined it.

Brows lifting, he said, "Werewolf syndrome?" He gave me a quizzical look. "You don't have werewolves on this continent. I would have known about it."

"It's not really a werewolf—" I began and then stopped, eyes widening. "What do you mean on this continent?"

Fynn's grin turned smug as he sat the bottle back on the shelf. "Nothing to worry about. So tell me, what are these werewolves that are not werewolves?"

"Wouldn't you know if you were suffering from it?" I said dryly.

He crossed the final distance between us, leaning one arm on the counter and invading my space with casual arrogance.

I didn't mind it one bit.

Instead, a little shiver ran through me, and I couldn't quite keep my gaze from dropping momentarily to his lips.

"Perhaps I need the physician to help diagnose me," he said, refusing to drop the bit.

Feeling oddly challenged, I couldn't resist going along, at least for a while longer. "It's just a condition where you grow excessive hair," I explained. "Usually on your hands."

"Ah," Fynn said, sounding intrigued as one eyebrow lifted. "I quite like excessive hair—do go on."

"Well, not everyone who grows it does," I said, fighting back a smile. "Although I agree."

Without meaning to, my attention dropped to his chest, concealed beneath a flowing, green shirt tightly strapped with leather. The fae never appeared to have much facial or body hair, but was that only an assumption? Was his chest hairy or smooth below that silky fabric?

I realized I was biting my lip and quickly stopped. When I returned my gaze to Fynn's, it was just in time to note the flash of hunger there.

Swallowing, I pushed away from the counter and walked around to the front, where I ran my fingers over the tops of several bottles. "You can have your choice of one of two tinctures. If you quite like the look of this extra, unusual hair on your body, you can take this one. It will ensure that your hair grows healthily, rather than patchy and dry. It'll be luscious. Shiny."

When I said the word 'luscious', Fynn's gaze dropped momentarily to my own lips.

I cleared my throat. "Or, if you don't like the look of it, you can rub this cream on your hands and the excess hair will fall away."

Spinning around, I clasped my own hands behind my back to keep from doing any more of this—whatever the hell I was doing.

Flirting, I supposed.

"Then it seems I'm in the right place," Fynn purred, folding his arms and leaning back so he was half seated on the counter. He made no move to cross the room toward me, even though I half wished he would. "No matter what ailment I may have."

"Unless you don't have any ailment," I pointed out.

"Oh, we're all suffering from something," Fynn said as he picked up a bottle from the counter and studied it. His words came out far too casual to be truly relaxed, and for a minute I was thrown.

I decided to continue as if I hadn't noticed. "Sure, except you—you're just... what was it?" I tapped my finger on my lower lip. "Sightseeing."

To my surprise, Fynn barked out a laugh, and from the slightly widened eyes, I suspected it had taken him unawares as well.

"You caught me," he said, setting the bottle down and spreading his arms wide. "I really am sightseeing, though. I thought I'd take a look at this human town we're in, since it's been..." He mulled it over. "Probably five or ten years since I was here last. I'll admit, though, until I saw you within this shop, I was glamoured."

I blinked at him.

"You mean you were invisible, walking out on the street with everyone else and no one knew?"

His eyebrow quirked, a subtle acknowledgement. I let out a slow breath. That possibility had never even occurred to me.

"I thought the fae couldn't leave the circus grounds," I pointed out, frowning.

Certainly, Sebastian had been forbidden to. It was disobeying that rule that had gotten him into the situation he was in now. For just a moment, something dark shadowed across Fynn's face, there and gone again in a flash.

Then he shrugged and said simply, "We all live under different guidelines."

Ah, I thought, *by which he no doubt means he has none.*

No rules to follow, no guidelines to live within... Whereas Sebastian was forever damaged by the ones he had broken.

Some of my joy melted away, leaving behind a strange sense of guilt. Sebastian had tried to warn me about the potential dangers of my choices, and here I was—fraternizing with them. While Sebastian was trapped in his tent, unable to even step outside freely.

I let my hands fall to my side, one reaching out of its own volition to toy with a dangling mesh bag of garlic at the front of the shelf.

"Well, you've found me," I said, studying the way the bag twirled under my hands. "So what can I do for you?"

Wait—was he here for payment? Did I have to make my decision now?

Before I could think of a way to distract him, he leaned back a couple inches more, his attention sliding to something behind the cash register. My stomach sank.

Fynn reached out and plucked the ticket from the counter, holding it up between two fingers.

"I just wanted to see how you were going with this."

A beat passed, then another. But Fynn waited in silence, neither mentioning my looming payment nor rushing me to speak.

"It's going fine," I said slowly. "If by 'going' you mean I'm staring at it and waiting for inspiration to hit."

He let out a low laugh, sliding the ticket back behind the cash register and winking at me, as if it were a secret we both shared. I supposed, in a way, it was.

"These things take time," he said. "Wishing to steal away with the fae is one thing, but it is quite another to do it. You still have four nights to make your decision. There's no need to rush."

I frowned at him. "It's like you knew I'd have trouble deciding."

"Of course I knew," he said, and for a moment genuine surprise appeared on his face. "It's not any old human that makes a choice like this, which means it is a difficult choice to make. I wondered, in fact, if you might have any questions."

"Questions?" My heart fluttered.

The way he said the word made me think of all number of

things I wanted to ask him. Like whether I was imagining that haunted, hungry look I kept seeing out of the corner of my eye. Or whether he was aware that he kept following the dextrous, fine movements of my fingers like they were his lifeline. Whether his hair was as soft as it looked, and if he liked the way it must fall like a curtain around whoever he chose to kiss. Or if, perhaps, he preferred to be the one kissed, shrouded by the privacy of someone else's touch.

I couldn't ask any of those, of course, but now that he was here, did I have questions? Perhaps he would tell me how the ticket worked, and what the fine print had meant. Disguise included. Do not tear, break, or bend.

"Well," I said carefully. "The disguise. What's that about?"

His eyes glittered. "Ah," he began.

But before he could continue, Merelda burst from the lighting fixture and began spitting a hundred profanities at him at once from midair.

He blinked at her, lips parted in shock, hand half raised as if to protect himself from the onslaught of her rage.

"Is this an imp?" he said incredulously.

"This is Merelda," I corrected him.

Instantly, I berated myself, waiting for the slap-down to come. Hayden had always hated when I corrected him, especially when I did it unkindly.

But Fynn, to my shock, shot me a delighted glance, his grin only growing wider.

"My apologies," he said. "Merelda, do you think perhaps you could back up..." He mulled it over. "...two feet?"

In response, she blew him a raspberry.

"Lovely," he said, staring at the ceiling for a minute. "It's been at least a year since I saw an imp in the flesh."

"Don't you have them over the water?"

"No," he said in a curious tone. "They appear to have all

migrated. Not just to here. There's a greater population on the other side of the mountains, and on an island, I think, to the south. If I'm remembering correctly."

Huh.

I thought it was only a few that made their way over the water, but it seems they all escaped Criera.

My eyes narrowed. "Why?"

Something unfamiliar crossed his features. His brows slid together, jaw tightening as he looked away.

"There are those of us who..." He raised a finger in Merelda's direction. "Don't bite me," he cautioned. "Use our impish friends in..." His eyes slid to the potions along the wall, and nausea flooded me.

"You can't be serious."

"Oh, I am," he said, an apologetic air to his tone.

Merelda had gone silent. Over the years that I'd known her, even though I couldn't understand her language, I'd begun to read various changes in her moods, and I could see now that she was hurt. Grief-stricken.

She was beyond anger, beyond rage. I wondered who she might have lost, and my heart broke for her.

I reached up without thinking, but with a final, wailing chatter, she dived back into the center of the lampshade, out of reach.

Fynn's head jerked up toward me, as if I'd said something. The furrow in his brow deepened, and his lips parted as if to speak. But then he simply closed them and shook his head.

"It is what it is," he said coldly. "Now, tell me, would you like to learn how to fight a lora beast?"

My mouth fell open at the sudden change in conversation. "What? One of those..." I jerked my thumb back in the rough direction of the forest we'd run through together. "One of those monsters. You want me to fight one?"

"No, I'd much rather you didn't," he said, running a hand through his blond hair and pulling a face. "But if you really are going to accept that ticket and cross with us over the bridge, then I imagine you'll be scurrying off to make your own way through our lands rather quickly. Which means you need to know what you might encounter, and you need to know how to survive it."

He paused at the sight of my open-mouthed expression.

"What?" he asked with a slow smile. "Did you think I was just going to give you *books* to read?"

A flush rose on my cheeks as my eyes darted to the pile of texts I'd been methodically searching through all morning. Was it so stupid that I had? I wasn't used to being helped. Even Sebastian had only offered to take me so far before making it clear that, for the rest, I was on my own.

I cleared my throat. "So we're going to train together?" I lifted one eyebrow, fighting to regain the upper ground. "And you're offering me this out of the goodness of your heart? This is going on four times now that you've helped me. It's starting to look suspicious."

Unease twisted in my gut as I realized how true that was.

He lifted his hands in easy defense. "Let's say I'm curious. You're the first human who's tried to stow away with us in, oh, decades, certainly."

An echo of Sebastian's words returned to me: you're a mystery.

My heart stuttered, and when my gaze met Fynn's, I swore there was a spark of something there between us. Something that made me realize I was diving in far deeper than I could possibly emerge from unscathed.

Sebastian, at least, had seemed to understand the walls separating us. He had his mission, after all: to save his father. And I refused to allow myself to be stripped bare again like Hayden had done to me when I forgot my oath. To be left so raw and so broken. Thus, it was an immutable truth that, no matter how many flirty exchanges or searing kisses we shared, Sebastian and I would never have more than this small handful of nights.

Strange though it was to say it, he was safe.

But Fynn... He was dangerous in a different way. Not only because of those unpredictable secrets that hovered beneath every word he said, but because I had the feeling that, if he wanted me like Sebastian did, it would not be so easy to convince him to let me go.

"How do you want to teach me?" I asked him as the silence of the apothecary descended upon us.

I could hear distant laughter out in the street, and it sounded like another world.

"Tonight," he said, tipping his head to the side. "An hour before sunset, you and me, in the forest where we met the beast. I'll show you what you need to do to survive us."

To survive us.

He didn't say to survive his world, or to survive those creatures. He said to survive *us*.

It felt like the truest thing he'd ever uttered.

Hesitation warred within me, cautioning me to run in the other direction—that I was already in too deep with this man. I had four tentative days left, in which I had to keep the balance of my oath so I could escape it forever. And every step I'd taken so far had been with that single end goal in mind: dissolve the oath. Become lost. Sebastian's touch last night hadn't threatened any of that, but Fynn...

Fynn was different.

If I followed the siren call that curled around the two of us, I wondered: would I even make it across the water? Or would the necklace at my throat sear a hole right through me as I stood there on the shore?

But if I didn't take what he offered, even if I did make it over the bridge to Criera, I might never survive more than a second on the other side.

I opened my mouth to answer, but then the front door creaked and stuttered.

The door to the apothecary had always been old and water-logged, taking a minute to open after the rain. I could hear the person outside giving it a shove with their shoulder before a muffled curse sounded.

My head whipped back to Fynn. He made no move to do the little disappearing act he'd used to enter my shop. Made no move at all except to stare at me, waiting for an answer.

I didn't have time for this.

If one of the townsfolk saw me in here with the fae, who knew what they would do to me? It was one thing for the fae to be a mysterious magical spectacle, safely behind their own walls, but to be here, in my shop, with me, when I was hardly trusted as it was...

I didn't think. I lurched forward, grabbed Fynn around the waist and shoved him over the counter and behind the curtain just as the door burst open.

"Gods!" Mrs. O'Leary muttered. "You need to get that door looked at, girl. My hip was bad enough before trying to get in here."

I tried to shove all thoughts of Fynn from my mind as I helped her, ringing up her purchases and recommending some new ointments before waving goodbye.

Was he still there? Had he just assumed my answer would be yes, or was he waiting to be sure?

The second the door fell shut behind Mrs O'Leary, I swept

through the curtain and found him standing there, back toward me, gazing down at something in his hands.

My heart fluttered again, stomach swooping. He'd waited.

"She's gone," I said.

He didn't answer me for a moment. Then he slowly turned, and I saw what he was looking at. Ice slid down my throat.

I should have smashed that fucking photo. Should have done more than just turn it face down, but I couldn't. I couldn't, for the part of me that remembered all the good times. For the part of me that saw through the ugliness to the beauty within, and who naïvely, foolishly, stupidly hoped that one day in the future I would be able to focus on that beauty instead of what my sister had done to me.

"She looks like you," Fynn said, glancing up from the photo to my face and then back again. But his eyes lingered on mine, the same as they had outside when he jerked his head up, acting for all the world as if he could hear my inner torment without me saying a word.

Maybe he could. Maybe that was one of the fae's abilities.

"Your sister?"

"Yes," I said tightly, making it very clear that I didn't want to talk about her.

He glanced up at me, one eyebrow raised. "And what did she do?"

"Leave it," I growled, looking away, my hand clenching the fabric of the curtain between my fingers until my knuckles hurt.

"No," Fynn said, lightly.

I glanced at him in astonishment. "What?"

"I said no." His eyes challenged me. "What did she do to you, Bailey?"

He was the complete opposite of Sebastian, pushing me where Sebastian would leave me be. And I found myself rising to it, fire curling within me, growing from the embers into a raging inferno. Fire I'd never felt before—never dared to.

"She destroyed me," I hissed, anger blazing through me.

Fynn's eyes flared, glinting in the light. He gave a soft hum of acknowledgement, low in the back of his throat, and then set the photo down on the table—face down like he'd found it. "What a cow," he said, his tone light and airy.

The sheer light-heartedness of it shocked me, piercing the flames within me and, against all odds, making me laugh. I didn't understand it. When anyone else pushed me, it just made me hate them. When Fynn pushed me, it felt like lancing a wound.

But I couldn't deny that I liked Sebastian's gentleness, too. Fynn felt like lancing the wound, but Sebastian... he felt like healing it.

Fynn stepped forward, tracing his fingers down my face, catching a lock of my hair between them as he studied it.

His eyes were like fire, and my breath caught as he said, "You don't look destroyed, though."

The way he said it, it was though he was doing more than dismissing what I wasn't. It was as though he was telling me what I *was*. And what I was... did not belong here, in this dingy shop, in this human world.

Not going by the expression on his face, at least. Or the tentative, new thoughts that filled my mind.

The necklace at my throat was cool, calm. That was all I needed to know. The only metric that mattered alongside my own, precious desires.

His eyes flicked to mine. "Will I see you tonight?"

"Yes," I breathed.

The word sounded powerful. Certain, in a way I never had before—at least not to myself. I would see Fynn tonight, and I would learn how to navigate the dangers of their world with power and grace.

And, by the time the full moon rose, I would be free.

My earlier concern about Sebastian returned to me, tugging at my thoughts, shifting the tone of them as I examined old ideas through this newfound lens of strength. Perhaps, the way to achieve all of this might result in helping someone more than just me—if I was smart about it.

Fynn's lip curled. "It's a date."

That little puff of air rose once more, and he vanished.

CHAPTER 16

Bailey

THE REST OF THE DAY PASSED IN A BLUR OF MUDDY MEMORIES AND unsolved questions. Before I knew it, the sun was high overhead, and I was sitting at the little wrought-iron table outside, eating a tasteless pastry and counting down the seconds until I could go home.

An hour before sunset, that's when I would meet him.

Pastry crumbled beneath my fingers, piling up at the sides of my plate as I layered the flakes into abstract pictures. Would he teach me to fight with magic? Or with weapons?

Which did I want him to teach me?

I swallowed down the last of my pastry, barely noticing that I'd finished it, and turned at the sound of a gentle knock on the side gate behind the apothecary. I looked up to see Sadey's head peeking above the fence, her hands hooked over the wooden palings.

"Hellooo!" she called. "I've come by to get that mirror."

Right, the mirror.

I stood, dusting myself off and removing the stray crumbs from my breeches, and then crossed to the back porch of the apothecary where I'd tucked the mirror this morning.

"Here you go," I said, hoisting it up and handing it over. "I'm so sorry, but I knocked it against the door when I took it down, and it cracked in the corner there. It still works though. I checked."

The broken shard had fallen somewhere near my bed, leaving a gaping hole in the top right corner where someone's face would sit. Even now, I wasn't entirely sure I hadn't struck the thing deliberately.

Sadey's face fell for a moment, and then she laughed. "Of course you did," she said fondly. "That's alright, so long as it still works."

"It definitely does. I checked it with Ella this morning."

Sadey leaned the mirror carefully by the gate, brushing off a cobweb from her skirt as she straightened.

"How was the dance troupe?" I asked.

"Oh, they were so good, Bailey. Gosh, I wish you'd seen them." Her eyes gleamed. "And their muscles, *gods*. They must do nothing but work out." She giggled, the sound ringing gently over the small courtyard. The trees overhanging the fence lifted in the breeze, rustling forward almost as if they were swaying closer to the sound of her laughter. She had that effect on people, and now the bloody plants, too, apparently. She lived a life I couldn't even imagine. "So anyway, thanks again for the mirror. I really appreciate it."

For a moment, her expression eased into a genuine, appreciative smile, and my heart softened. To be honest, I barely cared about the mirror anymore. It wasn't like I'd be here after the full moon. Hannah could keep it; it didn't matter.

"You're welcome," I said, and found that I actually meant it.

She hoisted the mirror under her arm, sticking her hip out to balance its weight, and then glanced at me again over her shoulder. "Oh, we've all decided to check out the circus tonight. Are you going again?"

My heart stopped, only to kick up again instantly with a rapid, staccato beat. "What, all three of you?" I asked. "How? You didn't Bargain for entry."

No one could enter if they hadn't already Bargained for a ticket that first night. It was the first rule.

"Yeah." She grinned excitedly. "But someone else did and they Bargained for all of us. Wasn't that sweet?"

A note of something strange entered her voice, but I couldn't work out why. Who would Bargain entry for four people, when three hadn't even agreed to come? And could that person really be called a friend? Without more details, I was a fifty-fifty split on whether dragging someone into the Lumière's twisted entertainment constituted an act of war.

Fynn was right, ultimately. It was a rare human who actually *wanted* to be stolen from her home in Aelor and carried across the water.

"Anyway." She flapped her hand. "We want to see how the dancing fae compare to the dancing humans." She laughed again. "Can't let you have all the fun."

This time, I could read exactly what was in her voice—it was sharp and stern, a cruelty tinged with reproach. It was also familiar, just not usually from Sadey. My chest swelled with an unnamed, unexamined emotion, and I pressed my lips tightly together for a beat before replying.

"Well, I hope you ladies can keep up with me." I let the corner of my mouth curve into a grin. "I've had two days on you after all."

Sadey barked out a laugh, thrilled by the challenge. "Don't tell me you've got the fae hooked around your little finger," she said, shaking her head. "Bailey, you are wicked."

Her tone was light, but I could sense the warning beneath it, building on the reproach from before. The Offering could visit the circus, and laugh and dance with the rest of them, but only if she remained in the background. A member of the audience, while the leading lady and her chorus took the speaking parts and collected all the bouquets at the end.

I never should have accepted Sebastian's hand so publicly.

A sliver of unease trickled down my spine. Had Sadey heard about that? What would she do if she knew I had the attention of not just Sebastian but Fynn as well?

In the space between one second and another, it was as though a weight descended on me, the sun hiding behind a cloud. Angrily, I shrugged it off. *No*—it wasn't supposed to be like that anymore.

Sadey paused in the midst of picking up the mirror, eying me strangely. "Are you quite alright, Bailey?"

"Never better," I answered in a smooth drawl.

I took in the gentle furrow of her brow—concerned both for me, and why I might be upset, and for herself, in case my reactions put her at risk. Sweeping my gaze in an arc, I followed the clutch of her hand around the mirror, the lift in her shoulders. The tap of her foot. She was nervous, and she only wanted to help. It just so happened that she couldn't help me. No one here could. They could only help themselves.

My breath slowly eased, and I smoothed the palms of my hands over my breeches. "It's a lovely skirt you're wearing today," I said breezily, finally recognizing her signature embroidery along the seams.

Her shoulders relaxed. "Thank you! I finished it last moon. The fabric's from Mosswilde; isn't it gorgeous?"

After a few minutes more, Sadey strolled away with the mirror, but the echo of her words remained as a sour taste pooling at the back of my throat.

Bailey, you are wicked.

It was said as a joke, but I knew she believed it.

That was the story Hayden had told. The story they all told, to twist the truth until I was the villain—even more than my own mistakes had made me.

I'd teased his friends and led them on. I was greedy. Selfish. The Offering, desperate to break her oath and take what wasn't rightfully hers. Hayden had finally stood up for himself, quit his misguided charity case, and shown me what happened to loose, greedy women who forgot their place. They got what they deserved: humiliation in front of everyone. Who cared if the Bargain Magic was so cruel, when it restored the balance? It was a wild thing, and she should never have let it go so far.

Did it even count as twisting the truth, when I could search the story for moons and find no trace of a lie?

I glanced down at my hands, turning them over and searching for a sign of the magic that had sparked from the ticket just hours before. It was a ridiculous hope, but I found myself begging for it to appear, even though the ticket was stored safely at the bottom of my satchel. I found myself hoping that, somehow, a piece of that magic had stayed with me.

But there was nothing.

My mouth twisted into a harsh slash across my face. Four more nights, then all this would be gone. It wouldn't matter what they thought of me then.

With a firm push, I rose to my feet and went to fetch my gathering basket.

As I strolled along the forest path, basket swinging against my hip, my body slowly relaxed to the sounds of nature's symphony. Trees swayed, animals scurried, and far above my head, birds sang, signaling that all was safe. All was well.

Inwardly, I tried to find that same feeling in the rush of my heart, the pump of blood within my veins, and the rhythm of breath that filled my lungs. I tried to recall Sadey's words without being overcome by an unfamiliar nausea, twisting low in my gut. Without feeling that sense of betrayal.

She was my friend, and while she wasn't always a good one, that was okay. It wasn't like she'd abandoned me after what Hayden and my sister did; she just... sometimes believed their version more than mine.

It didn't matter. No one was perfect, and given the historical Bargain—centuries worth of it—that was wrapped around my very existence, I understood why she was sometimes harsh. I was the Offering; I had one role, to protect the village from descending to the depths of Hell by humbly kneeling at their feet. If I were in her shoes, I'd be terrified at any sign the Offering was rebelling, too. She was only looking out for the rest of the village by chastising me.

Sure, I *wasn't* in her shoes, and understanding her position didn't make it any easier to be in mine... But I had nearly thirty years of practice keeping myself company when no one else would, and that made up for when my friends weren't enough.

When I was younger, I used to tell myself that if I just kept seeing through my neighbors' ugliness to the beauty within, one day, they would do the same for me. They would see past 'the Offering' and see *me*. Maybe they would even love me, too.

And if they didn't, that was okay, because I had myself.

I repeated the beloved mantra, taking pleasure in my own company as the soft thud of my boots echoed on the leaf-strewn path—a companionable sound. Out here, I didn't have to work so hard to keep my face still and unreadable. I could just relax and let it be. With each step I took away from the village, I felt the truth of that even more.

Soon, I found several of the little micro clearings that I knew held the herbs I wanted. I was sure to only take what I needed, leaving the rest to flourish in my absence.

After my basket was almost full, I ducked off the path completely, heading toward a little clearing that I knew lay further in and housed several of the mushrooms that I needed.

The forest grew quieter around me until even the birds' singing sounded distant. If I didn't pay attention, it was almost like they weren't singing at all.

I knelt on the ground, closing my eyes and breathing in the scent of the forest. Did they have forests like these over the other side of the water? They must. Their magic was rooted in nature, and the creatures that lived with the fae would need places of their own, too. I wondered if Fynn would tell me about any of them tonight.

My mind returned to the sensation of his hand trailing down my face, the gentle tug of his fingers as he took a curl of my hair and ran it between them.

I opened my eyes and began examining the mushrooms around the area. It seemed as though someone had already been through here, and they'd left less than they should have.

Not only that, but their footsteps had traipsed other spores through—or perhaps they'd been carried in on the wind—because there were other kinds of mushrooms here now. Thriving in the darkness and moist roots of the gigantic trees towering over me.

In fact... I narrowed my eyes. The patch of mushrooms that I'd thought were the ones I needed now had me questioning them. Was this the same patch I used to forage from?

I thought my patch was a little further over, and this one looked new.

There was a kind of mushroom that was similar in almost every way to the one I needed, except that it was deadly. The only way to tell the difference was by the faint blue tinge very close to the stalk. I knelt down, my hands pressed into the earth and my head tilted sideways. I couldn't see any blue, but that didn't mean it wasn't there.

Even just picking such a mushroom could mean grave illness, if no one found me in time. Some people were susceptible to these poisons by touch, and I wasn't sure if I was one of them.

I wished Master Skylark was here. She'd roll her eyes and lament how ill-fated and useless I was, but at least she'd tell me if it was dangerous or not.

What would be worse? Risking going back empty-handed when I knew we needed to restock these tinctures? Or risking that this was the wrong mushroom?

If I returned without them, Master Skylark would rant about my ill fate ruining her supplies, and possibly make me work overtime to make up for it. She'd already told me I was a fool for going to the circus... would she make me work at night, so I missed out entirely? My breath stuttered at the thought.

The soft chatter of voices reached my ears.

"I know! They all just dropped like flies. Boils, vomiting, the whole lot."

What? More illness? My stomach turned, the thick beat of my pulse suddenly audible, like I was about to keel over myself.

"Urgh," a disgusted voice answered. "Right there in the inn?"

"Middle of the floor. Hand to the gods, I'm telling the truth."

I turned in time to see someone emerge suddenly from the other side of the clearing, away from the path. After a beat, I recognized her as the baker's apprentice, Tiffany.

She stopped short at the sight of me, and the two people with her barreled into her back. The laden baskets that lurched forward, spilling over the ground, told me these were the people who'd found my clearing—and been here many times recently by the look of it.

Maybe Tiffany was lying about the illness. She did like to exaggerate a bit, after all.

Either way, it was best to change the subject immediately, before she pointed the finger at me.

"You know," I said, rocking back onto my heels, "you're meant to leave enough that the patches thrive after you've gone." I gave her a wry grin. "Otherwise, the imps will sulk and steal your milk from the breakfast table."

I bit down on my tongue to stop talking; a subject change was one thing, but to imps? And gently admonishing her as though she were a friend? My brain must have vacated my body in the last five minutes.

No one talked about imps in the village. No one even read about them, or cared about magic beyond the fae deals we Bargained for or the paid work of the Spell Masters in the city. They certainly didn't care about trying to keep imps happy, or about the natural balance of give and take when it came to foraging for potion ingredients.

Tiffany stifled a laugh—badly—and her eyes grew wide and incredulous. No surprises there, but she wasn't laughing *with* me.

"I'll note that for next time," she said in a very unconvincing voice.

I let my eyebrow raise, amused caution giving way to anger. Tiffany had always been the younger in our overlapping circles of friends, and acted younger even than her age. She never liked dealing with anything serious or caring about consequences.

"You should," I drawled. I could feel my expression stilling, the hesitant smile now like ice on my face. Familiar and cold. "Or you'll find that next time you come through here, the place will be barren."

One of the other girls snorted, but Tiffany's brow furrowed. "Is that a threat?"

Oh gods, she was an idiot, too.

"No," I said in a slow, measured voice. "It's an observation. I'm helping you."

"Oh, we don't need your help," she said. Then her eyes fell on the little patch of mushrooms before me. Her face brightened. "See, there's plenty left behind."

I glanced at the mushrooms and then back up at Tiffany. I could see no sign of malice or guile in her expression, but I had to check.

"You've picked these before?"

"Uh-huh, just the other day."

The other day? Well, then they had to be the same ones.

"And you ate them," I prompted.

"They were delicious," the girl behind Tiffany said.

She was from one of the neighboring villages. I didn't know her at all.

"So yum," their friend agreed.

"Hmm." I tilted my head to the side again, as if I might see beneath the mushroom from up here. They really were too low, though.

I hadn't wanted to risk it, but if these women were sure, it made me feel safer knowing that they had vouched for it. I glanced up at Tiffany one last time, searching her face for any sign of trickery.

According to my texts, when the fae weren't glamoured like on the first nights of the circus, their trickery was evident in their expressions. It was their faces that couldn't lie, not their words. So, when they were speaking with malice, their teeth would grow, their bones sharpen, and their eyes fade to black as the pupil overtook the iris. They came to resemble the monsters they were choosing to be.

Sadly, there was no such test for humans, and I simply had to trust her. But she was smiling sweetly at me, and who in their right mind would risk killing someone just because they didn't like them much?

"Well," I said, reaching for my basket. "That solves my problems."

"Happy to help," Tiffany said, and she shot me a beautiful smile. "And thanks for the tip about not foraging any more than you need." She shook her finger in a cute little waggle that I'd seen her do before, as if she was telling herself off.

My lip curled unexpectedly into a smile.

"Any time," I said, watching as the three of them traipsed off toward the path.

I turned back to the mushrooms, reaching out more confidently now—

—and then paused.

There was a light hovering near my hand, but as soon as I looked at it, it winked out.

Did I imagine it?

I waited, keeping my hand painfully still, but the light didn't reappear. I reached out again, and there it was—two of them now dancing around my fingers.

For the first time, I wished I'd brought Merelda with me. She would have shared her opinion whether I wanted it or not, and right now I desperately wanted someone else's opinion.

What the hell was happening?

A third light joined them, and I couldn't ignore it any longer. I pulled my hand away.

The lights stayed where they were, spinning around the mushrooms.

The way they swirled reminded me of the magic Sebastian had tried to draw free from me on that first night together. But this wasn't like any magic that he'd shown me. Fae magic was of the elements, and this looked more like witchlight. Like something the Spell Masters would create.

The lights buzzed, as though they were angry, and then suddenly they froze in place. There were more of them now than before. At least eight, I thought. Slowly, they drifted onto the ground.

The mushrooms were now surrounded by a ring of light.

As if moving in a trance, I leaned down, my head tilted at an angle, and looked up at the mushrooms once more. It was almost impossible to see from this angle, but there were signs of blue near the stalk.

I let my senses drift, listening further than the clearing, beyond the rustle of leaves and the panic of my heart. I heard in the distance, nearing the path—further than I should have been able to hear—a faint giggle.

They knew.

They'd known exactly what they were encouraging me to do.

My mind instantly began searching for ways to defend them. Hunting for answers that didn't transform the women I'd grown up with into cold-blooded murderers. Maybe they hadn't realized how dangerous the mushrooms were; they weren't the best foragers, after all. As I knelt there, my breath becoming more ragged by the second, I tried to search through the ugliness on the surface to find proof that it was an innocent mistake, but this time, I couldn't.

They knew. They knew, and they didn't care. Because it was me.

The pain I'd been resisting ever since my misguided Bargain revealed it to me surged, rising like vomit in my throat. My eyes flickered around the clearing, searching for something beautiful to hold on to, but there was nothing that countered this. Nothing.

After twenty-eight years, I could no longer bear it. It was too much, too great, too all-consuming.

And with it came, for the first time since this whole mess started, a sense of utter clarity.

When the full moon rose, I would cross that bridge, no matter what it cost. I had the power, I had the strength, and—between Fynn's training and Sebastian's warnings—I had the help.

I was sick of pretending there was anything left for me here. I was done trying to find the beauty in people. I had tried for so long, thinking that if I did, one day they would find it in me. That if I could just find the perfect way to act around them, the right expression on my face or the right words on my tongue, then they would get over their mistrust of the Offering and see me for who I was beneath.

But as I sat there, with the mud soaking my knees, and the deadly mushrooms a scant few inches from my body, I realized for the first time that maybe they would never see the beauty in me. Maybe there was none to see, because words, power, skills... those things didn't really have anything to do with desire—that indefinable quality that drew some people together and shoved others apart. They didn't have anything to do with being loved. Or loveable.

Acting on reflex, I turned my attention inward—searching for that quiet sense of familiar beauty that I'd always taken comfort in. The worth that I'd always hoped someone else would find. But I couldn't see it.

I couldn't see anything that was worthy of the world that I wanted to live in. I couldn't see anything beautiful or wonderful or kind. All I saw was fear and pain, and the simple truth that, in this entire human world, no one wanted me.

No one had ever wanted me.

My hands clenched into fists by my side, and I wondered, with a rising sense of desperation, why I was still trying so hard to follow their rules. In four more nights, I wouldn't be here. My existence would no longer matter to anyone but me.

So what if my necklace started to heat, warning me that I was taking too much? So what if the village came down with an illness or two? They'd get better. It took a dozen moons for the Bargain Magic to become as wild as it had with Hayden. Four days was nothing.

Slowly, I rose to my feet, and with the forest as witness, I took off the necklace of the Offering.

Then I finally walked away, leaving it lying in the dirt behind me.

CHAPTER 17

Bailey

I wound my way down the overgrown garden path, leaves crunching beneath my boots as I headed toward the mailboxes at the front of our little square of cottages. A strange hollowness had been building in my chest ever since this afternoon, but with a little careful effort I was managing to block it off. Both the hollowness, and the words that whispered at the center.

What was the point in listening to them? I knew what they said. I thought, maybe, part of me had always known.

It isn't the Offering part of you they don't like; it's everything else.

No matter how capable or clever you are, they won't want you.

People like you don't get good things.

Golden rays danced across the lawn as the sun set behind me, casting shadows where I twirled the letter between my fingertips. With each step, my mind became as blank as the expression on my face, and at last, an unusual sort of peace descended over me.

I could focus on what mattered now—the tasks laid out before me one by one. Research the fae, pay for my ticket to sneak across the water, and find a quiet life on my own where no one could bother me. Maybe steal some joy from Sebastian and Fynn before they realized who I really was, and that, for me, joy could only ever be stolen.

There was one more thing I had to do, too—this thing, casually written down in the most innocent way I could manage, so Stefan didn't suspect the truth. Merelda would shriek at me if she knew I was wasting what little precious time I had left on this. I could practically hear her trilling in my ear, like an enraged bat. But even though I couldn't completely explain why, I knew I had to do this, too. It felt like, if I could just do this one thing, then maybe everything else would fall into place. I'd prove that this world I was walking into wasn't as frightening as it seemed. I'd prove I was making the right choices.

Beneath all of that mess, though, was a simpler truth. One that was clean of subterfuge and self doubt and lies: there was a chance I could help Sebastian, and it didn't feel right to walk away without trying.

I stepped between the roses that hid the stone steps leading to our mailboxes, breathing in the scent as the last of the light vanished and slipped below the horizon. A surprising calmness washed through me, strengthening my resolve despite the undercurrent of pain that still ran so clear beneath it. I held onto the strength and let go of the rest.

I slipped the letter into Stefan's mailbox, nestled beside mine, and turned to leave.

"Bailey."

The calm, wizened old voice came from behind me; my limbs locked, my body stiffening while my expression grew—if possible—even more blank. Stefan was standing right there, pruning his lavender bushes, and I'd completely missed him because I was so lost in my own thoughts.

"I was just heading out," I said, taking another step back as I shot him an easy grin. "Don't let me keep you."

Stefan's eyebrow raised, and his lips pursed in a tight frown. He was having none of it.

"Oh, you're not keeping me," he said dryly, and then reached forward and plucked the letter from his mailbox. "This will be a welcome reprieve from the swarm of locusts that overtook my garden this afternoon and ate half my lavender."

My blood ran cold. Locusts? On its own, perhaps not so odd. But when combined with the sicknesses that Master Skylark had mentioned, and then the girls in the forest, too...

Was it a sign of something worse?

My hand, on reflex, lifted to touch a necklace that was no longer there. I dropped it as though I'd been burnt and shoved the thought from my mind, as far as it could go. I'd done nothing wrong. The Oath of the Offering was still intact, and nothing I'd done with the fae could be considered greedy or selfish enough to break it.

There was no reason to think a daemon was rising.

Stefan raised an eyebrow at the meticulous flourish of his name written on the envelope and the wax seal on the back. It was far more sophisticated than the notes we usually passed over the fence when we had a message to drop off. I silently kicked myself for raising suspicion before I'd even delivered the damned thing.

"I wonder what this could be that you couldn't simply say to my face," he mused.

Before I could stop him, he'd cracked the seal and popped the letter out. It was only a few lines; the coward's way out, asking my dubious questions where Stefan couldn't ask any back.

He read them quickly, then stared back at me, his face a still mask.

"Well," he said slowly. "It's not the goodbye I was expecting."

My heart stuttered in my chest. "Goodbye?" I asked him, trying to sound innocent.

Stefan grunted in response. "Thought you might have fallen for that pretty fae boy and gone running off into the sunset together."

To my shock, his tone sounded almost disappointed. Not disappointed that I would do something as foolish and ridiculous as that—but that I hadn't.

"You want me to run off into the sunset with a fae boy?" I asked him, taking a step forward and leaning on the fence between us. "Gods, Stefan, most people just curse me under their breath and go about their day." I shook my head, tutting. "This sounds like a needlessly complicated way to off me."

He barked a laugh. "You're in no danger there," he said, surprising me with his fierce surety. "I can pick the good from the bad. No," he said, looking down at the letter. "It's the rest of them I don't trust. And this here"—he shook the paper between his fingers—"is exactly why."

My breath caught and I fought to remain casual, leaning there on my folded arms, drumming my fingertips on the wooden fence. "Why do you say that?" I asked, tilting my head.

Stefan snorted a laugh. "Because you've still two days left to survive the circus, and you've already got yourself trapped in a Bargain."

"Oh, it isn't for me," I said airily.

"Then who's it for?" he asked, his tone disbelieving. Then his brows drew together, and a look of understanding crossed his face as he said, "It's the boy."

I swallowed thickly, not seeing any way out of this one but the truth.

"It's the boy," I agreed, then shook my head. "Man. Fae. *Sebastian*. It's Sebastian," I said firmly, nodding my head.

The corner of Stefan's mouth turned upward in slight amusement.

"I just wondered…" I took a slow breath. "You know so much about fae myths and mysteries, and while I've found some information tucked away here, there's so much I still don't understand."

Understatement of the century. Even days into my research, all I knew were lora beasts and cursed Bargains and never say 'thank you'—everything I had messed up the first chance I could.

"And yes, Sebastian is trapped in a Bargain," I continued, returning the steel to my voice so it didn't waver. "And he helped me when he didn't need to, so I just wondered if I could help him as well."

I cut myself off before I could give anything more away, like how much this actually meant to me. It wasn't only that it was fair and right, no matter that the people who'd made the Bargain didn't think so. It was something deeper. My stomach still flipped every time I thought of those words: *make it hurt, love*.

I didn't *want* to hurt him. If hurting someone made it fair, I didn't want to be fair.

The furrow in Stefan's brow had grown deeper. "You say you're not caught in a Bargain," he said slowly, "but you're certainly acting like you are."

"It's not a Bargain," I insisted, holding out my hands in earnestness. "I just want to help."

His expression softened, and unexpectedly, he said, "You always want to help, Bailey." He turned back to the letter, sighing softly. "And they're always the wrong ones. But…" He clucked his tongue. "This one isn't, I know that much."

He trailed off, a question clearly hovering there that he didn't know how to ask. *If this one isn't the wrong one, then who is?*

I kept my mouth shut and didn't offer any suggestions. It would only lead to a conversation that wasn't worth having, since I wasn't going to turn back now. Besides, it wasn't like I was riding off into the sunset with a man who would only stab me in the back. I wasn't that foolish anymore.

What I was doing was riding off into the sunset with me, *for* me, and I needed help from the fae to do so. No matter how dangerous they were.

"So," Stefan said, breaking me out of my musing, "you want to know how to break a Bargain when the gate isn't clear. I do know a thing or two about Bargain law, as it happens. They're twisted, evil things." He leant against the fence, glancing at me. "Does his Bargain even have a gate?"

He nodded when I confirmed it did. "Then there's a loophole, written with tricky wording that tells you how to end it, and I'm afraid that is the only way that I know of. But make no mistake, loophole or no loophole, the Bargain always wins," Stefan finished, unknowingly sending my heart plummeting to my stomach.

"How can you be so sure?" I insisted. "If there's a loophole, and the loophole is always the truth, why don't people ever win? Surely they can. They must!"

But Stefan was already shaking his head. "It's not the Bargain itself," he said slowly. "It's the Lumière. They won't allow a Bargain to be broken, even if they give cruel hope."

His brow wrinkled, and he scrubbed at it with one hand, wincing. "I wish I could tell you more, but my memory just isn't what it used to be these days. But I know this much: that troupe is vicious. The ones who are in charge have warped the rest of them and killed any they couldn't bribe into their twisted ways.

Killed them, ensnared them, trapped them in their own Bargains..."

He shook his head, rattling off all the ways that the Lumière were the worst of the fae.

"The fae can be kind." Stefan shrugged one shoulder. "Of course they can. They're like any other group of people; the whole spectrum of cruelty and kindness rests within them. Bargains can be broken or made in kindness, but the Lumière, Bailey... Listen to me. They are twisted, and they only ensnare."

A fire ignited in my abdomen, rising within me, and my jaw tightened. Stefan wasn't telling me anything I didn't know. People were the problem; people were always the problem. But that didn't mean that the Bargains themselves couldn't be won. It didn't mean that success was out of reach. It just meant there would be people trying to stop me.

Newsflash: there were always people trying to stop me. There were always people telling me what was fair and what wasn't.

But as I stood there, studying Stefan's wizened, serious face while the sun lowered behind him and silhouetted us both against the light, none of that seemed to matter. Impossible or not, I became more determined than ever to do this.

My arrival had heralded the gate that could free Sebastian from his Bargain, and even if I had no magic of my own, it didn't mean I was useless. He'd said it himself: the terms of his gate were likely to be a trick, which meant we could assume nothing about what Sebastian had to do next.

Ever since he'd told me that, I'd wondered if I might somehow still be the key to unraveling everything. If, magic or no magic, he might still need me to play a role in freeing his father. It would be just like the Lumière to somehow tie his father's freedom to the Offering's existence. To taunt Sebastian by hiding the key where no one would think to find it—with the one person who had no talent, no magic, and nothing at all to offer.

How could I know that, and still choose to stand back and do nothing?

"Bailey..." Stefan reached for me, resting his hand on mine, and for a second I nearly broke under the weight of his empathy. "What Bargain is this fae boy ensnared in?"

My shoulders sagged. "His father's lost," I whispered, unwilling to say the words too loudly lest anyone hear. "He broke the rules and his father paid the price. Now he's trapped here, chained somewhere in the human world, and this is the last season Sebastian has to find him."

Stefan's face crumpled into an even deeper grimace. "Breaking the rules," he said slowly, "and so there will be more rules now, I imagine, for him to follow. A Bargain made in order to keep his father safe. A punishment disguised as hope."

My breath stuttered. Sebastian had spoken about it so simply, as if it were nothing special, but Stefan had landed on the truth—neatly unwinding the twisting threads to expose the cruelty at the center.

Stefan leaned back. "If that boy steps even one foot out of line, he will never find his father again," he warned me. "But the Lumière will not let him win. And, Bailey..."

I looked up. A fierce light glinted in his eye.

"No fae would ever have been caught in a Bargain like that unless he was deliberately, expertly, trapped."

"Yeah," I said slowly, tapping my fingers on top of the fence. "I got that."

Stefan shook his head. "No, not caught, Bailey. *Trapped*. He didn't stumble into this Bargain like a fool, no matter what he may believe. He was hunted for it."

I sucked in a breath; what if Stefan was right? Sebastian had made it sound like he was just young and stupid, but that didn't fit with what I knew of the fae. They wouldn't be caught so easily within their own nets.

"So the question is..." Stefan pointed a finger at me. "Who hunted him?"

The last of the sunlight dipped below the horizon, and in the shadows of the forest behind our cottages, I saw him. Blond hair, an unearthly swagger as he folded his arms and leant against the tree.

Fynn.

My heart stuttered. "I have to go," I said gently, "but I'll be careful, I promise."

Stefan's frown deepened. He didn't believe me, but he let me go, as I'd known he would.

"Watch their faces, Bailey," he called after me as I set off on the path toward the forest. "And ask the right questions when you do."

His unguarded demeanor told me he couldn't see Fynn, even though he was facing him. Some piece of magic was concealing the fae from the man, and I was grateful for it.

"Bargains are a funny mix of truth and lies," he continued in a slow, measured way that told me he was thinking deeply about each word. "And we know, of course, that it is only a myth that the fae cannot lie. They lie as well as we do, but their faces do not. As the moon becomes full, the longer the Lumière stay on this side of the bridge, the more their glamors will fade and their lies will become apparent," Stefan said. "If you won't trust me, trust that. Watch their faces, ask the right questions, and lies and truth will become clear."

I nodded, unable to explain the shiver that raced through me. For just a second, in the shadows, it had seemed as though Stefan's face changed. As though it shifted—not dramatically, but simply into a face I didn't recognize.

But then he turned and made his way back up the path to

his darkened house, and I decided it had only been a trick of the light.

I turned to Fynn.

He simply watched me, waiting for me to step into the darkness with him.

Once more, that fiery strength surged within my chest, and I did.

CHAPTER 18

Bailey

For a moment we regarded each other silently. His piercing, jewel-blue gaze was fixed on my face, as if he were reading every emotion hidden there.

His eyes flicked to the fence where Stefan had stood, and then back again as he tilted his head to one side. "Daddy doesn't approve."

I blew a deliberate huff of air at him as I moved past, walking further along the well-worn path into the forest. Dappled shadows swayed with each step I took, the moon not yet high enough to give more than a faint glow beyond the trees.

"Grow up," I said over my shoulder. "Stefan isn't my father, and even if he was, I'm a grown woman. I don't need his permission to live my life."

Fynn hummed thoughtfully, falling into step beside me as the trees closed around us. The soothing coolness of the forest kissed my skin.

"Perhaps you should," he said lightly. "Perhaps you should consider the words that he says very, very carefully."

I glanced up at him, narrowing my eyes. "What are you talking about?"

He shrugged. "I only mean that the thoughts, opinions, and complex inner workings"—he said the words very slowly and deliberately—"of even our closest confidants can be a mystery to us, and sometimes we need to look closer if we wish to see the truth."

He stared at me, and I felt a ripple of unease radiate through my body. An unease that morphed quickly into frustration because I had absolutely no idea what he was talking about.

"Stop being so cryptic," I told him, lifting my chin and tilting my head to the side as we walked. "It doesn't suit you."

His eyes widened momentarily in shock—an oddly gratifying sight, since I was sure it was genuine. Then it faded away and he returned to the Fynn I knew. Watchful. Thoughtful. Dangerous.

We walked for a while in silence, the rich loamy scent of the forest enfolding us the deeper we went. Shortly, we passed through a clearing, and I couldn't quite keep from stiffening in repressed pain. It was the clearing I'd nearly picked the fatal mushrooms that afternoon.

They were still there—innocent flecks of white on an otherwise rich brown carpet of leaves and earth. I couldn't look away from them as we passed, and I couldn't stop the violent wave of buried grief that surged as I remembered what the girls had tried to do to me.

Fynn, of course, noticed.

He slowed his footsteps, glancing between me and the mushrooms, and finally came to a stop.

"Something you'd like to share?" he asked, lifting one eyebrow in polite enquiry.

"No," I hissed through gritted teeth. "Keep walking."

His footsteps remained firmly planted. "And miss the eruption of a lifetime?" he asked in that low, needling voice he got when he was being particularly stubborn. Strange that I knew that about him already. "I don't think so."

"What do you mean 'eruption'?" I squinted at him, turning my back to the mushrooms. "No one is erupting."

Fynn leaned around me, the motion exaggerated for dramatic affect so well he reminded me of Sebastian. "Then why are you trying to melt those with your eyes?"

I stiffened. As always, he saw far too much.

"What, are you a mind reader now?" I spat out, turning my head from him but remaining with my back to the mushrooms.

If I saw them again, I thought I might puke.

"No. But I can be."

My pulse spiked. His eyes met mine as my head whipped around toward him again. He was standing closer than I expected.

"You can read my mind?" My heart pounded in my chest, but behind the fear was the strangest thought: do it.

Hear what I can't bear to tell you. Take the choice away from me, because the silence is killing me.

Fynn took another step closer. "Not without permission," he said, prompting a ridiculous spike of disappointment. Then, he lifted a hand to hover over my cheek, and I forgot how to breathe. "But if you allow me to, I can sift through the thoughts you give me, in search of truth. If you try to lie with those thoughts, the magic will force you to speak honestly. So don't attempt to lie about anything you don't wish to share."

I stared at him. What was he waiting for?

And what were we *doing*? If it was that easy to avoid answering, we may as well just have a normal conversation.

His eyes glinted in challenge. "Are you game?"

I smiled sweetly, words I'd never dare say to anyone else spilling free. "Read my mind and find out."

His palm fell against my cheek, and I instantly realized this was nothing like a normal conversation. Fynn was in my mind, in my body. I could feel him everywhere I looked, in every breath I took.

"What's troubling you, Bailey?" he asked, his eyes fluttering closed as he obviously focused on the sensations building between us.

Meanwhile, I fought to push those same sensations away, terrified they would flood me when I was already drowning in him.

The mushrooms, I thought, catching hold of the simplest thought I could find and sending it toward that terrifying, overwhelming presence.

Fynn's brow furrowed. "The mushrooms are bothering you?" he repeated softly. The corner of his mouth ticked into a smile. "Simple. I'll pick the lot and fry them up in butter for you. How does that sound?"

"No!" I yelled, not even managing to keep the thought to my mind.

And then, I began to shudder. Waves of grief and pain shook me as violently as if I were standing in the snow. Fynn's eyes opened, but he didn't withdraw his hand from my cheek. I focused on the warmth of his touch, the beautiful, loamy scent of autumn on the breeze.

He didn't speak; he only waited.

Before I could stop it, dozens of thoughts flooded me, and I sent them all barrelling down the connection between us. Memories of the look on Tiffany's face; the giggle I'd heard in the distance; the sharp, vibrant blue of the mushrooms.

And the lights that had guided me—the only reason I wasn't dead on the ground where we stood.

Fynn's expression flickered at that, but he didn't interrupt. Slowly, I became aware that the clearing was eerily silent, filled only by the sound of my ragged breaths. Our conversation had been entirely in our minds, my confession propelled toward a rare honesty.

"So," he said after a beat. "They don't like you much."

I laughed—it sounded more like a sob. "Yeah, that's the problem."

Fynn tilted his head, but I didn't need the sudden interest on his face to know what had just happened. I could feel it. Somehow, that sentence wasn't true. But because I'd said it, rather than sent it to him through our connection, there was only a flicker of discontent from the magic. A warning.

From the sense of dread that stirred low in my gut, I suspected I should heed that warning if I didn't want to suddenly learn truths that were best left buried.

I clamped my lips tightly shut, but Fynn's smile only widened.

"Say that again," he said, voice almost a purr. "But like you mean it this time."

No.

The grin was sharp now—predatory. "You think they don't love you."

I know they don't love me, I answered against my better judgment, unable to stay silent in the face of his arrogance. *They don't even like me.*

"But that isn't the problem," he pushed.

My thoughts churned now, whirling so rapidly in my mind it made me feel sick. There was so much *feeling* behind what he was suggesting—so much pain. Years of it, all locked away until I made that stupid Bargain with the circus and accidentally unearthed the truth.

But Fynn didn't know everything; the villagers *didn't* like me, and while the nebulous, dangerous feeling at the back of my mind told me that was only part of a bigger problem, it was still huge. If I focused only on that, I needn't dive any deeper.

Of course it is, I threw back, almost mockingly, weirdly desperate to beat him at his own game.

But my mind rebelled, and suddenly I knew what he meant about the magic not letting me lie. It surged, a violent force wrapping around my mind and throat. Urging me to speak the truth I wouldn't face.

I ground my teeth together so hard it hurt, not caring that I was practically baring them at him. He didn't look away, and the touch on my cheek remained so very soft.

"Tell me, Bailey," he murmured. "Stop fighting it. What's the real problem?"

The words wanted to erupt—a volcano spewing lava all over the world. I wouldn't do it, even if holding it back sent me to my knees.

"Could it be..." His voice was deceptively quiet, gentle, and I felt the rising apprehension even before his next words hit. "...that you agree with them?"

I jolted at the force of the accusation, my body shaking, but he wasn't done; his voice lowered, tearing into me with savage precision. "Could it be that the girl who sees only the best in the world around her does not actually love herself?"

Of course that wasn't it, I thought. How stupid. I always saw the beauty in everything, including myself, and one day someone would see me like I did—not as the tainted Offering, but as something more. Humble and quiet, sure, like I was supposed to be, but *worthy,* too. And maybe I'd questioned all that after the mushrooms, but who wouldn't? It was a down moment, that was all.

But those weren't the thoughts I sent careening down the pathway to Fynn. Instead, I screamed, "What's to love?!"

The connection erupted, violently shoving both of us backward. I fell, panting, onto the ground, and only realized after I collapsed that I was right next to the mushrooms. Fear slid, cold and sickly, in the pit of my stomach.

I heard Fynn scramble to his feet on the other side of the clearing, but I couldn't look at him. I was too afraid; had I already touched them? Had I knocked them with my boot and sent the spores floating into my nostrils? Could I taste them on my tongue, or was that just fear?

"Ssh," Fynn said, crouching before me. "Don't move."

I was right in the center of the patch. There was no way I hadn't brushed them. No way that—

He whispered something under his breath, and one by one, the mushrooms sucked back below the surface. As if the earth itself had reclaimed them. Only when the last one vanished did I dare to take a breath.

I looked at him and found those eerie blue eyes glinting like fire. He held out his hand and I took it, the two of us rising to our feet together.

"So," he said calmly. "You think there is nothing worthwhile in you to love?"

I scoffed, ignoring the lingering swell of grief—calmer now but still devastating. "Well, that's what the world's told me, I suppose." I sighed, turning away.

Now that it was out in the open, it was strangely easy to lean into it. To face the truth I'd hidden for years.

Being careful to talk around the Offering, and all the details of *why* I had nothing of worth, I told him, "They see me as cold. Closed off. Unreachable, and not worth the effort of trying to reach." I laughed, the sound almost normal instead of bitter. I wondered if perhaps that was worse. "I am, I suppose. What's the point in letting them reach me when I have nothing to offer? I've never been very clever, and my jokes don't land. If I'm kind, it's generally assumed I'm after something in return. No one wants my friendship, really, so why should I bother thinking any differently about myself? It would only be a lie."

Fynn remained silent. When I finally looked up at him, his expression was unreadable. After a beat, he began to walk idly through the clearing, pulling a branch down to study its leaves. "Maybe, if they see you as cold, you could try being more affectionate. Reach out first, see where it takes you..."

"No!" I hissed, whirling on him, my voice already rising in volume. "No. You do *not* get to ask that of me."

Huh. Where had that come from? I tried to calm my face back into its usual mask, but it wouldn't move. My teeth remained partially bared, my eyes wide with anger I didn't understand.

"Oh?" Fynn asked, tilting his head. "And why is that?"

He sounded so neutral, it was making warning sirens wail in my mind.

"Because you—you—" I broke off, the words choking in my throat. It wasn't that I couldn't find them; it was that there were too many all at once.

Distantly, I registered the sharp edge of interest in Fynn's gaze. The almost hungry way he watched me, waiting for the next thing that would come out of my mouth, as if he already knew what it would be.

But he couldn't. Even I couldn't have predicted when what I said was, "Because you took it from me."

The clearing was so quiet, so still. The noise inside my mind was deafening.

I was no longer talking to Fynn; I was talking to everyone else.

My voice turned cold. Deadly. "Every time I laughed, you called it selfish. Every time I loved something, you took it away. You shaped me into this cold, unfeeling *thing*, and now you dare to ask for the nice, friendly one to come back?" I laughed, loud and bitter. "Now that you've realized what happens to a child when you deny them value for the sake of everyone else? Well it's too late, because you fucking killed it."

My chest heaved angrily, ragged breath drawing in and out as I fought for control. It didn't make any sense. And yet, it made all the sense in the world. Fynn hadn't done this to me, but he was one of the only ones who hadn't.

Hayden had, when he chose my sister. My friends had, when they cut me down time and time again. Countless names in the village, day after day, night after night. My sister had, and she'd done it gladly, until all that was left was what stood here now. I remembered a Bargain, when we were little, but oddly I still couldn't remember the details. It didn't matter. The result was always the same.

They'd told me the Offering was quiet, worthless, a failure —and they'd shaped me into exactly that, to make sure my destiny was fulfilled and all of their fortunes secured. The cold-ness, the distance... those had come separately. Incredibly, it had never occurred to them that it would be a package deal. That a person couldn't give up pieces of themselves for another without donning armor to protect the scraps that were left behind.

They'd killed that hidden part of me. They didn't get to ask for it back now.

There was more to say—I could feel it bubbling away inside me. An immutable truth that, at least for a short while longer, I refused to admit. I'd bared my soul enough for today.

I looked up, and as my eyes met Fynn's, I realized I'd been right, in those first few moments when we'd met. There really was something dangerous in him—something that made me think of a hunter, running down prey.

Stefan's warnings rang in my mind.

Unaware of my thoughts, Fynn shook his head and tutted.

Then, he began to walk in a slow circle around me. I held myself very still.

"You're right. You can't change who you are, Bailey," he said. "How did you describe it? Cold? Closed off? Unreachable?"

I stiffened, my hands clenching into fists by my side as my shoulders hiked up around my ears. Before I could speak, he stepped toward me. I could feel the warmth of his breath against my neck as he lifted a lock of my hair and twirled it around his fingers.

"But why would you want to?" he said into my ear. "Are you so sure that who *you* are is the problem, and not them?"

My breath caught, the low whisper of his words sinking deep inside me.

"Don't give them that affection," he continued, letting my hair fall and brushing his palms over my shoulders, holding me. "They don't deserve it. But someone else might." I turned my head slightly, and out of the corner of my eye, I saw his gaze fall to my lips. "Someone else *will* earn that from you one day, and if they have even an ounce of intellect, they will know how precious a thing they hold in their hands."

Gods. When he spoke like that, I almost believed him. As if that truth spell still surrounded us, and I couldn't possibly fight the sincerity of his words.

What if he was right?

Tentatively, my mind slid forth an offering. A possibility. Something I'd never dared consider before: in some ways, wasn't it already true?

With Fynn, I wasn't closed off. He reached me as easily as breathing. With Sebastian, I wasn't unreachable, either. And while the Oath of the Offering dictated that I had to remain humble, quiet, and free of accomplishment, nowhere—*nowhere* —did it say that I should suffer for it.

I'd never made the oath they held me to. I'd never agreed to be their Offering and all that came with it.

But I had still seen my responsibilities through, and now the Offering's mark lay buried at my feet—where it would stay forever.

My knuckles cracked, and I turned to face Fynn, somehow shocked to find him so close, even though I'd known he was there. With his calm, certain words ringing in my ears, I decided that I didn't have to wait for someone to choose me. I could do the choosing.

And there was nothing worth choosing here.

"I want to leave this place," I said in a low, deadly voice, "and I want to know how to defend myself on the other side of the water when I get there. Are you going to show me how to do that, or do I find someone else?"

A slow, wicked smile curled onto his face. "With pleasure."

CHAPTER 19

Bailey

THE CREATURE OF SHADOW LUNGED, SENDING ME HURTLING INTO THE dirt and leaves as the ground rushed to meet me.

"Nearly had it," Fynn called encouragingly from his perch on top of a rotting log. "Next time, twist your wrist a bit more."

The shadow monster was nowhere in sight. For now.

"If you don't shut up," I snarled, heaving myself to my feet. "I'll twist your gods damned..." I paused, letting the rest of that sentence die in my throat.

Especially when I saw the curious arch of Fynn's eyebrow.

There was no logical way to end that sentence except for the obvious, and I wasn't about to yell that at someone I'd only recently met. However, if he kept pummeling me into the dirt with his shadow monster, I might be tempted to.

"If you twist your wrist to the left," Fynn said with infuriating calmness, "you'll bare your hands in supplication to the willow dryads." He examined his nails, twisting his wrist this way and that, as if testing it out.

And the most annoying part was, I could feel it. I could feel the change every time he lifted his wrists skyward. The air grew a little more poised. The earth felt steadier.

I just kept forgetting to do it, gods damn it.

Fynn was trying to teach me the ways of the natural magic around me, and I was proving to be just as useless as I had been when Sebastian tried to call it free from my body.

At least this time, I had an excuse. Because every time Fynn looked at me, I remembered those charged moments from earlier—before he'd taken my hand and whisked me via magic to this solitary clearing. He'd held me close, his eyes fixed to my lips, and for a few seconds there I'd thought he would kiss me.

I was still thinking about it, and it was awfully distracting.

"All right," I murmured. "Supplication, dryads, willow. Got it. Try again," I called.

I rose to my feet, keeping balanced on the ball of my toes. Closing my eyes, I let the wind rush over me. Let it bring hints of the darkness and decay that rested in the small pockets of this forest. Like the log beneath Fynn's boots, and the crawling, burrowing things under our feet.

Like the shadows of the lora beast illusion that Fynn had created and sent charging toward me.

There—the beast was to the right. I could hear the willows whispering about it, their words folding like air over a space that looked empty but wasn't.

I turned, flinging myself out of its way just as it erupted from the darkness in a whirl of crimson and gray. And as I turned, I lifted my wrists skyward.

Pale, vulnerable flesh, revealed to the heavens. There was a crack, followed by an aching, groaning weight as a dead branch heaved itself free from the tree above us and came crashing down in the center of the beast.

The lora beast erupted into smoke, and with a soft hiss, vanished completely.

"Yes," Fynn called, leaping from his seat and applauding me, every inch the showman in that moment.

Oddly, he reminded me of Sebastian.

"You did it, Bailey. Brava." He stepped before me, blond hair falling in his eyes for a moment before he flicked it free. I swore he glanced at my lips again, and my whole body tingled.

"It almost sounded in pain," I said, frowning at the place the beast had been.

"It probably was," Fynn said, shrugging. "The shadow creatures have some sentience, after all. Sending them back to their dimension so roughly wouldn't tickle."

"What?" I rounded on him. "I don't want to cause it pain! No matter what it is."

He cocked an eyebrow. "Then don't. The choice is yours." He spread his hands wide before him, already moving on. "So, now you know how to ask the forest for help. Next, you should learn—"

He broke off, the words dying in his throat as he stared at me with a very strange expression.

"Did you know," he said softly, head tilted, "that you're glowing?"

My eyes widened. I looked down at myself, shoving my hands out to the side. He was right. There was a faint glow caressing my body.

"I'm not doing that," I insisted, terror bubbling free in my voice. I took a step backward. "Is it you? Stop it."

"It's not me," Fynn said, holding up his hands in easy deference. "And I don't think you need to be afraid, but please do hold still. Just in case I'm wrong, we need to know quickly."

I forced myself to hold still, my breath shallow as Finn slowly roamed in a circle around me.

When he was standing once more at the front, he paused, tapping his finger on his lower lip.

"It's you," he said finally. "You're summoning magic."

I blinked. "What? No, I'm not."

"You are," he said, the corner of his mouth twitching. "Which answers my next question—you don't know how. Interesting."

"You have this wrong," I insisted, forgetting to be scared when such outrageous things were coming out of his mouth. "I'm not a Spell Master. I haven't been trained, and I don't have the affinity."

Fynn's brow furrowed. "Affinity? What in Criera's name are you talking about? You don't need an affinity to reach for the earth's magic."

My stomach swooped. "Yes you do," I stammered. "The Spell Masters find you in your youth, and you're invited to train with them in the big cities. It's where every human with magic learns. The hearth witches, the Spell Masters, the curse breakers... all of them."

He pulled a face, and it looked almost pitying. I gritted my teeth together and fell silent.

"It seems the learnings of magic have become..." He paused, thinking of the word. "Somewhat twisted."

"How twisted?" I asked, heart fluttering. It almost sounded like...

"Anyone can have magic," he said gently. "I imagine that an affinity, if it exists, would only mean you found your access point quicker than most."

"Access point?" I stared up at him.

He sighed, shoulders collapsing. "It seems we need a crash course." He rolled his shoulders back, stretching his arms above his head as he thought. "Fae magic is the magic of nature, as raw and brimming with potential as the land itself. But while human magic can never be as strong as fae, it can briefly touch that same power, dividing itself along one axis. A central core that runs through the infinite scope of that power. Control... or the lack of it." He weighed his hands on either side of his body, like a scale moving up and down. "To control is simple enough, but you do need an access point. For you..." He looked around the space curiously. "I would suggest it may be this forest. You've spent some time here?"

I nodded. He seemed satisfied.

"Your connection to this forest allows you to tap into the magic, but an access point can be anything. A Spell Master may have a particular connection to a stone, or to a natural element. A jar of water, for instance..." He threw out the suggestion, waving his hand as he walked back to his rotting log and perched upon it. "It would be an odd choice, but if the water had particular relevance to the user... perhaps it was the water in which she lay to give birth to her child." He gestured dramatically. "You can see how it comes about. Something of particular significance, large or small, provides an access point to control the world around you, through the use of incantations. So long as you keep that access point nearby, you may take part in the magic that exists naturally in this world."

"By controlling it," I said cautiously.

He shrugged. "Controlling it or setting it free. That's the axis upon which your magic rests. Control and... a lack thereof. Simple."

The way he described it was so strange. It made what had felt like a secretive and powerful talent into something far more organic. Almost as though the magic had a mind of its own, and our use of it was more accurately a communication with it—a relationship. One that could go well, or could go very badly.

Did they know this in the cities? Or was the knowledge locked away and kept secret by the Spell Masters?

"We don't define it by an axis of control," I said hesitantly. "It's create or curse. Those are the two natures of our magic."

Fynn wrinkled his nose. "Create or curse? Even magic is

bound by the natural laws; it can't create something. It can only shape that which already exists."

"Yes," I said, my words steadier now as I began to piece together this new knowledge with what I'd once read. There was something there—something just out of reach, which was hurtling toward understanding at a frightening rate. "Maybe we use the wrong word, but it's the same result. We don't create something from nothing, but we *can* give new form to the elements—witchlight from water droplets, illusions from air and light, complex manipulations of fixed objects... Or we can curse them, and let their internal wildness take over to produce an unpredictable outcome."

He nodded slowly. "Wildness. Chaos. As in... a lack of control," he said thoughtfully, mulling it over out loud. "Which could also be referred to as bad luck. A curse."

"Yes," I said slowly, everything sliding into place with a neat *click*.

They were the same thing.

Gods, it made sense. The way humans understood it, it was about the outcome. You could curse someone with ill luck, or you could create something anew. The Spell Masters called it mastery, but in truth, the magic was a wild entity of its own, and our relationship with that entity could go in one of two directions.

Control or chaos.

And I, apparently, had that relationship.

My fingers twitched. How strange, that the Offering should have access to magic when the Spell Masters hadn't deemed anyone else in the village worthy. My sister had craved magic for years, and they'd always turned her down.

But Fynn had already said there was no such thing as an affinity. This wasn't a big deal.

"Okay, fine." I waved my hand. "So everyone can do it. It

doesn't mean you're special, and I've found my access point. What does that even mean?"

Fynn's eyes glinted. "It means, love..." A little shiver raced through me at the word. Once more, the air between us became charged, and it seemed as though the smallest spark might set the whole clearing ablaze. "...that you can fight the beast on your own, without asking for fae help at all."

Our training session went downhill from there.

I may have had access to human magic, but no matter how many times he threw the shadow beast at me, I couldn't use it. Every time I went to face the threat, a wave of inexplicable terror washed over me, and I shrunk away. If it had been the real thing—the lora beast in the flesh—I would have died.

"I think we need to quit," I said, my breath coming out of me in a rush as I braced my hands on my knees and panted. Who knew that trying to draw magic would hurt so much? "Let's go back to the supplication you were teaching me. You mentioned something about sprites. Teach me how to pray to them, or..."

I racked my brain trying to remember the things that Fynn had listed when we arrived.

"Seed pods," I said, snapping my fingers and pointing at him. "You said there were seed pods that could be used as explosives. Why don't you show me what those look like?"

"No," Fynn said simply, pausing in the middle of twisting a ribbon in complex knots around his finger and smiling pleasantly at me. "No, I think we'll continue with this."

I snarled, blowing a curl of hair out of my face, and then froze. For just a moment, I'd seen something different in him. Something like a shadow, or a lie.

Had it been his true face that I glimpsed, beneath the glamor? Or had it been my magic, still swimming around me even though I failed to use it right, and alerting me to something within that complex web of control and chaos that didn't fit?

"What are you hiding?" I said.

Fynn went very still, and when he glanced up at me, the light didn't quite reach his eyes. Even still, there was the strangest reflection of blue within them, glinting as though his eyes glowed with an inner flame.

I took a step forward. He still hadn't moved, the ribbon poised in an elaborate twist around his fingers, tangling them together.

"What is it?" I pressed. "There's something you're not telling me. I..."

But the sound was broken off as a small, angry, violent creature crashed its way into the clearing.

Fynn leapt off the log in alarm, his hands braced in defense as I whirled and snatched an irritated Merelda out of the air before Fynn could hurt her.

"What are you doing?" I insisted, glaring at the imp as she struggled in my grip. Her little blue face was puffed up indignantly, and she hurled what I assumed were deadly insults at me.

Fynn stared at the imp, a furrow once more in his brow. "She isn't a fan of me," he said with delight. "Thinks I'm ensnaring you in a..." He tilted his head. "What was it you said? In my filthy little snake grip? Very inventive."

My eyes widened. "You can understand her."

"Of course I can understand her." Fynn made a rude sound. "For all the good it does me. Absolute gibberish. I've never met an angrier imp."

I stared down at my companion. Not a creature at all—a friend. As she shrieked, I listened closely to the sounds, as I'd done a thousand times before. But this time, I listened with more than just my five senses.

There was magic in it. Sensation. As though she was speaking with auras.

Blinking, I looked up to find Fynn watching me shrewdly.

"What do you hear?" he asked.

"*Sh'rath*," I murmured. "But... it's colored by the wind. A rushing of leaves and earth."

A flicker of recognition crossed his face.

"What does it mean?" I pressed.

"Hunter."

My words died in my throat, and I stared at Fynn as if seeing him for the first time. Hunter—just as Stefan had said. But it couldn't be true. Could it?

A light glinted in Fynn's eye, and he took a step backward.

"Oh yes, now there's a thought," he said, his tone abruptly casual again—a change in conversation I wasn't ready for. "She'll do nicely."

"Do for what?" I asked, drawing Merelda closer to my chest. She'd gone quiet in my arms.

In answer, Fynn smiled. "Did you know that imps have two forms?" He took another step backward. "And typically they can change between them at will, but your little friend" —Merelda was no longer quiet, but now screaming in my grip —"seems to have been... What do you humans call it? Cursed."

Cursed. Out of control. Bad luck.

"You mean she can't change?"

"I mean she can't change," Fynn agreed. "Perhaps your magic is not forthcoming because you have no real interest in saving yourself."

His eyes shot to mine, alight with a fire I didn't recognize as his words pierced me through the chest.

"You only care about running away and living small, but saving your friend... that could be a different story."

My heart began to hammer in my chest, and for the first time since I'd come here with him, I felt afraid.

"What are you doing?"

"Oh, I'm not doing anything," Fynn said easily. "I'm merely letting you know that if your friend were in her usual form, then a lora beast wouldn't stand a chance. But in her current form, they are one of the beast's favorite snacks."

"You wouldn't," I hissed.

"Wouldn't I?" he asked in a low, careful voice. "What makes you so sure? You are convinced that I am hiding something after all."

"Because you are," I said, no longer questioning the truth of it. Simply knowing.

He allowed me a small grin and a token bow of his head. "But what do my secrets mean? How far do you think I will go to get what I want?" he said slowly.

My grip on Merelda loosened in shock and the imp flew free, darting like an arrow straight for Fynn's eyes. He snatched her out of the air without even looking, and my heart leapt into my throat, squeezing painfully as I cried:

"No!"

I stumbled toward him and my only friend. But his fingers were clasped loosely around her, like the bars of a birdcage. And although she scrabbled and scratched and bit at him inside it, and he did not open them, she wasn't hurt.

"Ask the question, Bailey," he said, his voice oddly distant as he stared down at the imp in his hands.

"What question?"

He looked up at me, no longer distant—painfully, terrifyingly, here. "The one you're too afraid to ask."

I swallowed.

"Why did she call you a hunter?" I asked, my voice barely above a whisper.

My stomach roiled, my body sensing the answer before he gave it.

"Because I am," he said simply. "And to put you out of your torment, I'll answer the rest, too. What your friend suggested back there by the woods, and what you were too afraid to accept." He leaned forward. "I hunted Sebastian. I reported him to the Lumière and ensnared him in a cage."

"Why?" I breathed, the word a rush of fury. "Why take his freedom?"

Fynn's lip curled in a sneer. "Freedom." He studied Merelda as she sank her teeth into his finger. He didn't even flinch. "Such a complicated thing."

He'd done this to Sebastian. Taken everything from him. Punished him for something that should never have been a crime.

And yet... I thought a part of me had known that from the beginning, and I was still here. Because I could hear a hundred words that he wasn't saying out loud, and I wanted to know what they were before I cast my judgment. Because he clung to his own performance of danger like a safety blanket, but he had never once turned that danger on me.

Because I sensed something hidden beneath the ugliness of this truth. Something beautiful.

Perhaps that just made me a fool.

Abruptly, Fynn loosened his hands and flicked them, sending Merelda flying across the clearing as if she were nothing more than a mild annoyance. When she hurtled back at him, screeching, she hit an invisible wall. Her claws dug into it as she slid down with a mute glare.

Anger flared, bright and fierce, in my chest as my senses hooked onto Merelda and *listened*. When I heard the power that answered, I forgot to be afraid. Even though it wasn't my magic, I felt Merelda's claws tearing at the barrier as if she were clawing at me. I felt the way Fynn had woven the wind and the condensation into an invisible wall.

I felt how I could take it apart with a thought.

My brow furrowed, and I took a step backward; it was so easy, once you knew what you were looking for. Easier, even, than the Spell Masters had ever described.

The Offering shouldn't find magic *easy*. No one did. People studied for years to access this sort of power, and all I'd done was reach out and take it.

"Bailey."

My eyes snapped up to find Fynn watching me.

"I have never lied to you. You know who I am, what I am, and what I offer. So the choice is yours."

"What choice?" I wondered, breathless, but I already knew that too.

It was the choice that had been looming over my head for the last hour. The promise I had felt closing in ever since Fynn pushed me to that proverbial edge and caught me, the wind raging around us.

I'd sworn off men. After Hayden, I'd learned my lesson and finally accepted what my village had tried to drill into me all those years: love was not part of my destiny. Anything resembling it could only be a lie that would end in terrible pain.

And yet, here I was again—falling into the orbit of not just one man, but two. Just as greedy and selfish as they'd always told me.

I was in danger of losing every bit of solid ground beneath me, and the sad fact of it was, what Fynn had told me earlier was true: I couldn't change who I was. I would always crave this, even knowing it wasn't mine to have. Even knowing it was greedy and selfish.

But maybe...

A tiny flicker of hope surged within me.

Maybe knowing that was enough. I couldn't keep him—I couldn't keep either of them—which meant love was off the table. This ending was already written.

It couldn't surprise me and stab me in the back.

So, maybe this time, I could walk into this, whatever it was, with eyes wide open and simply enjoy it for what it was. I could have everything I craved, from both of them, knowing that in a handful of days it would end.

But there was something I had to know first, and only one way I would trust the answer. With Sebastian, I had made a Bargain. With Fynn...

I took a step forward. There was no invisible wall separating me from Fynn. And although I knew she would never let me live it down, I ignored Merelda's little fists pounding on the other side of hers.

In here, there was only Fynn and me.

When I stood before him, so close our toes were touching, I lifted my hand and hovered it over his cheek, mimicking our positions from earlier—when he'd cast his magic and seen inside my mind.

"Show me how," I demanded.

He watched me silently for a moment, then he lifted his hand and curled his fingers around my wrist. Moving slowly, he maneuvered my palm so it lay against his cheek. "Picture a spring rain," he murmured. "Washing away the last melt of winter. Picture the crocus buds bursting from the soil beneath, and the simple truth of an earth that cannot be taken by any but those who deserve her."

Shivering, I closed my eyes and did as he said. The air shifted between us.

"It won't be quite the same," he continued. "You can't command me to tell the truth. You aren't strong enough. But you will sense a lie."

I heard the warning behind the words; if he wanted to, he would lie and keep his secrets without a shred of guilt. I had to choose carefully.

Watch their faces. Ask the right questions.

Logic told me to ask the question in my heart: do you regret hunting Sebastian? Instinct told me Fynn would lie. Or construct his answer in such a way that it was true but only just. He would make me think he was the crafty hunter, because for some reason he was attached to this idea of being both dangerous and honest. I knew better. I knew there were a thousand ways to lie, and only a handful were dishonest. There were a thousand more ways to lie to yourself.

"I'm going to save Sebastian," I said, ignoring the surprised hitch of his breath. "I'm going to break his Bargain and set him free. Should I?"

I opened my eyes at the last second, and Fynn clearly wasn't expecting it. The mask he wore so carefully had cracked, and through it I witnessed something else. Something wretched. Something pained.

"Yes," he breathed, and although my magic might have been new, and weak, I sensed that word was the absolute truth.

A swirl of emotion coursed through me, too complex to understand. But most of all, I felt relief. His secrets were ugly, but whose weren't? There was beauty beneath it, and that's what mattered.

I let my hand fall away, and in that time, Fynn regained his calm, familiar arrogance.

"So," he challenged, smoothing his shirt. "Are you going to do it?"

"Do what?" I asked, lifting an eyebrow in faux confusion. He blinked in surprise. "Oh, are you referring to that choice you mentioned before?"

I let my lips curve into a slow smile. The kind I never dared give in the village—confident. Hungry. Fynn's eyes darkened as they followed the movement.

"You know I am," he replied, voice low.

"And what choice would that be?" I asked, stepping closer, so my legs bracketed one of his own.

His breath caught. "The choice that has been building between us ever since the sun set," he said, holding still as I studied his face. "A simple one, really. Will you kiss me anyway? Knowing who and what I am?"

"Why should I?" I challenged him, eyes falling to his mouth.

For once, there was no amused smile there. He wet his lips. With the answer he'd given me, and the fact that my village was far away—another lifetime away—I felt I could kiss him without guilt. But I wanted to hear his answer anyway.

"Because you can," he said simply. "A kiss can be just a kiss. It is neither greedy nor selfish to want something—especially if it is being offered."

Especially if it is being offered.

I reached up, curling my fingers into his collar and pulling him down inch by inch. He didn't hesitate, didn't stutter. But neither did he close the gap between us.

He merely watched me, eyes heavy-lidded with desire. With need.

"Face the fear, Bailey," he murmured in a voice I barely recognized. "It's the only way to transform from hunted to hunter."

I leant closer, feeling the rush of warm breath against my mouth. Merelda's indignant screeches had stopped, and I heard her huff. Practically felt the roll of her eyes as she fluttered off into the darkness and left me with my bad decisions.

Eyes wide open, Bailey, I reminded myself.

With that in mind, I didn't kiss him. Instead, I took his

lower lip between my teeth and bit it gently, as a slow, stunned moan dropped from his mouth.

I pulled his lip between mine, sucked, and then let it free.

He stared at me with wide eyes, lips still parted, breath ragged. My gaze lowered for just a moment, and I saw the evidence of his desire pressed tight against the front of his soft, dark gray breeches—brushing against my hip. He didn't bother trying to hide it. Neither did he move away. His hands fell to my waist and immediately tightened, fingers driving into my skin sharper than he'd ever touched me before.

In the quiet privacy of that embrace, I caught a final glimpse of something: a truth, carefully concealed. He was holding back. Fynn was holding back *everything*, and the sheer magnitude of that restraint momentarily floored me.

Fynn wet his lips, and the moment of shock passed, leaving me with only the memory of his lips and the now gentle grip of his hands pulling me close.

I let the magic of that half kiss wash over me. The syllables of Merelda's language filled my blood, a thought without a name, and I stopped straining to make sense of things that could only ever be felt. I stopped begging for the magic to find me worthy, and I simply decided that I was.

A twinge of fear—the knowledge that this magic represented a far bolder, greater, *better* life than the Offering was allowed—rang through my body, but it was muted against the power of Fynn's touch. A distant warning that I was all too good at ignoring.

Something moved in the darkness of the forest. I smelled rich earth, and the sharp scent of fungus. Fynn's shadow beast was on the hunt, and my mind conjured images of raising spears from the ground, formed from tree roots. Of taking the sparks of minerals from the earth and lighting them into an inferno. Of bending the wind to my will, strong enough to scatter the shadows to the ends of the continent.

At the last second, I remembered the hiss of the beast's pain. And when it burst from the foliage, I reached for the deadened branches that had once fallen on the beast's head.

A cage sprung from the earth; in a second, the thing was trapped.

I stared at the cage, my head tilted in curiosity. Such a simple thing. I could have done so much more with this magic. Could have speared it straight through the heart. The twisted cage—so brutal and confronting—was a kindness.

I turned to catch Fynn's eye, but he wouldn't look at me. With a flick of his hand, the evidence of our magic, lora beast included, vanished.

A split second later, so did he.

CHAPTER 20

Sebastian

A HUSH FELL OVER THE FAIRGROUNDS AS THE LAST OF THE HUMANS slunk out the gates to return to their mundane lives. I watched them from the shadow of my tent, a sheen of sweat still glistening on my skin.

She hadn't been in the crowd. I'd searched every performance, ducking from tent to tent when I wasn't in the spotlight. And when I was, I'd woven a web of light and illusion to search the crowd there, too.

It shouldn't have mattered. We had made no promises to see each other again, even though I'd urged her to consider trusting me over Fynn. And even if we did see each other a final time or two before the full moon, what purpose would it serve?

I wanted to kiss her goodbye, it was true, but I could do that on the other side of the water. Once she'd safely bought her passage to Criera and escaped whatever demons haunted her here.

But no amount of rational sense could wipe the blasted thoughts from my mind. Irritating, swirling beasts that wouldn't leave me be. I'd gone ten years never bothering about a single person other than myself and my caged father—I couldn't afford to—and now *this*. Worry after worry, hounding me like dragons at my heels.

What if she'd tried to enter the archives, and the Masters had caught her?

What if she'd paid for the ticket, and Fynn had trapped her somewhere far, far away? I didn't think he would do it, but I didn't know for sure. There was so much about him that I'd thought I'd known, and I'd been wrong. So very wrong.

I turned from the doorway and let the curtain fall, passing a hand over my face and wincing as my nails dug wretchedly into the skin. None of this should matter. She had her life to live, and I had mine.

And yet, I stared at the mirror hanging on my velvet wall and wondered.

She had one just like it, she'd said. When I had proposed destroying the curse on my lonely mirror and searching for a fresh partner, it had been nothing more than an idle comment. Why would I bother? In ten long years, I'd never fought against any of the Lumière's curses.

I lifted my hand, passing it across the glass until it fogged with condensation. The Lumière no doubt wanted me to try breaking the curse. I'd always assumed that was why they had installed the thing in my tent the second my Bargain took—so that I'd try to hunt down my father and speak to him.

So they could laugh from the shadows while they held him just out of reach.

Anger rose inside me, and a lick of flame overtook the condensation, stripping it free. Before I knew it, I was chanting, muttering beneath my breath foul spells that I had pulled from the dredges of the archives.

They wanted to watch me fail? I'd watch them burn.

Suddenly, there was a soft *pop*, and the fire vanished. I

stared at my reflection in shock. There was a shimmer to it that hadn't been there before—a shimmer of magic.

I frowned. It shouldn't have been that easy. Shouldn't even have been possible. But then... my magic hadn't yet formed when they trapped me, and I'd hardly submitted to the Masters for training once it did. Was it possible that I was stronger than they thought?

Moving carefully, cautious for any traps, I pressed my palm against the glass and reached through it.

There she was. After hours of searching, skipping through mirrors all across Aelor and a terrifying couple from Criera, I caught a familiar scent: rose petals and old books. It took me a moment to narrow my search, eyes pale with scrying and fingers bloodless from being held against the glass for so long.

But when I did, the room shifted.

Darkness folded around me, suffocating the orange glow of my lamp. Even though I hadn't physically moved, and was only looking through the mirror, the magic filled all my senses. As though this lonely mirror had been yearning for company.

I blinked, adjusting to the pale light of the moon that streamed through her bedroom. The angle was somehow wrong, and it took me a moment to work out why. The mirror was on the floor. And... with a squint, I calculated the distances branching out each side. It was too small.

Had she broken her mirror, and I was only looking through a fragment?

I closed my eyes and let the mirror's yearning pull me forward, no longer resisting its desire for companionship. Succumbing to the desires of an object was dangerous, but so long as I took care not to let the mirror keep me, it would be fine. And necessary, for all its danger. My current view wasn't enough; I needed to see what the mirror saw.

At first, it was an indecipherable kaleidoscope, but as my senses adjusted, it began to slowly make sense. I was right in my first estimation: this was a fragment of mirror left behind, and through its jagged edges, a myriad of new angles were reflected. The room wavered, my senses now full of not only what I could see through the thin sliver, but of what the mirror itself observed and understood.

Floorboards, cool and dark. Clothing piled in the corners, and perfume bottles strewn across a dresser. A bowl of rose petals by the window, and something half made with them beside it. Spilled lotions and ink spots on wood.

Loneliness.

My fingers froze against the counter, gripping it tightly. Huh. A mirror never lied, not when it came to matters of the soul. For all those who saw our many masks worn in public, only our reflection saw the truth.

I hadn't expected to find such a familiar truth in this bedroom.

My gaze drifted upward, and when I realized Bailey was safely in bed, sleeping, the most unexpected surge of relief washed through me. For a second, as my eyes adjusted, it had seemed as though the shadows stretched around her like a beast, a daemon crawling along the walls, but it was only my frantic imagination. The shadows filtered away, leaving nothing but cozy darkness and stillness. I could leave now, knowing she was safe. There was no reason to stay.

Rubbing the bridge of my nose, I leaned a little closer to the mirror, letting the shard's presence guide me and reveal more of the room.

It was a cozy room. Cozier than I expected from the cool, graceful way that Bailey held herself. I'd expected to find a space that was meticulously organized. Not removed of warmth, as such, but not cozy either. Instead, I found lace curtains, pillows piled high on the bed, and small knick-knacks strewn around the windowsill and shelves. Tiny carvings, glasswork, you name it—if it was cute and unnecessary, she had it.

I blinked, losing the vision for a minute, and was slapped over the head by the reflection of my own stupid face grinning into the mirror.

I cleared my throat, wiping the smile from my mouth. I was tired, that was all. Perhaps a little slap-happy from tonight's performance. It made me fonder than I would otherwise be.

I leaned closer, resuming my examination. It hadn't been my goal when I first touched the mirror, but it occurred to me now that I might find a clue here as to the whereabouts of my father. It wouldn't be a stretch for the Lumière to place him near Bailey. Those traces of magic I'd sensed on the first night could mean he was trapped fifty feet below her floorboards. But after a few minutes I found nothing and saw no lingering signs of magic.

It was as our disastrous first meeting had proven; she was utterly human.

Slowly, my gaze fell back to her, watching the rise and fall of her breath. Once again, I couldn't ignore that rising sense of loneliness that permeated the room, seeping from every corner. It was baffling. This was not the room of a lonely person. This was the room of someone whose life was filled with warmth, and yet, I had already noted that 'warm' would never be the first word I used to describe her. She was calm, collected. Intelligent and poised.

I propped my elbows on the counter, balancing on one foot as I lost myself in thought. Could it be that appearances were deceiving?

Movement caught my attention, and I looked up to see

Bailey stirring in her sleep. I should have let her slumber on, comforted by the knowledge that Fynn had not stolen her away and Heillon had not caught her among the archives.

Instead, I opened my mouth and called out, "Oh, lovely lady."

She stirred further, and a soft, sleepy sound rose from the nest of pillows and blankets as she came slowly awake. A warm feeling arose in my chest, and I fought valiantly to keep the goofy smile off my face.

Bailey sat up, hair mussed, blankets falling down beside her as she blinked in confusion around the room.

"Down here," I called.

I watched her crawl to the edge of the bed and kneel over it, eyes widening as they landed on what was clearly a forgotten fragment that had fallen near the wall.

With my luck, it had propped up against it, and the view I had of her was splendid: limned in moonlight, cheeks flushed with sleep, her gaze soft in a way I'd never seen it.

She blinked, and in an instant her cool composure returned, taking me by surprise. I was right; she didn't exude much warmth, typically. But seeing her here, now, among the space she had chosen and crafted, I realized that was not for lack of it.

"Sebastian," she breathed. "What are you doing"—she frowned—"in my mirror?"

"A question for a question," I offered, grinning slyly. "Tell me why your mirror has been reduced to such a lonely fragment on the floor, and I'll tell you why I'm in it."

Her lips twitched. She hooked her feet over the edge of the bed and stumbled off it. In a moment, she was seated cross-legged, holding the fragment up carefully between two fingers. I could see her thumb pressed against the glass like a giant's.

"Careful," I warned her. "Blood on glass holds memories."

Her eyes widened, and she adjusted her grip cautiously.

"I dropped the mirror, and a piece fell out." She shrugged. "I didn't think it would work anymore, or else I would have glued it back in." Her nose wrinkled, one eye squinting in thought—familiar gestures mixing with more instinctive ones as she remained poised halfway between sleep and awake. I held my breath, soaking in every movement like a secret shared. "But I'm sure the girls have been chatting, and I haven't heard their voices come through this broken piece like you have."

"I dare say the mirror set is clever enough to work out who to speak to," I said thoughtfully. "But you see..." I pressed a hand dramatically to my chest, leaning my other palm against the counter. "I've used my very clever magic to locate your particular mirror, not what counts, percentage-wise, as *the* mirror." I gestured toward her reflection, admiring the way the light softened the angles of her face, catching on her lower lip. "And your mirror happens to have been reduced to this pathetic little thing."

She laughed, and then bit back the sound. That warm feeling stirred in my chest once more.

"Okay, that explains how. It doesn't explain why." She raised an eyebrow.

It was fascinating, but piece by piece I could see the Bailey that I knew falling back into place. Calm, collected, almost emotionless... But only if you were a fool and believed what she was trying to show you.

"Ah, the why," I murmured, leaning on one elbow now and gazing toward the tent's entrance. "The why, my dear Bailey, is because you did not show tonight. And since I happen to know that your hobbies for the immediate future do not include such tame activities as flower arranging and collecting library books, I thought it best to check that you were still..." I wrinkled my nose, widening my eyes in faux shock as I finished in a hushed whisper, "alive."

Once more, that laughter burst free. I reveled in it, drowning in the sound.

"I can confirm I'm all in one piece," she said, adjusting herself in search of more comfort. She reached back with one hand to pluck a cushion from the bed and bring it beneath her. "But it is nice to see you again."

She blinked, as if surprised to hear the words come from her own mouth. I had the sensation abruptly that I was dealing with a wild animal. I needed to move very slowly so as not to spook it.

"It is a delight to see you again," I said, my voice dropping to a seductive murmur. "But what a shame that it is through glass, when there are so many ways that I could otherwise"—my gaze dropped to her lips—"touch you."

That kiss still haunted my dreams. I didn't understand it, but in the last few hours I'd finally stopped resisting it.

"What?" Her eyebrows lifted in exaggerated surprise. "You're telling me you can make a cursed mirror locate a new, highly specific partner, but you can't come through the glass yourself?"

My breath hitched, and suddenly I felt that the dynamic of power between us had abruptly flipped. I could come through the glass. There were spells for it.

But it was one thing to sneak beyond the circus bounds when the ribbons had spread on the wind and the moonlight still touched my skin. It was quite another to take the forbidden step Bailey was asking me to—one that would catapult me miles beyond the circus gates, into the shadows of a human's room.

I cleared my throat. "That type of magic would come with far too many consequences, I'm afraid," I said reluctantly. But the words cut off in my throat as I saw the disappointment flash in her eyes. My chest tightened.

Gods, this was ridiculous. I shouldn't be reacting like this; I barely knew her.

I turned my attention away from Bailey's face, searching for some way to ground myself, and my eyes landed on a slip of paper that was pinned beside her bed.

Even from here, I recognized my own chicken scratch scrawled across the paper.

"You kept my note," I breathed, and my voice was absent of the seductive drawl I'd been hiding behind ever since she opened her eyes. Instead, there was a note within it of something entirely different. Something that frightened me.

Bailey glanced over her shoulder, and in the curve of moonlight across her cheek, I caught the most beautiful flush rising.

"Oh," she stammered. "It's just..." She swallowed. "It was a reminder."

"A reminder of what?" My voice was low and persuasive—filled with more and more of that terrifying emotion.

She chewed on her lip. The cold, distant Bailey was far from sight. I wanted to erase her from memory, leaving nothing but this—this warm, open, flushed woman who had pinned my note to her bedside.

"At first," she said tentatively, shooting me an apologetic glance, "it was to warn me not to trust you."

I jolted. Well, that hurt. Not that I could blame her.

"But then it was a reminder that I could," she continued. "A reminder to always look below the surface and find the beauty within."

I gaped at her, lost for words. The beauty within. That was what she thought when she saw me? This twisted, useless, trapped idiot caught in the darkness of the Lumière, thanks to his own mistakes? There was no beauty here. Only a fool.

I looked away, my fingers clutching at the counter beneath me. "I don't think I quite deserve that," I said.

"Of course you do. Everyone does."

The warmth in my chest cracked, and something I didn't recognize spilled out. I looked up, my attention landing on the corner of her mouth, where a hidden smile was beginning to bloom.

Oh.

Oh fuck.

I was a fool twice over, because I'd somehow convinced myself this wasn't romance—that I wanted to see her smile and nothing more. But falling for someone's smile wasn't the opening night; it was the curtain call. The siren song that would have me returning over and over for an encore, if I wasn't careful.

I'd been careful for so very long.

Too long.

Bailey reached out with her free hand, fingers trailing along the shard of glass. She seemed on the verge of saying something, but then her face smoothed over.

My palm twitched against the surface of the table, fingers sliding just a little closer to the mirror.

"You know…" My voice was hesitant, but even though a tiny part of me rattled its fists and demanded I fall back in line, I knew I wouldn't. "Perhaps I can't completely come through, but—" I reached forward, pressing my palm against the mirror.

As I whispered the right words beneath my breath, my hand slipped through.

Bailey gasped, nearly dropping the shard of glass as she stared at the palm that now reached for her.

"Hold still," I breathed. This mirror is…" I chuckled. "Smaller than it should be. I don't want to slice my hand open."

She held so still, I wasn't sure she was breathing. Good sign? Bad sign?

Who was I kidding? Everything about this night was a bad sign, in the most enthralling of ways.

Leaning forward until my elbow disappeared into the mirror, I cupped her cheek. When she didn't flinch away, I traced my thumb along her jaw and then higher, marking the shape of her cheekbone.

Her eyes fluttered closed, brown and green disappearing into darkness. In the safety of knowing she couldn't see the expression on my face, I let my thumb trace along her lower lip. They parted on a gasp, breath sucking in with a ragged intake.

This was dangerous. If I didn't stop now, I'd be stepping through that mirror and taking her where she stood.

My hand trailed lower, over the hollow of her throat, fingers brushing her collarbone. I could feel her chest heaving with air, betraying the stillness of her expression. And still, she kept her eyes closed, as if she couldn't quite bear to see me. To see us.

Was there an us?

The question caught in my mind, spinning around and around until I finally broke through the fog in my mind and saw reason once more.

This wasn't like me. This was nothing like me, and I couldn't afford to explore the novelty, no matter how tempting.

I clenched my teeth and drew my hand back, as slowly as I could bear, but a hiss of pain still escaped me as my finger pulled through. I was too distracted, and at the last second I had caught it on a jagged piece of glass.

As her eyes fluttered open, I sucked the tip of my bloody finger into my mouth, smiling wryly.

"Forgot about the glass," I offered.

My voice sounded husky, raw, broken. She looked the same. If I didn't end this conversation now, I'd be risking a lot more than one night in her bed.

"Time to go to sleep, Bailey," I said, lowering my hands and leaning casually on the counter, thankful that the small window she had into my room couldn't possibly reveal the racing of my heart.

"If I must," she answered, eyes heavy-lidded.

A shiver raced through me, and I knew I should put an end to this now. Forever.

Nonetheless, as I ended the spell, I murmured, "Dream of me."

CHAPTER 21

Bailey

It was only a handful of seconds after he left that I noticed the blood on the mirror. It pooled slowly against the reflection, twin droplets rotating like a crimson galaxy—one on the surface, one within the glass.

Blood on glass holds memories, he'd said. And as I stared at the swirling droplet, I saw it was true. Shapes moved within the liquid, opaque and hidden for now, but instinct told me if I touched the glass, I would see.

These were Sebastian's memories... I shouldn't look without permission. And yet, I couldn't bring myself to set down the shard of glass.

To survive in Criera, I had to learn the secrets of an entire world in only a handful of days. Its magic, its creatures, its dangers... none of which had really become apparent in my training session with Fynn or the books I'd combed through from the library. And most of all, I needed to understand Bargains.

I needed to find a way to break them—to outwit the fae before they outwitted me.

I'd already committed to helping Sebastian destroy his

Bargain, whether he knew it or not, and here was a potential clue in pursuing that end. If I let the blood dry and the memory fade, then my only remaining source of information was the fae archives. A gamble at best. Sure, I could just *ask* Sebastian, but he was fae. He didn't know what his world looked like to an outsider. The most innocuous memory could hold a key, and he would never think to share it.

The blood slipped, running down the mirror, and I slammed my palm over it before I could talk myself out of it.

"If it's private, I'll just stop watching," I murmured as the room began to blur. "Simple."

Then, the world turned dark.

It stayed that way for just long enough that I began to panic, but then, drip by drip, images filtered in. A tall figure with long red hair, eyes of night, and leather straps wrapped around his body appeared: Heillon.

I sucked in a breath, going rigid even though I knew he couldn't see me. Was I about to witness the moment of Sebastian's Bargain? Surely my luck wasn't that good. But after a few minutes, the memory remained unmoving, its edges murky and strange. Not a fully formed thought, but more like a feeling.

When I looked at Heillon through Sebastian's eyes, I was deeply, chillingly afraid.

Swallowing thickly, I forced myself to study his features. To learn why the other fae were so terrified of him, and how I could survive him long enough to reach the other side. It was a face that spoke of both cunning cruelty and exquisite hedonism. Flashes of Sebastian's thoughts and memories raced around me: exile, barbarism, ritual. After a dizzying beat, they finally pooled together for long enough to create meaning.

Heillon had been exiled from multiple fae courts before he transformed his troupe of skilled outcasts into the Lumière. Banned from countless provinces for his barbaric rituals, sacrifices to old gods, and selfish exploits, he had created his own sanctuary where none but the Lumière were welcome. That was when Sebastian had joined.

More memories, more images. I shivered as Sebastian's swirling thoughts coalesced into a single warning, carried at the front of his mind: more than one human had been cut down in their attempts to stow away with the Lumière and seek Heillon's hedonistic pleasure for themselves.

He was worried for me.

I tapped my fingers against my leg, barely even noticing the movement. Restless and anxious, I recalled the signs from the fairground. *No human after midnight, on pain of death*. Here lay the evidence that the threat wasn't a lie.

Warning received: don't get caught.

I shifted, distantly acknowledging that it was time to let the memory go. I'd learned enough to make it worthwhile, and anything more felt like an invasion of privacy. But as I tried to break free of the memories, they shifted again. And this time, their grip held me tight.

The darkness pulled out to the side, like fog, and left me looking at a familiar face.

"Sebastian," I breathed, my attention fixed on his joyful, rakish smile.

This memory wasn't a conflicting jumble of words and thoughts; this was as clear as an image in my own mind.

He was younger, the sun lighting up his face and giving it a boyish charm. I'd seen him give this smile while performing, but it seemed hollow then; in this memory, it was blinding. His surroundings materialized in a dreamy fashion, wispy trees stretching up toward the sky and towering over the small clearing.

Sebastian wasn't alone, and when I realized who was with him, my breath caught in my throat. Fynn dropped down from an overhanging branch and tossed his blond hair out of his eyes. The smile he gave Sebastian was hesitant, almost shy.

They couldn't have been much more than teenagers, and all I could think as I looked at them was: what the hell happened? The lighthearted joy in each of their faces was completely absent from their adult selves. I couldn't imagine them looking like this, let alone at each other.

The Lumière, I supposed. That was what happened.

Fynn spoke, the sound distorted at first, as though he was underwater. "You really don't believe in it?"

Sebastian roamed the edge of the clearing, leaning in to examine the nooks and crannies of every tree he passed. His expression was one of rapt attention, as though the entire world was a fascination to him.

When he answered Fynn, he had his head half stuck on the hollow of an oak. "Nope! Not at all."

Fynn watched him silently. I couldn't help noticing how still he held himself. How small he made his body compared to Sebastian's lithe form, which was ever moving, traversing the clearing with broad sweeps of his limbs. Almost like a dance.

"What about in the legends? Magedara... she fell for the witch as soon as she heard her in a dream. And Ashonwy? Her prince was fated in the stars."

Shock rippled through me; were they talking about...? They couldn't be.

Sebastian snorted, spinning around and leaning back against the tree with a dramatic flourish. "Those are *stories*, Fynn. You can't tell me you believe that crap."

He moved to turn away, but at the last second took a closer look at Fynn's posture—the way he folded in on himself, eyes on the ground. A furrow appeared in Sebastian's brow, and he pushed off from the tree to come and kneel at Fynn's feet.

"Hey," he said softly. "I didn't say I don't believe in *love*. Just not love at first sight."

Fynn's gaze lifted to meet Sebastian's. The sunlight caught the blue of his eyes, making them glisten like flame. He gave Sebastian a wan smile. "I know."

The words were dull. Flat. Sebastian's frown deepened.

"No, I don't think you do," he said slowly. "What you're asking is... not what you think it is. I believe in *lust* at first sight."

He gave Fynn a smoldering look that had even my body warming with residual heat. Fynn's cheeks pinkened, and I watched him sway a little closer to Sebastian, as if powerless against the fae's charm. Sebastian slid a hand along Fynn's knee, up his thigh.

"But love at first sight," he continued, voice lower now, "is a lie. It has to be. You can't love someone you don't know; you can only want them."

"And do you want me?" Fynn rasped.

I almost drew back, dispelling the memory. It felt too raw, too intimate for me to witness.

"Yes, I want you," Sebastian murmured in response, leaning closer. They were only a few inches apart now. "But more than that, I want you to listen to me, you arrogant bastard."

Fynn gave a surprised laugh, the expression transforming his face. Even Sebastian's softened in response, his attention roaming every feature as he appeared to drink the rare laughter in.

"Love is like a budding flower," Sebastian continued.

With a flourish, he produced something from behind his back: a tightly furled cherry blossom from the trees at the edge of the clearing. Fynn stared at it, transfixed.

"You might have an inkling what will bloom," Sebastian

said quietly. "You might even be right. But you'll never know unless you cherish and nurture it into life."

Fynn had grown very still, his face uplifted to Sebastian, his eyes shining with emotion.

"And that takes time," Sebastian finished, the words barely above a whisper.

I couldn't hear Fynn's response as he surged up to crash his lips against Sebastian's. But as the memory faded, he repeated the words into the encroaching darkness, making my heart crack with empathy as the sound drifted all around me, lingering long after the image had faded.

"We have time."

CHAPTER 22

Bailey

I DIDN'T DREAM OF SEBASTIAN; I DREAMED OF FIRE.

Fire that spread and engulfed everything I'd ever touched, ever dared to love. I watched as the flames caught on the tree-tops, burning them to ashen piles in the way that Sebastian's magic by the lake should have but hadn't. The cold slide of tears ran down my face, but although I was clearly weeping, I couldn't feel it. I couldn't feel anything at all.

There was a mirror standing by the wayside, angled so that the only thing I would be able to see in it was my own face. But no matter how much I tried, my body wouldn't turn to face it.

When I woke, I lay there and stared at the ceiling while the sun slowly crested the horizon. As the golden rays kissed my face, I thought of all that I had seen these past few days, all that I'd done. With Fynn, with Sebastian. With myself.

My life now was unrecognizable to the one I'd had before, and in just a few short days, it would be nothing more than an obituary carved on a tombstone. Perhaps, if I was lucky, they'd make my painting in the town hall gentle and serene, but more likely it would appear as my dreams had: fire engulfing a wedding gown, and the shameful Offering carried across the water by the untrustworthy fae.

Three nights left, and tonight was the big one: I would sneak into Heillon's archive and raid it for answers.

Answers to the mystical world of Criera, to the Lumière's strange ticket—offered amidst warnings of terrible death—and, most of all, to the Bargains. If I could only find a way to outwit those, then nothing across the water would defeat me. Not lora beasts, not tempting whispers, not fae deals brimming with treachery. It would bring me power where I had none, and it would free a man who deserved so much more than the cage he'd been confined to.

Nothing else mattered.

To that end, I now perched on the kitchen counter of my little cottage and stared at the imp currently smashing all of my crockery. Stared at her and wished for that tiny spark of magic within me to bloom again and uncover the hidden form that Fynn told me was locked away.

Because breaking a fae Bargain? It needed either a miracle or magic, and the gods knew I wasn't blessed.

"Find the access point," I muttered to myself, ignoring the commotion as Merelda took yet another of my dinner plates, heaving it with both hands until it made her drop two feet in the air, and then hurling it at my fireplace. Needless to say, she wasn't happy about yesterday. If she'd discovered that Sebastian visited my bedroom last night, I suspected she'd have dumped my entire bed in the lake—with me still in it.

"Find the access point and take control."

Magic couldn't create, according to Fynn, but it could direct. It could control or set free. Somewhere within Merelda was a lock that just needed picking.

I closed my eyes to the symphony of yet another crash and a

screech, and I felt for the forest that grew only a few meters from my garden path. That was my access point. My connection.

My breath caught—I felt it. Like a seedling growing beneath the soil, there was a hum of power buried inside her. A physical sensation that, if I just reached out my hand, I could hold.

And so, I did. I ignored the disquiet that hovered in the back of my mind, reminding me that there was no way the Offering should be able to use magic when no one else in the village could, and simply reached for what was mine.

With a thought, I took control of the thread, and—

It was the quietest sound in the room, only a faint *snick* beneath the crashing and shrieking of my companion, but it stopped both of us in our tracks. Merelda froze, her mouth falling open, and I...

I hardly dared to draw a breath as, before my eyes, Merelda began to change.

Her little blue body began to grow, taller and taller, limbs stretching out as her face became apoplectic with rage and fear. And more than that—a fiercely guarded hope. Something I'd never seen on her before.

All this occurred in a handful of seconds, but before her shape could solidify into something I recognized, she spun on her heel and ran from the room, the door slamming behind her.

By the time I'd got my wits about me and run to catch up, she was nowhere to be seen.

My nails dug into the wood as I stood in the doorway, hanging onto the architrave and leaning around the corner. The front door swung gently on its hinges, a cobweb in the corner wavering in the breeze. Plants rustled, and the soothing scent of lavender drifted over the garden.

I did it.

I actually did it.

Slowly, wildly, I began to laugh. The sound startled a nearby bird, sending it racing from the bushes, but I barely noticed. The dream from this morning had long since faded from my mind, and all I could think about was tonight. Fear or no fear, it was happening.

I would either infiltrate their archives successfully, or die trying.

The sounds and smells of the Lumière folded over me, and without Stefan's slow, steady pace to my right, I moved easily through the crowd. Goblets bumped into my hand, begging to be drunk. Small stands of delicious smelling food and drink popped up among the tents while fae dressed in golden fabric danced and sang and played instruments I'd never seen before.

I stopped as a bubble floated before my head; within it was a perfect contraption of clockwork, mechanical cogs whirring as tiny figures danced and swayed. I didn't know how much of it was real, and how much of it was pure illusion.

My fingers twitched, itching to poke it. I glanced around; no one was watching. What was the harm? I reached out and nudged the contraption.

It fizzed and sparked, doubling in size. The dancing figures were now the size of my head.

I recognized their faces.

Gaping, I leaned in close as my sister and Hayden whirled in each other's arms, a pretty veil atop her head and a smart bow tie adorning his neck.

"Are you fucking kidding me?" I breathed.

But where this harsh reminder would have only recently sent me into a fit of tears, now, all I felt was rage. Anger rose within me, swift and cruel, and I found myself rising with it. Standing taller. Straighter.

That *asshole*.

And Katerina—how dare she?

Somehow, the lines of my world became blurred here, in this place that was neither one world nor the other. I knew I was the Offering, that I deserved the reminder Hayden had given me, but in this fairground, I had once become someone else. Someone who deserved so much more than the dregs they gave me.

The memory of Fynn's words echoed in my mind: *Are you so sure that who you are is the problem, and not them?*

No. No I wasn't.

With a whisper of a thought, I popped the bubble and sent the brass machinery clattering to the ground. Magic hummed over my skin, glowing faintly. Several people looked over in curiosity, and with a jolt, I realized they were my friends. They hadn't recognized me yet, their eyes drawn to the commotion of the whirring pieces at my feet.

I should have walked over to them. Said hello. Fallen into my place behind them as we strolled among the sights and sounds together.

I turned and walked away.

It didn't take long to lose myself in the crowd. The grounds were filling up, the guests relaxed now that four nights had passed without harm. I let myself fall among them, another wide-eyed human in awe of the fae.

As I did, I kept one hand slipped into my pocket and pressed my fingers to the ticket there.

It had warmed when I first stepped through the gates, and I

had known without looking that it glowed as well—those same sparks of magic emerging like they had in the shop. My theory for tonight, while I waited to bust into the archives, was to follow the magic of the ticket and see what it revealed. Perhaps there were places other than the gate that it would respond to, and if there were, then I might learn more about what kind of magic fueled its power.

Understanding the ticket's magic seemed vital, with all that I had discovered about Fynn last night. Not to mention Heillon himself, and the gory exploits that had been suggested in Sebastian's memories.

He'd killed them. Murdered the stowaway humans in cold blood. And while part of me held onto the hope that their punishment was only because they had no ticket, whereas I did... another part of me was confident he would kill me, too.

And so, the question remained as it had been from the beginning: did I trust Fynn and this ticket, with its nebulous promise of a disguise, to keep me safe as we crossed the water? Or should I take Sebastian up on his offer and find another way?

I roamed the grounds, searching restlessly for a sign that would make sense of this magic and give me a clear answer. But the ticket remained as lifeless as ever, giving me no clues at all. There was no sign of the magic that had surged when I stepped through the gates, and even if there had been, I needed more than that. A handful of dull sparks weren't enough to give me the information that would keep me safe.

But then, as I hovered near three caravans tucked to the side, I felt it: heat beneath my fingertips.

I paused, looking over at the caravans. There was nothing strange about them; they just looked like storage wagons. Off limits by implication, but there were no signs explicitly telling me to leave.

I took a breath, steeling myself as I glanced over my shoulder. No one was watching. I hadn't seen a single sign of Sebastian all night, and I assumed the moon hadn't been kind to him.

Even as it grew to full, it was almost as though the shadows increased even when the light did. For him to leave his tent, he would have to duck and roll, leaping from moonbeam to moonbeam—drawing attention to himself and, eventually, to me.

I briefly considered returning to his tent and asking him about the caravans, but quickly dismissed it. If he'd known more about the ticket, he'd have shared it last night. And besides, what if we picked up where we'd left off? Who knew what would happen then?

A little shiver of temptation ran through me, pleasant heat curling in my abdomen. The touch of his palm against my cheek still lingered, even now, and I allowed myself to enjoy it, knowing it would come to nothing. Then, in a heartbeat, I slipped between the shadows of the caravans.

A terrified second passed and then another, but no one emerged from the shadows to shout at me or trap me with their magic. So I took the ticket from my pocket and held it up in the thin sliver of moonlight that fell between the caravans.

The ticket glowed, sparks dancing from it, and it felt... happy. I didn't know how to describe it, but the ticket felt relieved. Like it was home. It hadn't felt like that before, not even at the gate.

Holding it up like a guide light, I turned slowly until the ticket was in the shadow. The glowing light carved a way through the darkness for me, and, acting on instinct, I followed it to the back of one of the caravans.

It was closed off by a thick drape of fabric, a heavy red velvet lined with gold. I lifted the corner and held the glowing ticket up to look inside.

It was empty, but the rows of carefully designed shelving

and brackets suggested that, at the end of the circus season, it would become storage for the tents themselves. Which meant that no one would be looking inside it on the other side of the bridge, because there was nothing in here they would need until they came back again.

My heart began to pound.

This was it.

If I could use the ticket for only its passage, paying for it legitimately so that its magic protected me, then perhaps I could slip away here and hide. I didn't have to accept the disguise, or take whatever passed as a seat in this transaction. The Lumière would think I'd simply changed my mind and run off, and I wouldn't be in danger of whatever trickery awaited me during the passage.

I would be like a legitimate stowaway. Someone who had paid their way, but couldn't have that payment abused.

A touch breathless now, I slid the ticket back into my pocket. My entire body prickled with urgency. Now that I had a plan, the thought that someone might come and ruin it terrified me. There were only three. Anything could go wrong.

I had a plan now, and I had to protect it at all costs.

All that was left was to conquer the Bargains and free Sebastian—something that had never been done in the history of fae and human deals. No pressure.

I turned, but as if summoned, I stepped straight into a hard, lean chest. Strong arms came up to steady me, and Sebastian's dark gaze looked down, his face lined in moonlight.

"Gods," I muttered, clutching my chest, "you scared the life out of me."

"Well now, we can't have that," Sebastian said with a wry grin. He looked up at the caravans surrounding us, a faux thoughtful look on his face. "A strange place you have here," he said, shoving his hands in his pockets and making a show of looking at the other side. "Do you come here often?"

I rolled my eyes, making sure he saw. "Do you always joke in the face of near-death experiences?"

"Frequently," he said, returning his gaze to me and grinning. "But I'd hardly call this near-death. Near slap-on-the-wrist, maybe?"

Pointedly, I stared down at his feet, which were currently resting in the only circle of light within these caravans. To land behind me, he must have leapt through the darkness.

I had no idea how I hadn't heard him, but then I supposed that was acrobats for you.

"I think it would be a lot more than a slap on the wrist for you," I said, aiming for amusement, but the seriousness of the statement hit me too quickly to hide.

I stared at the darkness that lay between him and the exit—felt the weight of those shadows like a chain around my neck. As I stared, I found myself imagining Sebastian losing all that he had worked for, all that he had hoped for, for something so meaningless as standing in the shadows with me. The thought chilled me.

Sebastian followed my gaze, but the angle of his face made it so that I couldn't see his reaction. I didn't know what he was thinking, and when he looked back, it was with that same joyful smirk.

"I've been thinking about your predicament," he said, lifting a hand and twisting it in the air so that it caught the moonlight from every angle.

I watched, faintly spellbound, as he somehow managed to traverse all the different angles and secrets of this pool of light. Once more, that somberness hit me as I realized how often he must navigate circles of moonlight, if he could know them this intimately. He knew where each beam of light would land—

where it was safe to put his hand, and where it wasn't. It was like watching a fish swim through water.

"Oh," I said, fighting to keep the emotion from my voice and stick to my usual, laconic drawl. "Don't suppose you've come to tell me you've hired an escort with three imperial guards and an anti-magic ward."

Sebastian barked a laugh, dropping his hand and shifting his weight casually backward. His posture was so relaxed now that his body almost slipped into the shadows, and my breath caught in fear.

He didn't seem to notice.

"Not quite, but you aren't far off. I was wondering why you've chosen the Lumière to travel with when we are undoubtedly the most dastardly of the bunch." He raised an eyebrow.

Another shiver of heat went through me.

I cleared my throat. "Well, it's not like we have fae pounding down our doors out here," I said, looking away. "I'll take what I can get."

Sebastian tapped his lip. "Yes, but that's what I've been thinking about. Why don't you have fae here? We used to be all through these woods. You couldn't throw a stone without hitting a summoning or a Bargain or, hell, just a merry little tea party. So why are the Lumière your only option?"

"Are you seriously asking me for a brief recap of the last five hundred years of human history?" I said, leveling him with a glare. "I've read a few books in my time, but even I don't know all the ins and outs of that. All I know is the fae are few and far between out here in the countryside. I could go to the city, but..." I shrugged. "I'd have to get there first, and I don't love my chances traveling alone among humans."

"And yet you will travel with the Lumière," Sebastian said. There was something odd in his voice. Not a question, because we'd covered this already, but a sense of melancholy that I couldn't quite ignore.

I opened my mouth to tell him it was irrelevant—I'd already thought of a plan. It wasn't a plan that he would love, but that wasn't his decision to make. It was mine.

But then he lifted his chin, and I caught the look in his eyes. My words froze as Sebastian took a very slow, very deliberate step toward me.

Into the shadows.

"What are you doing?" I breathed, noting the slight hiss he gave as the shadows hit him.

I took a step forward so that he didn't have to do whatever idiotic thing he was doing, but he held up a hand. This time, the hand didn't caress the moonlight. It was shrouded in darkness.

Sebastian took another step forward. His body was cloaked in shadow. I could see the pain in the grit of his jaw, in the flash in his eyes, but I didn't understand any of it. I didn't understand all the layers of *something* that I was reading there.

There was a fire within him; something that hadn't been there before. As though he'd come alive again after years of sleepwalking.

"I thought," he said slowly, "that tonight, I could show you how to summon another fae."

"Okay," I said, holding up my hands and trying to shoo him back into the moonlight. "Message received. Let's do it, but first —" I pointed to the gap between the caravans with both hands. "May I direct your attention to this beautiful pool of moonlight, barely three steps away? Look at it glow. What a delight. Come experience it with me."

I stepped forward, but Sebastian stopped me with a hand firmly pressed against my collarbone, his palm open and loose. I swallowed, moving backward with him as he took another step into the darkness, and then again.

The moonlight was out of reach now; four meters away, at least. His lips parted on a small gasp of pain.

Without meaning to, a whimper of pain dropped from my own mouth. I reached for him, intending somehow to help. To soothe him, to fix him—to shove him back into the moonlight and slap him silly, I didn't know. Just anything that wasn't this.

But as I did, his hands came up to clasp my jaw, and he lowered his head to kiss me. It was far softer, far gentler than before, but he moved against me with an urgency I couldn't quite name.

I melted into him, as lost as I always was—as I always would be—at the first hint of desire.

Of someone wanting me, choosing me.

"You weren't followed by guards again, were you?" I asked, cracking a weak joke to try to diffuse some of the shock racing through me. What was he doing? He had no reason to kiss me, now.

"No," Sebastian agreed, lips curving into a smile against mine. "This one's for me."

I groaned, completely unable to stop the sound escaping. My hands slid to his chest, taking in the shape of him, the warmth of his body through his soft clothing. He smelled like jasmine and mint, the soft curtain of his dark curls falling across my face. If I twirled a finger between two locks of our hair, it would be like a corkscrew of shadow and light, pale and dark.

I drew back just enough for air, and then lifted my hands to his curls, driving them deep and pulling him to me. He groaned, a long dark sound, and dropped his hands to my waist, pulling me in.

"Shouldn't we go somewhere safer?" I whispered against his mouth. "Someone could walk in at any second. You're risking everything right now. There better be a good prize, or else my estimation of you just dropped into the sewers."

He laughed, the sound a low rumble from where his chest pressed against mine.

"There is," he promised, and then he pulled back just enough to gaze down at me. "I'm seeing how much I can withstand."

"Of what?"

"The pain the shadows bring."

My brow furrowed. "What? Are you serious? Why not just play with knives like any other self-respecting masochist? You don't have to risk—"

The words caught in my throat. I forced them out anyway.

"You don't have to risk losing everything you've worked for these last years. And what are you even doing it for? Who cares if you can withstand the pain? It isn't the pain that's the problem, is it?"

It's the punishment, I thought. The loss of his father.

But my words didn't seem to be sinking in. The light in his eyes glinted, darker and deeper than before, as he pushed me back into the side of the caravan, hooked my leg around his waist, and began to kiss me again.

"Maybe it is," he murmured, barely making sense. "Maybe I want it to be."

This time there was no mistaking the purpose of this kiss— where it was going, what he wanted.

It was what I wanted as well.

He ground forward, the hard length of him unyielding evidence of his desire, his need, as he thrust between my legs.

"This summoning can't happen here," he said, "and there's been no wind tonight. No convenient stretching of the circus bounds, and no magical one I can summon either. They're all ignoring me tonight; I asked too much of them last time."

Through his ramblings, the answer hit me. He was seeing whether he could withstand the pain long enough to break the rules. To show me how to summon fae that weren't as dangerous and deadly as the Lumière.

Too many thoughts and feelings twisted around inside me, their jagged edges slicing me open.

He was doing this for me, and it was by far the smartest option if you looked at it that way. Finding a way across the water that didn't rely on the Lumière... It was the most sensible option for everyone but him, and that was when it hit me.

He wanted to break the rules.

My eyes snapped open, and I stared up into his fiery gaze. All the tiny contradictions in his personality made sense now.

He followed the rules because he had to, but it wasn't who he was. It had never been who he was. The problem was that it was precisely those traits that had landed him here—that had cost him his father, his freedom, his life.

But he didn't want to follow their rules anymore. I was temptation for him, just as the pure ecstasy of his touch—wanting me, claiming me—hit every forbidden, lost, and stolen hint of desire in me. With a dawning horror that still wasn't strong enough to make me walk away, I realized: I was bad for him.

He was going to risk it all, and I was going to let him.

He bit down on my lower lip, desire making his voice rough as he said, "Besides, I can't very well let you leave without saying a proper goodbye, can I?"

"Are you sure this is a proper goodbye?" I said, my fingers twisting in his collar and dragging him closer to me. Begging him without words.

He chuckled, and for a second I thought I'd convinced him.

But then he said, "No, Bailey, *this* is not a proper goodbye."

His lips trailed up my jaw, toward my ear. "*This* is not what I'm talking about."

My stomach swooped, hips grinding up into him without even meaning to as his hand moved round to the front and slipped below my breeches.

"But while we're here..."

His fingers weren't hesitant. His touch was light but deliberate as he slid them between my thighs and ran them over my core, back and forth, building up a slick, hot need.

I moaned, losing the ability to think. To know anything except this moment.

"That's what's so good about a situation like ours, Bailey." He breathed the words into my ear. "We know when it ends. So, if we aren't allowed to keep anything, then there's nothing to stop us from simply enjoying the moment. Every. Last. Second." His teeth trailed across my neck as he asked in a lower voice, "and are you enjoying it?"

"Yes," I breathed.

"Are you having fun?" he insisted, curving two fingers and sliding them into me.

"*Yes.*"

"I want you to take everything you can from me," he breathed, the words a low rasp. "Take it, and remember this night when you leave. Remember how I made you feel."

I wasn't sure I could even describe how he made me feel. My ragged breathing filled the night, my mind foggy with pleasure. And through it all, he was relentless—fingers moving in a slow, aching slide, slipping inside and then out again. His thumb traced over my clit as he kissed and sucked and nipped at my mouth, and suddenly I couldn't bear it anymore.

I clutched at his chest, tiny whimpers dropping from me as my hips ground into him, writhing on his touch. I took everything he offered me, every last drop.

Only a handful of minutes passed, but he wasn't teasing; he was going for the kill. I came with a hoarse moan, trying to bite back the sound and failing, only for him to capture it with his mouth.

He slipped his hand free and stepped back, into the shadow and then further. When the moonlight hit him, the sharp, tense edge to his body relaxed in one breathless swoop.

Gods, he was so beautiful.

The expression on his face was hardly complicated at all this time; it was pure, satisfied male.

"Meet me at midnight," he said, "by the lake, where the shadows are deepest." He paused, tilting his head to the side. "Unless you have another way."

Unless I had another way.

I did. I had a way to use the ticket safely, without walking into a trap. I could pay legitimately, and then stow away where the magic was strongest and no one could find me.

But as I stared at him now, I realized that the way I was planning was, while perhaps not *breaking* the rules, certainly bending them. If I told him that, would he be complicit? Would they punish him if they found out?

Worst of all, did he even care?

Because as I looked at him now, I found there was no denying the conclusions I'd come to tonight. He'd been at breaking point for years, and I was the thing that had tipped him over the edge. I'd reminded him of everything he was, everything he wanted to be.

He was done playing by their rules, but he had to. He *had* to, or he would lose everything. It was up to me to convince him that this way was folly, and I could see in his eyes that there would be no convincing him now.

Silently, I vowed to talk to him tonight, where danger didn't lurk around the corner. Where we could take our time and be clever about things.

I shook my head. "No other way."

Sebastian turned to leave, but then he seemed to see something in my expression and halted. Tilting his head to the side, for a shining moment, the ever-present darkness in his expression faded.

"Did I ever tell you about the time I stole my father's boat, back in Criera?" he asked, giving me a rakish grin.

The expression was almost unrecognizable, and yet I thought, wildly, that it was the truest one I'd ever seen.

"No?" I shook my head, confused by the sudden change in topic.

He leant in close and, with a theatrical whisper in my ear, said, "He had to summon the north wind to chase me down, but he didn't account for how strong it was." Sebastian stepped back and made a wild gesture with his hand. A rush of light appeared, whooshing upward as the sparkling outline of an illusory robe flying up over his head appeared. I was struck by the image of a young Sebastian, paddling for dear life, while his father chased him in his altogether—robes tossed blindly over his face—and yelled at the north wind to behave.

Laughter escaped me; I clapped my hand over my mouth to stop it, but I couldn't. It bubbled out of me, and I had to double over to keep it to a faint wheeze. Muscles I'd never used came to life in my cheeks, and it was almost painful. I wouldn't have traded the feeling for the world.

When I finally got myself under control, I rose to find Sebastian waiting for me, standing only a foot away. As I straightened, he cupped my cheek with his palm and scanned my face. His smile was breathtaking.

"There it is," he murmured, leaning in for a slow, unexpectedly sweet kiss.

I melted, my heart fluttering as I leaned into the warmth of his body. "There's what?" I asked as he pulled away.

"That beautiful laughter," he replied.

Then, with a wink, he was gone, leaping free into the moonlight on the other side of the caravans, as he left me standing there with my heart rending in two.

He wasn't like the others, who all told me to smile. Who called me cold and lifeless. They demanded I laugh. That I be grateful. That I show them some affection.

Sebastian gave it to me. Even in the middle of danger, while breaking all the rules and daring the consequences, he stopped to make me laugh.

I was falling for him. Not just a whisper or a hint—I'd crash landed on the shattered ground of rock bottom. My eyes were wide open, alright, and I couldn't change what I was seeing.

I couldn't keep him. This end was written. And walking away was going to kill me.

I took a long, slow moment to compose myself, but I was still in a daze when I left the seclusion of the caravans. Immediately, I ran up against something hard, not even seeing what it was. For a second, I thought I'd walked into Sebastian again. That he'd lingered, ready to test fate a second time. But then I realized the hard chest I was pressed against wasn't Sebastian's. It was Fynn's.

Fear coursed through me, sharp and painful. I looked up into his eyes, but I couldn't read what I found there. Had he seen us? Would he report Sebastian?

I forced my breathing to slow, reminding myself that it didn't matter if he suspected; he had to have *seen*. Those were the rules of the Bargain. And Fynn had arrived too late. Sebastian was long gone.

I wet my lips. "Fynn. What are you doing here?"

For several long seconds, he didn't speak. Then his expression shifted into lighthearted amusement, just like always. He leaned down and whispered in my ear.

"I wonder, Bailey, do you want a mouse or a lion in your bed?"

My breath caught. He knew. Had he heard us? Heard the sounds I'd made?

Unexpectedly, it wasn't embarrassment that rose within me. It was desire. I wanted him to have heard.

Gods, I was just as bad as Sebastian, breaking rules that would squash me like a fly.

He leant to my other ear and whispered, "A lion would have sniffed out that secret you're keeping in a heartbeat." He drew back, glancing at the caravans with a knowing expression. "It's a good choice," he murmured. "The tickets welcome each other home in these wagons. No one will think to look for you here, especially if you throw off the scent by hiding beneath one of the blankets." He winked at me. "Promise I won't tell."

I stared at him, lost for words. Should I deny it? It seemed pointless.

Or perhaps I should argue his assumption about Sebastian. I could point out what I'd just discovered tonight; Sebastian was no mouse, no matter what I might have thought of his passive, obedient nature before.

But that would give him away. It would alert his captors to the fact that something in Sebastian had broken, and he was now a threat. I couldn't do that.

The secrets were piling up, one after the other, and I couldn't even tell what were mine and what were theirs anymore. Even Fynn had shared secrets with me, only I didn't know what they were. They'd been wrapped in layers of truth and untruth, twisting around on themselves and cobwebbed until I had no idea what was at the core.

But he *had* shared secrets with me, and it was that which

kept me from turning him away entirely. And so I answered with the truth, foolish though it was.

"I don't know who I want," I told him, searching his face as if it might present me with an answer.

Sebastian made me laugh; Fynn made me fight. And I needed both. Gods, I *wanted* both.

A flicker of surprise appeared there—at my honesty or at my answer, I wasn't sure. Whatever it was, it seemed to have thrown him because he had no more pretty words for me, no more challenges.

He simply melted into the night like Sebastian, one in light and one in darkness.

CHAPTER 23

Bailey

IT FELT LIKE A LIFETIME BEFORE THE BUSTLE OF THE CIRCUS PICKED UP enough that I trusted those secret passageways to be empty. Even still, my body was taut with fear as I snuck in the back entrance Sebastian had shown me, my footsteps horrifyingly loud in the echoing mud room. My confidence from earlier still thrummed in my veins, but it was distant, muted in the face of this strange, echoing place between worlds.

Bravado was easy when you were casting forbidden magic in the safety of your own cottage, but here in these hidden walls, I'd never felt so far from home. It was hard not to question myself when it was a habit that had been built into my survival for twenty-eight years.

"Act enthralled." I whispered the words like a mantra as I crept through the shadowy archway. "Act enthralled."

I'd already come up with a cover story, and, assuming I could convince the fae of anything, it was a good one. I only hoped they wouldn't shoot first and ask questions later, so I'd still be alive to tell it.

I slipped the correct key from the hook and tucked it into my pocket, and then I strolled airily down the corridor, letting my head lilt back and forth as if I were dancing to inaudible music. I even paused a moment or two, spinning around, letting my hands trail along the stone walls just in case invisible eyes watched me.

And then, when I reached the wooden door at the end of the corridor—such a contrast to the shadowy alcoves that led from one room to another in the rest of this place—I leaned back against it in a swoon. The key lay concealed in my palm, and with my eyes closed and my hands tucked behind me, I worked feverishly to unlock the door.

It was almost impossible without looking, but finally it gave a soft *click* and the pressure eased. I turned the handle, a dreamy expression on my face as I braced myself and let the door fall inward. I drifted through, whirled on my toes, and shut it with a quiet thud.

Now came the hard part. Relaxing every feature of my expression into a look I had never worn before, I gave a soft, airy smile to the door—blissful, safe, and clueless—and turned around.

Thank the gods the archives were empty. It was a small enough room, and from the odd shape of the shelving around the walls, slightly domed, I wondered if it matched up to one of the caravans outside.

Of course, just thinking of those caravans sent a wave of remembered desire flowing over me.

I shivered, barely managing to keep a calm expression for whoever may be watching, instead of biting my damned lip. If everything failed because I couldn't stop thinking about Sebastian's fingers, I'd have to run back to those archers and tell them to aim at my face.

Once a measure of composure returned, fueled entirely by that mortifying image, I drifted into the room. There was a single-person desk in the center, complete with a golden ball of faelight hovering above. I ignored it for now, just as I ignored the red velvet arm chair—although I did let my fingers drift over the back as I passed—and the sepia photos that lined the wall nearest to the entrance.

Instead, I went straight for the shelves, working my way around the room in a clockwise direction, letting my fingers run along every spine as if by a compulsion. As if someone had enthralled me and commanded me to come here and touch every one. And as I did, with my head lolling dreamily to the side, I scanned the titles for a clue.

Very few of them had their titles lettered on the spine, and only a handful of those looked useful. Mindful of the time that I had—or more likely didn't have—I plucked out every book that mentioned a Bargain and an oath, ruffling the shelving to conceal what I'd taken, and then I selected three books from the top row nearest the door. Setting those on top of my stack, I dropped into the velvet armchair, took a book from the bottom, and began to read.

Within seconds, I knew that this would not be like the library at home. A chill raced down my spine as I took the words in, and with every passing second I had to fight to keep the languid expression on my face.

These books were not instructional manuals—textbooks outlined in a dry, unattached voice. These were the archives of the fae, and they read like the exploits of war. I propped my chin on my hand, keeping my eyes wide and guileless, and ran my finger down the center of the page, skimming the words on either side.

They were written in Criari, but apart from a word here or there I had no trouble reading them. At first, I found only records of rituals—dark, horrible things that spoke of daemons and blood summonings. Terrifying monsters were etched into the panels, as page after page of twisted maws opened before me. And after the monsters came the symbols. Tangled glyphs that sent dread and fear coursing through me at the mere sight of them.

Some, I even recognized. Three symbols, at least, were identical to those carved into the plaque in the town hall where the Oath of the Offering was recorded. I didn't even want to think about what that meant.

Ultimately, though, the rituals didn't help me; all they did was chill my blood and make me regret every decision I'd ever made to come here. So, I moved on as quickly as I could, setting those books back on the shelf and searching deliberately for information on the Bargains.

It was then that the pieces began to come together, and a sense of dread and overwhelm rose alongside new understanding.

Fifth night of the frost in the year two hundred and three; convinced two lost humans to part with their wedding night for a chance to stay by my fire.

The tone quickly became gleeful.

I fed that memory piece by piece into the flames until the magic surrounded them. They were entranced, caught by the power of that fire—by a yearning they couldn't quite taste. That which had been lost and could never be restored. Their love for each other began to sour, twisting into doubt and uncertainty. The vows they had spoken were lost, and the scattered pieces of all the memories that anchored onto those vows became untethered by the light of that fire.

I fed off them for days, while they refused to leave its warmth, neglecting both food and drink for the chance to savor one more flicker of the flame. Of the memory they could not recapture. And then...

The pause between one word and the next was luxurious. Anticipatory. It sent a violent ripple of disgust surging through me, and for the first time my expression faltered.

And then I doused the fire.

Pain wrenched through my chest as I forced myself to read the remaining words—how the couple had died there, yearning for what the flames had promised them, and how the fae had gone along their merry way. I noticed with dull interest, even though it was precisely the kind of information I'd been looking for, that this feast resulted in the addition of several decades to the fae's lifespan.

I paused, forcing myself to push past the pain and re-read the words until they sunk in. My heartbeat kicked up. Their Bargains with us weren't just power, or a trade of service. They were the source of their immortality.

I read on, each entry more sickening than the last as I consumed what they had done until it felt like I, too, had taken those memories, those feelings and passions.

What the humans had lost I devoured, each bite bringing me closer to understanding precisely what I was walking into. This was a world built on the power of exchange and, therefore, the exchange of power. And the fae were at the top of the chain.

A mother lost her firstborn child; a daughter lost her music; a father lost his aging parents, bricked up behind an impenetrable wall. He never found out if they survived, and I turned the page quickly so that I needn't either. Offering after offering spun past on the pages, all taken by the fae and consumed until their lives on the other side of the water were infallible. Pure power, pure pleasure.

The Lumière, I quickly realized, were gluttonous with it. What small mention came of the other fae over the water read in opposition to the Lumière. Their Bargains were softer, quieter; an exchange that felt, although I was loathe to say it, fair.

Passed by a naiad building a complex Bargain with a human that had gone seeking her, I read. *I tried to interject but the power of the Bargain remains sacred. Pitiful thing. She traded water from the wellspring of life in exchange for an oath by the human to trim the birch trees by the mountain pass. Sorely neglected, their occupants were becoming sour and gnarled.*

The human gladly gave this service and walked away feeling richer.

The word was underlined, and the passage split off in disgust. The Lumière Bargains were never like this, and as I read book after book, my head slipping from its dazed position and becoming more alert despite my efforts to hide, I noticed that most of the Bargains were about impossible choices. Choices that either couldn't be made, or that the victim didn't have the power to make.

When I read one line, I couldn't help but laugh—a soft, bitter huff of a thing. This human had been bound up in a curse where he had to wait to be chosen by the one person who would never choose him. Wasn't that my whole life? Wasn't that exactly what the Offering was when it came down to it: a curse to wait in perpetuity for nobody to ever choose you?

I swallowed, my hand clenching into a fist, my dreamy expression entirely forgotten. Perhaps being caught here would be an acceptable end to the Offering. The final poetic period on a sentence that could barely be called a life. I could offer myself up to the fae and go out with a bang. Perhaps I should; if I couldn't break my Bargain or find a modest life on the other side of the water, I could at least ensure this suffering was over.

The dread within that thought speared me, and I shook my head violently, coming awake as if from a dream. No, that wasn't why I was here. I was here to find an answer. I was here to fight.

The handle of the door rattled, and I lurched forward in my seat, fear rising like vomit in my throat. Oh, gods, someone was here. I only just managed to school my expression into that dreamy daze once more before the door swung open slowly, with great suspicion.

It took everything for me to swallow my gasp of horror when those familiar coal-black eyes and long red hair appeared in the corner of my vision. As I did, a delirious thought struck me: hardly anyone else would have managed it. It was only through years of keeping my expression still and poised, rid of any emotion, that I managed to keep myself safe.

As Heillon stepped into the room, legs braced wide and scowl fierce, I kept my hand steady and slowly turned the page. He stood there for what felt like an age, and all the while my heart pounded. Screaming at me that I'd been caught, that I had to run. Had to dive around the predator standing between me and the door and get out of here before he destroyed me.

I turned another page, humming to myself.

"Well," Heillon said in Criari. "What have we here?"

The words were accented, harder to understand than any before him, and I strained to hear every syllable so that I might have an inkling of when the trap was about to snap closed.

He rounded the little wooden desk, tapping the orb of fae light so it spun in the air. Flickering shadows danced across the walls as he came to rest standing just behind me. His hand curled over the back of the chair, his fingers brushing my shoulder.

I latched on to the tuneless humming sound as an anchor; it was the only thing keeping me going. Could humans die from the sheer weight of their stupidity crashing into them? If they could, my obituary would read: *died as she had lived, making every wrong decision and somehow still believing she might win.*

The tuneless song rose in pitch. Hopefully, Heillon thought it was a bold artistic direction, rather than terror shattering my vocal cords.

He stood there for a very long time, and then, in the common tongue, he said "What are we doing here, my dear?"

My carefully prepared answer dropped off my lips. "Counting pages," I said dreamily, "One hundred eighty-one, one hundred eighty-two..."

A low chuckle came from his throat; he believed me. Of course he did. Heillon had no idea I could read their language. If he did, I'd already be dead.

But even though relief began to kindle desperately within me, I kept my body still.

"I see." His hand lifted to rest on my shoulder as he leaned forward and scanned the words of the page.

He read a few sentences aloud, outlining a Bargain that had been struck between three fae and a coven of Spell Masters. A Bargain that had kept them busy for three long, ecstatic, sweaty nights. The way his accent caught on certain words highlighted a couple of unknown phrases that had struck me, and even though I was seconds away from death, I soaked up the knowledge for later.

"The pleasure of the immortals and mortals alike," he murmured, his finger twirling idly and caressing my hair. I couldn't quite keep the shiver from breaking free, and I hoped he would take it as an involuntary bodily response.

For good measure, I leaned into his touch, squashing the nausea that threatened to rise.

He laughed softly again. "I shall have to commend whichever one of my vicious darlings sent you in here. It is quite ingenious. Who is your Master tonight?"

Once more, I had prepared my answer. Sing-song, I said, "Never caught their names. Two to a pair, brunette hair, and eyes glinting in the firelight."

All the while I spoke, Heillon's hand caressed my hair—the idle pet that one would give a beloved dog seated by the fire. I didn't feel an ounce of that love within his touch now, and doubted he even knew what it would feel like.

"The pleasure of immortals," he murmured again, once more in fae, as I turned the page. His nostrils flared, breathing in deeply. "I can smell it on you."

My heart stuttered, and terror clashed violently with desire. He could *smell* Sebastian's touch. My lingering pleasure. Gods, it was all I could do not to vomit in fear and shock, and yet, what he smelled was confirming my story. I had been with one of them tonight, and after, they had sent me here for their own twisted joy.

"I could give you pleasure, too, little mortal, and what a treat that would be." He leaned in, his nose all but buried in my hair. "The scent of you is so twisted. So deprived." His laugh was louder now, riddled with genuine amusement. "There is something wrong with you."

Another shiver raced through me. The fear was becoming unbearable; I wasn't sure how much longer I could hold out. Was he smelling Fynn's Bargain or the Oath of the Offering? There was so much wrong with me, he could practically take his pick. Beneath the cover of the book, my left hand clenched uncontrollably, fingers curling into a rictus of terror.

I couldn't outlast him. How had I ever thought it would be worth it to come here like this? Heillon's appearance had finally forced me to admit the truth that had been solidifying ever since I began reading about the Bargains.

I had been searching for the knowledge that would empower me to outlast the fae on the other side of the water. That would give me the strength and cunning to carve out a humble, free life for myself, where no one could touch me. Where no one could ever hurt me again.

And all that I had learned was that this was impossible.

There was no way to break a Bargain. At least, none that

they would tell me. There was no escaping the Lumière, who were cruel and delighted in offering impossible gates and twisted choices. There was no way to beat the game I'd joined, and with Heillon's hand caressing my neck, I wondered if this truly was my destiny—to walk straight into the arms of the beast and to die there.

Heillon straightened and then crossed the room to pluck a book free from the shelf.

With a start, I realized I knew it. It was the one I had read just before. The one with the symbols that matched up to those on the Offering's plaque.

Tucking the book beneath his arm, Heillon crossed the tiny room to the doorway. But before leaving, he paused and spun to regard me once more.

I turned another page, pressing my knees together to keep them from quivering. I was certain the expression on my face by now was a grimace. Certain I was about to be discovered.

But all Heillon said was, still in Criari, "I doubt this is the last I'll see of you. I do love a sense of poetry—that euphoric lust found only in completion." He smiled, his gaze flicking back and forth between my eyes, as if noting one and then the other. Comparing the colors of each. "I look forward to our reunion, oblation."

Oblation.

It took me a breathless second to make sense of his wording. His accent wrapped around the syllables, changing one that I typically knew as emphasized to something much softer. The word wasn't a perfect translation, but I was certain it shared a similar form... too similar to ignore. Sacrifice. Gift.

Offering.

Heillon knew who—and what—I was. And as he said those words, permeated with such certainty, I recalled Stefan's warning only days ago.

Being wanted is no picnic. The Lumière would snatch up every human here in a heartbeat if they could. Their desire to own us knows no limits.

As Heillon's cold, infinite eyes pierced me, I had the undeniable feeling that I had just been added to his list of desires.

After a beat, he finally left. The second he vanished, I didn't bother with my disguise any longer. I dropped my head onto the book, gripping it fiercely with fingers that threatened to tear the pages in two.

I had to get out of here. I'd learned all that I could, and none of it helped. Meanwhile, Heillon had collected a book that spoke of the darkest rituals blood magic could offer, with the same nonchalance as I might collect a library hold.

Not to mention a book that recorded the symbols of the Offering—my oath to give myself up so that my village could prosper.

I didn't yet know what it meant—what it *would* mean—for me, but I had seen enough of the Lumière to be deathly, terrifyingly afraid.

CHAPTER 24

Bailey

At first, I thought Sebastian wasn't going to come. With the way the forest grew around the lake, and how low the moon was on the horizon, the shadows stretched into every corner. There was only the thinnest sliver of moonlight on the lake shore. To reach it, Sebastian would have to move through complete darkness.

He'd have to be a complete fool to come. A total impulsive, brattish fool.

There was a rustle among the trees. The branches parted, and Sebastian stepped through.

Quite without meaning to, my body stiffened, my breath coming a little faster than before. Even though I'd seen him several times now—had stuck my tongue down his throat, gods damn it—every time was like the first. Like that moment on the bridge.

He called me a mystery, but had he looked in the mirror?

He was dressed differently to his usual style. His pants, while still loose, didn't flow quite the same as the ones he performed in. They wrapped around his leg in layers, almost like leather riding pants, but they were far looser. More fluid.

Across his chest, a loose white shirt billowed, pressing against the contours of his body as the wind caught it.

He was easy to spot in the shadows, and my heart beat faster in fear for who might see. Still, his walk down from the circus was unhurried, his steps sure and steady. As he walked in the shadows beside the path and came to a stop before me, the moonlight finally reached him, bathing his skin in its silvery glow.

The second the light kissed his body, he softened—shoulders lowering, fists unclenching.

"It really does hurt, doesn't it?" I asked.

He gave me a crooked grin, suddenly looking so very different to the dark and devastating man he appeared to be. This was the man who liked nothing more than to make me laugh. Who bent all the rules and transformed the terrifying new shapes they made into art.

"Nothing like a little pain to liven up a relationship," he said with a wink.

I wasn't buying it. I held up my hand and examined my empty palm, as if searching for something. "I don't see a gavel in here—you know I'm not a judge, don't you? You don't have anything to prove to me."

Sebastian flicked his arm, producing a ball of golden light that appeared from his shoulder and rolled down to twirl around his upheld finger.

"No," he agreed lightly, flicking the golden light ball from one finger to the next. For a split second, it danced into my open palm and changed shape into a gavel.

I narrowed my eyes, closing my hand to catch it, but the light was too quick. It bounced back to Sebastian.

"If you were a judge, you would be far easier to convince," he said, amusement in his tone.

He flicked the ball over his head, spun, and bent forward to catch it on his foot, poised in a half bow with one leg in the air.

Reluctantly, I gave him a slow clap.

He shook his hair free from his eyes, flicked the ball into nothingness, and rose.

"For you see, I am a model citizen." He arched his brow. "And any who claim to have seen otherwise are nasty liars."

The lighthearted mood vanished as I remembered just who had been the one to see him last time.

"I know that it was Fynn who caught you," I said quietly.

The smile slowly faded from Sebastian's face. He tucked his hands in his pockets and gazed out over the lake. "The one who turned me into the Masters and got me trapped? Yes, it was Fynn. Must have run screaming all the way back to camp, he reported it so quickly."

A bitter smile twisted onto his face. "I suppose it was too much to ask that he possess a working heart, given what we were to each other at the time, but there you are. Valuable life lessons and all."

I frowned. "You were dating when he betrayed you?"

My blood felt like ice. The wind rustled the leaves around us, creating a small cocoon of sound in the midst of a night that felt abruptly barren.

"Yes, sadly. I never thought to hide what I was doing from him." He shrugged, that same bitter smile appearing once again. "It doesn't matter. It's history."

A memory slid to the front of my mind, unbidden. Hayden —a malicious grin on his face as he wrote the auditors on his last business trip and told them about an associate he'd discovered engaged in backroom deals. He'd had no reason to do that. The man's actions had no impact on him one way or another.

And he'd taken such joy in delivering the news anyway.

Was this who Fynn really was? What on earth had

happened between these two, to ruin everything so brutally? I knew better than anyone that love could be cruel, but this was beyond anything even I had endured.

But when I'd asked Fynn if I should free Sebastian, he'd said yes. He'd *meant* yes. And I hadn't sensed a trap—not with the agonized look on his face, as though it pained him to admit his own mistakes.

"But..." Sebastian trailed off, running a hand through his hair. He sighed. "Ah, I can't explain it. He's the one who caught me, but if I were ever in a true bind, it would be Fynn I turned to. Never trust him with a secret, but if you need help—he'll help." He laughed softly, the sound tainted with a bitter chord. "Maybe I'm just a fool. Forget it."

Huh.

I shuffled my feet, fingers clenching at my sides as I glanced over the water. If he was a fool, then that made two of us. Fynn had revealed who he was to me—*hunter*—and I still hadn't walked away. But at least I had my eyes wide open, this time. I knew what he was, and I knew what the Offering was allowed to have from him, and I wouldn't be led astray again so easily. I could take what I wanted without guilt, while guarding my back at the same time.

The squirming sensation in my gut rose, bringing with it unpleasant memories. Memories that called me out for the liar I was.

I could tell myself not to trust Fynn all I liked, but history dictated I wouldn't listen. I had a talent for believing the pretty lies of men who wanted me. That, or reaching greedily for things that couldn't be mine, inviting the kind of punishment that felt even worse than betrayal.

Three more nights. Just three more nights.

"Hmm," I said, keeping my voice to a lazy, unaffected drawl. "Sounds complicated."

A surprised snort escaped Sebastian as he glanced at me over his shoulder. "Speaking of complicated," he said, warmth infusing his tone. "Have you taken any solo expeditions through treacherous hidden pathways, yet?"

He meant the alleys, and he clearly thought I hadn't. I raised a brow. "As a matter of fact, I have." I lifted my bag, heavy with the book I'd stolen, and wiggled it.

His eyebrows shot up, the moonlight catching on the shock in his face and highlighting it as he froze mid step. "You're joking," he said.

"Unfortunately, no. Don't suppose you'll bust me out of faerie jail when Heillon catches me?"

I'd barely known what possessed me when I took it—only that my time was running out, and my knowledge was even more skint. If there really was a faerie jail, I'd just booked myself a cell.

Sebastian's mouth fell open and shocked, broken laughter escaped. For a long moment, he simply stared at me. Then, he shook his head, and this time when he met my gaze, there was something unreadable there. Something I'd never seen on him before. "'Fraid not. You'll need to be on someone like Fynn's good side for that. I'll put in a good word for you when they clamp you in irons."

Sebastian turned and took a step toward the shoreline. "We need to be in the water," he called over his shoulder, and then he began to pull off his shirt.

My lips parted.

"Oh, I see through your ploy," I called to him, my words echoing across the water, "Mr. Abs For Days. We're not all going to fall for it."

Shirtless, he turned and gave me a wicked grin. "Then stay on the bank for all I care, but if you want to learn how to summon the fae that will help you cross the bridge…"

He pulled the drawstring of his breeches—holding them up for a lingering second as he scanned my face in silent question. I didn't look away. He let go, and the breeches slid silkily off his body.

He was not wearing anything beneath.

I swallowed, fighting to keep my eyes fixed to his face as he backed shamelessly into the water.

"Then I suggest you join me."

Only half a second passed before I pulled the shirt over my head and dropped my breeches in a rush. The cool night air kissed my skin, making me shiver.

I wondered if I should leave my underclothes on, but there was nothing worse than getting out of a cold lake into sodden clothing. It wasn't a freezing night, but it certainly wasn't warm—barely warm enough to drip dry on the shore.

Making a disgusted sound, I stopped dithering, tugged my camisole off, and dropped my underwear on the pile. Then I strode quickly into the lake water.

Sebastian hadn't even turned, simply continuing his steady pace into the water. When it was at chest height, he stopped and faced me.

His eyes glinted as they fell to my breasts, just before those, too, slipped beneath the water. And then we were standing before each other, bodies gently swaying up and down with the ripples, half floating, half standing.

Through the cloud cover and the trees, a thin sliver of moonlight caught his face. It was almost as if he wasn't breaking the rules. Except, if anyone saw him, it would be obvious that the only way out of here was through shadow.

All they would need to do would be to keep watching, and they would see.

From the darkened clouds above us, I thought it might even rain soon, and then the last of the light would truly be gone.

"Is this where we say goodbye?" I asked when the silence felt too full, my voice steady even though my mind screamed.

Sebastian gave a low chuckle, his eyes darkening. "No, love, you'll know when it's time. Trust me." He winked, moving closer through the water. "I'm *really* good at goodbyes. The lingering hug, the honest confession of just how much I've loved our time together..."—his voice grew lower—"...the begging for just a few more minutes before you go."

My body shivered, and I caught my lip between my teeth, biting down the sound that threatened to escape.

"Am I the one begging, or are you?" I asked him, barely recognizing my own voice.

A wicked light appeared in his gaze. "That's for me to know, sweetheart. We have to keep some mystery, don't we? But make no mistake, someone will be." His eyes fell to my mouth. "Just because I can't keep you, doesn't mean I won't have you."

"You mean *I'll* have *you*," I interrupted.

Clearly caught by surprise, Sebastian's brow lifted, his expression shifting for a moment into open wonder.

In a rasping voice, he said, "Oh, we are going to have some fun, I promise you." He cleared his throat. "But for now... Now I'm going to show you how to summon a water sprite." He held up his hand, and a tiny spout of water spun above his finger. "Not one of the ones that migrated here, but one from across the bridge. It's their magic that enchants the water, allowing us to cross from one side to the other. They were the first to ever migrate to your land." He frowned, glancing toward the center of the lake. "Strange we haven't seen any from your side, actually. Even the sprites are absent." He shook his head and turned back.

I blinked at him, intrigued despite all the emotions churning through me. I'd always wondered why Criera lay across the water. "So, does their magic create portals or something?"

He glanced at me, the thin spout of water still spinning. "Basically," he said, tilting his head in agreement. "It creates pathways. Sometimes they're straightforward pathways from here to the place in front of you." He tilted his head toward the darkness of the forest. "Sometimes much, much further."

He lifted his other hand and the spout transferred from one finger to the other, but without leaving. Before my eyes, it became an archway; I stared, transfixed.

"You're going to tell me I have to create that, aren't you?" I said, lifting an eyebrow as I stared at his hands.

But Sebastian didn't know I could create magic. So why would he tell me to do it?

I trailed off, looking up to find his gaze fixed to mine.

"Not quite," he said. "Although, if you wanted to learn how to use human magic, I'd be all too happy to teach you."

My heart thudded. I hadn't realized it, but I'd been comparing Fynn and Sebastian in subtle ways. And one point in Fynn's favor was that he had shown me magic, while Sebastian had taken it away.

But here he was, proving that all I had to do was ask. With Sebastian, it seemed, all I ever had to do was ask.

"But in the interests of time," he continued. "I thought I could make you a few of these archways to take with you." His eyes slid away, and I thought I saw a flicker of something there —sadness or regret, I wasn't sure which. "That way, when you finally do reach the fae who'll take you safely to the other side..." He gave a wry smile, still staring down into the lake water. "Maybe then you'll think of me."

"I'll always think of you," I said without meaning to.

His head whipped up, eyes wide. The archway of water faltered, dripping into a half collapse before he caught it again.

Long moments passed, and this time when he looked away, it wasn't in sadness, but with an undercurrent of fire that was already beginning to blaze.

A jolt of regret ran through me as I remembered this was meant to be a goodbye. A clean, simple goodbye, where neither of us broke the rules we were bound to live by.

But before I could speak, he whispered a handful of words and then blew, and from his lips emerged a silvery pearl.

It hovered in the air, and as he twisted his hands, the spout of water shifted, flowed into the pearl, and disappeared. Breathless, I caught the pearl as it dropped before me.

Sebastian repeated the movement, somehow turning the simple action into an acrobatic performance. A twist of his hands, a twirl of water, an arch, a spout, a breath of air—and then a pearl.

He did it three times until I had three different archways.

And then he produced a thin silver chain from the air once more, water droplets rising to become metal links, and threaded the pearls onto it.

Wordlessly lifting my hair, I turned and let him settle the necklace around my neck. When it was done, his hands fell to my shoulders, resting there. The warmth of his body was a burning heat between us.

"When you're ready to cross," he said quietly, "simply trace the pearl through the air, and, when they arrive, step through the arch. Make sure you're at least within sight of a body of water when you do, and the water sprites will hear you."

"How can I repay you?" I asked quietly, knowing that I couldn't.

He huffed a laugh, the sound somehow transformed by the fact that I couldn't see him—it sounded harsher than it should have. Almost bitter. "You could tell me what that magic was that I sensed in you, before I go mad from hope," he muttered, clearly not believing that I could answer any such thing.

I froze.

I hadn't considered that such a small thing could have such devastating repercussions. That Sebastian might be clinging to false hope, all because of me. Abruptly, I couldn't bear it.

"It's an Open Bargain," I said before I could stop myself, the still water carrying my whispered words so it felt as though they surrounded us. "I have an Open Bargain with Fynn, as my entry to the circus."

Sebastian's hands tightened on my shoulders.

I felt his entire body stiffen with restraint, shudder with it, and I remembered in a heartbeat that while I knew he was good, and that he would only ever do what was right and true, he was still a Lumière. Something had drawn him to this troupe, to these fae, and no matter what he would choose, there was something in him that called to that darkness.

"You don't mean that," he said, the words so quiet I barely heard them.

"I do."

A rough sound erupted from him, but still he didn't move, didn't turn me to face him or drop his hands from my shoulders. It was as though we were frozen in time.

"I could have anything from you right now," he finally said, the words low, laced with both a faint air of disgust and a raw, trembling need. "Do you know that? Do you understand what you just gave me?"

"You could," I whispered, and I meant it in more ways than one, because I knew there was nothing he could ask for that I would not gladly give.

"I could tell you to run away with me," he continued, his voice a deep, thoughtful hum. "I could tell you to forget your human life. To be mine. To keep me company in the long years locked inside my tent, with my father lost for good." He swallowed, thumbs trailing back and forth over my shoulders. "Or I could tell you to leave now. To run the ends of this land until your feet bled. To find my father in his chains and free him. And you would do it gladly."

"I know," I whispered.

He let out a low, bitter laugh, and the dark atmosphere between us cracked. His hands fell from my shoulders.

"I would never do that, Bailey. How could you think it for a second?"

I turned in his arms, catching him by surprise. The twist of self-hatred was still evident on his face.

"Of course you won't," I said. "But I know that part of you wants to, not because you're cruel. Not because you're weak. But because you are alone."

His eyes widened. I kept going.

"You've been alone and trapped and forgotten for a very long time, and whatever we have here ends in two nights—as lost to you as your father will be if you don't find him."

Sebastian's jaw clenched. "If you think that, then what makes you so sure I won't claim the favor you just offered me and keep you anyway?"

I lifted my hand, resting it on his chest. Water beaded from my fingers, slipping away to drip into the lake surrounding us.

"Because I know who you are," I said, holding his gaze, "even if you have forgotten."

His breath caught. For just a moment, Sebastian's expression became something raw. Surprise flickered there, and I had the impression he was seeing me in a way he hadn't before now. A truth that, perhaps, he hadn't allowed himself to see.

Slowly, he leaned down, brushing his lips over mine. The touch barely registered, it was so soft.

Even as my heart beat with fire, a part of me remained cold, because I had meant what I said: I knew who he was, even through all he pretended to be. And I knew he only needed one reason to destroy everything that mattered to him.

His cruel punishment may have fed the darkness within him, but he was good. He would always choose to be good. To follow the rules. To do the right thing. Deliberate, calm, measured. Unless... the only person who would be harmed was himself.

Himself, and the nebulous memory of a father he already believed was doomed. And with everything I was offering him, with every step we took toward each other, I was giving him a reason to break those rules. I was giving him a reason to be trapped forever.

With all my careful planning, all my awareness that I had to be on my toes lest I do what I always do and choose the wrong man, I never once considered—I might be wrong for him.

And still, I didn't pull away. Because I was selfish. Because I was greedy. Because I *wanted*.

Sebastian's lips moved, brushing against mine as he murmured. "In payment then, tell me one thing. Tell me this is just for fun, and both of us can walk away unscathed when the moon rises in full."

I swallowed, heart hammering. "This is just for fun," I repeated back to him, my body shaking with the lie. "When the moon rises in full, both of us can walk away unscathed."

His brow furrowed, almost like despair. Then a moan crashed through him as he brought his hands to either side of my face and pulled me into a dark kiss.

CHAPTER 25

Bailey

WATER CHURNED AROUND US AS HIS HANDS SLID DEEPER INTO MY HAIR and our kiss became more urgent.

Every time I tried to come up for air, Sebastian followed me, kissing me again and again with a ferocity that bordered on desperation. It was terrifyingly easy to tip over into that and just go with it, to let his touch guide me and the tender embrace of his hands on my shoulders—then my waist, then my hips— draw me in.

It would be so easy to fall under this spell with him, which was why I shoved my hand between us, covering his mouth and leaning back.

"You can't," I said, breathless and weak, even to my own ears.

Sebastian raised an eyebrow. "I think if you give me a solid five or ten minutes, I'll show you that I very much can."

It was on the tip of my tongue to volley his joke back with another, to call him a one-pump chump and challenge him to last an hour or more. But I couldn't. I had to fight this urge and the growing sense of belonging I felt in his arms, or Sebastian would pay the price.

"If they find you like this..." I warned him.

Sebastian moved my hand away from his mouth, holding my wrist lightly as he swooped in and pressed a kiss along my neck, and then another—this time with teeth.

"They'll think: look at Sebastian go, maybe he isn't such a boring old bastard after all?" he suggested, lip quirking with amusement.

He reached for me again, and I held him back with a finger against his lips. "They'll think we've got him," I said, in the harshest, darkest voice I could muster.

It wasn't half bad, given how much I regretted that I couldn't have even this. This one small moment with him.

I could see his answer forming; it was practically on the tip of his tongue. He was ready to say 'fuck the lot of them', no matter if they caught him. He loved the risk of danger.

But then he looked at me properly, and the amusement fell away.

"Is this about me or you?" he asked slowly, the touch of his hands softening to become more reassuring than desperate. His thumbs stroked a line back and forth over my hip, as the water lapped at our necks.

"Both," I said, my voice catching. "You can't risk them seeing you here, Sebastian. Not for something so..." I bit back all the words I wanted to say, and instead said, "fleeting."

He stared at me for a long, long moment. And then, it was as though a light came on behind his eyes. Something visibly shifted.

"Well," he said, and just that one word sent shivers down my spine. "Perhaps we'd better go somewhere a little more discreet."

Before I could say a word, he scooped his arm around my waist, pulled me to him and dropped.

The world fell away, and we sank like a stone—not to the

ground that had been beneath us but sideways. Deeper, toward the center of the lake. I spluttered for air, desperate and choking. But just as it got to the point where I couldn't bear it any longer, the water slid away.

I stared up at Sebastian, who lay braced over the top of me. Dark ringlets dripped water onto my face as he grinned.

I looked over his shoulder. The air in the distance shimmered strangely, swirling and undulating. My lips parted in shock; it wasn't air. It was water.

We were in the center of the lake, caught in a bubble of air. Completely private.

Completely hidden.

I looked back at Sebastian and found him watching me, waiting. The urgency was still there, but it simmered this time —embers in a carefully stoked fire.

Controlled. Waiting. Dormant.

"It's just fun, Bailey," he repeated, his expression oddly shuttered this time. "Where's the harm in enjoying this when —" He broke off, his gaze trailing over my face and then lower, catching on my lips, the hollow of my throat. He reached out to trace the same path with his fingers, pausing just above my breast.

I realized abruptly that we were both completely naked, and no longer hidden by the water.

"It's been so long for either of us," he murmured. "So long since we had any joy or affection."

He returned his gaze to me, and I heard the echo of the word that he didn't say. The word he wouldn't say, and neither would I.

"So long," I repeated.

And I wasn't even embarrassed to hear the deep pit of yearning open up within that one phrase.

Because it *had* been so long. Six moons since Hayden, and a lifetime before that. Long lonely years before, after, and even with him. When had I ever had what Sebastian promised me? Just simple attraction. Mystery. Affection.

Love.

It didn't have to be true love, or lasting love. I wasn't asking for a fairytale or a happily ever after; I knew they could never be mine. But, *gods*, I just wanted someone to care. I wanted someone to *want* like I did, and to not throw me into the trash as soon as it was over. To say goodbye like I still mattered, even if they wouldn't keep me.

My breath caught, and I felt the corners of my eyes growing embarrassingly warm, and so before I could lose whatever impression of stability I'd given him so far, I grabbed Sebastian by the back of the neck and pulled him into me.

He met my kiss with a groan, lips parting. My hands fell, lowering from their subconscious position of defense to rest on Sebastian's hips and hold him against me. Without words, his body answered my silent plea; he rocked between my thighs, a low sound dropping from his mouth. It was a sound I'd almost heard from him before, at the caravans and in the hidden alcoves of the Lumière, but I'd never heard it like this.

He hadn't allowed himself to give this much before. To be as loud, as unfettered. But below the surface of the lake, hidden from all watching eyes, Sebastian could finally let his guard down.

Nobody would find us here.

Nobody would interrupt or see that he was shrouded in darkness instead of moonlight. And it *was* darkness. This far down, the lake was a murky cave of shadows, lit only by a few tiny balls of faelight that Sebastian had conjured. They bobbed in the water outside of our little bubble, flowing back and forth with the current as dark shapes swam past our covert sanctuary.

I tilted my head, looking out into the shadowy depths as Sebastian licked a line from the hollow of my throat up to my ear. You couldn't see much beyond the first couple of feet. Plants drifted back and forth on the lakebed, and clusters of rocks transformed the silt into a series of cliffs and valleys rather than a flat, open plain. But every now and then I could see within some of those dark shapes the buggy eyes of a fish. And once, for an unnerving, terrifying second, the far more haunting and intelligent gaze of a creature I didn't recognize.

"Ignore them," Sebastian murmured into my ear, tilting my head back toward him with one finger placed against my chin. "This is where they live. We must trust them to be polite."

"Can I trust *you* to be polite?" I asked tartly in response.

He laughed, the sound oddly intimate in our tiny bubble, and leaned down to bite my lower lip. "That, my dear Bailey, depends entirely on what you want from me."

What I wanted from him...

Of its own volition, my mind returned to our first meeting, and those little silvery ropes that had wrapped all around his body.

Yes, I wanted that, but perhaps not here. Perhaps that was for another time.

I forcibly ignored the voice that piped up and asked me what the hell I was doing, imagining another time when everything we'd said had been clear: this would be it. We had two nights, and no more.

So what did I want from him? The question haunted me. Gnawed at me as he pressed soft, sweet kisses down my breast, over my hips. As he parted my legs and licked a teasing swipe on the inside of my thigh, close enough to taste me but nowhere near close enough at all.

I realized what I wanted from him.

"I want you to break those rules you so desperately wish to

shatter," I whispered, feeling him grow still. "You can't break them up there, you mustn't, but down here it's just you and me. So I want you to let go and be who you really are."

I looked down at him, where he lay braced over my hips, his expression shadowed by the hair that fell over his eyes. For a second, a spike of fear shot through me—had I misjudged him? If I said those words to Fynn, I had no doubt that danger would hover between every breath, but that wasn't what I expected from Sebastian. Unless I'd been painfully wrong.

But then he swept the hair from his face, leaning his chin on one hand propped by my waist, and looked up at me. There was an expression of such hesitant joy on his face that every one of my screaming questions fell silent. My whole body fell silent, waiting for him to speak.

"Break the rules, you say?" he asked me, mouth curving into a wicked grin. "But there are no rules down here." He arched a brow. "Which means we'll have to make some."

Suddenly, he grabbed me by the hips and spun us, rolling back into the wet sand and pebbles, so that I was braced over him with one knee on either side of his waist.

But he didn't let me settle. Before the shock had even passed, he'd pinched me on the ass, making me squeal and shuffle forward.

"Higher," he said, grinning and giving me a sharp smack on the other cheek.

"Oh, you little ass," I said, inching forward a little further.

He smacked me again, so I reached down to flick one of his nipples. "Use your words."

"Oh, but Bailey," he said, voice darkening as he slid his hands over my hips and thighs and tugged me higher still. "I don't intend to be able to speak at all."

With a final hitch, he brought me up until one knee was on

either side of his face. I gaped down at him. The only possible description of his expression was smug, self-satisfied male.

"If these are your ideas of rules," I said, forcing my voice to strengthen from the breathless, weak thing that wanted to appear into something more assured. "I'll have to reevaluate my opinion of you as a rule breaker."

I put my hands on my hips, fighting back a shiver as he idly traced his fingers back and forth between my legs, brushing over my clit just enough for me to know he was there, and not enough to do anything more.

"Oh, I'm not going to be the rule breaker," he said lightly.

Minutes had passed, and still his expression was completely transformed to what it would be above the surface. Gone were the darkness and shadows. The second I told him to let himself free, there was only joy.

"You are," he finished, and then he ran his hands up the side of my body, capturing my arms and guiding them above my head.

From this height, my fingers just skimmed the edge of the bubble, dipping into the water that flowed above it. It was the strangest sensation, like trailing my hands through a bath, except the bath was above me.

I gasped and pulled them free, but he shook his head with mock disapproval. "You have to keep them there," he said, and then he dipped his head to lick a single swipe over my pussy.

My lips parted on a strangled inhale, and I nearly pulled my hands down again but stopped at the last moment.

"Why?" I breathed.

"Because I said so," he said, warm air brushing over me.

He noticed me shiver at the touch and blew deliberately this time. My eyes rolled back in my head, back arching as I moaned.

"You'll kill me like this," I protested.

"What a shame," he said, his gaze roaming my body again. "I rather like you."

This time, he flicked his tongue in a fast pulse over my clit. My body went rigid with pleasure, desire coursing through me in time with every lick.

Then, I came to the faintly horrified realization that, to keep my hands above me like this, I would not be able to move.

"What happens if I don't?" I asked breathlessly.

"Then when I make you come, you'll *thank me* for the privilege," he said, and while his words were still in that light, joyful tone, his eyes held just a hint of that same darkness he'd shown me on the surface, where I'd already offered him one favor.

I shivered, knowing that I was perfectly safe, even if he did ensnare me. And knowing, too, that the fun of this moment together had nothing to do with safety.

I stretched my hands above me, sinking them deeper into the water and arching my back. Sebastian moaned in appreciation, reaching up to brush his fingers over one of my nipples. I writhed beneath his touch, never letting my hands slip free.

And then he began to kiss me.

His lips caressed me, teasing and taunting, as if it was my mouth he was exploring—tasting me almost sweetly. His tongue plunged into me, and I braced myself, body rigid, every nerve on fire, as he licked me fully from core to clit.

I was right, I thought as he flicked his tongue over me—fast little kitten licks that already had me soaring far higher than I thought possible. Hidden within Sebastian was a side of him that had not been allowed to emerge in a very long time. A side filled with joy and harmless danger, filled with challenge and fire; and gods, he wanted to let that part of himself free.

I got that. I really, really got that.

But apart from here, in this rare moment of privacy, I couldn't let him, because I knew that he would regret it. I knew that if he was thinking clearly, if he wasn't already on the brink of collapse after spending so many years simply surviving the Lumière's taunts, then he would never risk losing his father like this.

And that was my last conscious thought as Sebastian slid one finger over me and slipped it inside. He followed it with a second, curving them upward as he sucked and tasted. I writhed over him, and the pressure to keep my hands in the air was abruptly too much.

The water lapped at my palms—a delicious, anchoring coldness. I wondered if I should just pull them free, bring my hands to my side, and shout his name in a prayer of gratitude as I came. Then I could see what sort of Bargain he'd trap me in. What other things he might delight in making me do.

I felt the pleasure rise within me, building like a tide, crashing against my body until I was drowning in it. My breath came in tiny whimpers, my fingers clasping into the water, seeking a hold on solid ground that I wouldn't find. I rose to my knees, riding his mouth, feeling his lips curve in delight.

I dropped my hands.

He clenched my hips, fingers driving into my skin hard enough to bruise. I wrapped my palms over his, holding him there as I rocked back and forth.

A lifetime passed before I shattered.

Wave after wave of pleasure coursed through me, my eyes snapping open as I stared out into the twinkling light of the dark lake. Ripples of water surrounded our protective bubble until it was like I was drowning inside and out, pleasure hitting me, consuming me, while all around us a whirlpool of water ebbed and flowed. As I came down slowly from the high, I did as I had promised, thanking him over and over.

Within our bubble of air, I felt another kind of pressure take over. The pressure of a Bargain, and the magic that bound it.

As I slid down to sit over his hips, he rose, holding me there with one arm around my waist as I slumped against his chest. My body shook, and I swore I could feel tiny shivers running through Sebastian as well.

"What will you have from me?" I asked, my lips pressing into his chest as I spoke.

Sebastian traced soothing circles over my back. I felt the curve of his smile against my hair, and when he spoke, I could hear the wicked edge within it.

"Tell me what you really want," he murmured. "That secret I can see in your eyes."

I started to laugh, thinking I was about to magically confess my dream of the silver ropes. But then... I thought of another secret.

And of the two of them, I knew which one was more powerful. I knew which one the magic would choose.

My body stiffened, and I felt Sebastian's tender touch grow still in response. "Hey," he said softly, drawing me back so we faced one another. "You don't have to—I take it back, I—"

"I want you to tell me what you see in me."

His breath caught, and inwardly, my heart shattered. I knew what he saw in me: the only thing he *could* see in me, because I was the Offering. Not special, by design. Mediocre. Boring. Cold. And yet, my body believed his, and my mind had been fooled in the process. I believed that he saw something wonderful in me. I believed it just enough to ask for it. And I was about to be destroyed for that belief.

But then he spoke, and although his words were gentle, kind, and true, they flayed me in another way completely.

"I see a woman who has been hurt so much and for so long that she's closed herself off from any hope of happiness," he said, lips moving against my shoulder. He lifted them to my neck. "I see a woman who has been made to believe she's nothing, and that her place is the shadows and the silence." He met my lips, barely brushing mine as he spoke. "I see a woman who is so tangled up in their lies and hatred that she can't see the truth: that she is brave and strong and kind. And that, one day, somebody out there is going to love her so much that he never lets her go." He pulled back a fraction, the corner of his mouth giving a wry twitch. "That he would risk everything just to see her smile. Because that's what she's worth."

A shiver ran through me. I couldn't look at him; I kept my eyes tightly shut as he kissed me, sinking into his touch and believing that as I fought to believe his words as well. Impossible words that couldn't be true. Not only because it was me, and I was ostensibly less than he described. But because if what he said was true, then I had damned my village to Hell. And a brave, strong, kind woman would never do such a thing.

It was a perfect paradox, but down here, where no one could see us, I believed.

Sebastian shifted in the sand, his hands cupping my thighs as he pulled me closer to him. His hard length pressed against me. I lifted my chin, my gaze meeting his as he claimed another soft, slow kiss and threaded his fingers through my hair.

"Up for round two?" he asked.

"Yes," I breathed without hesitation.

It was slower this time. Sebastian whispered some kind of spell—presumably for protection—and I felt a shiver of magic wash over me. Then he lifted me just enough to position himself at my entrance and lowered me back down, sliding inside.

We stayed as we were, with me above him as I'd been moments before, and him holding me with one arm around my waist. Braced backward on one hand, he rocked slowly up into me.

I clutched his shoulders, holding on for the ride, still feeling languid with pleasure from before. But as the slick slide of him continued, relentless, it became too hard to hold back. Soon, I was kissing him with the same urgency that he'd shown me ever since this night began.

For his part, Sebastian seemed almost destroyed from this simple touch alone. His eyes fluttered closed, his lips parting on rough moans. He succumbed to every touch I gave him, every eager pull and kiss and nip. He wanted it all, melting into me, and I gladly gave it.

Then his eyes snapped open, and he fell back onto the sand, hands clasping my hips as he held me in place and thrust up into me. I braced my hands on his knees behind me as he slid his feet up to brace, flat, on the sand. The angle was perfect, his hips driving up with a punishing force. A beautiful flush rose along his chest and up his neck, and he wouldn't take his eyes from my face.

The joy hadn't faded, the darkness hadn't reappeared, but there was a hint of some kind of desperate edge there. Something almost bordering on despair.

A shiver raced through me, and it should have been marked by dread, because I knew what that look was. It was the same thing I felt rising in my own chest, the same inevitability. The same thing we'd sworn wouldn't happen.

But it wasn't despair that I felt. It was pleasure, need, desire. They flooded through me in equal measure, filling me as I rose above him and felt myself shatter and crest.

It didn't take long before Sebastian, too, was stilling, body rigid as he moaned his release, gripped me tight, and drew me down for one final, hopeless kiss.

He didn't let me go for a very long time.

After, we rose to the surface again and dressed quickly in the shadows. I stepped into his embrace, tracing a hand over the shadow of his jaw and kissing him. My heart beat erratically. I didn't know what this was anymore. Didn't know whether to admit, either to myself or out loud, what I thought had changed, or whether to stay in the safety of the lie.

I moved to pull back, to say goodbye, but he stopped me with a hand on my wrist. I looked at the open expression on his face. He still hadn't quite recaptured all the walls that he needed up here. All the careful rules he had to follow.

Fear skittered through me at the thought. "You can't," I said, shaking my head, forcing him to pay attention. "You only have two nights left to find him—" I broke off, the words dying in my throat.

As the hope faded in his eyes, he looked away. "I know." He paused, as if steeling himself, and then gave a wry laugh. "Speaking of—I'm due an update. My allies are reaching out tonight, to share what they've found. I wish I could search with them, but..." He shrugged. "These stolen moments with you are all I can spare outside the boundaries, and they certainly aren't long enough to search one end of this land to the other for a man who could be chained in all manner of ways." He swallowed. "Before I meet them, I should make an appearance back at camp. The Masters check on me regularly, and if they see I'm not there..."

"I know," I pressed, "which is why you have to—" I took a breath. "You have to let me go."

He looked at me then, eyes glinting sharply as he said, "And what if I can't?"

The moment stretched between us. I found I was shaking my head over and over.

"You said I was a mystery," I told him, the words tearing through me. "What will you do when the mystery is solved?

This is a good thing. When you know me inside and out, you'll get bored. You'll feel trapped."

The words were like knives now, ripping through me as I remembered all the things Hayden had thrown in my face. All the ways he'd reminded me who and what the Offering was. I laughed bitterly.

"This is a good thing," I repeated. "It's a good thing we can't last, because then we never have to see what that looks like."

I moved to leave again, but this time he pulled me to him, fiercer now than I'd ever seen before. He lifted a hand to gently trace the angles of my face, as if committing them to memory.

"Mysteries aren't meant to be solved, Bailey. They're meant to be explored." My breath caught, his words surrounding me until they were all I could feel. "I know I can't keep you, but I don't know how I can walk away." His fingers paused at my lips. "How can I say goodbye when I have a hundred more ways to make you smile?"

Against my better judgment, I smiled. A real smile, like only he had ever given me.

His eyes darkened, becoming oh so serious. "It's rare to feel hope in the way you do. Trust me. I've seen the worst of the fae, and in all the secrets you haven't shared with me, I suspect you've seen the worst of your own kind, too. And still, you manage to find beauty in things that have sent me to my knees in despair."

He gave an incredulous laugh—a small huff of a thing.

"You sneak into our hidden alleys, and steal from our archives, and make devastating Open Bargains with fae you've only just met. My father would call it brash and foolish, but that's not what I see. You've given me hope when I had none left—reminded me that there's always a way forward, and it doesn't have to be the way they choose for us. We don't *have* to do what they say."

A shocked expression crossed his face, and he fell quiet suddenly, struck by realization. Fear spiked within me, and all of a sudden I didn't want him to say it, didn't want him to speak the words that I knew were coming.

But I couldn't bring myself to stop him, because I couldn't change who I was. What I wanted.

"I think I'm falling for you," he said, and I drank in every gods damned word.

Was it a memory echoing through my mind, or did I hear thunder cracking in the distance? Was the sulfur I smelled real, or only a nightmare given life by the strength of my fear?

Was my village already burning?

I reached for a necklace that wasn't there to warn me, and found only heated, damp skin. There was nothing left to warn me, no one to help me. Should I have seen this coming? I'd thought I calculated it perfectly, even accounting for both Fynn and Sebastian. Five nights of fun, of seizing the life I wanted before I left Aelor behind... It should have been safe—except for this. Never in a hundred years would I have imagined one of them would want to keep me.

The Oath would never allow such a promise.

"Stay with me tonight," he begged.

I couldn't have this. I wasn't allowed this. Just one word, and it would all stop. Everything would go back to how it should be.

I couldn't bring myself to say it.

"What about when they check on you?"

"Screw the lot of them," he snarled, flaunting the rules like they were nothing. Like he wasn't risking anything more than a warning. "Stay with me anyway."

His conviction broke through the fog of need.

"No," I said, and with more strength than I thought I was capable of, I stepped out of his arms. "Not tonight. I need to think. I—" My expression twitched, emotion clawing free in a way it never had before. "I told you from the beginning, I won't do this. I know how it ends. I know what I'm allowed, what I deserve, and it isn't this."

But gods, what if it could be? What if there was another way?

When I spoke again, my voice cracked. "Just let me think."

Sebastian's face fell, but he didn't follow me. Didn't force anything. With one final look over my shoulder, I stepped onto the path and all but ran from the clearing.

I'd barely made it free when there was a sound in the forest beside me. Fear rose, the acrid scent thick on my tongue as I thought of the lora beast. Of the eyes I'd seen at the bottom of the lake.

I whirled, and for a second I thought I saw a flame-filled gaze staring at me from the shadows, but then he stepped free and it was only Fynn. My heart pounded so hard, I thought he must be able to hear it, because behind him, shrouded in shadow but still so easy to see, stood Sebastian.

Sebastian stared at us. The whites of his eyes were visible through his fear, and he didn't dare move, didn't dare make a sound lest Fynn turn and see him.

Fynn took another step closer. His back was to Sebastian, his gaze fixed on me, and all I could think was that he couldn't turn. I couldn't let him turn, or he'd trap Sebastian forever. The Bargain would be eternal.

"What are you doing out here on a night like this?" Fynn tilted his head, all shadows and secrets.

I stammered, searching for an answer. My body still sung from Sebastian's touch. His words still ricocheted through me, taunting me with everything I wanted and could never have— not with all that stood between us.

"A moonlit stroll," I said, the words somehow remaining steady.

Fynn cocked an eyebrow, eyes dark, and for a moment I swore he knew exactly what was happening. Knew exactly who stood behind him.

"What strange fancies you have," he said. He stuck his hands in his pockets and straightened. "While you're here, I should tell you that the clock is ticking. You have only until tomorrow night to pay for your ticket."

My pulse stuttered, and I tasted ash. Would he demand I pay now? Should I even pay it at all, when Sebastian had given me another path across the water?

But I didn't yet know if the water sprites would answer.

"What... What is the payment?"

His mouth curved in a smile. "Something I know you can afford, don't worry." He took a step toward me, eyes roaming my body as if he could see every lingering imprint of Sebastian's touch. But he didn't call us out. When his eyes returned to mine, he merely said, "Until tomorrow."

And then he strode past me and back along the path, never once turning to look behind him.

CHAPTER 26

Bailey

Noise washed over and around me. Sadey and Christine were deep in conversation, chattering and passing tiny plates back and forth, while Ella and Hannah—heavily pregnant and glowing with it—reclined by the river bend near our table and sipped chilled tea from patterned glasses. My own glass was already warm from the palm of my hand, the ice within it almost gone and the drink untouched as I stared vaguely into the distance. My thoughts were with Sebastian, twelve feet below the surface of the lake.

What was I doing with my life?

This was meant to be an easy way out. Find an escape that constitutes 'lost', so the Offering Oath is fulfilled, leave this place behind, and find a modest life over the water. But there was nothing modest about what had happened with Sebastian last night. Worse: I didn't want there to be.

There had been no sign of hellfire when I returned to my village, but that didn't mean it wasn't waiting in the shadows, ready to pounce the second I took too much. The Oath had never let me get away with having anything beautiful before, and Sebastian was the most beautiful thing I'd ever held.

Restless, my fingers tapped back and forth on the slippery glass. I took a sip for something to do. How long would I have to stay here to be polite? I hadn't realized they were planning something today. Sadey had shown up at my door first thing, picnic basket in hand, and told me I had three minutes to get changed into decent walking trousers and boots before we were all leaving for lunch.

My body had still burned from Sebastian's touch.

"We couldn't even find you last night," she had called after me when, after a few moments of blank staring, I had hurried off to my bedroom to get changed. "One minute you were in the distance and next, *poof*, you were just gone. And don't think we didn't see that gorgeous man you were with. Well…" She laughed airily. "I shouldn't say 'man' at all, should I? We want all the details and we want to actually see you this time, Bailey. Somewhere you can't run away."

Her words had floated through me, much like their conversation did now, leaving my body strangely ringing and numb. Which man had they seen, and would I survive the conversation about him?

But if I hadn't agreed to come, it would have been considered a snub. I couldn't afford to upset anyone right now; what if it ignited the magic of the Offering to punish me? I was already balancing on a knife's edge, poised between punishment and obliteration.

But every second I spent sitting here was a precious, wasted second of research that I would never get back. I only had a handful of hours left to master the magic and the knowledge both Fynn and Sebastian had shared with me. Only a handful of hours to wrap my head around the dangerous, terrifying unknown of Criera.

There was nothing for me here, with these people who had never wanted me and never would.

I set my glass down on the picnic table with a firm thud and straightened. "I—" I began.

Ella paused mid sentence, her timid voice making me stumble and flush as I realized she'd already been speaking—to me. I'd talked over her without even realizing.

"Sorry," I said calmly, smoothing the stutter from my voice with ease. "What did you say?"

"I said," Ella repeated, a strange smile on her lips. "Who is the mysterious blond?"

Blond... So it was Fynn they'd seen me with. But where?

My heart sank as I realized there was only one place she could have: by the caravans.

"Oh, he's just one of the ushers. He wanted to know if I would come to the next show," I said airily, waving my hand.

Ella looked skeptical, and if I hadn't convinced Ella then I was in deep shit. She took everyone in good faith. Deeper still, because then Sadey leaned over, an odd light glittering in her eyes.

"You are lying," she said triumphantly, sticking her finger in my face. "Do you know how I know? Because I've been learning how to read lips."

Huh. This was either about to get really funny, or really bad.

"Oh?" I said, stalling for time by plucking a grape and popping it in my mouth.

As I did, I noticed that Hannah was watching me shrewdly, her eyes narrowed. They had been since I first sat down, now that I thought about it. I hadn't paid much attention, assuming the scowl on her face was to do with discomfort or nausea, but no—it was definitely directed at me.

"And I think what you said to your pretty blond fellow was that you didn't know which to choose," Sadey finished with another triumphant stab of her finger.

Suddenly, all eyes were on me. The fact that this was almost exactly what I had said was disconcerting to say the least. The fact that I'd said it with the echo of Sebastian's fingers inside me was far worse.

"Yes," I said slowly. "He was asking me which show I would choose." If I doubled down, would I dig the hole deeper or escape?

Sadey's lips curled into an unattractive smile. "No, he wasn't. I think he was asking you something personal, and I think he's waiting very carefully for your answer."

"What could he possibly want from me?" I asked after a beat, playing it off with a laugh even though my heart pounded like a mallet. "A five star review on the town notice board? My highly qualified human opinion on the electrifying acts performed by the fae illusionists?" I plucked another grape. "Sadey, I hope you haven't been paying too much for those lip reading lessons."

My stomach sank when the triumph in her expression didn't fade.

"No." She shook her head slowly. "Because I didn't actually see it, sorry. Hannah was standing around the corner, near enough to hear."

My body stiffened, my hand poised halfway to my mouth with another grape. I looked at Hannah again, and there it was once more—that tight, flinty look of... I froze.

Hatred.

It was hatred.

"You're toying with him," Hannah accused me. "Because you just can't stop, can you?"

The world felt like it was closing in, and all I could do was swallow and pretend I didn't notice. Pretend the faces of my friends hadn't transformed into those of hungry wolves. How much had they seen? What did they know?

Sadey chimed in again, and her words rang like a death

knell. "You disappeared into the shadows with one man," she said, very slowly and deliberately. "And came out with another."

It wasn't even technically true. I'd gone in alone, and come out alone, and the rest had just happened. But they were right in every way that mattered.

"It's not like that," I said, and I didn't need a mirror to know my face looked like stone.

Sadey's eyes narrowed, scanning my still expression with a faint sneer of her lip. I'd never seen her look at me like that before. "You actually lied to us. Hannah told me to pretend we weren't sure, just to see if you would try to conceal it, but I didn't believe you would." She reeled back, as if she couldn't get far enough away from me. "We're your friends, Bailey. And when you saw us in the fairground, you practically ran the other way!"

My eyes widened faintly. So that was how they had found me; they'd noticed I ignored them, and Hannah had followed close enough to eavesdrop.

"I didn't run from you," I said, holding myself tall and forcing my restless fingers to still. "I was busy."

Christine made a rude noise. I stared at her in shock.

"You did," she said, in a voice I'd never heard from her. "You turned right around and left. All to go and play with two deadly fae, who would love nothing more than to ensnare the lot of us in a cursed Bargain."

"Do they even know you're the Offering?" Hannah asked acidly.

All my protests died on my lips; so that was what this was about. The worst part was, I couldn't argue it, even if I did have the words. They'd be a lie.

I tried anyway. "I'm not doing anything I shouldn't," I

insisted. "When the fae leave, I'll never see them again. It's not like I'm taking something from anyone else."

A note of pleading almost entered my voice. I didn't let it. It would be more vulnerability than I had ever shown them.

"Except that you did," Hannah said, her words spitting out like venom. "Anitha told me that you were the acrobat's assistant on the first night, when it was meant to be her. And then again two nights after, when you disappeared with him." Her scowl deepened. "Are you fucking them both, or are you playing them off each other like you did to Hayden and Michel?"

I couldn't breathe, couldn't think. I knew that most of the village believed the lies that Hayden had spread. Of course they did; I was the Offering, and it fitted. But for Hannah to believe them as well... She wasn't my close friend, but she was close enough.

An unfamiliar pit of dark, deadly emotion opened up in my stomach. It was hot and raw. I wanted to scream. I wanted to lurch myself across the picnic rug, hands wrapped tight around her throat.

The second the thought hit me, I reeled back as if I'd actually done it, horrified that I would think to harm not only one of my friends, but a pregnant woman at that. I didn't want to hurt them. No—I didn't want to *want to* hurt them.

But for just a second, the rage had burned so bright.

I squeezed my hands tight, plucking reflexively at the paper napkin beneath my glass and trying to steady myself. I tried to let the ugliness wash over me, so I could see what was truly beneath it. Hannah was upset. She thought I'd done something wrong—something cruel that would have repercussions for the whole village—and she was standing up against it. That should be praised. It should be rewarded.

I just had to find a way to make them understand. They

needed to know it wasn't like that; no one was going to lose here except me.

"Sebastian and Fynn," I began, but I was interrupted by a gasp from Sadey.

"So it's true."

When I looked at the face of my oldest friend, I found her lip curled in disgust.

"Have you learned nothing?" she said.

It felt like a slap. Like a burning, painful slap to the face, and I couldn't move. Couldn't even breathe as the words kept pouring out of her mouth.

"We wanted to help you, Bailey. We thought you were tricked by the fae, and they were manipulating the Offering to abandon her Oath. But you're choosing this. You're choosing to play with people's hearts again, like they don't matter. Like they're nothing." Her voice choked with emotion. "And you're damning us all while you have your fun."

I gaped at her soundlessly, until finally, dreadfully, words did spill free. Unfortunately, they were the wrong ones, stuck in the pain of a past I couldn't escape, no matter how far I ran.

"What about my heart?" I snapped. "You're all so quick to believe *him*. What about me? What about your friend? Do you actually think that's what happened with Hayden? I never—"

"Katerina's our friend, too," Hannah insisted, cutting me off. "And before you ask, she saw you last night as well, and came to the exact same conclusions."

The words were like a spear of ice, straight through my heart. I realized with a sick jolt that Katerina must have been the friend who Bargained for their entry; that was why Sadey had been so shifty about it.

"She told us the truth, back then," Hannah went on. "That you'd seen how Hayden looked at her and swooped in because you can't stand to see any of us happy. And then you weren't content, even with that. You had to toy with Michel, too."

I never did. I never toyed with him. He just looked at me, and I liked it.

I wanted to scream at her: anyone can look at you. *Anyone*. But no one looks at me, and when Michel had... I couldn't help but smile back.

Instead, I didn't say a thing. My face was stone, and when Hannah's gaze roamed my expression, whatever she saw there made her sneer.

She leaned forward. "You could give our whole village a good life, Bailey, if you just stopped being so selfish, but instead you'll damn us to Hell just because you can."

"I didn't—" I began.

"Have you even looked at the Oath recently, like you promised you would after Hayden?" Ella asked softly.

Oh. The rage burning inside me died with a fizzle. They had planned this. There was a reason they'd arranged lunch by the town center. A reason they'd cornered me and lulled me into a sense of safety. Because I had a responsibility, and they intended to make sure I kept it.

Slowly, I stood. One by one, each of them softened in relief.

"I'll just do that now, shall I?"

They rose to follow, filing after me one by one as I climbed the steps to the town hall, where we kept our most historical Bargains on display. The silence of the hall was overpowering. It sank deep into my bones, where the hum of dread was rising. Behind me, I felt every one of my friends' footsteps as they trailed in. Making sure, no doubt, that I did what I had promised.

The caretaker watched us curiously, looking up from the worn soft-cover novel she was reading behind the desk, where volunteers sat to take deliveries and help visitors. She didn't speak to us—I didn't know her by name—but her beady stare was familiar enough. She knew who I was, and would take note of why I was here.

The string of illnesses Master Skylark was treating returned to the forefront of my mind. Were they really that serious?

Was it really my fault?

I swallowed and came to a halt at the foot of a small alcove. Two wooden steps led the way up to a display case and a small plaque. Around the walls were dotted various newspaper articles describing terrible events that had occurred whenever an Offering tried to seize fortune for themselves. Fires, floods. One memorable time, a plague that nearly wiped out the village.

In all the years since the first Bargain, though, the town had never descended into Hell—because there was always someone to put an end to the Offering's greed before they went too far.

I wasn't sure the last time I'd visited here. Certainly not since I was an adult. I remembered clutching my mother's hand, Katerina on her other side, and listening solemnly to the honor and responsibility of my role. Listening to my mother explain how me and my sister could be considered scales, swaying on the balance of our village's health.

She told me that I would always know I was fulfilling my oath if I turned to my sister and found her prosperous and healthy. That my sister would look out for me and make sure I was both protected and content—humbly satisfied—until the day a new child was born to take my place. She conveniently left out that this would only happen when I died or vanished to ill fate, but at the time, I hadn't cared. I felt honored to play such a role. To help the people I loved by being selfless and sensitive to their every need.

I couldn't remember when I stopped feeling that way, but I could admit to myself now: it was long before I met Hayden.

Perhaps I'd never truly been selfless at all; I'd always wanted far more than I deserved.

I swallowed and scanned the room, not yet ready to face the glass sphere that controlled my destiny. My eyes fell on the small ledger that lay open on a pedestal at the foot of the alcove. Several events were recorded in a shaky hand—omens, tracked to ensure that the Offering was kept in line well before danger struck.

The list was longer than I had ever seen it. I scanned it, finding everything Master Skylark had mentioned and more. Illness spreading through the village. Money troubles. Poor grades in the elementary school.

At the bottom, someone had written in large, hasty letters about a crack that had opened up near the well, reeking of sulfur. It was underlined.

Someone shifted restlessly behind me, their foot scraping along the floorboards. Like awakening from a dream, I blinked rapidly. Then, I climbed the stairs.

The orb was exactly as I remembered it. Slightly larger than the usual Bargains, and the flame within was paler—evidence of its age and power. As I leaned in close to study it, I breathed out a sigh of relief.

The Oath written into the plaque was intact, and the flame shone as brightly as ever. Beneath a series of strange symbols were familiar words.

I swear to always and forever uphold the lives and fortunes of my neighbors. To fill of their cup from my own, to replenish their plate from mine, and to trust and submit to their kindness and mercy. The joy of many will outshine the greed of one, and with the scales in perpetual balance, our village shall prosper. Always and Forever.

. . .

I ran my fingertips over the plaque, tracing the symbols. I'd seen three of them in the book Heillon chose, but as I stared at them now, I realized something else about them. About one symbol in particular, and why it had looked so familiar.

If you turned it sideways, it matched the symbol of the soul eater—the one that was warned about in Master Skylark's book.

I shuddered, stepping away from it. I must be misremembering, seeing omens where there were none. And, truly, there were no bad omens here—because the plaque containing my oath was completely, irrefutably, whole.

Legend said that if the Offering were ever to become an oath-breaker, the plaque would crack, but it was whole. Nothing I had done had damaged the magic protecting the village.

I began to turn, so I could let the others know and then escape, but a flicker of familiar power caught my attention. I frowned and tilted my head, unfocusing my eyes so I could see within the flame.

It didn't feel right.

Or, more correctly, it didn't feel fae.

I knelt before the display case, pressing my nose right up to the glass. I recognized this feeling—it was the same one that Fynn had shown me inside Merelda. Indicating a curse, or perhaps something trapped.

My heart kicked up rapidly. Had the Oath become tainted over time? There should be no human magic here, and yet it was all I could sense.

Without questioning it, I reached for my connection to the magic. It took a moment, being so far from the forest, and it was weak. But with care and patience, I wove that thread around my finger, twisting it in the air as if I were fidgeting while thinking.

"Bailey?" Sadey asked quietly, her tone cautious but not yet suspicious.

In another life, I stepped back and deferred to my friends. To the caretaker, and the people whose lives I'd sworn to protect with my sacrifice. But Sadey didn't know what I did, she didn't have my knowledge or my skill.

She was wrong, and in this life—in *my* life—I chose to listen to me.

Something wrong with this Bargain, restraining or constricting it in some way. And if I could just get to the heart of it, like I had with Merelda's curse, maybe I could fix it. Maybe the oath would let me go without me having to fight the whole way through.

If they worked out what I was doing, they'd never let me back here again. They'd think the fae had ensnared me and tricked me into breaking the Bargain, unleashing chaos onto the village. They wouldn't believe that I still wanted to play within the rules. That, while I wanted an escape from my oath, I didn't want to hurt anyone in the process.

The fae hadn't ensnared me at all; and I was going to break this Bargain if it was the last thing I did.

I unleashed my magic, and the orb cracked.

"Whoops," I whispered, rising to my feet, but it was too late.

The flame within the glass fizzled and puttered out until it was only a handful of sparks puffing up every few seconds. The crack widened, and Sadey screamed.

"She broke it!" Sadey whimpered, lunging for me as I tried to run past.

I could feel the orb calling to me, screaming. The cracks widened, still joined together but now unmistakably divided into pieces. Those pieces rose in the air, lurching forward, reminding me of my shattered Bargain that first morning after the circus. It was following me.

The attendant, leaning unashamedly around the desk to watch, began yelling at us, her eyes wide and panicked. Hannah backed away, shaking her head, her hand resting on her stomach as she pleaded with nobody in particular to save her baby.

Christine and Ella were in shock, and that was my only saving grace as I dodged Sadey's clutching hands and ran for the door.

With a clear view of the orb now, they balked, staggering backward at the horrifying sight. I whimpered, whispering random words under my breath, hoping I landed on a combination that would hide the orb from sight. Eventually, I just hissed "Hide! Hide!" at it, knowing that if that village saw it following me, cracked open and dying, I would be killed.

Either it worked, or the damn thing faded out of existence, because the next second, it vanished. Which left them with nothing to distract from chasing me.

Sounds reached my ears—the dull thudding of my heartbeat. The pulse of blood in my veins. I opened my mouth to speak as I backed toward the door, Sadey's piercing gaze frowning in confusion and pain, and then froze; I could see it. I could see it floating from my lips... the softest hint of smoke, the softest whisper of chaos...

A curse.

I didn't want to curse them.

Suddenly, the hall burst into loud yelling. It was a familiar voice, although I couldn't understand the words, but it was so loud. Unusually loud. Why was that voice so loud when it should be quiet and small and—

I whirled, recognizing it: Merelda.

But she wasn't as I had ever seen her. Gone was the little blue imp, and in its place was a tall, willowy sprite of a woman. She was very clearly not human, but she didn't look a thing like any fae I had seen before.

Long red hair flowed down her back, reaching below her waist, and her skin was tinted an opalescent blue that glittered a different sheen depending on which way she stood. Her eyes were full of fire as she turned on Sadey, who had been edging toward the exit to block it.

Without a word, she stalked forward. Her shoulders gave a subtle shimmy, and magnificent blue wings erupted from her back, glistening in the light.

Her audience was too stunned to respond or do anything as she hooked her arm through mine, and without another word to anyone, launched the two of us out the door and into the sky.

CHAPTER 27

Bailey

It was only when we crash landed on the front step, sending vine leaves scattering over the verandah, that she finally faced me.

My heart beat erratically. I didn't know what to say. I'd never been lost for words with Merelda before, but I didn't know this woman. This beautiful fae creature.

A deep pit of shame opened up in my stomach at the idea that I'd ever thought an imp was an animal—that I'd treated her like a *pet*. I should have trusted the evidence of my own eyes, not the words of those ancient scholars who had probably never even met an imp.

"Bailey," Merelda said, the word revealing a flash of sharpened teeth.

I'd never heard her say my name before, didn't know she could speak my language at all. Perhaps in her other form she couldn't.

Merelda paused, running her tongue over her teeth and frowning, as if the word felt wrong. In the slanting beams of sunlight that broke through the vines, I could see those teeth clearer now. They weren't completely pointed, but they were far sharper than a human's. As though each one was a canine. By contrast, the curves of her lips and teal-colored face were soft and full. She was like nothing I'd ever seen before.

She'd thrown her arms around my waist and sprung me from that hall without a second thought.

"Bailey, we need to get you inside," she said again, her voice more certain now. "They'll come looking for you."

"You don't know that," I whispered.

She didn't bother correcting me—merely stared as I turned from her, slipping my key with shaking hands into the lock and rushing inside.

It was dark within my cottage, the familiar warmth oddly stifling. She was right; they would come for me. And I didn't know if staying inside here would be enough to escape their reach. But...

I glanced out the window, taking note of the sun's position, already dipping below the horizon. Another day had passed, another night closer to the full moon. The circus was upon us.

They could come for me if they wanted; I wouldn't be here.

Restless, I walked to the kitchen, setting the kettle on the stove and refusing to look at the place that I would soon be leaving behind. Merelda's calm, measured footsteps trailed me inside, and it was all I could do not to turn to her and stare.

Gone was the tiny imp who had lived with me for years. Chaotic, irascible, and most of all angry—that final trait was the only familiar thing about this wild, powerful woman who had saved me.

Realizing that my fingers were clenched so tightly into the wood of the counter that they threatened to carve holes in them, I let go, smoothed down the front of my sweater, and turned.

"I'm leaving tonight," I told her quietly. "You know this, I think."

Part of me wondered if I should leave now—track down the sprites Sebastian had found me and just run for the hills. But no —at the very least, I had to return to the circus to pay for my ticket. Because if I went to the sprites and they couldn't help me, then I would have nothing. The circus might slip through my fingers while I wasted precious time betting on the wrong horse.

Merelda said nothing, but there was no change in her expression either. No parted lips, no flinch of shock. Only a steady, angry resignation. She knew.

"It isn't safe over there," she warned me as she perched on my small dining table, her wings swaying back and forth.

They became iridescent in the lamplight, I noticed. The gentle drift held me captive, my gaze fixed on the mesmerizing sheen of color.

She was pure magic.

Ever since I'd made that fateful Bargain, the magic of this world had been opening before me. With a hitch of my breath, I realized: I wanted to cross the water. Not only to escape my old life, although with each passing second that became more urgent. But more than that, I wanted to discover what else this strange world had to offer. Even knowing the dangers that awaited me, even knowing that humans couldn't possibly face off against the fae and hope to win, I wanted to try.

I wanted, gods help me, to live.

The kettle whistled, but halfway through pouring my mug of tea, I froze.

Glancing over my shoulder, I asked, 'Would you like one?"

A wry grin hooked into the corner of Merelda's mouth. She nodded. "Milk, please," she said innocently.

Another wave of guilt washed over me.

I busied myself making two mugs of tea and then carried them over to the table. Elegantly, she dropped down and perched on the guest chair. It was rarely used, and I wondered whether the sight of her in it now—blue, sparkling, and with devastatingly sharp teeth—would be stranger than seeing someone from the village or not.

Even though we sat in relative peace compared to what we'd left behind, there was a tension bubbling inside me. Like the kettle on the stovetop, I felt as though I was about to start whistling—a high-pitched screech that would echo on and on. And one look at Merelda told me she wasn't far off screeching either.

At least that much was familiar.

I tapped my fingers against the tabletop, each nail resonating with pain as I hit it with satisfaction against the wood. I took a sip from my drink, hissing as the too-hot liquid burned me.

"You aren't trying to stop me," I suggested.

She spoke so quickly over me, I knew she'd been waiting.

"It's not like you're giving me the choice."

"Should I?" I asked, brow deepening incredulously. "I didn't even know you were..." I waved to encompass all of her. "This."

"Did it matter?" she spat back, slamming her mug onto the table. "You knew I was your friend."

"I knew you were—" I stopped, squeezing my eyes shut tight. How could I possibly say the words churning through my mind?

I thought you were an animal. A pet. I thought it wouldn't matter if I left you.

Gods, it was wrong on so many levels, because I wouldn't have done this to a pet, either. And yet, I'd never once thought of what would happen if I left Merelda behind.

When I opened my eyes, she was watching me with a knowing gaze. The pit of shame churned within me, thick and hot.

"I assumed you would stay with Stefan," I said quietly. "I admit I didn't think as much as I should have. If I had, maybe I would have worked it out. But please believe me, Merelda. I didn't think—" I swallowed, trying again. "I didn't think you would miss me."

The honesty in my voice wiped the expression from her face. The words rang in the air between us, possibly the truest ones I'd ever spoken to another person.

How could I have thought she would miss me? I wasn't supposed to be missed. It wasn't *possible* for me to be missed. And yet, as I had stared upon that oath today, it had felt wrong.

Being in the presence of the altar below the surface of the river—that was magic. That was honor and fairness and truth wrapped in one. Something that could not be fought. Could not be broken.

I hadn't sensed any of that today, and I didn't know what it meant.

Merelda's fingernails, long and black, tapped against her mug in thought. Her brow was still wrinkled in a furious expression, her jaw tightly clenched. She took a sharp sip of her tea and didn't even flinch.

I wondered, distractedly, what the climate was like where she was from. Whether she'd been freezing cold for all these long years.

"So you're just going to run away then?" she said slowly, each word spat out with venom.

"Yes," I said tightly, surprised by the challenge in my voice.

Apparently, the anger that Fynn had ignited still lingered. There was a fire burning in my chest, and if I wasn't careful, it would blaze through this entire village.

"Right," she said, taking another angry sip. "So whenever I try to get you to stand up to them, you simper and cower and ignore me. But the second one of those dick-swinging assholes appears and offers you a way out, you take it. Even though they bloody stink of secrets, the both of them."

I stared at her, eyes wide. "What on earth are you talking about?" I asked her, gaping. "You weren't offering me a way out. You were just—" I shook my head, searching for the words. "Trying to make me angry."

"Yes," she snapped. "Anger that would have helped you. And you refused every gods damned time."

Even as I opened my mouth to argue, I saw the flaw in my logic. Because wasn't it the anger that Fynn had kindled within me that made me do what I had done today? To reach for the *wrongness* I'd seen in the Oath's magic, instead of merely accepting it and renewing my vow?

I'd known something was wrong, and I'd fought back. Because I was angry.

"But that's not—" I spluttered. The words were all muddled in my mind. "It isn't like that," I insisted.

"It's been like that for years, Bailey," she shot back, shoving her drink aside to lean into my space across the table. Her wings beat an agitated rhythm, making the cobwebs in the corner sway. Dust eddies swirled along the floor. "Year after year I've watched you suck up to them for no good reason. For no reason at all."

I scoffed. "I've had a very good reason, thank you very much. Or are you just conveniently ignoring what would happen if the Offering turned her back on the village?"

My voice choked at the thought—at the image of the Hell that would descend upon this place the second the Offering broke her oath. The Hell that the most stubborn parts of me refused to admit might still descend, even now, if I didn't make sure I was lost to them in a way that satisfied my promise.

"The Offering," she spat acidly. "That's right. It's always about the Offering."

"Of course it's about the Offering." I gaped, incredulous.

"Yes, yes." She ignored me, her voice rising in, not just anger, but rage. "Because the Offering is such a worthy cause," she snarled. "Such a perfect, sanctified promise that you made."

She leaned back in her chair, disgusted. For the first time, she looked like her old, one-foot-high self.

The fire in my chest was burning and burning, and I didn't know what to do with it.

"Bailey, I'll always stand by you. I'll always support you." She shook her head as she spoke. "But I swear to the gods, if I have to watch you submit to them for a single second longer, I'm going to lose it. And you still, after all these years, are convinced that it was a fair trade. A fair Bargain. An oath that you would gladly uphold in all of its stinking *fairness*."

"*It's never been fair!*" I yelled at her, slamming my hands down on the table.

Finally, she fell silent, eyes wide, lips parted as those words hung in the air between us.

They'd been building for a long time. It was the echo of these words that I'd heard in the clearing when Fynn poked at me. An echo of those words that had whispered to me when I had finally seen my life without the Bargain—when I'd felt what it could be like to walk without its weight.

"It's never been fair," I repeated, each word gritted out through clenched teeth. I pointed out the window, dimly registering that my finger was shaking. "And if I walk out there and think those words, or *dare* to breathe them out loud, then I will burn this fucking place to the ground."

I closed my eyes, focusing on the sound of my breath. The rough, shaking inhale; the heavy exhale. Mice scratched in the walls, and a breeze whistled in the crack of the kitchen window.

In the quiet darkness behind my closed eyelids, I said, "And I don't want to do that."

When I finally opened my eyes, Merelda's skin had turned a pale cyan, glittering with orange flecks of light. The whites of her eyes shone in the darkness of my tiny kitchen. The sun must almost be set.

"I know I never made the oath personally, but it is still mine." I pushed away from the table, restless, my mind spinning. "And whether I said the words or not, it doesn't make it right for me to hurt the people who are kept safe by them. It doesn't make it right for me to turn that violence around on them and risk triggering the curse that would be unleashed if I break that promise."

My fingers twitched, tapping the back of the chair. I needed a distraction. I only had to last one more night. One final night before I escaped into the terrifying, thrilling world across the water; the only one I'd ever wanted.

I plucked one of the titles I'd stolen from Master Skylark free and flicked through the pages, idly searching for what I had seen. Searching for the one mystery I felt I could safely poke at.

"I don't know what you want from me." I spoke as I turned the pages, flicking them sharply, one after the other. "I'm not staying here, and I'm not going to face up to them. There's no point. I'm just going to get out of here in a way that seals my oath and tidies everything up. I'm going to find another life over the water, and then everything will be fine, and—" I broke off, my fingers landing on a familiar symbol.

I wasn't misremembering. The symbol of the soul eater matched the one from the Offering plaque today...

And the one etched in the book under Heillon's arm.

How lucky was I feeling tonight? How much weight did I want to put against the balance of coincidence?

I swallowed, ignoring the taste of bile that landed, thick, on my tongue. I was the Offering; when it came to ill luck, there was no such thing as coincidence.

Heillon was planning to summon a soul eater.

I stared into the face of the daemon that was etched there. Its vicious maw and gaping eyes made the lora beast look like a carnivorous plant after all. Shuddering, I skimmed the rest of the page, my brain refusing to accept the words written beneath it—words that filled me with dread. Because this ritual needed an offering, and the word 'offering' was capitalized.

Heillon had told me himself, although he didn't realize I was listening, that he loved a sense of poetry. What would be more poetic than summoning a daemon in the town of Broodshire with The Offering?

I slammed the book shut. It didn't change anything. This fresh hell was clearly a warning from the fates: if I got greedy, if I tried to take something that belonged to someone else or that was more than I deserved, then my village would fall, just as the first Bargain had warned.

But without an Offering, Heillon's plan would fail. And, all going well, there would not be an Offering for him to take for much longer.

As long as I took care not to ruin the balance in these last two remaining days, so the Bargain Magic had no reason to lash out and hasten the oncoming damnation, then... everything would be fine.

Everything was fine.

I would return to the Lumière tonight, pay Fynn for my ticket, and then speak to the sprites. That way I was assured of at least one successful crossing. And if the sprites couldn't take me, I would hide in the caravans, waiting for the final night to rise. Out of reach of my neighbors; out of sight of Heillon.

My pulse steadied, calming from the raging thunder of the last few minutes to a companionable, enduring pulse. I shut the book. There was no point telling Merelda what I'd discovered; she'd only get mad.

"You don't know what I want from you," she repeated slowly when I finally sat down again.

It took me a second to catch up. My mind had long since raced on from our argument.

"No," I agreed, softening as I slid back into the chair across from her.

"I need you to do something for me," she said, her voice lyrical and accented, almost like the people to the north of the mountains.

"Okay," I said, all witty retorts dying on my tongue.

"I need you, for once..." Merelda tilted her head and—unexpectedly—reached across the table. Cautiously, I slid my hand into hers. I wondered how long it had been since I'd held someone's hand, if I ever had. "To stop trying to see the beauty in people, and instead see the ugliness they keep showing you."

I stared at her, a thousand responses whirring in my brain and threatening to come out at once. I'd anticipated anger, even a fiery argument—which we'd both delivered on spectacularly —but not this...

Merelda wasn't asking me to stop what I was doing, or to change my plans. She wasn't insisting I go back into the shadows, or even that I go down in a blaze of glory, demanding to be allowed a place in the light.

Perhaps I should have seen this coming. She'd always hated my friends and the people who took advantage of me. I just hadn't realized just how deep that hatred ran. I hadn't realized that she'd seen so clearly through it to the heart of the issue— that they might have hurt me, but I gladly let them.

But I didn't want to stop seeing beauty in people. I wanted the world to be beautiful, even when it didn't feel like it, because if it wasn't...

"But if I do that," I whispered, "then there'll be nothing beautiful left at all."

Merelda's face softened into an expression I'd never seen on her before as she leant forward to rest her hand at the center of my chest.

"What about the beauty in you?" she said.

Once more, that fire within me flickered into life. This time, I let it.

I let the flames rise until the lamplight itself seemed to glow brighter than before. Until a charged atmosphere entered the cottage, sparking and glittering at the edges. Merelda's expression turned fierce—hungry. It felt, for a minute, as though something brushed against the back of my hand. Something that felt like smooth, cool glass, and that hummed with both magic and recognition. But when I looked down, there was nothing there.

"Alright," I said softly, facing her again. "I will."

Merelda shook her head. "Say it," she insisted.

I swallowed, strangely timid. "I—"

"*Say it.*"

"I deserve more than this."

The hungry expression shifted, the corner of her mouth lifting into a feral smile. "I almost believe you."

I leant back in my chair, oddly drained as I clasped my mug of tea and waited for the sun to vanish.

"You know what?" I murmured, glancing out the window and marking the seconds. "Me, too."

The sun had long since set, but I hadn't been able to bring myself to leave. I knew I should. Ironically, I would be safer from the mob of torches and pitchforks within the bounds of the Lumière than I would anywhere else. But once I entered the circus, one way or another, I would never leave.

And that was a sobering thought.

Dirt filtered between my fingers as I toyed with a leaf by my feet. At least Merelda was coming with me, now. Such a strange thought, that for once I wouldn't be alone. That I never truly had been. She'd left to take care of some things, and we planned to meet up in Criera once I safely crossed. Whether that was with the Lumière or—as I'd described to her, not wanting to get into more details about the fae men she couldn't stand—my contingency plan.

The leaf crunched into tiny pieces, catching in the breeze and flying off toward the clearing entrance.

Another sound echoed back.

I looked up, fear pulsing in my chest, but found only familiar blue eyes and hair that glinted blond in the moonlight. For a moment, he stilled, as though he hadn't expected to find me here.

Then, he raised an eyebrow and resumed his usual smirking demeanor. "I regret to inform you the circus is in the other direction," he said lightly. "If you're lost, I can find you a map, but it will be written by the fae so there might be a nasty word or two directed at your favorite landmarks." He smiled, leaning back against the tree behind me and crossing one leg over the other. "You know how it is when someone bans you from all the nice places. You get mean."

I laughed, leaning back so my head fell against the trunk and I could look up at him. "You mean you actually listen to those old bans?"

"Me?" He pointed to himself. "Absolutely not. But I am uniquely gifted."

He didn't elaborate, and I didn't ask.

We fell into an unexpectedly comfortable silence. In the

distance, laughter and music carried on the breeze. The sounds swirled through the clearing, bringing the rustle of leaves and the gentle cool of the night air.

"Who were you looking for?" I asked, toying with the folds of my shirt. "If you didn't realize I was here?"

"No one," he answered calmly.

I frowned. "Then why are you here?"

"Same reason as you, I expect."

Lifting one brow, I offered, "What, because you have an army of people chasing you down with torches?"

To my surprise, he didn't skip a beat, only bared his teeth in a smile. "Always."

The silence stretched further, less comfortable this time. Poised with something unsaid. Glancing sidelong at Fynn, I realized he had closed his eyes.

Seconds ticked past, and it occurred to me that I should probably leave; he'd obviously come here wanting privacy. I rose to my feet, dusting off my breeches, but Fynn immediately said: "Stay."

"And if I don't want to?" I asked, folding my arms and studying him in the darkness.

"Then go," he replied easily. "It's hardly complicated."

"On the contrary: everything with you is complicated."

His mouth twitched, but he still didn't open his eyes. My heart fluttered, and I took a step closer. Then another, until my legs bracketed his.

"Why don't you open your eyes?" I asked, the words almost a whisper.

"Full of questions tonight, aren't we?" he murmured.

For a long moment, I thought he wouldn't answer. Then he said, so quietly I barely heard it, "Because he doesn't get to have this, too."

Before I could ask what he meant, Fynn's arms had scooped around my waist, and he spun me back against the tree. A rough sound escaped me, and I waited for his mouth to descend on mine.

It didn't come.

Instead, he tilted his head so his face was angled down into my hair, and threaded the fingers of one hand through mine, holding it by my head. Then, he lifted the other from my waist and trailed a long, slow line up the side of my body.

"I know Sebastian was there, last night," Fynn whispered. My breath caught, but before I could panic, he added, "Don't worry. We have to see it, remember? Rules of the Bargain, bound by truth."

Slowly, my shoulders eased down from around my neck. "Then, what of it?"

His lips curved into a smile against my hair. "Don't you want to know how I know?"

"Villainous instincts?"

The laugh he gave was almost surprised. Soft. His hand continued to trail upward, over my ribs now, just below the swell of my breast.

"Maybe," he confessed. "But mostly, fae can get a sense of the energy in a space. The feeling that drifts on the air currents. And I know how Seb feels when he wants someone."

A dark shiver raced down my spine, and the memory of their time together hammered for my attention.

"Because he wanted you once?" I asked.

"Because he had me once," Fynn corrected.

His fingers spread, palm cupping my breast so that his fingertips traced a ticklish, hardly there line over the bare skin at my open collar. He trailed them back and forth, my pulse no doubt fluttering beneath his touch.

"Do you want to know why I didn't turn?" he asked at the same moment he slipped his hand inside my shirt.

I gasped, arching up into the warmth of his hand. His thumb brushed over my nipple, and I had to bite my lip to stop from crying out. The hand that was still in his squeezed so tightly it must have hurt, but he didn't tell me to quit.

"Yes," I whispered.

His thumb and forefinger came together, squeezing my hardened nipple. This time, I couldn't hold back the sound— my sharp cry echoed through the clearing, and when I writhed beneath his touch this time, I couldn't help the way my hips moved too.

His leg was already between mine, as if he'd been waiting, and I didn't stop to consider how desperate I must have looked. In that moment, I didn't care at all.

A whimper fell from my lips as I slipped one leg up his side, wrapping my calf around his hip and grinding shamelessly against him.

His eyes must be open now, I thought, because I could feel how ragged his breath had become. There was no way he would keep his eyes shut through this and still be so affected. His hand on my breast remained so gentle, it might hardly have been there at all—and yet the fingers that pinched me again were hard and unyielding.

I wanted more. I wanted him to claw into me, tear me apart. To pinch and bite and take.

I cried out, lifting my hips so I could feel the hard, thick length of him against my core. A sound escaped him, rough and desperate, and his hips moved—an impulsive, instinctive thrust against me, the force of it so hard that my lower back grazed the bark. At the same time, that gentle hand against my breast lost control and squeezed. As if he had forgotten himself, for just a second. He thrust again, and again.

I shattered.

Frotting like a teenager, without even a mouth against mine, I came completely undone.

Fynn lowered his voice, murmuring into my ear as I was still riding the waves of pleasure. "One day, I'll tell you."

His voice was far from steady, despite the amusement in it. I didn't call him out, because the pot-kettle of it all would have slapped me in the face.

Instead, I reached up to grab him by the hair and pull him down in front of me. His blue eyes glinted wickedly, as if they glowed with their own inner light.

"Are you going to kiss me now?" I asked, my gaze falling to his mouth.

It looked soft and warm, completely unlike the unpredictable, acerbic faerie before me.

Fynn smiled. "No." Before I could respond, he stepped out of the reach of my arms and added, "Not yet."

Then, with a flash of golden light, he was gone.

After a minute, I drew the coronet free from behind my satchel and stared down at the pink petals, unseeing. I'd planned to throw it into the river tonight, before I left, giving one final offering to the altar beneath the surface before I became lost. But maybe I wouldn't. Maybe I would keep it, and tuck it away in my satchel to carry with me until this whole thing was over. Because the coronet wasn't the offering; I was.

Whatever magic this had, it was fueled by my prayer, my dedication, my servitude.

On my last full night spent in Aelor, blasphemous though it might be, I would pray for me.

CHAPTER 28

Sebastian

THE CLOUDS PARTED, COATING THE FAIRGROUNDS WITH LIGHT. FOR once, I had almost complete freedom to go anywhere I wanted. Every deviant shadow, every shimmering luminescent sign, every gaudy, shining button on the ushers that waited by the tent entrances—it was all lit up with moonlight, ready for the big show.

By contrast—and yet, for much the same purpose—the faces of my fellow Lumière were overtaken by darkness. Teeth had turned a little sharper, eyes a little blacker—swallowed almost completely by pupil. The final night was almost upon us, and by the end of the evening, the unglamoured faces of the fae would appear in full strength, and the Bargains would begin.

I had to find Bailey.

The Bargain Night ritual was hardly a peach, but something was very wrong this season. I kept hearing rumors that it had changed, the key details altered in a way that had my companions practically salivating behind their feathered masks.

And I didn't like what had nearly happened last night, by the lake. Why hadn't Fynn turned around? He'd known I was there; I could feel it. Fynn could have had everything he'd always wanted—my ass locked up in a cage, for good—and yet he walked away.

I passed a hand over my face, wincing as my nails dug into my skin a little harder than I'd meant. I'd always told myself that, for all that he was a hunter and Heillon's lapdog, Fynn's hatred belonged to me alone. That the games he played were twisted and unfathomable, but to everyone outside of me, they were not cruel. *He* was not cruel.

But maybe I was wrong. I'd seen how he'd looked at Bailey across the grounds, and I couldn't help wondering: had the hunter turned away from me last night because there was a bigger prize on the table?

If he hurt her, I'd never forgive myself.

Fire erupted from pillars placed throughout the circus ground, lighting up the sky as gold mixed with silver, and I took the chance to slip into the crowd unnoticed. Stunned humans pointed upward, ignoring me and gazing in wonder at the little images that flickered in and out of the flames. Such a strange sensation, to be in a crowd of avid onlookers and hide from the spotlight. Couldn't say I liked it.

"Ladies and gentlefolk," a familiar voice rang out across the fairground.

It was the last one I wanted to hear right now.

When I turned, Fynn's eyes were already bearing into mine, their depths flickering oddly, even though he was faced away from the towers of flame.

"We have a true spectacle for you on our penultimate evening before we return to our homeland." He gave a sultry little pout, like he was devastated to leave, and then winked at a group of giggling humans by his right.

Roaming unfettered amongst the crowd now, with each

step Fynn lifted higher into the air, until he was floating above us all.

He angled himself so his toe was pointed straight at my head, positioned so he could look down and pretend he was simply watching the crowd, when instead his words were clearly meant for me. A challenge of some kind, but for what, I didn't know.

It was tempting to consider grabbing his ankle and spinning him into a sharp roll. Tragically, I refrained.

"Alongside our gifts of refreshments, you will now find various fancies and adornments. For, tonight, *you* will be part of the performance."

My heart thudded in my chest, its pace quickening despite my efforts to play it cool. Nothing was out of the ordinary yet. The Bargain Night rituals always began on the sixth night with a party, easing the humans in with dancing and debauchery to relax them and make them pliable. But no actual Bargains were to be struck until the seventh night, when the actual ceremony rose with the full moon...

And yet, every fae face I looked at had eyes that glinted with hunger, teeth that elongated into fangs. There was no more pretense of humanity here; the Hunt had risen.

It was happening too quickly, and with an undercurrent of gleeful apprehension that chilled me to the core.

Fynn raised his hands above his head, as if calling out to the stars, or the moon that bound me. "And so, choose your disguises," he finished grandly, "and join us tonight on the dance floor for merriment and wine. For tomorrow will surely be"—he winked—"a night to remember."

And with that, he stepped forward and vanished in a puff of shadowy smoke.

The crowd squealed, and as floating trays of drinks and fancies—masks, jewelry, fabrics—began to distribute among them, the energy rose even higher. My stomach turned at Fynn's little parting joke; the humans wouldn't remember a thing. The magic prevented it. And like lambs to the slaughter, they suspected nothing.

I grit my teeth harder, practically grinding the damn things, as I searched the crowd and still didn't find Bailey. The urgency propelling me forward had taken on a frantic edge, and I tried desperately to quell it. No good could come from acting rashly. It would only make things worse.

I turned, only to smack straight into Fynn.

He glared at me, eyes glinting. "If you're looking for your lady love," he said in a crooning voice. "Might I suggest there are plenty more fish in the sea. So many beautiful women who look just like her." He shrugged. "Well. At least one." His eyes widened in faux shock. "Make sure you don't mix them up. Wouldn't that be ghastly?"

Gods, I was so sick of his arrogant shit. I shoved him in the chest, ignoring the gasps of surprise from around us.

Fynn's scowl deepened, and he walked closer to me, shoving me back. My breath caught as I reflexively checked to make sure he hadn't pushed me into shadow, but no. By coincidence, he'd shoved me just as a cloud above had moved. If anything, he'd saved me, shunting me back into the light.

"What's your game with her?" I hissed.

"No game," Fynn said, grinning brightly. "I've been naught but honest with your beloved."

"She isn't my beloved," I protested, ignoring the heavy weight that appeared in my chest at the words.

Even if I could keep her, she'd sworn off love. She had a life to live, far away from me and the disaster that trailed my every move.

"Insecurity is an unattractive trait," Fynn said flatly. "Time is ticking."

"I don't love her," I snarled, even as the words *I'm falling for you* echoed through my mind. "And she has better things to do than fall for a circus brat."

"Oh, give her time." For a second, Fynn's face turned deadly. "After all," he said, taking a step back and spreading his hands wide. A grand gesture of showmanship. "Does the hero not always get the girl?"

"Only after the villain has kidnapped her," I answered in a low rumble. "Tell me what you're planning."

Something flashed in Fynn's eyes, but all he did was give a low, mocking bow. "I would so hate to disappoint."

With another turn, he was gone.

Before I could move any further, a tray appeared with a mask on it. The hint rang loud and clear: with the moonlight so bright, I was to join them, helping in their task of seducing the humans and lulling them into a false sense of safety.

Fighting back the shudder, I picked up the mask and slipped it over my face, using those precious seconds to scan the crowd once more for clues. Beyond a rising sense of anticipation that had me wanting to wrap Bailey up in cotton wool and hide her away, I found none.

The seventh night—Bargain Night—*should* have been a frenzied ritual of Bargain hunting, collecting every last drop of power from these humans before we crossed back over the bridge. Hundreds of deals were passed on Bargain Night, few of them fair.

I'd thought it sounded so grand when I was a youth. When I was bitter and jaded, eager to get out from under my father's thumb. He'd cautioned me, warned me, and even followed me here to this troop he'd hated. Just so that the Lumière never ensnared his son completely.

And he paid the price for it.

Worst thing was, he needn't have. When I got my first look

at a real human, I realized what the Lumière were doing was wrong. These weren't vicious killers out hunting faeries, like we were told. They were just people. Now, Bargain Night was a source of crippling shame, reminding me of every single one of my failures.

Despite the drunken laughter as they accepted our gifts of clothing and jewels, it was only the sixth night, and no Bargains were to be made yet. The glamors should still be held firmly in place, and each human seduced until they were on the cusp of begging. Until the promise of only one... more... night... sent them into the kind of panic that would have them give up anything for a taste of Lumière magic they could keep forever.

But a whispering hum of anticipation crept across the crowd, glittering in the face of every fae present, and the glamors were falling.

There was no longer any doubt in my mind; the ritual had shifted.

Well. I supposed my best chance at learning what was happening was to avoid drawing attention to myself by resisting it. And so, my body riddled with despair, I adjusted my mask and let the music take over me.

Giant silver hoops rolled through the crowd of their own volition, subtly scattering the humans from the safety of their huddles. I caught one as it passed by and leapt inside, spinning with it. The dizzying swirl of earth and sky was familiar and comforting. I used the moments where I was upright to pause, twirling the hoop around and behind me so I could face one way and then the other.

In this way, I discreetly searched for a flash of her golden hair, or her friend's wizened face, but I found nothing.

My stomach sank; had I scared her off last night? Maybe that was for the best. If I had, at least she would be safe. She could give up this foolish endeavor with the Lumière and go straight to the sort of fae she could trust.

It would do her more good than sticking with me and risking a fate as doomed as my own.

My mouth twisted, becoming a harsh slash of bitter humor that I couldn't quite wipe free. I kicked up the energy of my performance, trying to lose myself in it. If I could only dull the frantic buzzing of my selfish, impulsive urges, I might be able to think. But they were so loud. Impossibly loud, yelling at me to throw away the mask and *find her*.

Not just find her—keep her.

The bitter scrape of my laugh startled the nearest humans. I wanted to stop those urges? I might as well have tried to control the moon.

Acrobats leapt through the crowd, prancing and lifting each other up, forming impossibly high towers and tumbling down into shapes that humans could never possibly hold. I wove among them, dancing and searching.

But after nearly half an hour, I was forced to admit I needed a new plan. Or at least, a new activity. Perhaps one with a little more height—and heat.

Grinning almost ferally beneath my mask, I dropped out of the hoop and sent it whirling across the fairground with a flick of my wrist. Shocked humans darted out of the way with indignant cries as I walked slowly to the center of the fire-twirlers.

"Evening," I said pleasantly. "Mind if I join?"

There were no rules for our performances tonight. It was a showcase of skill—but more than that, it was a hunting ground. We were using the opportunity of lowered inhibitions to sniff out the humans' desires. To uncover what they wanted most of all, so that we could use it against them.

Another performer on their stage would mean more eyeballs their way, more excitement—more opportunity.

Kris glanced at me from the top of his whirling circle of fire and grinned. "Hop right on up, Seb," he rasped in his distinctive voice—throat burned from too many fire eating mishaps in his training. "Let them get a good look at your pretty face."

I forced a laugh, letting it ring out over the crowd, and then leaned in close. Kris angled into my welcoming embrace, long black hair pooling against my shoulder, as I crooked a finger toward the flame. Two puffs of fire split from the main circle and rose toward me.

While the crowd was distracted by the movement, I whispered into Kris' ear. "What's the game tonight? Something's changed."

For a moment, Kris' face turned sour. The expression was gone as quickly as it came. "Can't tell you," he replied. "Don't know myself. But Heillon's got something planned."

I caught the twin flames and began to spin them between my palms—a smaller version of the ring in Kris' hands. "What did he say?" I muttered, barely moving my lips.

With a mighty shout, Kris hurled the ring of fire into the air. It split into three, and when they dropped down again, he caught them and began to juggle.

"We'll never have to hunt again," he said with a grin that didn't meet his eyes, playing up the vision for the crowd who wouldn't be able to hear his words over their own gasps. "Feast up, darlings. From now on, the lion grows fat off the lamb."

"Fuck," I whispered, turning away to hide my face.

I left Kris to his performance, spinning my twin flames while I caught my breath. It was only half an answer, but it was all I needed. What Heillon had described wasn't a Bargain. It wasn't even an unfair Bargain.

It was a slaughterhouse.

Swallowing down my fear, I silently renewed my vow to find Bailey and get her out of here. Calm, logical movements.

Discipline. Strength. I could do this—I wouldn't let my impulsive urge to burn this entire fucking place to the ground ruin her chance of escape.

But the fear wouldn't stay down.

I plucked a fresh rope of fire from the fire-twirler on my left and sent soothing whispers of magic to my hands so they didn't burn. Then, I began to twist and shape the fire, much like the twirlers beside me, but I had a different purpose. Soon, it lay suspended in midair above me—a shimmering curtain of flame cascading from the air. And as the crowd watched in fear and awe, I wrapped that curtain of flame around one leg—twisted, flicked and rolled it—and then leapt into the air.

It didn't burn. Barely even tickled. And still the humans' eyes were lit with wonder as I used that curtain of flame to roll up and down in thin air.

It was at the very top of one of those spirals that I saw her.

My breath caught, my pulse stuck in a staccato beat. From up here, it was as though I were part of a different world—no longer bound by the rules of my cage at all. I could pretend that I could keep her.

I could acknowledge, however briefly, that I wanted to.

With a flourish, I rolled down to the ground, took a bow, and left the ring.

The crowd had grown even drunker in the time that I was performing on high. The wine flowed freely, and many of the humans were dancing—some of them even with fae. Naughty creatures.

I heard it then, a whisper in the back of my mind.

Indulge all who are willing.

Bile rose at the back of my throat. That was our primary command tonight, then. No human would be turned away. No curiosity left untouched.

I turned and spat on the ground, ignoring the shriek of

horror from the human beside me. It was better if she was disgusted; then she wouldn't want something from me that I didn't want to give.

Bailey stepped before me, her golden curls filling my vision and sending a wave of unexpected pleasure and comfort through me from head to toe. I couldn't help smiling, and I knew it wasn't the charming, brilliant smile I gave my audience. It was softer, gentler. A smile just for her. I lifted one hand—and then froze.

It wasn't Bailey. She had the same hair, but the smile, the stance, the aura—it was all wrong.

Her eyes were both brown, and the soulless depths of them made me shiver.

"Could I have this dance?" The woman gave a soft, airy laugh that might have been seductive to anyone else.

With only a faint hesitation, I immediately turned on the charm and bowed to her.

"Of course, my lady."

We began to dance, twirling among the other humans. Our steps were seamless, even as theirs grew more and more erratic.

"You looked so clever up there," the human said, startling me. I'd practically forgotten about her. "Oh?" I arched a brow above my mask. "Is that why you came here tonight? To see all the clever fae?"

I twirled her out and in again. She laughed, the rich sound tinkling over the heads of the dancers, many of whom turned this way.

They were drawn to this human, I realized. Several of them clearly knew her, and others simply liked what they saw.

Doing what my masters desired me to, I let my hand slide lower, to the small of her back, and pulled her in close. I could scent the jealousy rising on the wind, muddying the energy of all those close by.

Several Bargains tomorrow would be made with this woman in mind.

"It'll take more than a clever fae to impress me," she said, clearly flirting.

And because it was my role, I dipped my head toward her, encouraging the fantasy. Foolish woman. She reeked of need and pain in equal measure; the Lumière ate women like her for breakfast. Her only chance at survival lay in running far, far away.

I froze, my attention landing on a person hovering alongside the edge of the crowd: Bailey. And this time it really was her.

The tightness I hadn't noticed ripping through my chest softened, the tension across my shoulders seeping away. *Finally.* Now, I just had to ditch this distraction and find a way to reach Bailey so we could talk properly.

But why did she look so tense? And why was she not out here dancing? I'd have guessed she was listening to my advice from days ago, but it didn't appear that way.

All the humans were giving her a wide berth.

My brow furrowed. It was like they wanted nothing to do with her. Was this the other half of the reason she was so desperate to escape her world?

Rage burst in my chest, and I gripped the human woman tight enough that she squealed.

I looked down in apology, offering a rakish grin as I murmured, "Apologies, we fae sometimes forget we have claws."

From across the grounds, I immediately sensed the most overwhelming wave of sadness. It shocked me, leaving me speechless and stumbling as the woman in my arms took charge and whirled the two of us deeper into the crowd.

Was that Bailey? Was she upset I was dancing with some-one? Surely she understood I had no choice.

But then my brain finally woke up, and I looked back at the woman before me—those golden curls, the shape of her chin. There was a reason I'd thought this was Bailey.

It was her sister.

Bailey's pained confession, spat through gritted teeth, shot through me.

He left me at the altar... for my sister.

My lip curled back in a sneer. But before I could speak, Bailey's sister spoke again, interrupting me. "I see you're quite the popular one. My sister hasn't been able to take her eyes off you, but..." She gave that soft, airy laugh again, the sound putrid now that I saw it for the manipulation it was. "She's not the one out here dancing, is she? Neither she nor my..." She waved her hand dismissively. "Current suitor."

Current suitor? She must have meant Hayden, Bailey's ex-fiance. They weren't even engaged. She'd stolen Bailey's fiance and hadn't even bothered to keep him.

The rage was already building, but I could feel that little tingle at the back of my head that told me the Masters were watching, observing the most important night so there were no mishaps.

If I stepped one toe out of line, they would be on me in an instant.

"And since neither of them are out here," the woman continued, truly oblivious. "I think it's well within my right to claim what they cannot."

What on earth was she dribbling about?

I lifted a hand from her waist, intending to politely end the dance and walk away. But then she reached for me, forefinger and thumb on either side of my chin, and dragged me down into a kiss.

I froze.

It was as though a thousand eyes pierced me; that was how intently I knew people were watching. If I broke this kiss, the Masters would know. I would lose everything.

But for Bailey to see this, for her to see what I was doing with her sister. The same person who had already betrayed her...

A sound escaped me, full of regret and anguish, but the woman in front of me took it as an invitation and only gripped me tighter.

Through that faint connection between myself and the Masters that were watching, I felt a hint of intrigue. They noticed my resistance, my desire to break the rules. Like a cat watching a mouse through half-lidded eyes, they wanted to see what I would do.

But even with those bastards watching, and the danger climbing, the strongest voice in my mind wasn't one of caution. It was a voice that screamed: fuck it all.

How dare they trap me in their twisted games and then blame me for losing? They were the ones who did this to my father. I should just cut the lot of them down and make them tell me where he was instead of playing by their rules.

But that was what got me here in the first place.

My hands clenched into fists, twisting the fabric of the woman's dress within my grasp. My father had always said I was too hasty in my actions. A child, not a man. As the words assaulted my mind, the old familiar shame curdled low in my gut.

I was the reason all of this was happening. From my father's years-long torment to Bailey's current despair—it was all me and my foolish actions. Bailey shouldn't even be here tonight, not if what Kris had said was true. The danger was too great.

I couldn't keep her, and even though I'd said that from the

beginning, I'd indulged in the fantasy anyway, like the impulsive brat I'd always been. And once again, it would be someone else who paid the price.

I had to end this, so she would be safe.

And so, I did what I had been told time and again to do, despite every part of me resisting—I followed the rules.

I let my hand fall to the back of Bailey's sister's head, and I eased gently out of the kiss in a way that was still indulging her. In a way the Masters would approve of, so they didn't bring their wrath down on anyone else I cared for.

And I smiled.

CHAPTER 29

Bailey

When Sebastian's lips met my sister's, my body froze. My heart, previously pounding out a rapid beat of fear, disgust, and everything in between, suddenly just—stopped. And in its absence, a cavernous pit opened inside me.

It was happening again.

I didn't run. I gave myself ample time to be logical. Sensible. I gave Sebastian ample time to pull away, to shove her back and tell her 'no'. But he didn't.

And as I took a deep breath and let it out, slowly turning away from him, he didn't look at me once. Even though I knew he'd seen me only moments before.

I had to get out of here. I had to get so far away from here that not even the fae could find me. Somewhere I could think. Somewhere I could let the familiar ice cold granite take over my features and keep me safe.

But as I moved blindly through the crowd, I couldn't find the exit. Somehow, I'd ended up on the other side of the fairground where there were no paths outward. I tried to move back through the crowd, but a dozen figures closed in around me, the warmth of their bodies already suffocating. With the masks and jewels hiding their faces, I had no idea if I was looking at human or fae.

In the shadows, bodies writhed in pleasure, laughter and soft cries spilling out over the crowd. It had taken me too long to notice, but the tone had shifted this night, moving from wonder to rapture. Wicked and sinful sounds surrounded me, drifting from private nooks filled with silken cushions and sheets, and I couldn't fucking breathe.

"Excuse me," I began, pushing my way firmly through the center. The faces leered and drew closer, but I kept shoving until I burst out the other side in a flurry of fabric, laughter, and tinkling glass.

At the last second, I managed to right myself before I crashed into the nearest performer and sent the crystal balls they were juggling shattering to the ground. But as I straightened, shock tore through me; they weren't crystal balls. They were Bargains, ablaze with iridescent blue flame. The fae were flicking them around like they were meaning-less. Like they weren't holding people's lives in the palm of their hand.

Static hummed in my ears. I'd come to a halt without meaning to, staring open-mouthed at the callous insolence of it all. I forced myself to keep moving, but a woman stepped before me, her body as tall and willowy as the instrument in her hands.

She began to play, the song crooning from her mouth and the strings in unison, and—unwilling—I began to sway and drift. Golden hoops appeared on her arms, spinning and jangling with the music. She raised one hand above her, swaying like a snake, and I watched with intoxicating languor as the hoops lifted off, hovered in the air, and spun and spun.

It felt like my body was spinning too.

There was somewhere I had to be. But how could that be so?

Clearly I had to be right here. I swayed a little further, falling deeper into the trance.

No, I had to move. I had to get out, away from these vicious, cruel people. These fae who had never once lied about who they were and what they did—and I'd gone and fallen for them all the same. Every last one of them.

I stumbled forward, ducking beneath a wall of flame, and then twisted around another of water. The music was cacophonous, a jingle of sound and merriment that enfolded around me. Three sets of eyes for three different fae turned my way.

They were all pupil. No iris to be seen, no sclera—nothing. Just pitch black eyes, hidden behind glittering masks.

They stepped closer. One stretched out his hand, clawed and covered in feathers, reaching for me.

Why wasn't anyone else seeing this?

Because they were all so drunk, and I was the only one not partaking in the wine and the dancing.

And, because no one else wanted to see. Why would they? To see this would be to admit that every choice they'd made when they stepped through the circus gates was stupid. It would mean facing up to their own failings, and having no one to blame but themselves.

I'd been so certain that I could get away with this. So sure that my choices were noble and right and *good*. That I could take what I wanted for once and no one would be hurt.

How easily I'd believed my own lies.

The fae reached for me. I turned toward him, thinking I may as well let him. What was I even fighting for anymore? A goblet appeared in my hands, and I raised it to my lips.

Fynn stepped before me.

With an irritated little slap, he cast the goblet from my hands, threw the reaching fae's palm away, and then reached for mine with a gallant bow.

"I'm here to kidnap you," he said mildly. "Shall we escape with gallant secrecy or treacherous haste?"

I stared at him, my chest rising and falling with ragged breaths as I waited for him to haul me over his shoulder like everyone else had tried to so far. He didn't move. The seconds ticked past, and I broke. Taking his hand, I began to run; this time, the crowd parted before me.

I had no idea where I was taking him. Had no idea if Sebastian saw us tearing through the circus ground. I just ran. Ran and ran until we reached the shadows out the front of the gates and well beyond.

As I suspected, Fynn hadn't been prevented from leaving. Was he one of the only fae who could?

What did that mean?

Especially—what did it mean with what I now knew about fae hunters, and Fynn's role in that. Was I being hunted even now? And instead of escaping from danger, I'd stepped right inside the mouth of the most dangerous beast there.

Slowly, watching me as though I might implode at any moment, Fynn let go of my hand and knelt down to perch upon a low rock. We were completely hidden from the fairground out here, tucked behind the weeping willows that lined the riverbank before it joined the lake.

"May I ask what animal is apparently more terrifying than the lora beast?" he asked politely. "You know, since you can already fight one of those." He gave an exaggerated shiver. "How terrifying this new creature must be if it could send you running."

I didn't answer. I stared into the shadows in the rough direction of the lake, where Sebastian and I had come together only last night.

Merelda had told me these men had secrets. She'd said she could smell it on them. But we all did, didn't we?

What I couldn't work out was which secret to listen to. Which secret to chase and insist they share with me, and which to allow privacy and respect. Which secrets of my own to share and trust I wasn't giving away the means to my own destruction.

I cleared my throat. "My sister came tonight," I said.

"Ah, yes, the charming Katerina," Fynn murmured. I turned to find him examining his nails. "I did see her flirting her way through the troupe."

"Then you saw her kiss Sebastian."

He shrugged. "Can't say I'm taking notes, but I believe it."

He didn't say anything more—simply watched me, head tilted, as he waited for the rest of my secrets to come blaring out.

They did.

I couldn't hold them in any longer.

A tear slipped free and slid down my cheek, and I watched as Fynn's eyes traced every inch of its path.

"Everyone always chooses her." I said quietly, in a voice I barely recognized.

If I hadn't been watching him so closely, I might not have noticed, but something in him flinched at those words. No— recoiled. His eyes snapped up to mine, and there was such darkness there, I had no idea what he was thinking.

After a beat, he spoke.

"You know that Sebastian was commanded by our..." He paused before gesturing grandly to the sky. "Ineffable lords and masters to indulge any human who took an interest in him tonight?"

Even his voice was unreadable. The tone was completely different to the usual humor that marked it. It was humor at everyone else's expense, to be sure, but this was different.

This was dark.

He sounded like I'd thought Sebastian would be when I first saw him, before I knew him better. Like I thought I heard from Fynn the first time he spoke, before he turned on the charm.

Then his words sank in.

Relief washed over me. I'd guessed as much, but it was different to know for sure.

"Even still," I said, reaching out to pluck a leaf from the tree and turn it over and over in my fingers. It was easier to stare at the leaf than at Fynn, at his unreadable expression and the dark edge to it that I didn't understand. "Just because that was the reason for tonight, doesn't mean it will be the reason in the future."

"What makes you so certain there will be a future between them?"

"Because there always is," I snapped, throwing the leaf away and glaring at him. "It always happens. With all of my friends, with all of my boyfriends in school, with my—" My voice choked. "With my fiancé. They always choose her. They all believe I'm fickle, greedy. That I want more than I deserve, and so I flit my way through men I shouldn't have and"—I threw my hand up, letting it fall with a loud slap—"Look at us. Aren't they right? Here I am complaining to you about Sebastian, when I know that you want—"

I broke off, squeezing my eyes shut tight.

The reparation the Oath demanded of me was worse than normal, this time. At least with Hayden, I'd gotten so far into things, it was obvious why the Bargain's magic had seen fit to knock me down. But why was it so bad now? I had nothing real with either of these men, no actual hope for the future, and I'd refused to use the magic Fynn had shown me except in self defense. I'd said no when Sebastian asked for me to stay.

I didn't have anything worth taking away, for gods' sake,

and still the cruelty of that first Bargain ripped into me, carving me into pieces for the world to see.

Was this my punishment for breaking the orb, perhaps? Was the world reminding me, in vicious clarity, that my oath—and my fate—could not be so easily undone?

"I am everything they say I am." I said slowly. "And I've been here before. I've seen this pattern before—I take what I shouldn't, and it is taken back with reparations on top. They are right about me and I am right about them, and there is nothing that I can do."

A rustle of movement sounded, but I didn't open my eyes. Not even when I felt his presence before me, felt his clothing brush my skin and his hand fold carefully around my bicep.

His thumb with a soothing anchor, stroking back and forth. Part of me resisted, seeking that familiar coldness that had always protected me. The steel of a mask that let nothing in.

But I didn't want the mask, the cold. I'd been cold for so long, and I wanted warmth.

"There is something you can do," he said, still in that dark voice.

Reluctantly, I opened my eyes to face the world, but the world wasn't there; there was only Fynn.

My breath caught at the sight of him, because his eyes no longer held that secret, shadowed look. They glinted with fire—for a second, I thought almost literally.

He lifted his hand and ran his thumb over my chin, pausing at my lips.

"Pick me instead," he said, and there was no humor in his voice at all, no amusement, no challenge.

The words were raw, dark, deep. I forced myself to breathe again, not sure how long I'd been holding it.

Could I do that?

Could I believe that he wouldn't turn to someone else the

second he was bored of me? Could I do that when I knew that at least some part of Sebastian wanted me to be his?

"I," I began, but broke off partway because he didn't know.

He thought I was being dramatic. Insecure.

Fynn didn't know I was the Offering, and that everything I touched turned to dust. That to have anything good in this world, anything like these two fae had shown me, I'd have to steal it and damn my entire village to Hell.

That perhaps I already had, and my greed and selfishness had destroyed the happiness of an entire town.

I should tell him.

I opened my mouth, but I couldn't. I couldn't do it— couldn't bear to have him finally understand, and to look at me like the selfish mess I was.

Fynn tilted his head, a wry twitch of amusement finally appearing in the corner of his mouth as he marked my hesitation. "I'll give you a reprieve from answering," he said slowly. "We have one more night together after all. But at least trust me to keep you safe. Will you accept my pass?"

His pass. It took me a second, and then I realized he meant the ticket.

My heart hammered. In all the mess, I'd forgotten: Fynn had demanded payment tonight. And now I had to choose.

I'd thought I'd have a chance to test out the water sprites, but I hadn't. And I didn't want to lose this opportunity in case that went nowhere. But he still hadn't mentioned what the payment would be. And I knew now, looking at him, that he wouldn't. Not until I promised to pay it.

"Trust me," he repeated, softer than before.

That was why he wouldn't tell me; because this was the price. Whether he realized it or not, he was asking me to trust him. That was the payment for this Bargain.

To trust that the price he would demand of me wouldn't hurt me.

The world seemed to slow down, time crawling to a standstill. This was the war I'd been having with myself about him. I knew I always trusted the wrong man, and everything about Fynn screamed that he was the wrong one.

That I was falling for the same tricks, trying to seize the kind of joy that could never be mine.

And yet, I'd spent six long moons ignoring my heart, only to realize that I couldn't change who I was. That running from myself only meant I was abandoning myself; knowingly or not, I had been abandoning myself for years.

And the man who had told me that was him.

"I'll pay," I said, and the words filled me with relief.

Something in his face softened. His hands slid around behind my neck, and my breath caught.

"Is payment another kiss?" I asked, waiting for him to tilt his head for another peck on the cheek.

The quirk of amusement on his face deepened. "No," Fynn murmured. "Not that kind of kiss. Not this time." And then he pressed his lips to mine.

A sound escaped me, raw and broken. I could still feel the tears glistening on my cheeks, but where another man might have pulled away—might have tried to wipe them and make me smile before kissing me again—Fynn didn't stop. He didn't ask me to be anything that I wasn't.

He devoured me whole, tears and all. Pain and anger and all.

I had been in pain my whole life, I realized; I didn't know how to live without it or what it might feel like. And Fynn was the only one who had seen that. Of course. Because Fynn wouldn't just ask and wait for an answer. He'd hunt for it.

He'd seen the truth in me and hadn't asked me to ignore it—to squash it, to hide it. To admit I deserved it. For the most terrifying heartbeat, I wondered if I could tell him about the Offering. If I could tell him, and he'd still choose me.

I moaned, arms looping around his neck as I pulled him closer. I felt something that sounded like a gasp erupt from his mouth, but that had to be impossible. He must have kissed a hundred girls just like this.

He drew me nearer, one arm falling around my waist, and began to walk me backwards, slowly, slowly, until my body met with the tree behind me. And still he kept kissing me.

Kissing me like he didn't need air, like he didn't want it.

Finally, when I thought I couldn't bear the aching desperation of it any longer, he pulled back. In the shadow of the willow tree, he traced a line of my hair back from my eyes and simply watched me for a moment.

Then he said, "I know you're still keeping a secret or two, and I won't demand you share, but tell me: why do you keep telling yourself you only deserve the dregs of this life?" His eyes glinted. "I would give it all to you, Bailey."

A shiver raced through me, and for a heartbeat I allowed myself to pretend this was real. To pretend I could take what he was giving without damning the world.

But the heartbeat passed, and I couldn't help the bitter laugh that escaped me. "To answer that would be to share my secrets," I said quietly. "How about we just say: because that *is* what I deserve. Because it is my place, and my oath, and to take anything more would be to go against the needs of my entire village."

"So, you're telling me they want you to fail?"

"They *need* me to fail. The fact that they also want it only makes it easier for everyone."

He regarded me for a moment, expression unreadable. Then, he smiled. A slow, arrogant smile.

"Doesn't that make you just want to rage, Bailey? Don't you want to storm out there and make them all pay?"

This time, my wry laughter got caught in my throat, tangling up with all the thousand feelings there that I wasn't allowed to let out. Of course it did, but that wasn't the whole truth of it. It wasn't even the deepest truth. Embarrassingly, I choked off a sob. Fynn's face flickered with a gratifying flash of surprise.

"No I don't want to make them pay," I hissed, no longer caring about holding back. Something he'd said had triggered the most primal need inside me. A fury I hadn't even known I was carrying, and it wasn't the one either of us expected. "I want to *want*, Fynn. I want to feel again, and want things, and open up my arms to someone instead of willing myself into stone."

I wanted the life they denied me, and I wanted that desire to not be so utterly, disgustingly, unforgivably selfish.

For a long, long moment, he was silent.

Exhaustion flooded me, and I realized I had nothing left to say. So I simply dropped my head to Fynn's chest and squeezed my eyes shut tight around the pain that wracked me.

After a hesitant pause, his hand came up to the top of my head and he stroked me gently.

"There are many kinds of strength in this world," he said, the words murmured into my hair. "I forget that sometimes. Rage and fire is one kind—my favorite," he added with a low chuckle. "But to soften in the face of pain is another entirely." He pressed a kiss to my head, his lips lingering. "Mercy, forgiveness," he continued, quieter now, almost distant, ending in a faint laugh as he said, "All things I don't understand."

We fell silent, Fynn holding me as I struggled against the confusion of everything I thought I knew. Would it really be so wrong to steal this happiness? The broken oath in the archives said that it would. Sebastian's desperate expression as he'd contemplated giving up on his father for me said that it would.

The kiss he'd given my sister—evidence, yet again, that the world would remind me of my place when I forgot it—said that it would.

But Fynn... Fynn told me to seize it anyway. To take what I wanted, and who gave a fuck whether it was what I deserved.

The two of them were worlds apart in the way they chose to live, to love, but it was strange... In the darkness of Fynn's arms —where there was nothing to prove and I was hidden from the world by the safety of his body—I had the most profound sensation that, without looking, I couldn't tell the difference between him and Sebastian at all.

<h1 style="text-align:center">CHAPTER 30</h1>

<h1 style="text-align:center">Bailey</h1>

We made our way back to the fairground together, both of us silent and lost in our thoughts. I kept darting glances at Fynn, wanting to ask about the expression on his face, the sense of unease that had lost its armor.

But I didn't get a chance to, because the second we stepped inside the gates, someone else appeared. My body stiffened.

"Hayden," I said as he looked me up and down.

Moonlight glinted off his auburn hair, shadowing his features, but I'd know him a mile away. I'd know him in the darkness, by nothing more than the feeling that came over the air as he entered the space and strangled all the life within it.

He didn't even answer me; he just turned to Fynn, the corner of his mouth twisting into a sharp little smile. We were hidden from the rest of the circus, here. Overshadowing branches drooped and concealed our small clearing from the merriment of the fairground. My nerves burned, the ice cold edge of fear making them sharp and fragile. I forced my shoulders straighter, my back taller.

"Hayden," I said again.

I was relieved to hear that my voice came out steady. Even my expression felt as calm and still as ever.

After a long pause, he finally turned his attention back to me. "Bailey," he said, a charming grin sliding onto his face. "How funny I'd run into you here."

Don't give me that shit, I thought. *I know damn well Katerina told you I'd be here.*

"Are you finding enough pretty things to hold your attention?" I asked sweetly.

A flash of some darker emotion appeared on his face, but he hid it quickly. His smile softened, and he stepped forward with his chin lowered, his fingers sheepishly tucking his hair behind his ear as he said, "You know me, Bailes. Always too wrapped in my own head to see the beauty around me."

My blood froze; what was he playing at? The last time we spoke, he called me a whore and grinned the whole way through.

Fynn shifted, moving almost imperceptibly in front of me.

Hayden stuck his hands in his pockets and glanced back at the mingling crowd. Illusions of imps and dragons danced above the tent tops while the central square the fae had carved out for dancing churned with joyful bodies.

"I think this place has been good for me," Hayden continued, turning back. Before I could sift through the shock enough to speak, he added, "It was because of you that I came, actually."

The calm, controlled expression wiped clean from my face, and I gaped at him. Faintly, I registered Fynn stiffening; the air around us turned a little cruel, a little dark. But I couldn't look away from Hayden.

"What on earth are you wittering about?" I forced out.

He shrugged and took another step toward me, ducking

around Fynn so that he was practically cut out of the conversation.

"You know, you were always talking about the Lumière," he said, pronouncing the word with a slight twang, as though it tasted funny in his mouth. "Always banging on what it must be like, to live across the water." His expression turned sad. "I've been finding myself a bit lonely," he said in a hushed voice, like a confession, "so I thought I'd come and see what it was all about. See what *you* were about."

My breath caught. So many emotions swelled inside me, fighting for dominance. All I'd ever wanted was for Hayden to know me, to understand me. To see beyond the Offering and see *me*.

I'd thought he had, and I'd been proven so cruelly wrong. But was this a sign that he regretted his actions?

I didn't want him back. Too much had passed for that—but just to know that he was sorry…

But then Hayden said in a very different tone, slightly dazed, "I just need to know, Bailey—help me."

I blinked, startled.

Fynn remarked in a bored voice, "He wants something from you." With a graceful sweep, he lowered his hand from where he'd discreetly placed it on Hayden's arm—enough of a touch to read his mind, and force the truth past his desperate lies— and everything fell into place.

My mind grew still. The warm ray of happiness that had been uncurling inside me suddenly snuffed out, like a flame. I'd been tricked again.

Shame quickly whirled up in response, and because I didn't know where to direct it, I snapped at Fynn. "You read his mind. Don't you think I can handle this?"

Fynn laughed—a delighted sound as he arched one brow and looked me over. "That's your takeaway?"

I looked away from him. Hayden watched the exchange between us with something bitter on his face.

"What do you mean he read my mind?" He snarled, the wheedling expression vanishing in an instant. "He used his magic on me? How dare you?"

"Leave it," I said, shoving him back with one hand. Somehow, we'd ended up in the shadows beneath the tree. Hayden must have backed me into it, and I never even noticed. "What do you want? Get it over with."

Instantly, his eyes turned mournful again. "Bailey, don't be like that."

"Don't be like what?" I said, each word cutting and cruel.

"I just wondered if you'd seen the imp lately."

I paused, the fight I'd thought we were building to suddenly disappearing in the wake of confusion.

"What, Merelda?" I asked, frowning. "Of course I've seen her. Why?"

Hayden had never cared about Merelda before. She'd lived down the back of Hayden's garden for several years, but he'd never thought her more than a funny little creature, good for a laugh when she got riled. And when she'd chosen to follow me instead of him after the breakup, he'd said 'good riddance'.

Hayden shrugged, glancing off to the side for a minute before returning those same puppy dog eyes to me again. "Just a passing fancy, nothing important."

"You can't leave it at that," I snapped. "Why do you want her?"

His eyes widened in momentary surprise. Clearing his throat, he drew himself a little taller. "The Lumière are agitated," he hissed, darting a glance at Fynn and back again. "Someone's been thieving, and we both know what she's like."

My heart fluttered in my chest. *Someone's been thieving...*

Had they noticed the absence of the book I stole? But then surely Heillon would know it was me?

Unless my performance had really been that good.

"Merelda has nothing to do with it," I said coolly. "She would never mess with the fae like that."

Hayden scoffed a rude sound. Then, his tone turned wheedling, almost desperate. "If something's happened, Bailey, you can tell me. You're always forgiven, you know that." He swallowed, and it struck me that he was genuinely afraid. "But if the magic is striking out, we need to know. We need to stop it."

Ah. He'd heard about the fae's misfortune and thought my presence was the cause. Not because I'd stolen it—although I had—but because I was the Offering, and all misfortune could be traced back to me.

My lip curled. "I told you," I said in a quiet, steady voice, "you're looking in the wrong place for answers."

Anger darkened his features, wiping the fear clean. He stepped forward, reaching for me with the calm surety of a man claiming what was his.

Before he could reach me, however, Fynn stepped between us, his body like a rock wall, and with one flick of his wrist he sent Hayden hurtling across the ground.

My gasp rang across the quiet clearing. Before I could speak, or even think what I might say, there was a commotion off to the side; a figure burst from the dance floor, and I looked up to see Sebastian.

My heart began to pound, and I felt sick. If Sebastian was here, was Katerina close behind? Or had she abandoned him for someone else? I saw Fynn cast me an uneasy glance—for once, the mind reader seemed to have no idea what was about to happen.

On an ordinary day, I would have shared his concern, but

my stomach was churning too wildly, my mind racing too chaotically, and I just didn't care. I had to get out of here.

I had to.

I whirled on one foot, determined to leave before anyone could stop me, but then Sebastian ran to my side, his hand closing around my wrist as he silently begged me to stay. If I took another step, I'd be standing in shadow.

He would follow.

I swallowed, fighting the urge to fold in on myself and hide. My face was stone—the only wall I could stand behind.

"What's happening?" Sebastian asked.

Fynn glanced into the distance, where Sebastian had come from, and then back at us, before letting his lip curl up in a sardonic smile.

"A bit of human drama, my friend," he said in a voice that suggested anything but friendliness. He strolled over and clapped Sebastian on the shoulder. "I say we see how it unfolds."

Sebastian shrugged him off, sending Fynn stumbling with how violent the gesture was. "Drama you started, I'm guessing."

"Not technically," I said, my voice quieter than I meant it to be.

At the same time, Hayden finally found his feet, and he stalked back over to me.

"You're acting like a child. Whatever the imp stole, just give it back." He lowered his voice to a hiss. "Before the Bargain takes it back with interest."

"She. Stole. Nothing," I snarled. "You're looking in the wrong place for the wrong answers." Quieter, I added, "This has nothing to do with any of you."

For a long moment, he just stared at me. Then, his gaze

flicked to the two fae standing behind me. Something darkened in it.

"The star of the show and the emcee," he said, quiet enough for only me to hear. "Two of the most important fae in the Lumière, Bailey?"

Then, the worst person I had ever had the misfortune to meet shook his head at me.

Somehow, I found the strength to stand taller. To look him in the eye and lift my voice.

"Why don't you tell us why you're really here?" I told him. "And spare us all the delight of your company any longer than we need."

It was as if a glamor fell away. He bared his teeth at me, eyes flashing with anger as he stared from Fynn to Sebastian and back again. And then the anger simply faded as he began to laugh.

"Why bother?" he said tartly. "You can see it for yourself. You know what you're doing to them, even if you'll never admit it. How long before this crashes down as well? It all works out in the end, no matter how hard you try. The Bargain was too strong."

I waited for him to tire, to spit out all his cruelty and run off. But then... he looked at me. The whole time he'd been speaking, even though I'd stood my ground, I hadn't been able to look at Fynn or Sebastian. Hadn't really been able to look at anyone, my eyes fixed, instead, to a spot just to the left of Hayden's face. When he said the word 'Bargain', I flinched.

And Hayden, who had always noticed me when no one should, who had always seen right through me in the cruelest way possible... he saw.

And he knew.

His eyes lit up, a malicious fervor filling them. "They don't know, do they?" he asked, his voice far too loud.

I felt everyone turn to me, but I couldn't look away from him. My blood ran cold, and all the accusations that my friends had thrown at me came rushing back.

I was leading them on. I was everything they claimed me to be.

"They don't know!" he crowed. "Nice going, boys—you've picked a real winner here." He turned to them, a grand performer on a self-constructed stage. "You recall the first Bargain you ever made with us, here? Gods, you were probably there, you immortal bastards." He laughed at his own joke, already on a roll. "Remember how it was one child traded for the good of all? One child who would live a quiet, humble, peaceful life, so the rest might flourish and reach heights never dreamed of? Who would be the anchor point of our village, grounding us to humility, so that we could shine in the light?" His words grew quieter, colder. "One child who protected us from damnation, by knowing and holding her place in the shadows?"

He gestured grandly to me, and with the moon shining down, it felt like a spotlight.

"I give to you, the Offering. Now a woman of twenty-eight, who should know *fucking* better than to act like a child," he snarled. "A woman who could have lived a quiet, humble life by my side—helping me, supporting me. Serving the people she swore to protect, while we kept her safe under our wing. But she didn't. She couldn't. She was so selfish, so greedy, she had to take it all."

He dropped his hand to his side in a triumphant little flourish. "That's who you're fighting over. That's who's turned you against your own kind. Pathetic, isn't she?"

Something in me crumbled—not like a shattering of glass, but like a soft, desperate, pathetic little puff. A cliff falling into sand. A tide pool fading in the sun. I was nothing; no one. They would see right through me, now.

It was all over.

Fynn and Sebastian glanced at one another. I saw Sebastian mouth the words 'The Offering' like a question. Fynn shook his head mutely in response, brow furrowed.

Was it possible they hadn't heard of it?

Before anyone could ask, Fynn stepped forward.

"Whatever little human games you like to play here," he said, sounding utterly bored, "you can rest assured that the fae do not bother with these petty jealousies. What about her actions tonight are greedy? I see only a woman taking what she deserves."

Hayden drew himself up taller, jaw tightening in repressed fury. "Then you haven't seen how she flaunts the two of you, playing you off against each other. Making fools of you both. By all means, keep going if you think it's worth it." He gave a snide laugh. "You'll be covered in boils before the moon is out."

Fynn tilted his head, a polite smile on his face. I could practically feel the intricate cogs in that devilish mind turning as he weighed up what Hayden was saying—what it meant—and made a decision.

"You call that greedy?" he asked in a voice of deadly calm. "Selfish?" He looked over his shoulder at Sebastian and let his gaze fall across the fae in a slow, deliberate once-over. Unmistakable for anything but desire. "I call it sexy." Then he brushed a hand casually over my hair and pulled me into a scorching kiss.

Sebastian went rigid with shock, and I waited for... what, I wasn't sure. An explosion? Someone to get punched? Sebastian to walk off on me?

Anything to match up with all that I had feared this whole time.

But then he turned to me, and his eyes bore into mine, filled with an earnestness I'd never dreamed of as he said, "I want what she wants," before kissing me, too—soft, slow, and lingering.

My breath caught, but Sebastian wasn't done.

"Besides," he said, giving Fynn a wicked smile. For the first time, I saw Fynn falter, hesitation casting a shadow across his features as Sebastian leaned in close to him. Close enough that his breath must have run across Fynn's lips. "How can I blame her?" Sebastian's head tilted up in challenge as his eyes fell to Fynn's lips. "When her tastes are so divine."

As the last syllable left his mouth, he let his lips brush softly against Fynn's, and then eased back. I'd never seen Fynn so still.

A bubble of laughter surged within me, and I had to force it back down by covering my mouth. Whatever challenge was going on between the two of them, I still didn't completely understand it, but I thought Sebastian might have just won.

And then he turned to me, and I saw a depth of feeling there that I'd never seen before. I remembered the glimpse I'd seen of their past, and how Sebastian said he didn't believe in love at first sight with Fynn, even though he was clearly head over heels. I thought about how he'd fought so hard to insist that the two of us were only having fun, that we were saying goodbye seconds before he promised me forever.

Had he ever believed a word of his own lies?

And Fynn… The expression on his face was broken open. Raw. But when he finally composed himself, it wasn't to return to the cool, aloof fae he'd been since I met him. Finally, his gaze burned with the heat I'd craved for so long. The heat I'd sensed simmering beneath the surface, hidden behind that haunted, hungry look he reserved for the shadows. Now, he was searing with it—for Sebastian, and for me.

As I had in the clearing with him while learning magic, I

tasted the breeze. Desire's scent mingled on my tongue, and it tasted like all three of us. They'd kissed each other to piss Hayden off, to get one small win for me over the small-minded man who meant nothing, but they'd awoken so much more.

I wet my lips, fighting to ignore the pulse of heat between my thighs, and the way both Seb and Fynn had seemed to close in on me without moving. Bracketing me, their bodies angled to protect.

To take.

With a magnificent force of effort, I turned my attention back to Hayden. He was gaping at all three of us, shock and rage twisting his pretty features into something ugly. The idea of not one, but two, men choosing me, even in the face of his accusations, was incomprehensible to him. An unfamiliar sensation washed over me, warm and vibrant—triumph.

"Exactly," I said, my voice like ice. "No promises have been broken between the three of us. No one was left waiting to make their vow, believing in the chance of forever." My expression cracked, the stone giving way to fury. Rage. "Not like I could say for some."

Hayden flinched, but he didn't back down. Instead, his expression took on a strange emotion, glinting with fervor even in the low light.

"So you're working with the fae to bring us down then," he said, the words clipped—shoved through gritted teeth. "Just like everyone is saying."

My heart thudded in fear. He'd heard. When he hadn't accused me immediately, choosing to focus instead on rumors and half truths, I'd assumed he mustn't know, and I was safe. But I'd forgotten one central truth: when it came to cruelty, Hayden was as patient as the fae. Always waiting for the right moment.

Hayden shook his head. "I didn't believe it, but the evidence is right in front of my nose, and I owe it to our people to witness."

I had to leave. I'd wasted long enough here, listening to his crap. If he was telling the truth and the fae were searching for a thief, I had to get the hell out of here. Now. I'd hide in the forest, or run to the next village or—

But before he could continue, someone else stepped in front and silenced him with a single hand lifted between them. All the air punched out of me in a single gasp, and the tips of my fingers went numb with shock.

My sister had been hiding in the shadows.

"I spoke to Hannah," she said softly. My body shrank under her stern gaze. "She said you broke the oath."

Something brushed my fingers, smooth like glass; I yanked them away.

"I did nothing to the oath," I insisted, stepping forward, out of the protective circle of their bodies. "There was something wrong with the orb."

Her eyebrow lifted. In the moonlight, we looked far more alike than we should. She'd taken off her mask, and the shadows highlighted how we had the same nose. The same lips.

But where I was short, she was tall and willowy. Where I was sharp edges and harsh corners, she was grace and ease. Where I struggled to make good grades, she passed with honors —as was good and right.

Where I slouched in the darkness, she shone in the light.

I'd always known the Offering was about the entire village. My life for theirs. But to me, it had never been about them. It had always been about her.

I would have given anything for her, once.

"So you broke it earlier than today," she murmured, her tone suggesting she was piecing together a puzzle that had plagued her for some time. "No wonder we've been under such duress."

I swallowed. "I don't think the illnesses have been because of me," I insisted, forcing my words to remain steady. "There was something wrong with the orb when I got there. I think—"

"Of course they're because of you." She cut me off. "It's probably been festering since your failed engagement. And now you have to fix it—it's your duty. You swore an oath."

The words bubbled up inside me, screaming: *I don't want this duty!*

"Actually," I said, my voice calm. "I never swore an oath. If we're going to be technical."

The thing brushed my hand again, and I stopped pretending I didn't know what it was. It had hidden, like I told it to, and then followed me—just as it had begged for.

As the orb brushed my hand again, like a lost puppy, I stopped silently rejecting it. Whatever it was, wanted or unwanted, broken or unbroken, it was mine. Perhaps it was time to see what it really was.

With a flash of brilliant light, the shattered pieces of the Bargain from the town hall burst into the clearing. As if in answer, the coronet tucked into my satchel warmed and began to rise.

Hayden's eyes widened, and even Katerina broke her usual calm, graceful demeanor as she stared at it and clearly recognized it. When she spoke, her voice was high-pitched and shaky. "Swear it, Bailey! Fix the Bargain!"

I gritted my teeth together and shook my head. For a moment, my sister's face was tainted with rage. The coronet struggled against my palm pressing it down; rose petals flew off, fluttering to the ground at my feet.

"You'll damn us all to Hell for your selfishness," she hissed.

Briefly, the rage building inside me popped. Guilt flooded

instead, sickening and swift. I didn't want to make them pay. I didn't. But it was Merelda's voice I heard in my head, screaming at me to see the ugliness—and I saw it. It had been there all along. And maybe it was just because I'd never had the chance, but I couldn't imagine making someone suffer like I had, just because an ancient oath demanded it. I couldn't imagine making a child suffer like I had.

But I wasn't a child anymore.

I glanced at Fynn, saw his eyes glint with rage and remembered his words: *Doesn't that make you just want to rage, Bailey? Don't you want to storm out there and make them all pay?*

Gods, there was a part of me that did. I suspect there would always be a part of me that did—that would take and take and take if it could, and call it fair.

I had no idea what was fair anymore.

"Swear it, Bailey," Katerina insisted, the whites of her eyes large and clear. She was terrified.

"I—" I began, but I couldn't force the words out. Couldn't promise that I'd swear the oath and make everything right again.

Katerina shook her head, lips pressed tightly together, "You've always been my problem to bear." She straightened, speaking almost to herself. A regal figure encased in moonlight. "It's my duty to guide you when you stray."

She raised her hands, and, standing there, she looked as though she were facing an altar in supplication. Dread curled in my stomach, and once more I reached for a memory that wasn't there. What had we sworn to each other? Why had I lost it?

But whatever Katerina had planned, it was lost as the orb began to scream.

The shattered pieces rose, doubling in size, tripling. And the blue flame that should have burned in the center of the glass reignited, eclipsing the orb and half the clearing in a cerulean bonfire.

Hayden and Katerina staggered back on one side, while Sebastian, Fynn, and I fell away on the other. Petals cascaded in a miniature tornado around us, the coronet tearing to pieces in my hands. I could hear Katerina screaming at me to swear the oath, to fix the Bargain. Even the magic called to me. Begging me, silently, to join with it. To renew what was lost.

I pressed my lips tightly shut, my teeth clicking together, and said nothing.

Fynn and Sebastian exchanged a glance, their brows furrowed.

"That's not..." Fynn said, his voice low.

"I know," Sebastian agreed quietly.

Before I could ask, they stood and murmured several words in quick succession. The flame fought them, kicking up in anger, but then, with a low rumble and a hiss, it went out.

Fynn waved his hand lazily, and the broken shards began to shrink.

Hayden recovered, rising to his feet. A mean grimace twisted his face into something unrecognizable. I knew what was coming. My friends and family had tried twice to convince me to renew my oath; now they would force me. The village depended on it.

He snatched for me, hands closing around my wrist.

"Get your hands off me," I snarled, yanking away.

But his grip was a vice, fingers digging into bone.

"Never," he hissed, beginning to drag me forward. "You owe us. You're *ours*."

Several things happened at once. Fynn glanced at Sebastian, some kind of knowledge passing between the two of them that I couldn't read. Then, moving in synchronization, Fynn whirled to face me as Sebastian stepped behind him, into the darkness where Hayden stood.

Out of the moonlight, and into the shadow.

My lips parted, eyes wide. All that would need to happen would be for Fynn to turn and see it, and Sebastian would be done for. But Fynn's eyes were locked on me, as they had been the night by the lake, while Sebastian drew back his fist, wound up, and punched my ex-fiancé right in the nose.

Katerina screamed, and I squealed as well, clapping my hand over my mouth. Hayden's hand around my wrist went slack, freeing me as he stumbled backward. I moved on impulse, about to walk forward, although I wasn't sure which one of them I was walking to.

But then a hand clasped my bicep, warm and firm. I stopped level with Fynn, the two of us staring at one another. Behind him, Hayden and Sebastian were yelling, squaring off in a vicious fight. Sebastian was winning, and the expression on his face was one of pure, wicked delight.

"Let it happen," he said with a bright smile.

"But—"

"No."

I rounded on him. "Sometimes I think that's your favorite word," I hissed.

His smile widened. "Well, when one hears it enough, one does become attached."

A frown dipped in my brow, confusion rippling through me, fighting for presence against the sheer adrenaline flooding my veins. I turned to see Hayden howling, sobbing as he clutched his crooked nose, while Sebastian gave an elaborate bow and my sister swatted him uselessly.

Then, as Hayden finally stumbled to his knees in defeat, everything changed.

Soft, orange lights twinkled into existence from pillars that I swore hadn't been there before, and beneath our feet...

Silk.

I stumbled back, catching myself before I fell onto a pile of cushions. "What the hell?"

If I looked upward, the forest still loomed over us. The breeze still hit our skin, bringing night scents and the crisp taste of the lake after dark. Everything that had been there before was still here, only now, we were in some kind of gently illuminated spotlight.

"Don't move," Fynn said in a low, urgent voice. He lifted his chin, scanning the circus over the top of my head, searching for something. "They're coming to us."

"Who?" I murmured, my voice tight and low.

When Fynn finally glanced down at me, he wore an expression so strange, I had no idea what to make of it. Equal parts shock, fear, reluctance, and... want.

"The party," he replied.

Bailey

LAUGHTER SPILLED OUT OVER THE NIGHT, AND GLASSES CLINKED together as half a dozen fae and humans threw themselves from the shadows onto the silken bedding. Bottles appeared in the air, pouring fresh glasses until the bubbling, golden liquid overflowed. Music rang from a quartet that sounded as though it came from the trees, although I swore there was nothing there.

"The sixth night is a party," Fynn said under his breath, still scanning the distant crowd. "Designed to distract and seduce, in preparation for the final Bargains. If they've brought the party to the gates to stand between the guests and the exit, then there must be humans here who need a little extra persuasion."

He glanced back to where Hayden and Katerina had stood, but they were long gone.

"Fynn!" a rough, male voice called, seconds before a fae with long blond hair appeared and smacked him on the shoulder. "Should have known you were keeping all the best corners for yourself."

I watched the change come over him, so smooth it was almost imperceptible. A cocky grin appeared on his face, and he slid a hand around the back of the fae's neck and squeezed—

just a little too aggressive to be friendly. But the fae was clearly used to it, since he only laughed and leaned into the touch.

The newcomer leaned in close, almost whispering. "Heillon's roaming early tonight. Someone's stolen from his archives, and anyone suspicious is to be checked, human or fae. Keep your eyes open."

My blood ran cold; Hayden hadn't been lying. The Masters had discovered the theft, and if trespassing was rewarded with death, I didn't like my odds of escaping intact.

I flicked a glance at the gates, but all of a sudden, it felt as though a thousand eyes were pinpointed on me. How would I possibly get out of this alive?

Then, the newcomer's eyes fell on me. "And who is your friend?" His voice was a low, sensuous purr.

A shiver raced down my spine.

"Yes," another voice called as several more people sidled up to us, stepping over the giggling, lounging humans at their feet. "Who is your delicious friend?"

Now, my blood ran cold. It was the archers. The ones who had nearly shot me in the face, all for the chance to prove I was ripe for the plucking.

A steady, firm hand appeared around my waist, pulling me close. I nearly shoved them back until I caught the smell—warm, safe. Familiar.

Sebastian.

"Hands off," he snarled at them.

The archers laughed in pure delight. They'd only just arrived, and Sebastian was already playing into their hands. A trap that had been laid for me would catch more than one, if we weren't careful. And Sebastian was becoming less careful by the hour.

Adrenaline coursed through me, making my hands tremble with the need to move. To act. I picked at the leather ties on my breeches, knuckles white with tension. Several pairs of glittering, malicious eyes landed on me, studying every inch of my features; did they know who they were looking for?

No. They wouldn't, or else they wouldn't have instructions to search for anyone suspicious. Slowly, I forced my muscles to relax. I just had to remain innocent in their eyes, and I would live to fight another day, one step closer to my freedom.

A sliver of trepidation unwound within me: they had brought the party to us, guarding the exit under the guise of their hedonist pleasures. To appear innocent here would mean to act as quite the opposite... I shook my head. Surely not. There would be another way.

"Come now, Sebastian," the first archer said, lifting his chin. "You heard the Masters. Indulge all who are willing, yes? And we have quite a few women here who would love to spend the night with you." He turned, lips parted ready to call to any number of the women lounging across the makeshift bed...

And then Fynn stepped forward. "Not tonight," he murmured in a tone that sent fear and desire roiling through my blood in equal measure. "Tonight, he's indulging me."

A flare of heat ran through me, and the hand at my waist clenched harder, fingers digging into the skin above my hip. I hardly dared to breathe.

What was Fynn doing?

Sebastian stared at him, expression shadowed, and a long, painful silence passed between them. I had the impression they were weighing each other up. Testing what the other would do. Until finally, minutely, Sebastian's tense muscles relaxed. He trusted him, at least for tonight.

Meanwhile, the expressions on the archer's faces froze into open violence.

"Indulging you?" the one at the front lifted a brow. "Then that leaves the two of us free, does it not?" He reached out to tug lightly on the end of one of my curls, smiling down at me with pure arrogance. "And with enough music and wine, I think this beautiful lady could be quite enticed into what I have to offer her."

"And yet she is not," Fynn sneered, and the archer pulled back with a flinch.

He looked between us, all three of us, and understanding crossed his features.

"You greedy fuck," he murmured.

What was *happening*?

I knew what was happening.

My chest rose and fell as my breathing grew heavier. He'd whisk us away to privacy, surely. There was no way we'd join this group of giddy, rapturous bodies.

But then our eyes met, and beneath the wicked glint of his smile, I saw the truth. If he took us away, it would raise suspicion.

We stood on a razor's edge, surrounded by enemies on all sides. Out of the corner of my eye, I saw a tall dais rise from the ground, draped in black velvet. A figure climbed slowly to sit upon it, dragging a pliant body into their lap. The twinkling faelights caught on red hair, and I clenched my fists.

He was watching, and there was only one path forward to allay his suspicions.

A human acting strangely, of their own free will, and trying to leave... that would get me captured in seconds. But a willing participant in this wild night of debauchery? A human who was safely contained within the arms of Heillon's men, being seduced to return for Bargain Night tomorrow? That human was safer than ever before.

It was like being with Sebastian in the room of masks all over again, only a thousand times more dangerous. And no illusion of light would save us here; it would get us killed.

Heat pooled between my thighs. The chaste kisses we'd shared moments before still burned on my lips, and I could hardly think straight.

"Go on then." The archer rolled his eyes in disgust. "Have your fun."

Before I could even process what had just happened, they left. My feet shifted nervously, pooling into the silken pillows and layers of luxurious covers strewn across the ground. Now that I wasn't staring in stunned incomprehension at the threat before me, I finally noticed the surroundings were still changing.

Silver poles rose, inch by inch, from the ground. Some were topped with swinging lanterns of faelight, others hooked gauzy drapes onto the elaborate metal flourishes of their arms, dividing the clearing into private corners. As the seconds passed, our lonely clearing by the gate transformed into a decadent, alfresco palace.

In the shadowy distance but still near enough to reach out and touch, hidden bodies giggled, drank, kissed, and more.

"Are they drugged?" I asked in a hushed, horrified voice. "Is the wine making them—"

"No." Fynn shook his head. "That wine does not come out until the final night." He cut a glance to me. "And it is not used for this."

Bargains. It was used for Bargains.

Fynn took a step closer. "We can leave," he said idly, "and they will question what my real game is. Or we can stay…" His voice lowered. "And you can trust us to look after you."

Trust us. Since when were they an 'us'? They'd been at each other's throat from the moment I stepped through the gates.

I expected Sebastian to cut him off. To turn their threatening words into violent actions. But instead, he pulled me closer to him and whispered in my ear.

"Heillon is watching, sweetheart."

Heillon was watching. They had brought the party to us, whether as a test or a trap, I had no idea. And the safest way out was to give them no reason to look closer.

It was also, I realized with a sudden shock, what I wanted.

I met Sebastian's gaze, and an unspoken understanding passed between us. His expression flickered with surprise for an instant before it was overtaken with heat. Then, his other hand came round to clasp the opposite side of my waist and turn me slowly to face him.

"Nothing that you aren't willing to do," he said in a low, urgent voice.

In the background, I heard several giggling people join the pile of bodies on the cushions, deep in conversation. Not everyone was as depraved as the fae claimed to be. Some were eating. Some were simply lying and enjoying the sights.

Two, I saw behind the shadowy layer of their gauze curtain, were slowly peeling clothing off layer by layer. Those two seemed to especially enjoy the audience.

But it didn't have to be like that.

I scanned the clearing, still surrounded by gently sweeping branches and vines, but overtaken in its center now by decadent finery and willing bodies. A group of three in a dark corner had pulled one of the silken sheets over themselves, and in the shadows there, illuminated only by the dappled light of the moon and the low kiss of faelight in our tiny corner, no one could quite tell what their hands beneath the sheets were doing.

I noted the outlines of their bodies, the slow, rhythmic movements of their limbs, the gasps that echoed from them...

And I yearned.

"Only if you promise me the same," I told him, glancing from Sebastian to Fynn until I was certain they understood.

This might have been a disguise we were using to slip between the cracks, but I would not have a lie. Not from them.

With slow, aching tenderness, Sebastian's hand slid higher over my waist, brushing against my breasts, unknowingly tracing the path that Fynn's hand had taken only hours earlier.

And then he kissed me, fingers clasping my jaw, mouth sweet and desperate.

It was almost more than I could bear, to be kissed in front of so many people, whether they were watching or not. To be *wanted* in front of so many people, only minutes after my sister and my ex had demanded I reclaim my oath.

I would not reclaim that oath. Instead, I would claim this.

I felt two hands settle low on my waist as Fynn stepped in behind me, and a mouth I'd barely begun to know—to taste, to feel—descended on my neck. A low, rough sound escaped from my lips, captured instantly by Sebastian.

He pulled me closer to him, and behind me Fynn followed.

The two of their bodies became hard, unyielding barriers between me and the world.

"An hour would be enough to deter them," Sebastian murmured in a low voice, only for mine and Fynn's ears. "If you think you can last."

That final, cutting comment was not directed at me, and I felt the man behind me stiffen before lifting one hand and tucking it beneath Sebastian's chin.

With deliberate care, he angled Sebastian's face until they were glaring into each other's eyes.

"You've had your games with me tonight," he said in a low, raw voice. "This one's mine."

Then he kissed him.

It wasn't the soft, tender challenge of the one they'd shared before. This was a kiss that reminded me of that single memory —of what they must have once held so preciously between them. Of what, I realized, part of them must wish to share again, no matter what lay between them.

Fynn's hand threaded into Sebastian's hair. He kissed him deeper, harder. And then with a desperate sound, he wrenched free, chest heaving as he stepped back. One step, then another.

"Go on, then," he murmured. "Make her comfortable. I know you're dying to."

My breath escaped me in a rush. They really were working together; it wasn't something I'd ever thought to see.

And perhaps I wouldn't, not ever again, because no matter what they might want, the chasm that lay between them was greater than they could cross. We had only this night, and one single, priceless illusion.

The noise of the circus fell away as Sebastian lowered me onto the cushions. Somewhere behind me, three humans were entwined with a single fae, clothing askew, hands and lips shared over and over. Their shadows fell through the curtains onto us, illuminated by the soft golden glow of faelight.

I didn't pay them a single thought, and they didn't care about me either.

I stretched out across the sheets, noticing with relief that Sebastian had chosen an alcove where the moon still shone through the trees. He was breaking no rules, and our hidden corner felt both tenderly hidden and exhilaratingly exposed.

Warmth pressed against me, a second body joining me from behind, and Fynn's arm looping over my waist as he breathed a word and encouraged the silken sheets at our feet to rise and cover us.

My hair pooled on the pillow beneath me as I lay back and looked up at the two men who had promised to be mine, if only for a night.

Time seemed almost to stand still, and then Sebastian kissed me. His hair fell against my skin, my neck, my collarbone. His fingers threaded into my hair, pulling hard enough to hurt as he kissed and devoured me right there, for all to see.

He pulled back, just far enough to speak but not enough that our lips didn't brush together at the movement.

"This dance lasts until closing time," he murmured. "But the players ebb and flow. So long as we keep you here enough to play and be enjoyed..." The words rolled on his tongue. "They won't question when we leave."

"Stop talking about leaving," I snarled, and beside me I heard Fynn laugh.

"You are still so full of excuses," he said in a voice that was so utterly sick of it all, I couldn't help laughing too.

Their expressions stilled, each of them turning toward me as the sound rose like bells above our warm clearing.

"Do that again," Fynn murmured, eyes glinting.

"I can't laugh on command," I pointed out dryly, "so play your role"—I hooked a finger into the front of his shirt and pulled him in, kissing him soundly, deeply—"and make me scream."

A sound rasped at the back of his throat, as if something had broken in him. He stopped holding back. Covering my body with his, he shoved Sebastian aside and kissed me how I'd wanted him to in that clearing, how he had the moment he took payment for that ticket. A wild thought rose within me, and I wondered now if I even needed the sprites, or if I was right where I was meant to be.

Taking every last drop, everything I deserved.

I shoved all lingering thoughts of my broken Bargain from my mind, all memories of sulfur burning and illness spreading. It was wrong; they were wrong. There was no necklace around my throat to burn and terrify me into obedience. There was nothing that I could take tonight that would ruin it, no matter what my sister said, because everything I did served a single purpose: to become lost.

To sever my ties here and be taken by these two men over the water, to another life.

I kissed Fynn with those thoughts surging within me, arching beneath his touch as he explored my body with cautious fingertips.

Pulling back enough to raise an eyebrow in question, he lifted the corner of my shirt and waited.

Swallowing thickly, I nodded, and then the shirt was gone, thrown off somewhere into the crowd who cheered and laughed in response, no doubt losing their own clothing too.

Moonlight bathed Sebastian's face as he watched the two of us in open wonder. But things were not fair yet, and what was the Offering if not the epitome of fairness?

I tugged at both of their shirts. "Go on then."

They barely wasted a second, stripping free with a performer's grace, before they slid down to enclose me from either side.

It was skin against skin, and I had never felt so warm and protected in all my life. The faint scent of crushed rose petals drifted upward, and I felt the scratchy texture of the broken coronet beneath me, tearing apart every time I moved. I didn't know which way to face, but they made the decision for me as Sebastian turned me with one hand and began to kiss me again.

He didn't stop.

Not even when Fynn carefully moved the hair from my neck and began to kiss there too, eyes closed, lips plush. Softer and sweeter than I ever imagined.

I moaned, arching beneath their combined touch. I kept waiting for something to ruin it, for something to take them away—whether that was their own stupid arguments or something worse. But it didn't come. The archers left us alone, and in our small circle of moonlight, nestled on either side by pillows and drapes, it was as if we were alone.

Fynn's mouth moved lower, kissing my shoulder, a hint of teeth digging into my skin.

A sudden flash of fear went through me. Their instructions tonight were to indulge all who were willing. What if someone else interrupted? What if someone else asked to be indulged?

"Tonight," I breathed, "you're mine. No one else's."

Fynn answered instantly, murmuring the words against my skin, "Consider it a promise," while Sebastian snarled in response: "Anything you want, my love."

That final word broke through me, shattering and remaking me in one. Whatever the future held, I would have this.

With rough, desperate movements. Fynn pulled me back, leant down, and licked a swipe over my breast, teeth grazing skin as he cupped the curve of it and stroked.

Sebastian kissed me once more, swallowing whatever I might have said as the two of them began methodically, deliberately, to devour me.

Scattered drifts of moonlight waved over my face, tree branches moving and blurring above me, shadows in the dark of night. The full moon was somewhere above us, but beyond the strip that haloed Sebastian's face, it did not reach us.

Fynn's hand moved lower, his lips caressing my nipple as he sucked it into his mouth and bit gently.

His hand moved lower, over the swell of my ass—still clad in breeches—and behind, slipping under the fabric. I realized his intent only a second before he slid his finger over the slick wetness of my core. Back and forth at first, teasing me, making me ready. And then he slipped his finger inside.

I was nowhere near full enough.

I arched back into him, trapped by Sebastian's relentless mouth on mine, caught between the two of them. Our bodies writhed beneath silken sheets, my clothing slipping further down beneath Fynn's touch until the waistband of my breeches was around my thighs. The hot press of his hand against my skin was a brand. It was both too much sensation and not nearly enough.

Fynn's teeth grazed the side of my breast, biting a little harder than I thought he meant to and making me cry out.

Sebastian pulled back with a wicked grin on his face, sweeping his hair free of his forehead. "He's a biter, isn't he?" he murmured in a low, husky voice.

Heat swelled within me, desire unfurling. Desire I'd never been allowed to have before. Sebastian tilted his head to the side, watching as Fynn's mouth moved from my breast, his finger still an aching, steady slide inside me. Sebastian seemed to come to some conclusion, grin widening and eyes little more than darkened shadows. His hand moved lower, down my front, skating across the junction of my thighs before—

I sucked in a breath.

His finger slipped in alongside Fynn's.

Fynn lifted his head, eyes flashing in the darkness. "I was here first," he said sardonically, flicking his hair out of his eyes with a rough twitch.

"And I was here second," Sebastian said breezily. "Do I still get a ribbon?"

A surprised laugh escaped Fynn. The sound completely transformed his face, eyes flying open for a brief moment. I caught a sight, there, of who he had been in that memory. In their dreams.

Young, carefree, in love.

Then the expression vanished, and he angled his mouth upward this time to kiss me.

The kiss deepened, his hand behind my head to hold me in place, while the pace of his finger inside me quickened, sliding alongside Sebastian's, the two of them caught in tender synchronicity.

I cried out, but Fynn didn't let me go, and I felt Sebastian's mouth descend on my collar and lower still, carving a path between my breasts, lapping over one nipple while the two of their fingers inside me still thrust an aching rhythm.

I wanted more—needed more. One night wasn't enough, so at the very least I had to take all they could give. But when I reached, fumbling, for Sebastian's loose, flowing breeches, he gently stopped me with a palm against my wrist.

"Not here," he murmured. "Not like this."

"But—" I breathed, reaching behind me desperately, searching for Fynn as well. I palmed his hard length, eliciting a delicious groan into my ear.

"Don't tempt me," Fynn warned in a low, wretched voice. "Or I'll have you face down in these cushions with your pretty mouth wrapped around his cock."

He kissed the whimper from my mouth, almost biting me into silence.

"Please," I begged.

But he only smiled, half-lidded eyelashes practically kissing his cheeks as he said, "If I give into you here, I'll lose all ability to watch over us."

Sebastian hummed in agreement.

Watch over us.

Suddenly, the way they kept glancing at the shadows took on a different tone. They weren't simply absorbing the sights and sounds, like I was. They were making sure no one inter-rupted. That the Masters were appeased, while I was kept safe.

"But you," Fynn murmured into my ear before casting a surreptitious glance over his shoulder once more, "should let go."

At the same moment, Sebastian's thumb brushed, featherlight, over my clit.

I thrust forward, lost once more in first Fynn's kiss and then Sebastian's, my body overwhelmed by the heightened awareness of both the game we were playing and the desire that shadowed every shared breath. Their hands quickened, touching, caressing, while their mouths moved to taste every sweat-soaked inch of my skin.

Too soon, I cried out, the sound as quiet and hidden as I could make it. I wrenched my mouth free from Sebastian's and turned, muffling the cry in the pillow beneath me and dampening the silk with my mouth. It wasn't enough to mask the unrestrained whimper of pleasure as I shattered on their fingers, coming in waves over and over.

Soft sounds came from above me, familiar and yet not. When I finally lifted my head again, I saw the two of them kissing desperately. Fynn's hand twisted in Sebastian's hair, clutching it, while Sebastian's palm gripped Fynn's jaw so tight it looked like he'd never let him go. Something ached inside me, but I couldn't have named it if I tried.

A fresh wave of laughter carried over from the entrance, breaking the moment. I looked up to see a number of newcomers stumbling in, finding their places upon the sheets and pillows.

Fynn wrenched his head back, brow furrowed.

The silken sheet lay pooled around their waists, each of their bodies angling over mine and hiding me from sight while they remained blessedly visible.

I'd never seen such a beautiful sight.

"That's our cue," Fynn murmured. "The new wave has come. They've seen enough." The upper curl of his lip twisted. "They don't get to have any more."

My heart thudded in my chest, but I didn't question it as we quickly regained our clothing and slipped out of the clearing. I stumbled a little over the cushions, the faelight too shadowy to see by and somehow still blinding.

When we landed back in the vibrant sights and sounds of the circus proper, my dizzy mind fought for solid ground. Where was I? What was I doing? I had a whole plan, and it had been completely derailed by silken sheets and smooth skin.

Piece by piece, I wrestled my mind back into place. I had to speak to the sprites, uncover their secrets, and decide my path forward. Because this night was coming to an end, and I was either to hide among the caravans here until the seventh day rose, where I would cross with the Lumière and my ticket safely in hand. Or I was to leave tonight, and all of this would become a memory.

I glanced at the two of them, their faces equally still and serious. They wouldn't look at each other, one standing on either side of me as if whatever had allowed them to come together before had already been lost.

"I have one final performance," Sebastian murmured to me. "But it's too dangerous for you to watch. If they have any clue at all, they'll expect you there."

Fynn's brow furrowed. "Who will?"

Sebastian ignored him. "Don't trust anyone from now until tomorrow night," he murmured, before pressing one final kiss to my lips. "And don't let Heillon get you alone."

Finally, he lifted his attention to Fynn, but still, he didn't speak. Another of those unreadable looks passed between them, a silent assessment that I had no hope of deciphering. However, with the way Sebastian's jaw tightened, lips pursing just a little, I wondered if he didn't truly know what he was seeing either. Didn't know what to make of this man who had so betrayed him, and yet who he would still trust with his safety when it mattered most.

Then, with a final lingering glance my way, his fingers slipped free and he disappeared, weaving among the moonlit path.

When I turned to Fynn, there was something shuttered about his gaze, something uncertain.

"I... I should go," I murmured, my mind racing ahead of itself, already tangled. Stick to the plan; keep moving forward. It was a new mantra.

But as I turned to leave, Fynn said, "Stop waiting."

"Huh?" I spun slowly to face him.

"Stop waiting to be chosen," Fynn said, each word low and fierce as he walked toward me. A bitter twist curled to his mouth as he added, "Some of us may be cursed by that dilemma, but not you. Stop letting their petty words affect how you see yourself, Bailey. Their twisted oaths, their manipulations... None of it matters, and even if it did, they aren't fucking worth it.

"You've been waiting for people like that idiot back there to choose you, to make you feel worthy." He shook his head. "You're already worthy. So who do you choose, Bailey?"

His words ricocheted through me; it was like I'd been hit by lightning.

I stared up into his blue eyes, and something began to unfurl—the quiet feeling of possibility. All my life I'd been searching for a bold statement, a grand gesture. Flowers delivered publicly for all to see. A ring.

But that, it had been proven to me beyond a doubt, was not love. Love needed to bud before it could bloom, just as Sebastian said in that memory.

That was what it was with these two. A bud. The beginnings of something that, no matter how we'd denied it, could be very, very real.

I didn't need to wait to be chosen. Instead, I just had to

reach out and choose which bud to pluck. And perhaps I couldn't take it now, with the Bargain Magic rippling all around me, waiting to drop around my neck like a noose. But in one more night, that Bargain would be dead. I'd be living in Criera, and anything I wanted could be mine.

As quickly as it rose, the hope within me fizzled, shrinking back in on itself. My heart stuttered, because as I looked up at Fynn, I saw that same glint in his eye from before. When his words had echoed through my mind—*don't you just want to make them all pay?*—and I'd realized there would always be a part of me that did. An ugliness, festering deep inside, that I didn't want to choose.

This was why he was dangerous. It wasn't what everyone else had tried to tell me—it wasn't that he was cruel, or untrustworthy, or a hunter.

It was that looking at him was like looking into a mirror. But where Sebastian's mirror had been the fire of desire, Fynn's was the fire of rage.

Fynn watched me, and I didn't think he even had to read my mind to know what I was thinking. Something darkened in his expression, as if he knew which one of them I'd silently chosen.

"You don't want to make them pay," he said softly. "You want permission to want." He gave a low, bitter laugh, the twitch of his lip wry as he simply said, "I can't fault your choices. Would that I could."

He straightened, a furrow appearing in his brow. When he spoke, his next words were thoughtful. "What did that man mean, when he called you the Offering?"

I swallowed, the words racing away even as I reached for them. "It means I'm the Offering Child," I said slowly. "The debt of the first Bargain, made centuries ago. I'm the town's sacrifice, so that they may prosper, and if I ever falter in my duty to serve them, they will fall to Hell."

The words were dull. Empty. I watched them land, the furrow in Fynn's brow deepening. "But," he began slowly, "that doesn't—"

He froze, eyes wide. He glanced at me, then at the clearing we'd just left, where Heillon's midnight dais stood, then back again. "No," he breathed.

Time stretched between us, his gaze fixed on the distant sights, something unknown passing through his mind. For a moment, I felt the most aching sense of sadness spilling from him. Of something ending, never to be found again.

As quickly as it had appeared, the glimpse behind the wall vanished. He cleared his throat, and something inside me felt like it was shattering. No—not inside me. Something *outside* of me. Something that lay all around.

Fynn watched me, eyes blazing like blue flames.

Then, he stepped away, and I realized abruptly how much I didn't want him to go. The shattering thing ruptured. Between us, around us—a crack split the air like thunder. Something tearing that could never be healed.

Agony wrenched inside me, even as that twisted sense of hope still bloomed—the two emotions thudding together like twin heartbeats. I couldn't help it. I couldn't control it; it just was. It was how he made me feel. How both of them made me feel. Equal parts hope and agony.

And even as that thing cracked, I felt a quiet, calm, hopeful pull toward Sebastian instead.

I turned back toward Fynn, but he was backing away into the shadows.

"The night is over," he said, still in that strangely calm, steady voice. "Best to run while you still can. Goodbye, Bailey."

I frowned, my heart stuttering. "No—wait."

He shook his head. "Be polite," he chided gently. "Say goodbye."

A frustrated sound escaped me, and I felt like a toddler stamping their foot. "Fine! Goodbye, already. But—"

"Uh uh," Fynn shook his finger, almost completely encased in shadow now. "Say my name."

"*Goodbye, Fynn*." I snarled. "Now get your cowardly ass back in here before I make you."

Fynn smiled, the sight so cold, so devastating, I felt frozen.

"Your debt is paid," he murmured. "Go and be blessed."

And then he was gone.

CHAPTER 32
Bailey

I ENDED UP SLIPPING OUT THE SAME GAP THAT SEBASTIAN HAD LEFT BY, when he came to the lake that first night, and making my way along the river toward home. Even though the path was shadowed and still, it no longer frightened me. I'd faced lora beasts near those shores, both real and illusory. I'd heard the words of the imps on the breeze, and prayed to willow dryads who answered in the language of shadows and earth.

My ties here were fading, and I was ready to cross the water.

But in the hours since I'd left, Fynn's words had played over and over in my mind. I couldn't make sense of them any more than I could make sense of my response to them.

Say my name.

Was that really what he'd meant when he made the Bargain with me, all those days ago? *This* was what he'd planned? I couldn't fathom it, and the finality with which he'd said goodbye terrified me.

But really, I was the one who made no sense, because what did I even want from him? I was leaving forever, and this thing between us was never made to last.

The moon glittered across the garden beds as I stood

beneath the forest canopy and stared at the darkness of my cottage. I hadn't intended to come back here tonight, but then, I hadn't intended to come apart on both Fynn and Sebastian's fingers, crying their name into their mouths, either. The night was full of surprises.

At one point, I saw torches draw close to my windows, heard the shattering of glass and muffled shouts. But the sounds faded soon enough, and they didn't return. The villagers hadn't found me there, and so they probably assumed I was in some wicked fae's bed. No doubt they'd come for me tomorrow night at the circus. Bargain Night.

Whether they found me or not, only the gods could tell.

Rubbing the goosebumps along my arms, I took a breath and lifted my wrists in supplication. The wind caressed my skin, and after a moment, the ancient tree above me creaked and lowered its branches—just enough to block the icy autumn wind that came from the river. A small thrill ran through me; it worked. Everything Fynn had shown me, everything I was learning, it *worked*.

With the willow's protection, I could wait here until just before dawn, and then ask the sprites for help when my village would be in the deepest sleep. If they couldn't carry me to Criera, then my choice would be made. I'd simply sneak back into the circus and hide among the caravans.

But as I stared at the darkness of my cottage, it occurred to me that there was one tie still tethering me to Aelor. Stefan.

Hissing under my breath, I rose to my feet and crept along his garden path. However, it didn't take long to work out that he wasn't home. Frowning, I hovered in the arch of his verandah as I thought. Could he be in danger? It wasn't likely... And he did often take midnight walks by the lake.

It was also possible he was looking for me. He'd suspected

once that I was leaving; it wouldn't surprise me if he'd worked it out again.

Leaning around the corner, I studied the darkened shadows of my cottage. Nothing moved, and there were no sounds apart from the gentle night noises from the forest. If I were to guess what those noises meant, I'd say it was safe.

I slipped inside and began to pack the bag I hadn't bothered with before. Part of me wondered whether I hadn't truly believed I was leaving until now.

I thought about taking the trinket box from the cupboard, but I couldn't bear to, and so instead, I buried it in the garden where no one would look. At the last second, I picked up the tiny shard of mirror and stared at it, my own dubious expression reflected back at me.

It wasn't a tie keeping me here, but my last moments with Sebastian still felt unfinished. If the water sprites took me across with them, then I'd never see him again. I was already churning with guilt and unease over Fynn; did I really want to add another name to that mess?

Eventually, I slid the shard into my bag, careful not to let it cut me.

Then I slipped back into the forest and searched for a place to summon them. As I came closer to the lake, the distant sounds of the quieting fairground returned. It must have been close to midnight by now, with only a few dwindling humans muddling their way to the gates. It was a strange thought, that I was safer here, near the Lumière, than in my own home.

I chose a spot on the other side of the lake, in the darkness, and then took the broken mirror from my bag and held it before me. As it caught the moonlight, I finally admitted one final hidden truth to myself: I'd always wanted this. Magic, wonder. Enchantment. I'd been told I could never have it, and so it was the one thing I'd always refused to give up. It was why I had a

Talking Mirror when no one else did. Why I learned Criari, why I'd loved Merelda from the moment I saw her. It was why I'd come running for the circus the second they looked in Broodshire's direction.

I'd always wanted this, and now I would have it.

When I whispered Sebastian's name, it shimmered with an inner light, before a dozen images sped across the surface. I frowned, staring at the whirl of color and sound. It was as though the circus was full of mirrors, and my little shard couldn't find the right one. It spun all around the circus, from every angle, until the near-empty grounds seemed to sparkle beneath the string of globes that strung across the center.

I froze, staring in silent fixation at the circus grounds. From this new angle, I saw what I had missed before. The globes had been here every night since the fae arrived, but I'd never looked at them, and now I saw: they weren't globes at all.

My breath caught in my throat; they were Bargains. Bargains waiting to be filled. Even as I watched, more and more lit up, not with faelight as I'd thought every night before this, but with a different kind of magic all together.

They were being prepared for the seventh night. The full moon, when their magic was highest, and the Bargains would begin.

I hardly had a chance to think about that, when the mirror finally stopped its search and brought me face to face with Sebastian's wide-eyed expression.

"Bailey," he breathed.

I stared at Sebastian, not knowing what to say. Judging by the wild look in his eye, he felt the same. It had only been hours since we saw each other, but nothing about the passage of time in this last seven-day had been normal. I'd made choices that felt like they were years in the making, even though I'd never thought about them before the Lumière arrived. I'd spent what felt like moons in a single performance tent, changing beyond my recognition. My nights had become my days, and I couldn't remember when I'd last slept properly.

Eventually I took a deep breath and said, "Hello."

His face broke into a smile. It was so cherished and familiar, I wanted to cry. "Let me guess," he said softly, a touch of sadness in his voice. "You're here to tell me we're running away together."

I let out a laugh that sounded more like a sob. "So you know why I'm calling, then."

"Of course."

We fell into silence, neither of us wanting to say the words we knew were coming. In the distance, I caught sight of a familiar lantern bobbing along the lake trail; Stefan was here. When I was finished speaking with Sebastian, I would find Stefan, too. One by one, my final tasks were being completed.

"Have you..." Sebastian began, wetting his lips. "Have you said goodbye to Fynn, as well?"

All at once, the thoughts I'd been desperately trying to ignore rushed at me. I closed my eyes. "I think I did worse. I think I rejected him."

He smiled sadly. "Is this not rejection? Because it feels like it."

This was where I should say that it wasn't. Where I should tell him that, as soon as I stepped foot in Criera, I could finally have anything I wanted, and that included him.

My gaze fell to a piece of paper clutched in Sebastian's hands—what he must have been reading when his mirror began to glow. Only two words were visible through his grip and the tiny window I had into his room: *possible match.*

They'd found his father, or hoped they had. There was a chance, at least, and that knowledge solidified the choice I knew I had to make. I hadn't chosen Fynn, but that didn't mean I had chosen Sebastian either.

Fynn had been right: I had to stop waiting for love to choose me. I had to stop running into the arms of romance, just to find a shred of self worth. I had to choose myself.

"I have to leave," I said quietly. "You've always known that."

Sebastian straightened, speaking quickly—impulsively. "I'll come with you. Protect you."

The earnestness on his face was like an arrow through my heart. Sebastian had to be here, waiting to receive the man who could be his father. If he wasn't, everything would fail.

And he still, impulsively, recklessly, chose me.

"You have to think with your head, not your heart," I cautioned him, shaking my head.

Sebastian flinched, shoulders hunching forward as his eyes slid away from mine. "We still have Bargains to break. You have to save your father, and I have to break the oath of the Offering in a way that doesn't doom my village."

"The Offering," he repeated cautiously. "I'd never heard of it until tonight."

"It doesn't matter." My words were harsher than intended, but they needed to be. "I've seen what will happen if I become an oath-breaker, and I know what to do to avoid it. My path is clear."

After a beat, he said, voice flat. "You could doom them, if you wanted. I wouldn't blame you. Burn it all down."

I only looked at him. He sighed.

"But I know that you won't." He gave me a wry smile.

"I won't," I agreed.

"Are you leaving with the sprites then?"

I smiled softly. "I'll ask, but if they say no, I have my ticket. Only..." The tone of my voice made him look up sharply. "I have to lie low until the crossing. Heillon is up to something, and he needs an offering… I think he's chosen me. Whether I cross with the sprites or the Lumière, I can't let him find me."

He straightened, eyes wide, lips parted. "Go," he breathed. "You have to go. Now!" He backed away from the mirror, glancing over his shoulder as if Heillon was already waiting.

"I will. I am."

Emotion danced in his eyes. "When I break free, will I find you again? Over the bridge?"

Here it came.

"Perhaps," I breathed. "But…"

"I'll find you," he promised. "I swear it. Nothing can hold me back."

His words filled me with hope, with the promise of a future I'd never thought I could have. And yet, if I hadn't been watching him so intently, I might not have seen it. But something shuttered in his gaze; a heaviness that hadn't been there before. One that affirmed everything I'd been thinking on this long, confusing night.

Nothing can hold me back.

And yet, so many things did. So many rules. The ones that trapped him now were a Bargain, but at the center of that Bargain was a wound. A mistake, made in the folly of his youth, that both shamed and shaped him even now.

"Sebastian," I asked quietly. "Do you actually want to be like your father?"

If he didn't, then we could have everything we wanted. Every wild and wicked future that was building between us. We'd break his Bargain and find our way back to each other once the Offering was nothing more than a memory. But if he did…

Even if we found our way free of our Bargains, the road on the other side of the water wouldn't be easy. There would be rules to break, chaos to embrace. Disasters and mishaps every step of the way, if I was involved. And Sebastian would still be faced with a choice. Become who he always was and always had been—impulsive, brave, reckless. Loyal. Or be the man his father wanted him to be.

Sebastian stared at me, something complex dancing in his eyes, and said, "Of course I want to be a good man. Of course I do."

He sounded so broken and twisted that my own heart shattered in response. A good man; that was how he saw the choice.

I tempted him. Tempted him to break everything he stood for, every promise he'd made.

Even if we won, and somehow defeated every evil standing between us and freedom... Would I make him lose his father all over again because I was too wild? Because I was too impulsive, and once more Sebastian failed to live up to those expectations?

I was sick of being called wicked and selfish. I was sick of being a temptation no one wanted to keep. Maybe the mystery would never fade for Sebastian and me. Maybe the allure would always be there. But it could always become tainted, and I wouldn't let him resent me for his choices, no matter what I felt.

I was worth more than that.

I lifted my hand to the mirror, pressing my fingertips against the glass as if I could reach through it like he once had.

"Goodbye, Sebastian. Knowing you has been..." I shook my head, letting my hand fall. "Everything I ever wanted."

And before he could stop me—his face twisted in grief, his hand already reaching for me in my absence—I set down the mirror and left to sever the final tie binding me to Aelor.

CHAPTER 33

Sebastian

SHE WAS GONE.

Everything had changed in one small moment—one that slipped through my fingers before I even realized it was there.

I tried to reach through the mirror, but it was too small; my hand sliced open instantly and found only sodden earth for my troubles. She'd left the mirror behind.

Panicked now, I stumbled to my feet, racing to the entrance of my tent. Shadows encroached long fingers over the pathway leading through the grounds, and there was no moonlight. The clouds were too thick and although I wasted precious seconds standing there, waiting for them to pass, the night was still.

Hissing in agitation, I fell back, pausing for only a beat before I spun and created an archway leading into the back alleys. The magic was so rushed and haphazard it practically tore through the walls of my tent. I stepped through, scanning for a moonlight path outside, and when I didn't find one created a new arch. Then another.

I scoured each tent, always following the rules of my curse, so I never risked capture or failure. But the moonlight didn't reach any of the entrances, and, as always, I had to wonder if

Fynn was behind it. If the clouds in the sky were just a little too perfectly placed. If the moonlight that flowed down upon the dancing crowd but never reached the tents was just a hint too pristine.

I searched the dwindling crowd for his face, anger rising with the slow thud of my pulse. But although I thought I felt a ripple of triumph from somewhere within, it was gone too quickly to be sure. Possibly, it was my own imagination searching for a scapegoat because I knew deep down this was all my fault.

I hesitated too long. I didn't listen to the voice inside me telling me what it would mean to let go of this moment—of Bailey.

The last of the humans were leaving, tired and dazed, but the fae left behind showed no signs of slowing down. The glamors across their features were shedding, dripping away bit by bit as the light exposed them for who they really were. I still didn't know the details of Heillon's new ritual, but by the end of the seventh night, dozens of these poor humans would be caught up in Bargains they didn't remember making.

Bargains that the drink and the dancing drew out of them. Hopes and dreams they'd never shared with another, whispered in exchange for promises that seemed, at the time, so small a price.

The name of a child, the memory of a first kiss, a favor to be granted on the full moon.

I shook my head, and as I went to turn away, I saw a familiar face, topped with a head of blond hair that was ruffled and slick with sweat. Fynn paused, staring at me across the fairground.

That fierce look in his eye seemed to be telling me something, but I had no idea what it was. There was no triumph in his gaze. Arrogance, sure, but not triumph. Instead, there was an echo of something else, something deeper.

With a wry twitch of his lips, he lifted his hand and gazed to the stars. The clouds parted, and moonlight bathed every shadowed corner of the fairground, but when I looked back, Fynn was gone.

I didn't waste a second. I burst free of the tent and began to search.

Where was Bailey? I had to find her, had to stop her before the sprites took her to the other end of Criera and out of my reach forever.

But with the moonlight aiding my movement, I soon scoped the entire circus and its walls, and was forced to come to the sorry conclusion: she was nowhere in sight of the fairground. Whatever water she'd chosen to greet the sprites, it wasn't the lake.

My pace slowed, each footstep coming heavier than the one before as I walked slowly toward the entrance. No one paid any attention to me, the world lost to a blur of frenzied dancing, but that didn't matter. There were always eyes among the Lumière. It would only take one of the Masters seeing me for my Bargain to be broken and my fate sealed forever.

Movement caught my eye, and I turned to see a hole had been torn in the velvet fabric that served as a barrier near the entrances. It wasn't human-sized—more like accidental-fireball-at-head-height-sized. But through the gap, there stood a figure. My heart sped up before I realized that although they were familiar, they were not Bailey. It was the older man who had accompanied her that first night.

I rolled my shoulders back, schooled my expression to something approximating neutral interest, and strode toward the gap in the fabric. He heard me approach and turned slowly, his brows knit together in a frown. I noticed he was very careful not to touch any inch of the barrier, even as I came right up to it.

I leaned one hand above the gap, fingers twisting into the fabric so I half hung there, and smiled.

"I'm looking for your friend," I said. "Have you seen her?"

"Depends why you're asking," the old man answered after a pause, lifting his chin. "You have the look about you of a man apologizing, and I wouldn't mind knowing why."

Gods, perhaps he was her father after all. He certainly acted like it.

"That's between me and her," I said tightly. "Do you think it your right to know all of your friend's business?" I emphasized the word *friend*, wondering if it would get a rise out of him; it did.

He puffed his chest and came closer, almost touching the fence now.

"I don't trust the damn lot of you, and you know quite well that I'm right not to. In there you might make the rules, but..." He gestured down at his feet. "I'm not in there, sonny. So I'll be telling you when and how you'll see her, and what the conditions are."

Reluctantly impressed, I took a minute to think, gazing over his head to see if there was any sight of her. Perhaps they'd been talking and she'd slipped into the shadows at the sight of me. But then, why would she? She'd been honest from the beginning about what she wanted and what she would do to get it. She faced every challenge that came at her and didn't back down.

I was the slimy one.

I was the one who hid and snuck around and tried to fight in ways that made no sense.

Something in me deflated at the thought. My body sagged, and I leant fully against the fabric and gave a wry laugh.

"Fine, you've caught me. You want to know my crime?" I didn't wait for him to answer. "I let her go, old man. I let her go because I couldn't bear to admit to myself that I hadn't changed a bit. That I was still selfish and impulsive. Wild. An overly dramatic brat." I exhaled with a wry grin. "Everything my father warned me not to be."

The old man huffed, irritated laughter spilling out into the night. "Oh, the folly of youth," he muttered, sounding genuinely annoyed.

The anger rose within me again. I pushed off the fence and turned to him. "Who are you to judge me? You don't know the first thing about me. Perhaps I have good reason to be wild and impatient."

Even as I said the words, the thick slide of guilt sank low in my gut. I didn't believe my own words. I had no good reason to be like that, and every reason not to be. And still, the frantic urge within me pulled me further down that path—foregoing sense and logic for action.

But then I realized he was shaking his head. I frowned, stopping short in the middle of my argument.

"Sorry, boy," the old man said, tugging in agitation on his beard.

He took another step away from the barrier, and I felt bizarrely like I was losing something precious. I leant against it, both hands threaded in the fabric as I pressed my face up to the gap.

He didn't notice, lost in some distant memory.

"I was referring to myself, believe it or not. I used to think how your old man did about impatience... Brattish behavior, wildness, haste, fire—I thought they were things to be controlled by discipline. My memory might not be quite what it was, but I know that much." He glanced at me shrewdly. "I was a younger man. Older than you, but younger than I am now. I thought it best if those sorts of fires were squashed out. If a man acted with discipline and poise, then he would create order in a world that was determined to be chaos. But I was a fool."

The words struck me. My body felt numb, and I found myself hanging on his every word, my fingers turning white where they clenched the velvet.

"You can never truly know what choice to make," the man continued, watching me now, no longer lost in his hazy memories. "Whether to choose haste or patience. Boldness or discipline. Times change, we change. What I thought an absolute truth at your age wasn't even close.

"But we do always know one thing. We know how to remain true to ourselves, no matter what lessons our elders might throw at us. What truths they might try to convince us are absolute.

"There is no absolute truth in this world but the one between your soul and yourself. What your heart desires most, and the values you'll maintain to get it. You know how to be true to yourself, Sebastian. All that remains to be seen is whether you have the courage to do so."

I stared at him as the carefully built structures of my life shattered around me.

He sounded so like my father in that moment, and yet he was saying words that I never expected to hear from those lips. Words I never would. And yet, it seemed so plausible when he said it.

Did my father think the same? Had he changed his mind about the discipline and order he'd forced upon me? About the ways in which he'd encouraged me to hide my true nature?

And if he had... then why the fuck was I clinging to it?

Was I even honoring my father by being the man he'd once told me to be? Or was I only abandoning myself and my future by clinging to that one juvenile mistake, and the advice I assumed my mentor would give me?

I realized I was gaping at the old man, and I forced my lips shut. He chuckled, noticing the gesture, and shook his head again.

"Gotten through to you, have I? Look, I don't know what's going on between you and Bailey, but I can see that you care for each other. If you really mean the apology that's in your heart, I'll tell you where she is. But if all you mean to do is to reject her once more, then you'll never see her again."

I swallowed, the sound loud in the silence between us. I knew what to do.

I didn't know how to do it or what it would look like, but I knew what step I had to take. As much as it pained me, terrified me... I was clinging to a lost hope, and I had been for years. The Lumière were cruel, their Bargains twisted and unbreakable.

I was never going to find my father. But I couldn't risk losing Bailey by clinging to what was already lost.

I stepped away from the barrier, and then again—toward the gate.

The old man nodded shrewdly and said, "She's in the clearing off Old Mill Track. By the river. If you hurry, you should catch her."

If I hurried.

The night was ending, but that didn't mean there was any possible way to leave without being seen.

But I couldn't let her go.

I had to break the rules and damn the consequences.

And as that thought hit me, I remembered another piece of advice my father had given me, about the ways in which the men in our family loved—deeply, truly, unchangingly.

My father would never want me to give up on Bailey, even if it meant we would always be parted.

I would find another way to ease his suffering, even if the cursed Bargain held and he would never be returned to me. There would be another piece of magic, something that could work within and around the constructs of that deal. Some way to save him at the expense of our reunion.

To me, he was lost and always would be. It was time to find Bailey before I lost her too.

I ran to the gate, not caring about the shadows that covered it, not caring that those ribbons bound the exit, marking my escape for all to see.

There was a commotion around and behind me, but no one stopped me. No blinding magic came into play.

It was wild. Reckless. I should have paused, should have thought of a smarter way to do it. A cleverer way. Should have taken a second to think and not been wild and brash and impatient.

But that simply wasn't me.

As I slipped into the night among the trees and heard the baying howls of the hunt behind me, I felt something in me break. And I knew—never again would I return to their rules, no matter what punishment they inflicted.

CHAPTER 34

Bailey

THE FOREST FOLDED AROUND ME, AS IF EVERY BRANCH WAS LEANING IN. To protect me or suffocate me, I wasn't sure.

Something in the air felt different tonight. Either it was my own concern given tangible form, projected outwards until every cracked twig sounded like danger. Or perhaps the magic in this forest was warning me.

I'd told Stefan I would be at the clearing off Old Mill Track, saying goodbye to him in a way that I hoped he would later realize had meant forever. But when I arrived at the clearing, it was full of people. They were still drunk and dancing, even though it was long past midnight, and something about them wasn't right.

I couldn't cast any magic near them, not just because they were throwing themselves around like buffoons, risking an interruption at any moment. But because something told me the fae were watching them, even outside the fairgrounds.

So I kept moving, walking deeper into the forest and letting instinct guide me. The sounds of laughter faded as I followed the gentle trickle of a narrow stream. It led deeper into the forest, away from the rushing of the river I'd grown up by.

I thought I knew the edges of this forest back to front, but soon I found myself setting foot onto a path I'd never seen before. I hesitated for only a moment, and then I followed it. When it ended at the foot of a crystal clear pool, perfect in every way for what I needed to do, I finally accepted that some other hand was guiding me tonight.

I only hoped it wasn't the oath of the Offering, returning to claim me.

The surface of the pool glittered with thin slivers of moonlight, although the clearing itself was dark; only a fraction of the full moon's glow had broken through the thick canopy above.

I stared at the water, wondering if I really dared to do this. And then I began to laugh, because for the last seven-day I had done nothing but dance with the most dangerous fae around—and here I was, scared of reaching out to the nice ones.

I didn't hesitate any longer. I folded my hands around the pearl at my neck, closed my eyes, and drew it through the air in the shape of an arch.

A soft splash came from before me. I opened my eyes and gasped; an arch of water had risen from the pool, its height catching those slivers of moonlight even more than the surface had, so the entire arch seemed to gleam. In the center, some kind of translucent film filled the space, like frosted glass. I couldn't see the forest through it, and the film shone with colors that didn't exist in the clearing at all—bright reds and oranges—as though it were a window leading out onto a sunrise.

I brushed my fingers over the pearl, and a shiver of magic caressed me. A message whispered from within it: no one would interrupt us until this magic was complete. No one would even be able to step foot within this clearing.

Immediately, an enraged hiss came from the trees. My head

jerked up to find Merelda prowling around the edge of an invisible barrier. She must have heard me talking to Stefan, and followed me to make sure I didn't do anything reckless before we left together. But I'd gone and prevented her interference without even meaning to.

She lifted her head, waves of red hair falling down her back, and glared at me with those emerald green eyes.

"Let down the wall, Bailey," she said, reaching up and scratching like a cat at the invisible barrier. "You're being a mighty idiot."

"You always say that," I countered, raising an eyebrow. "At some point, maybe you just have to accept that's who I am."

Merelda barked out a laugh. Trailing her hand along the barrier, she followed it all around me in a circle. It cut halfway through the lake, but that didn't stop her. She simply stepped a little higher, and the air rose to meet her, carrying her as she crossed over the water and around to my right.

Her glare deepened, glinting now with anger. "We're meant to be leaving together in a handful of hours, so why are you making a fresh Bargain with water sprites?" Her eyes narrowed. "They're the masters of love."

"Are you really going to assume the worst about everything I do?" I asked her, propping my hands on my hips and glaring right back. "I told you, I had contingency plans for the crossing." I waved at the pool. "This is my contingency plan!"

She laughed, the sound like bells tinkling. "How about this: when you can tell me that without a lovesick expression on your face, I'll believe you." She tilted her head. "What are you really asking them, tonight?"

My stomach sank.

Okay, so, maybe she was right.

"It isn't about love," I said slowly, ignoring her rude scoff. "It's for love."

That shut her up.

I wasn't going back to Sebastian. Not with what he'd revealed about his innermost desires; not with what I knew about my own. But that didn't mean I could just let him go as he was, when he needed help the most.

He'd had years of torment locked in that circus ground, unable to step free except for when the moonlight shone. And they were fae; they *controlled* the moonlight. His Bargain had never been fair, just like my own. I'd never been able to change my own circumstances, but with a little help, I might be able to change his. If I could just find an answer and get a message to him, perhaps I could have it all.

Maybe the world was right; I really was greedy. But for once, I didn't care.

Merelda stared at me, but whatever argument she might have given was lost as the arch in the center of the pool shimmered. The frosted film broke, parting as a leg stepped through, and I gasped as a sprite walked elegantly through the arch and stood in the shallows of the pool.

She was followed by two others, and, staring at them, I found I'd lost all ability to speak.

They were right: Stefan, Master Skylark, everyone who had told me that the Lumière were only a small facet of that mystical world on the other side of the water. They were right, because these fae were like nothing I'd seen before.

Green hair hung in large chunks, like seaweed, to frame their faces—which were as beautifully round as their bodies to protect from the cold of the depths. Their eyes were all pale blue, like the inside of a shell, and tiny flecks of mother-of-pearl glittered in trails and whirls along their skin. There were no glamors in place to conceal them from a human's interrogation. There was no need; they lived so far out of our reach that accommodating us was laughable.

Standing before me, they were eerily, beautifully alien.

I turned from Merelda, ignoring the sounds of her nails tearing at that barrier, and focused on the cool press of the pearl in my palm. I stared at them, at everything they were, at everything I didn't know as my world opened up.

Gods, my town was so tiny. Everything was so tiny. There was so much more waiting for me out there, and I could do it right now. I could leave with them and walk away from everything.

Sebastian hadn't lied; an overwhelming aura of safety rolled from the sprites. They weren't like the Lumière. But as I had that thought, it only served to solidify everything I'd already decided. Because I *could* walk away from everything. But I didn't want to.

I heard Merelda yell something beside me in a language I didn't follow. Still, I got the gist.

I glanced at her. "Merelda," I said quietly. "I don't want to walk away from him like this. I don't want to change who I am and the reasons that I care about people even when they don't deserve it."

She yelled something else, and this time I caught fae words sprinkled in. Words that made the sprites' elegant eyebrows lift.

Leaning against the invisible barrier, now, I followed her along the muddy bank of the pool, urging her to listen to me even when she tried to move away. Sweeping willow branches dipped between us; I swept them away. Finally she grew silent.

"I care," I told her. "I want to."

My whole life, I'd clung to the beauty around me like a life-line. I knew that Merelda hated it, and the gods knew that for so many years that desperate ritual had been naïve. A way to ignore everything I was really feeling.

But it didn't have to be. Even Merelda had told me to hold

on to the beauty in me, and this was how I did that. Fair or not, this was what I wanted from the world. It had been naïve to hope I could find it by simply blocking out everything I didn't want to see, but that didn't mean I could not make it.

She watched me, so still and quiet it was as if she were made of stone. Finally, she said, "And I love that about you."

It shouldn't have been able to, but her hand slipped through the barrier then, reaching out to cup my cheek. And then, moving calmly this time, she stepped through the invisible wall and stood beside me.

"Doesn't mean I won't guard your foolish back from attack, though," she grunted.

Heart swelling, I choked down the sob that threatened to escape and turned back to the sprites. They had witnessed the entire exchange, and I could see in their faces that they had thoughts about it.

The one at the front seemed to soften as she spread her hands in a placating gesture before her. When she spoke, it sounded like the river traveling down the mountainside.

"It is a good thing to care in a world that is so easily cruel," she said.

My breath caught again on another sob.

"A good thing and a hard thing to keep hold of, when, with every step, with every breath, the people in your life would demand you let it go."

Merelda stiffened beside me, but I knew they weren't talking about her. They were talking about people like Hayden, like my sister, who saw that depth of feeling in me and tried to carve it out. Who saw the label of Offering, and demanded I submit to it, body and soul, even as it took everything I was and destroyed it.

I nodded. "How does this work?" I asked hesitantly. "Is it like with the Bargains? Are there words that I shouldn't say?"

The two sprites at the back looked at one another, faces grim as the one at the front fiercely shook her head.

"We simply help." Her lip quirked. "Because we care. You may ask one thing of us, and there is no price."

Her eyes bore into mine, but I didn't interrupt as she kept speaking.

"There is one thing you should know. Danger hovers at the end of this forest, and our time together may be short." She glanced above my head and I had the strangest sense that she was seeing through the trees, through the foliage, through the entire world. "I'd say we have about thirty seconds."

My breath caught in fear. Long enough to run. Or long enough to ask the question on the tip of my tongue, and then stay and face what was coming.

I shivered, and I felt Merelda grow somehow more steel-like beside me. An anchor. A tether, holding me to her when everyone else from my old life pushed me away.

But instead of demanding I go with them to safety, like I knew she wanted me to, she slipped her hand through mine. Our fingers threaded together, and for the first time, I felt steady.

I took a deep breath, letting it out slowly. Roughly twenty-five seconds left. Time enough to make them count.

"I need to know if there is a way to break a Bargain."

The sprite's expression turned hard with knowing. "There are two kinds of Bargains, child. One that is made with honor and kindness, and one that is made with cruelty—a trap waiting to snap closed."

I flinched as she said the word 'snap'.

"If it is the second kind, you may already know about the gate."

"I do," I agreed.

Everyone knew. The gate was the loophole, the one bit of truth that the fae offered in their Bargains.

She nodded. "The gate is the truth, but if the Bargain is a trap, it will also have a lie buried in it. If you find the lie, child, then the entire fabrication will fall into dust."

My eyes widened. A lie.

There was a lie in the Bargain.

In that moment, I knew I couldn't leave Sebastian behind. Not like that. Not when there was a way to free him, and information he would never have without me.

"Ten seconds left," the sprite behind the first said, clasping her shoulder.

She nodded, reaching up to pat the hand with gentle affection. But then she froze, sniffed the air, and turned to me—urgent. The archway began to glow, beckoning the sprites back into safety. I couldn't go with them this time, but I had two pearls left.

If I could just outlast this danger, I could cast a second arch and leave tomorrow morning and...

"You are trapped here," the sprite said.

A numb buzzing filled my ears.

"You are trapped, child. You've made a Bargain. A Bargain that you have paid for, and so you must honor."

Oh gods. Fynn. The ticket. It wasn't just an option for me to take it; I had paid for passage, and passage must be taken.

Merelda's hand in mine squeezed so tightly, her nails dug into my skin, fear binding the two of us together. In the back of my mind, an imaginary clock counted down the final seconds.

"You must honor it, child." She looked so regretful, shaking her head and holding my gaze. "But look for the lie. When the truth fails you, look for the lie."

"Yes," I whispered, and then said it again, stronger now. "Yes, I'll find it. I won't just look for the lie, I'll find it."

She nodded, and then the three of them stepped back, vanishing into the center of the arch. It glowed for a moment longer. I felt the barriers that had separated me from the outside world disintegrate before the arch did, but it lingered—an imprint of light on a world that was growing darker.

The crashing of footsteps rang closer, closer. My heart leapt into my throat. Was it Sebastian? Had he come after me?

But when I turned, it was a head of blond hair and wide blue eyes that emerged into the clearing.

They weren't fixed on me; they were fixed to the arch, Fynn's chest heaving with breath as something dangerous glinted in his gaze.

CHAPTER 35

Bailey

I watched him, my pulse racing. There was something different about him, now. Something that made me hesitant to speak before he did. It was a rawness, a sense of truth he didn't often reveal.

Finally, his eyes tore away from the arch—to me. As if it had been held there by the power of his gaze alone, the arch collapsed, water sluicing down through nothingness and back into the pool with a rippling splash. He didn't even flinch.

I thought of the last time I'd seen him, probably no more than thirty minutes ago and yet it felt like a lifetime.

Perhaps now was my chance to find out exactly what had happened between us, and why it felt so much like an ending.

"An archway," he said, taking a slow step into the clearing and then another. His eyes flicked to Merelda, but neither of them made a move to attack. He seemed content to keep his distance, pausing while there were still several feet parting us. "Are you practicing your magic?"

I could have lied; I didn't owe him any truth here.

But I shook my head. "I was talking to the sprites."

There it was again—that glint of something. The same thing that had been there the second he burst into the clearing.

Hope. Confusion.

Fury.

I frowned. "What—" I began, but he'd already turned from me.

Before I could stop him or ask what was going on, he'd strode into the water, heedless of his clothing. His riding pants immediately soaked through, clinging to his skin, as did his pale green shirt when the stray flecks of water splashed up. Heedless, he swept his hands around where the arch had been, as if he could grab hold of it and bring it back.

"What are you doing?" I yelled.

Merelda's hand came to rest in caution on my shoulder, but I didn't shrug her off. I was glad of her presence. Something in him had snapped.

"Bring them back," he demanded. "Bring them back and tell me what you were after." He spun, his hair sticking to his head even as he clutched it, his eyes wide and frantic. "Why were you talking to them?"

I blinked at him, not pausing deliberately, just struggling to find the words. "They won't come back," I said finally. "They sensed danger."

Finn grew very still. His eyes closed for several long seconds, his hands clenching into fists. By the time they snapped open again, whatever change had come across him had faded.

He strode slowly from the water. "What were you asking them for, Bailey?"

Again, I could have lied. Again, I didn't.

"I was asking them how to break a Bargain."

The tight press of his lips firmed even further. I could see a muscle clenching in his jaw as his teeth ground together. His throat bobbed as he swallowed.

"And what was their answer?"

I shook my head, hair covering my eyes. Roughly, I shoved it back. "Hold on, you don't get to just charge in here and—" I broke off, pointing back into the shadows. "What's going on out there? What's the danger?"

For a second, Fynn's eyes widened as if he'd forgotten whatever hounds of hell had been at his feet. Then the expression wiped clean, and the corner of his mouth curved into a smile.

"I came to warn you: the circus bounds are open." He spread his arms wide, stepping, finally, onto the shore. Water dripped from him, turning the earth at his feet into mud. I saw, then, what was in his hand.

It was a length of ribbon—familiar ribbon. The kind that would have once marked the circus boundaries.

I lifted my eyes to his face and realized it still did.

"You set them all free," I breathed. "Where the ribbons go, the fae may walk. You've set the circus free. Why?"

He broke into laughter. "It is the night of the hunt, Bailey, and the pickings are simply too good in the fairground to resist. What more does your little town have to offer?" His eyes darkened. "I have never lied to you about who or what I am. Do not insult me by acting surprised when you can no longer ignore it."

"You sniveling little wreck of a beast," Merelda snarled, shocking me into silence before I could respond. She stepped forward, holding her hand in front of me, putting her body between me and Fynn. "I knew this would end in a hunt. I could smell it on you. I knew it from the beginning."

That was why Merelda hadn't trusted him. She'd smelled that he was a hunter.

"What's a hunt?" I asked quietly.

Merelda answered. "It's when the fae can no longer wait for Bargains to land in their lap," she hissed through gritted teeth, "and they go searching for them." She jerked her chin toward Fynn. "And he's at the very front."

My heart didn't want to believe what my mind had already known.

"Why?" I breathed.

Fynn ran his fingers through his hair, smile firmly set in an arrogant smirk. "I set them *all* free," he said.

There was something in his words that sounded like a double meaning. Something I was meant to get. But I didn't understand it. I looked over my shoulder as the distant sound of laughter echoed from the edge of the forest. They were near. I could hear the crunch of sticks, the rustle of leaves.

"They're circling me," I breathed.

"They are," Fynn agreed. Abruptly, the smile dropped from his face. "So we'd best be quick. What did the sprites tell you? What words of wisdom did they impart?"

"Why do you want to know?" I shot back at him. "So that you can trap us in Bargains so twisted we never escape?"

His eyes glinted. "Perhaps, or perhaps the sprites often give more than one piece of advice, and one must look within the layers of their words for the pearl."

"Can't you just summon them yourself?" I snapped.

He let out a bitter laugh. "Magic is not one size fits all, Bailey, even for the fae. We have our skills, and that sort of communication is not mine. I can create visions of people from nothing, but I cannot summon them."

It sounded as though it hurt him to admit that, and so I knew it must be true.

"Well, if you stopped being such a prick to Sebastian, maybe he could summon them for you," I threw at him.

The furrow in his brow deepened. "Ah, yes, Sebastian." He looked over my shoulder, narrowing his eyes in assessment as the encroaching hunt howled again. "Tell me, why is it that you two are so close to each other's hearts, and yet you don't seem to have a fucking clue how to keep each other? You should be far away by now, safe in each other's arms."

I let out a breathless, incredulous laugh. "You know very well the answer to that. Sebastian can't leave."

Fynn scoffed, a rude, rough sound. "Of course he can. He's free to do as he likes. There will simply be consequences if he is seen." He looked away, expression twisted into disgust. "And now, apparently, we have all seen his true character."

"How dare you judge him?" I snarled. "You were the one who trapped him here!"

Once more, that bitter laugh dropped free. His eyes closed, remaining that way for several seconds. "It doesn't matter," he said so quietly, I almost didn't hear him.

"What?" My brow furrowed. I took a step closer.

Fynn sighed and held out his hand. "I'll get you out of here."

I stood there, looking at him. I stared at his hand with incredulity. In any other situation, I would take his hand in a heartbeat. But there was something wrong with him tonight. Something that had started when we said goodbye earlier, and apparently only grown in the time since.

Was he only helping me because his Bargain bound him to offer me safe passage home every night until the circus ended?

But—I frowned—our Bargain had concluded.

Merelda put her arm in front of me again, but I hadn't made a move for him.

"And where will you take me?"

"To your waiting love," he replied, bitter and twisted.

Pain shot through me, piercing my chest. He'd never spoken to me like that before.

Maybe I'd never meant anything to him at all, if he could be so cruel to me so quickly. Had he got what he wanted and now he was done?

Heart pounding in my chest, I drew myself up taller. "You must think me quite simple," I hissed. "If that's all I am to you—someone who's incomplete without a man to cling to. Not that it's any of your business, but I said goodbye to Sebastian. Forever."

Fynn grew very still. "What did you say?" he asked me, and his eyes, which had been fixed at some distant point—glazed and disinterested—suddenly met mine and burned with a fierce fire.

"I said goodbye to Sebastian," I repeated through gritted teeth.

His lips parted, but he didn't speak. His breath rose and fell in ragged heaves. Lightning sang in my veins, struck into being from the expression on his face.

He looked away from me, quickly, then back again; and then he turned aside, his hand twisted in his hair. "Please do not tempt me again like this," he muttered in Criari. "I can't say no to you twice."

I reeled back. Through the shocked haze of confusion, I felt my heart twisting in pain.

"What are you talking about?" I breathed.

Even Merelda's hand had fallen, her expression soft with confusion, like mine. Fynn ignored me.

I lifted my voice, finding an edge of steel within it that I only held because of him. "You didn't say no to me. I said no to you."

He stilled, hand still clutched in the blond lengths of his hair, and then turned, excruciatingly slow, to face me. One eyebrow lifted in disbelief, and his mouth was a harsh twist of shocked anguish.

"Ah, Bailey," he said, in low, rapid fae. "A thousand years and I think you would still surprise me. How you ever thought you were unintelligent is a mystery." Then he laughed, the bitter sound riding high as he turned to stare out across the pool. "But sure, yes, you certainly did say no," he continued in common. "And now I'm afraid I must also say no—to whatever this is." He spun his finger in a circle, indicating our conversation. "There is no time, and there is no world in which I would risk the repercussions of that."

My head tangled with his half-said protests, and I had no idea what was happening anymore. The crashing of twigs and leaves was closer now. They were circling the clearing, right outside. When I looked to the shadows, I could see glowing eyes piercing the depths.

I stepped forward, shaking my head. "Stop walking away from me, I—"

All Fynn did was glance over my shoulder, his gaze meeting Merelda's. Something unspoken passed between them, and then her arms scooped around my waist, and those beautiful wings launched into flight.

"No!" I called out, reaching uselessly downward, as if I could somehow reach him. As if reaching him would do anything at all.

But he only watched. A calm, still figure in the center of the pool.

We burst up through the trees, just as the howling fae descended on the clearing.

CHAPTER 36

Bailey

It took until dawn to barricade the doors. Outside, the sound of fae laughing and howling sang like wind in a storm. The malevolent Lumière, now unbound from their human glamors, had inflicted some magic on the town as well. Their words carried as if they were right there whispering in our ears.

We're coming for you.

Except I could tell that in most people's minds, that wasn't a threat. It was a promise. A promise of all we desired. Because most people were still drunk on their wine, still had their music ringing in their ears, and still felt the siren call of their power.

Even I wasn't completely immune. As those long hours passed, I huddled with Merelda and Stefan, the three of us crouched around the tiny flame of my circular hearth as, outside, the town went to chaos. And still, that voice promised me everything that I wanted.

A way across the water.

A way to find adventure and bring love and happiness into my sorry little life.

I could see their lies for what they were, but that didn't make them any easier to resist. The words whispered to me until I had to shut my eyes and squeeze them tight, just so that I wouldn't follow the call.

How had I ever thought a Bargain would save me?

We crouched there, waiting for the sun to rise and bring something of a reprieve. I must have fallen asleep at some point, because eventually I woke up to a soft hand smoothing my hair back from my face and beckoning me to be quiet: Merelda. I sat up slowly, listening for the silence I'd hoped would come.

It wasn't there. I could still hear their laughter, even though the sun shone.

"They're still here," I breathed. "Even though it's noon."

"That isn't the sun," Merelda said stiffly.

Frowning, I lifted my head and saw that what I'd thought was the golden light of the sun was instead the full moon, risen at last to mark the final night of the Lumière. A harvest moon, its silver light turned golden.

"Shit," I breathed.

Bargain Night. The night we humans never remembered.

"They cast something upon us," Stefan said darkly. "Something to make us sleep through the day while they drew their net around us. There's not a person in this village who won't dance at their fires tonight."

Merelda stood, brushing down her dress as she crossed the room and looked out the sliver of glass, standing at the side so she couldn't be seen.

"I don't think we'll need to go far to reach them," she said darkly.

My breath caught. I ran across the room, stopping at the very edge of the window, beside her, and sucked in a breath. The ribbons that had once encircled the fairgrounds now lined the streets, and all down it I could see prancing fae—fire-twirlers and acrobats spinning through the streets. They were here, and they were waiting.

Through the crowd, I saw a familiar figure. Long red hair, broad shoulders, and eyes that absorbed all the light, reflecting none of it back. Heillon. He scanned the crowd idly from his perch on the top of the fountain at the end of the lane, where the trail opened into the town square. Waiting, I knew, for me.

There was no way out of this. I could try to hide among those caravans, hoping that whatever magic had seized our village would eventually fade and I'd be safe to stowaway. But I doubted it. This was his troupe, his magic, and the night they had all been waiting for. The ritual had begun.

"He's after me," I said, the words strangely calm in the silence of the room.

"Who is?" Stefan asked, frowning.

"Heillon. Their leader. He needs an offering for their ritual, and he's chosen me."

"How do you know, love?" Stefan asked, the frown fading into despair. He rose to his knees with a crack of his bones. "Has he spoken to you?"

"He doesn't have to," I said, studying the man in the distance. "He's summoning a daemon, for what end I don't know, and the symbols in the ritual he's chosen match the ones used on the Offering's Plaque. He's a man who craves a sense of poetry in what he does. He told me so himself, although he didn't realize I could understand him."

Merelda and Stefan shared a look, eyes wide. It was the most I'd ever revealed about my actual thoughts. The connections I'd made only to quietly file away. The opinions that weren't just regurgitated to make me palatable to whoever was listening.

"Whether the Offering Child *is* the key to this ritual, or whether he just wants me to be because it suits his poetic sensibilities, he'll come after me until he wins." I took a deep breath, letting it out slowly. "And I'm bound to cross back to the fae world with the circus. I bought a ticket, paid for it, and I have to see that Bargain through."

We were silent for several moments. Then Stefan asked, "So what do you plan to do? Because I'm not going to let you give yourself up, I'm sorry."

My flippant answer choked off in my throat. I turned to him, and the depth of feeling there floored me.

"I'm not," I promised him gently. "But hiding won't solve it; it's too late for that, and I'm too wrapped up in their world. I can't get out alone, and so... I need the fae's help." I steeled myself, knowing the backlash I was about to get from both corners. "I need Fynn."

Merelda snarled, animalistic fury rippling through the sound.

"It's his ticket," I insisted. "And he's saved me more than once."

"He's a hunter," she said, green eyes glinting in the flickering light of distant fires.

"I know," I said softly.

Her expression softened, and before I knew it, her arms had folded around me. I felt the firm press of her lips linger in my hair, and then she braced herself on my shoulders and held me at arm's length, staring at me fiercely. "I'm coming out there with you, then. If he wants to trick you, he'll have to get through me. They all will."

"But—" I gaped at her. "But you're an imp. They'll try to hurt you!"

My heart twinged. She should have been far across the water by now, waiting for me to cross. But instead she'd stayed to watch over my final days in Aelor, like she always had.

Merelda grinned at me, sharpened teeth blazing in the light.

"Let them try." Then she tilted her head to the side and studied me, one eyebrow raising. "But there's something else you have to do, isn't there? Before we face whatever this Bargain of yours has gotten you into."

"Yes," I said, swallowing thickly. "I have to find Sebastian and tell him what we learned. His Bargain locks him away forever tonight, because there's no way he found his father, not with the hunt taking over this town." I looked out the window again. "We need to go among them. We need to find him. And then..." I took in a breath. "Then I'll find Fynn and ask him to help me escape."

My announcement was met with silence; no one in the room shared my faith in him. Privately, I wasn't sure that I should. He was a hunter, and he'd hunted this Bargain from me magnificently—backed me into a corner without a single protest.

But there was more to him; I could sense it. Sebastian trusted him, even after everything, and I needed his help.

More than that—I wanted it.

"Never a dull moment with you," she muttered, shaking her head. "I swear I was better off when I was only a foot high."

We waited for Stefan to catch up with us, hobbling over slowly, and then fell onto either side of him as guards, because of course he refused to stay behind. We paced down the garden path together and entered the circus that had transformed our town.

I looked around in shock and wonder. The performers were no longer limited to the fae. Faces I recognized spun and twisted, wrapping themselves around ribbons, jumping through hoops. Bargains had already been made. Electrifying stunts performed.

We wound through the crowd, searching.

It didn't take long. As if something drew him to me,

suddenly, there he was, standing in a pool of moonlight. Prisms of rainbow reflections enfolded around him; someone was dancing with mirrors, spinning them around, catching and reflecting the shimmering moonlight, and I barely knew where to look. Through it all, he was like an anchor.

Sebastian.

He caught sight of me and grew still, chest heaving. He'd been searching for me. I could tell by the crazed look in his eye, and the way everything in him seemed to settle when he met my gaze.

I started to run, leaving Merelda and Stefan to catch up behind me. As soon as I reached him, he swept me into a hug, arms folding around me so tight I could hardly breathe.

"I thought I'd lost you," he whispered into my hair. "I searched for hours, and then there were signs of the sprites but no evidence of a human crossing with them."

Abruptly, he leaned back, staring at me so intently it made the whole world stand still.

"I came for you, Bailey," he whispered.

I shook my head, confused. "I don't—"

"I *came for you*. In the shadows, in the darkness, beyond the bounds of the circus before it spilled out to the village. I broke every rule for you, and I would do it again in a heartbeat. I was wrong to let you go, and unless you want me to, I'll never let you go again."

Stunned into silence, I couldn't do more than gape at him. Whether he took my stillness as hesitation, I wasn't sure, but he added, quieter now, "And if you want more than just me, then I'll do anything within my power to give you that, too."

I could have everything. All of it. Without compromise, without losing myself.

"But your father..."

"He's lost to me, Bailey," Sebastian said fiercely. "And whatever I do, I can't lose you too."

I covered his mouth with my hand, terrified of the words coming out of it—of how much I wanted to hear them.

"He might not be," I said, speaking low and quick. "The Bargains—there's a lie hidden in them. If the gate fails you, you need to find the lie. Then you can break free."

He stared at me, frown deepening even as hope flickered in his gaze. Slowly, he pulled my hand away from his mouth. "A lie? I've never made a Bargain with a lie. Are you sure about this?"

"That's because your Bargains weren't designed to ensnare," I said gently. "The sprites told me. It's true."

A loaded pause filled the space between us.

"You didn't leave with them." Sebastian drew back, apprehension dawning on his face. He was too smart not to have guessed what that meant.

"I can't. The ticket binds me to cross with the Lumière."

Seconds crawled past, my heart shattering at the look on his face.

"Then we need to break Fynn's Bargain," he said finally. "We'll find him now. Then we'll get you out of here."

Before I could speak, he outlined a plan to check the main streets for Fynn while I checked the shadows. Then he was gone.

With Merelda by my side, and Stefan keeping guard at our house in case Fynn came for me, we began to hunt. And all the while, I wondered—would he help me? He'd been honest about the hunt from the beginning, and Sebastian hadn't lied about his danger. But he'd also said that he trusted Fynn. Not with secrets—never with secrets. But to help him when he needed it most.

Well, I needed it most.

But no matter how far I roamed, I couldn't find him. The eerie faces of the fae loomed in and out of my vision, their pitch black eyes studying me too closely. Merelda grabbed my hand, squeezing tightly, and we fled deeper. Toward the town square, where dozens of humans were dancing around the fountain. People I'd known all my life, but never seen in this frenzied kind of fervor.

Then, my sister appeared.

"Bailey," she said, stepping free from the shadows.

She had a man on each arm, and neither were Hayden. And yet, even though she'd clearly drunk the wine and eaten the food, her eyes seemed as steady as they always were. Piercing and watchful.

"Katerina," I said cautiously, trying to move around her.

She held out a hand to stop me, fingers digging into my sternum when I attempted to push past. She leaned in close to my ear and whispered, "This ends now."

A flash of memory struck me: *this ends now.* Those were the words of a Bargain we'd made... down at the altar, with the strass beetles clacking their little wings all around us.

But I couldn't remember the Bargain. Even as I thought it, the memory slipped away, leaving nothing behind.

How long had I forgotten?

How had I forgotten?

"What?" I asked, my voice wavering. "What ends now?"

But she was already backing away, and one by one, melting from the shadows, came the townsfolk I had lived with all my life. A cold, wretched feeling turned over in my stomach. I took a step backward, but my foot bumped something, and when I turned I saw there were others behind me.

We were surrounded.

Merelda shuffled in closer, tipping her head back to scan the skies—presumably for a clear path out. But the fae had taken over the sky as well as the land; illusions filled the darkness, dancing with the unnatural light of the moon and creating a path so scattered and unclear I didn't trust we wouldn't be flying straight into a net.

I looked back at my friends, my family, and saw only cold eyes flickering in the light of the bonfires.

"Heillon wants you," my sister said calmly. She was barely entranced by the fae's magic at all. "Once he takes you, this all ends."

"How can you believe him?" I protested, spinning in a slow circle to face them all. "He's the Master of the Lumière; his life is steeped in deception."

Merelda's hand wrapped around my wrist, nails digging into my flesh. But it was a futile effort; we had nowhere to go.

The corner of Katerina's mouth twitched into a small, knowing smile. "I'm well aware of that. But he and I have an agreement."

"And you *trust* it?" I hissed, shuffling forward as the space behind me vanished. There were only a few meters separating me from the crowd in front now.

"I was quite specific in my wording."

I froze, ice sinking in my gut. Slowly, I turned to face my sister.

"You Bargained me for entry," I said.

I knew she'd Bargained something of high value, because it had been enough for our friends to enter on the third day. But I'd never thought... I hadn't imagined...

The forgotten memory—had he taken that too?

"More or less," she said, pulling a face. "There were negotiations, back and forth. It took time to work out what he wanted most, and then time to wrangle those desires into a foolproof Bargain." A cold smile appeared. "In the end, you only have yourself to blame. You might have escaped, but instead you became greedy. You've broken your oath, and reparations are due."

I gaped at her. "How could you?" I whispered before I could stop myself.

"Because this is your destiny," she said softly, and in the flickering light her face looked almost kind. "You are the Offering, traded to bless us until the day you die or are lost. That day has come, Bailey. Your purpose will be fulfilled tonight. Your offering will please the fae, and they'll leave us be."

"But you don't even know what they'll do to me!" I was yelling now, and I didn't care who heard me.

Hands clutched at my wrists, ignoring Merelda's enraged snarl. The snarl quickly became a screech, and I whipped my head around just in time to see them brandishing something that had her cowering in pain. They were separating us.

"Sebastian!" I screamed, tugging at their grip but failing to break free. "*Fynn!*"

I reached for the magic he had taught me, but I couldn't find the access point. We were too far from the forest, here, and I wasn't strong enough or practiced enough to manage without it.

My body rose into the air, balanced on greedy, rough fists. More hands reached for me, clutching at every part they could grasp.

"I don't need to know," Katerina called to me. I couldn't even see her anymore. She was handing me over to the fae, and she didn't even bother to do it herself. "Once the deal is concluded, you aren't my problem anymore."

You aren't my problem anymore.

My body went limp, and I stopped struggling.

As they carried me away to the waiting dais, where Heillon sat and waited, I fixed my gaze on the golden moon above me. Even when I felt those coal-black eyes settle on me, I didn't look away.

CHAPTER 37

Bailey

THE CROWD DROPPED ME AT THE FOOT OF THE DAIS AND THEN BACKED away into the shadows to continue dancing and drinking. I stared at Heillon's feet, resting by my head, and bit down the fear that threatened to surge and swallow me whole.

Rising slowly, waiting the whole time to be kicked down to my knees, I faced him.

He leant on his fist, gaze simultaneously bored and glittering with intent. On either side of his small dais stood two fae. Their hands were clasped loosely behind them, and their backs ramrod straight as they kept their gazes fixed over the dancing streets.

I presumed they were Heillon's guards. What would happen if I tried to run now? Would he chase me down himself—the predator delighting in the efforts of his prey? Or would he prefer to watch as his minions took me down and then delivered me straight into his lap?

The crackle of the bonfires—dotted all around our town by now—flickered as a background accompaniment to our conversation.

I swallowed, lifting my chin. "You called for me."

A soft, surprised laugh escaped his lips, and he rose slowly from his relaxed position to sit upright on his makeshift throne.

"More or less," he said, mouth curving in delight. "Word on the street says that you're the Offering." He gestured grandly toward me. "So offer yourself."

I had a face made of stone, so used to holding still, protecting me even as it condemned me. And yet, my lip curled in disgust.

"Well," he mused, "it would be no fun that way, would it?"

He crooked his finger toward the shadows near the back of the dais. The platform had been set up before the fountain, and the soft thunder of its flowing water had hidden from me any sign of movement.

I hadn't realized there were people behind it, not until they stepped out.

Not until *he* stepped out.

From the shadows, Fynn emerged, strolling up to lean one hand on the back of Heillon's throne. His blue eyes flickered, somehow reflecting hidden, eerie light back at me.

"There he is," Heillon said, hand reaching up to pat lightly on Fynn's cheek. "My eyes." He gave a low chuckle. "Fynn tells me you've been spending a lot of time with my people. I do so hope they've treated you well."

With a jolt, I realized Heillon assumed that Fynn had sent me in there when I raided the archives. He assumed I'd been sleeping with all number of the Lumière; it was likely one of the only things that was protecting me right now.

Heillon straightened. "And what a fortuitous pastime, for you are about to spend your final waking hours with us as well." He sighed, "and I do so hate it when they scream."

My lips parted in shock. My final waking hours; I wasn't just going to lose something in this ritual. He was going to sacrifice me for it.

My eyes flicked to Fynn, but there was no sign of what he was thinking. No indication that he was worried or afraid. The man I'd known before that charmed sleep fell over me was nowhere to be found.

"What—" I began, my voice cracking. I started over. "What do you plan to do with me?"

Heillon raised a single eyebrow, and it occurred to me that most offerings didn't tend to ask questions. He didn't seem bothered, however. If anything, he was interested. "How intriguing," he murmured in the fae tongue to Fynn. "It is rare for the food to ask how it will be cooked."

Fynn gave a low chuckle, and I forced my expression to remain still.

But Fynn already knew I understood them, and so I couldn't help but stare at him, my eyes watering as I fought not to blink. Begging for a sign. Anything to indicate that he was on my side.

He gave me nothing.

A commotion sounded from behind me. My head whipped around, and I saw Sebastian clasped in a guard's grip, tugging at the vice-like restraint of the fae's arms. Several paces behind him, dragged by two other guards, were Stefan and Merelda.

Moonlight cast Sebastian's face in an eerie glow, his expression torn. It turned to one of open agony when his eyes landed on me. "Let her go," he yelled, and if I thought Heillon's expression looked interested before, now, he was positively ravenous.

"Well now," he spoke in common tongue once again. "Do I detect a hint of romance in the air?"

Fynn answered him, his expression flat and uninterested. "She appears to have struck Seb's fancy. Can't imagine why."

His cold words cut through me, and I whispered silently in my mind: *he's doing it to protect me.*

Heillon regarded Fynn silently for several moments, but

even that scrutiny was ignored. I knew what it was like to act as though you were made of stone, but this was something else.

"Let her go," Sebastian roared again, and I silently thanked the gods that the moonlight shone so bright.

It would be almost impossible for him to step into the shadows. It would have to be done deliberately, rather than as a thoughtless mistake, and since Sebastian very clearly wasn't thinking at all, that was the only small mercy in a merciless night.

"Why?" Heillon asked, the single word carrying through the night.

"Because she doesn't deserve this," Sebastian snarled. "Because an Offering has already been sacrificed once. It shouldn't happen again."

Heillon's mouth curved into something smug and knowing, but he didn't elaborate.

"You've already flaunted your Bargain once tonight, running out of the gates at the same moment the wind broke the ribbons free," Heillon warned him. His lip twitched. "But I'm feeling magnanimous, since no witnesses could accurately pinpoint a timeline to your escape." He tapped his fingers on the arm of his chair. "I could, possibly, even be persuaded to make some adjustments to your situation, if you promise not to get in the way any longer. We are, after all, on the advent of a new phase of your contract."

My blood ran cold; Heillon was acknowledging that Sebastian had only hours left to find his father. And he was offering him a new Bargain.

Gods, he should take it. It would be just as cruel, certainly, but he might be able to find the lie within it, now he knew what to look for. It would buy him time, so long as he played along.

"Enough of this," Heillon said abruptly. To Fynn he said sharply, in quick, economic, Criari. "Release her mind. Ensure there are no more surprises. No one else who would defend her at the last minute." His scowl deepened. "I need full concentration."

Fynn pushed off from the throne and stepped off the dais toward me. As his eyes met mine, I realized what was about to happen. He was going to draw the thoughts free from my mind.

Over his shoulder, Heillon called. "Don't be afraid, little Offering, he's merely collecting the ticket you so studiously bought from us." That laughter rang again, sickening me. "It wouldn't do to have you run away at the last minute, would it?"

They were using the ticket to bind me, to keep me here throughout this ritual. Heillon had known all along.

I looked up into Fynn's eyes, and I couldn't read a gods damned thing. His palm came up to caress my cheek, gaze holding me still.

I bit back a sigh of relief. I could speak to him silently this way. I could beg him for help, and he would know it to be true. He'd never turned away from me yet.

Sebastian had told me to trust him, where it counted, but all I could think of was that moment in the clearing. When he'd muttered to himself that he couldn't say 'no' to me twice. He was pushing me away, twisting this into something broken.

It was hardly the time to question our relationship, and yet Fynn's help depended on it. I needed him to know that whatever he thought had passed between us—when he thought I'd turned from him and chosen Sebastian—that it wasn't the end. We weren't done here.

And so, when I felt his presence in my mind, the thought I sent his way was: *I'm not walking away from you.*

At last, the steel expression on his face cracked, his eyes widening. There was the Fynn I knew. Only a glimpse, the merest image, but it was enough. Without moving an inch, my mind surged for him, reached for him—begged him. He was still touching me, and the magic reacted, just as it had in the clearing. For an instant, our connection wasn't one way; I felt the ghost of his thoughts, and the wild, churning terror of them left me reeling.

I caught a glimpse of words, but they made no sense: stubborn, no, *must*.

And underneath it all, sadness.

Finally, he pulled his hand back as though it had been branded and stepped away. A beat passed. Then another. I swore that, for a second, agony appeared in the violently blue depths of his eyes. Then, resolution crossed his face.

And he smiled.

My stomach turned. The smile was devastatingly cold; I'd never seen him wear anything like it.

He backed away, his lip curving into a sneer.

"You should," he said in a voice of such utter contempt it tore through me. Then, speaking to Heillon, he said, "She has no one else who will come for her."

Before I could protest, a figure emerged from the darkness behind the fountain where the soft lawn lay hidden. Where many a couple would sprawl together on a summery afternoon, and where dozens of entwined bodies lay right now.

My sister emerged.

Her face was a familiar cruelty, her clothing rumpled and loose. She strode up beside Fynn, wrapped a finger around a loose lock of blond hair, and rested her chin on his shoulder.

I stared at that finger, unable to comprehend. Fynn had told me Sebastian had been commanded; surely that was happening again, to Fynn this time. But it wasn't. It wasn't, because Fynn hadn't been commanded.

Fynn was Heillon's lapdog, his eyes. He could go anywhere, do anything.

He had lied to me.

My vision began to tremble. It made my sister's hand look almost as though it was vibrating, flickering with light. My thoughts were moving too fast to grab, and through it all I could hear the low, delighted hum of laughter from Heillon on his throne.

He may not have known everything, but he'd picked up enough about our dynamic to know that this was hurting me. That when I had been apparently used by the fae, I had fallen for them, hook, line and sinker. And gods, I wondered if that was the truth.

Fynn had told me he would give me everything, but that was the biggest lie of all because here he was, taking everything away.

The thing I'd felt shattering between us earlier in the night finally, irrevocably, cracked and fell away.

I didn't argue, didn't protest. I didn't find steel or fire or magic. The only thing I could see was the pity in his gaze as he reached into my pocket—a gesture that was far too intimate—and plucked the ticket free.

Someone was screeching in the background—Merelda, I thought—hurling obscenities at my sister as she gave me a smug smile and disappeared into the shadows.

Sebastian, too, was hurling curses at Fynn, and I wondered how much more pain I could take. How many more people throwing my desires in my face, and reminding me that I could never be wanted. That I had been designed to be unwanted.

Hayden, Sebastian—though he hadn't meant to—and now Fynn. Even Heillon; he wanted me enough to send a crowd after me, but only so he could sacrifice me to his daemon.

There was no place for me in this world, no reason to fight. My hands clenched beside me, pain ripping my chest in two as I gritted my teeth and stood there, watching them all tear me to pieces. Fynn held up the ticket before the throne, and Heillon shifted as if to reach out and take it.

But—there was movement beside me. I heard shouting, saw magic sparking in fury. A cage crashing down and missing as Sebastian leaped and snatched the ticket from Fynn.

"You lying piece of shit," he murmured.

A dozen more words dropped from his lips, muttered in fae that was too quick to follow.

"Forget it," I said, but they both ignored me.

I glanced down, one eyebrow ticking up as I noticed feathers were sprouting along my arms. It should have alarmed me. Terrified me, even, but the world felt as though it were at a distance.

I was turning into a bird. The ticket was clasped in the Lumière's hands; of course. This must be the disguise. My time had run out, and I had been a fool to ever think I could outwit the fae.

I was born to be an Offering, and I would die an Offering, the scales forever balanced. I opened my mouth to tell Sebastian to back down. He had to at least make sure that he wasn't harmed in the process of my turning, not when he was so close to finding a way free. Not when it was vital that he play along for long enough that he could discover the lie in his own Bargain.

That was the most important thing. If I could not be free, at least he could. But when I tried to speak, no words came out, and my mouth felt hardened—a beak. It was a beak, and all that came out was a haunting song.

Sebastian looked at me, frantic. "The lie," he muttered to himself. "The lie—what's the lie?"

Good, he was remembering his priorities.

Fynn, expressionless once again, wagged his finger. "Tick-tock, tick-tock. Bailey's ours. We've won, Sebastian. When are you going to admit it? And besides, there'll likely be *something* left after the ritual is through. I thought you might like a little birdie in a cage to decorate your tent." He raised an eyebrow. "You're here forever now, after all."

For an instant, his expression flickered, twisting into something ugly. It was almost as if he had finally lost the fragile thread of his control. He appeared to be trying to tell Sebastian something wordlessly, although I couldn't for the life of me figure out what it would be.

Shadow loomed. I looked up to find that a cloud was passing over the moon, moving impossibly fast. They were taunting him—offering him devastating hope alongside terrible danger. He couldn't afford to be reckless; he'd lose everything, right on the cusp of a second chance.

I yelled out, the birdsong rising in agony.

Sebastian looked up, eyes landing on the cloud. But instead of following the moonlight, something fierce crossed his face. With a glint in his eye, he looked sharply back down at the ticket and began to smile.

"I'd better make my time count for something, then, hadn't I?" he told Fynn, leaning in close. "You can have me, but you'll never have her. And this, right here?" He tapped the instructions at the base of the ticket: *do not tear, break, or bend.* "That's a lie."

Then, as the shadow passed over him, he tore the ticket in two.

Light blazed.

It felt as though a ship had launched into the side of me, shattering me on the rocks. I fell to my knees, bracing myself on the earth as pain wracked my body. But it was the pain of a boil lancing.

A Bargain breaking.

There was a lie in the ticket; it had always been a Bargain made to trap.

The feathers receded from my skin, vanishing in a second, and the haunting song became a scream. Heillon winced, clapping his hands over his ears as he half-rose from the dais—a thunderous expression on his face.

And behind me, I heard a voice cough and splutter as someone I didn't recognize said, "Sebastian?"

I whirled around, rising to my feet, and stared at the wrinkled face of a man I'd never met before. Where had he come from? I looked around, leaning to see if there was a path through the crowd—the open front door of a house, perhaps. But there was nothing. Although... Stefan was gone, his captors looking at their empty arms in confusion, and—

My eyes widened.

"Stefan," I breathed.

"Not quite, love," he said, glancing at me.

At the same time, Sebastian stumbled forward, hands resting on the man's shoulders, and said in a voice of breathless wonder, "Father."

The ticket fell, forgotten, to the ground.

Oh, gods.

"How can this be?" Sebastian murmured, his eyes full of tears. And then he couldn't speak anymore. He swept the man into his arms, hugging him fiercely. From my position, I could see the man's face. His cheeks were stained with tears, glistening in the light, and he was smiling.

That smile... I knew that smile even though I didn't know the face. It had been Stefan all along.

That was the trick in the Bargain that bound Sebastian. His father wasn't chained somewhere, locked away in some cave. He was hidden in plain sight. No memories, no face that would be recognized.

Right here with me all along.

"You," Sebastian said, stepping back. "You were the hidden fae that I felt enter the circus grounds. It wasn't Bailey, it was you."

"You'll need to fill in a few gaps for me, son," he said, grinning. "But it sounds that way."

"And the lie…" Sebastian spun around, his face darkening with fury as he rounded on Heillon. "The lie was that I had to follow the rules. This whole time you made me think that the only way to get him back was to follow the rules, but the glamor would only be revealed when I broke them."

Heillon bared his teeth, spreading his hands wide in an exaggerated shrug. "Oops."

The Masters, lounging in the darkness behind the fountain with various humans and fae to keep them company, began to laugh. The sound rang across the crowd—it had grown, I realized, the dancing humans drawn ever closer to our circle. I drew my hands closer toward me, shoulders curving inward as I registered that we were surrounded.

Sebastian might have found his father, but we were still in the den of the wolves.

"Now," Heillon said. "If we're all done playing? I'd like to get down to business."

He spread his arm in a wide arc, and the square lit up with flame.

CHAPTER 38

Bailey

AS THE FLAMES SPREAD, SOMETHING CHANGED. THE CLEARING WE HAD been standing in before the fountain—with its distant bonfires, dancing crowd, and shadowed onlookers—didn't quite vanish. It simply shifted, as though an invisible force had taken the audience and shoved them back fifty meters.

I stood with Heillon in the center of my village, and I didn't recognize a single thing around us.

Flames licked over the surface of the ground. Rocks and gravel scattered, cracking as though we stood at the base of a volcano, bubbling over with lava.

"Are there to be any more interruptions?" he asked me, and his voice sounded disinterested, as if he were merely asking so he could tick off a box in a final administrative form. So he could mentally prepare for me to rise up against him and then bat me away like a buzzing fly.

In the face of his self assurance, I felt so weary. A bone-deep tiredness filled my body, and I kept seeing Fynn's cruel face in my mind.

But I couldn't see Fynn without seeing Sebastian, and

Sebastian had—gods—he'd done it. He'd found his father and broken his cursed Bargain...

And he'd done it all for me.

Slowly, a flicker of that burning fire rekindled. Not snuffed, as I'd thought, but only dormant. I could fight, at least a little. I could be brave, and clever, and magic if I tried.

Straightening, my body filled now with renewed purpose, I wondered how to answer Heillon. The clever thing to do would be to submit. To keep my wits about me for a last second diversion, so I could escape. After all, if there was no Offering, there was no ritual.

But my mind, it seemed, had other ideas, and what I said instead was, "No promises."

Heillon's eyes glinted with interest. He pushed himself up from the chair and strode off the edge of the dais until we were standing face to face. Whatever distant sounds carried from the crowd, behind the flames, I didn't hear them. There was only him and me.

"Well," he said, studying me. "If you're going to fight, I suggest stabbing me in the back. I'm in no mood for a duel." His lip twitched, and then he strode past me, forcing me to turn or leave my back to him.

"Where are you going?" I asked.

He ignored me, striding to the center of the giant space his circle of flame had carved. He reached a place where a giant crack had rended the earth in two, and then he knelt and peered into the crack. From the depths, something roared.

My heart skittered in my chest. This was it. He was beginning the ritual, and unlike the most typical of enemies, he wasn't bothering to inform me of what he was doing. I was less than nothing to him.

My mind whirred, searching for a way out. If there was a Bargain, I could find the lie, but there was no Bargain left to break. And therefore, the only piece of valuable information I had about fighting the fae was useless.

I was as free as a bird, and it was fucking useless.

Something landed at my feet with a quiet clatter that did nothing to distract Heillon. I glanced down, seeing that it was just a branch. A useless piece of willow. Then, I realized.

I looked up, and beyond the circle of flame I saw Merelda's glittering wings, iridescent in the moonlight. She had thrown a branch at my feet, a piece of the forest that was my access point to the magic.

Okay, so fae magic couldn't save me. But human magic might.

I'd get only one chance at this, only one opportunity to strike Heillon down where he stood. I didn't overthink it. I didn't question all the ways in which the Offering wasn't supposed to have this magic. All the ways in which I was surely sending my village to hell. I simply seized the magic right there at my fingertips and aimed it like a bolt of lightning right into Heillon's back.

It struck. My eyes widened in shock as the Lumière Master staggered.

Did I get him? Did I end it?

But then the figure slowly rose, and when he turned to face me, his expression was one of wry amusement. Not anger. Not fear. Amusement.

"Well, at least you can follow instructions," he murmured. Then with a snap of his fingers, the stick in my hands lit on fire, too.

I wasn't done; this couldn't be the end. I reached for the magic again, knowing it was right there, knowing the ashes at my feet were just as much a part of the forest as the living branch had been.

I hurled another bolt of power at him. He batted it away, tilting his head in curiosity.

"I said I wouldn't duel," he warned. "But I must confess: your fight is of more interest than I expected."

In a macabre twist of Sebastian's first meeting, where he tried to pull magic free from me, Heillon raised the earth around us. Giant pillars erupted from the rock, scattering stones over us.

I pulled my hands over my head as a shield and reacted on instinct. Control. Chaos. Those were my choices.

This time I reached for chaos. I pulled at the base of the earthen towers, cursing them and sending Heillon's magic back on himself.

He staggered.

My eyes widened in triumph. That was it; I didn't have the strength of my own magic yet, but I could curse him.

I didn't let up. As Heillon raised another pillar, and then another, I reached for the chaos at the center of each and set it free. He raised water, a towering whirlpool of it descending on me. I plucked that free too, and it became a storm, rising into the sky, shattering the night.

Moonlight and lightning lit the clearing, and beyond the circle of fire I could see my friend's faces, pale with fear and dread. The steel in my heart hardened into resolve.

"I'm not letting you take me," I hissed. "I'm not letting you raise that thing."

Heillon's eyebrow lifted.

"The Offering will protect her village from Hell," he murmured. "How very fitting. It is your purpose after all, is it not?"

Once more, he wore that smug, knowing smile, and in that moment I wanted nothing more than to wipe it from his face in the most violent way possible.

He shot a wall of flame at me, and I disintegrated it into ash with nothing but a thought. But as I did so, my body stumbled, a heavy weight dragging from the center of my chest, as though I'd been awake for five nights and counting.

I was exhausted, even though I'd barely done a thing. Heillon hadn't even broken a sweat, while I was on the verge of passing out. The curve at the corner of his lip deepened.

I blinked rapidly, sweat beading on my eyelashes, and frowned. He was right before me. How had he moved so quickly? Had I lost time? His hand cradled my chin, lifting it from where I realized sluggishly that it had begun to sink.

"I'm not letting you win," I hissed, as once more the daemon roared, shaking the ground with the sound.

Perversely, the dancing and music and laughter in the background never stopped.

If I died here, before the beast rose, would it be enough to stop the ritual? If I aggravated him into killing me now, would everything be tied up in a neat little bundle?

"Do you know why it is so very fitting that you are here, fighting for them?" he asked me, leaning close to whisper in my ear.

"Yes," I spat through gritted teeth, "because it's my destiny."

The low chuckle brushed my ear and filled me with a sense of dread. "No, sweet child, it is because the Offering is not real."

Shock slammed into my chest. "What?" I breathed before I could stop myself. "What do you mean?"

He drew back, fingers trailing along my chin. "The first Bargain is a myth," he said. "I should know. I was there." He laughed again, the sound vicious and cruel. "There is no reason for you to ever lay your life down for your neighbors. What you gave to them..." His hand lowered. "What they took from you... was all for nothing."

A ringing sounded in my ears. It couldn't be true. It couldn't. And yet, I knew that it was. I'd felt the orb, and it was not fae magic. I knew fae magic, knew it intimately, and there was none there.

I'd told myself it had just faded, or perhaps become warped because of what I was doing. But it was nothing to do with me.

Everything they had taken from me was meaningless.

I realized, there, that it was the one thing that had kept me going: the idea that my pain might have purpose. That while they might hate me, at least they had a reason for it. At least everything was as it should be.

But it was fake.

My body slumped, my hands unclenching. I knew that if I lay down here and shut my eyes, I would sleep and sleep. The exhaustion was overpowering. I lifted my gaze, expending every ounce of energy to do so, and found Heillon watching me.

"Quite the catch, isn't it?" he murmured. "You could have been so much more, Bailey. Could have had a life. Could have had meaning." He drummed his fingers on the hard ridge of his thigh. "Tonight, I will change you. I will make you something. How about that? That is my gift for you. You spent your life as the Offering for nothing, but you shall die as one for real."

His voice took on a prophetic edge.

"Because your blood will call to the daemon. Beneath the gold of the Harvest Moon, the beast shall rise and feast upon the souls of this village forevermore. Blood for blood, I will kiss your soul goodnight, and when the time comes, I will tell you to walk into the jaws of Hell and you will go."

I felt entranced, made dizzy from the weight of the truth he had revealed, coupled with my own exhaustion. Bargain upon Bargain, lie upon lie, all twisted around themselves.

"Yes?" Heillon prompted me, the single word wreathed in darkness.

"Yes," I agreed, as tendrils of magic wrapped around me and took hold.

He scanned my face and seemed to deem me no threat, because he turned and walked back to the crack where the daemon howled.

I didn't stop him. Sharp pain sliced through my palm; I hissed and looked down. Blood welled up in the cut, and drop by drop, it lifted into the air and floated toward Heillon. As it reached him, he sliced his own palm open with a violent flourish. His blood rose and joined mine, dropping into the darkness. Blood for blood.

My shoulders slumped in resignation and I came slowly to stand beside him.

What was the point in fighting it? If I was to walk into the jaws of Hell, I may as well at least face them. As I came to a halt by his side, the howling beast kicked up, and I saw within the dark depths two glowing yellow eyes.

The beast began to rise. I saw bone-white teeth, a glistening throat, and eyes that haunted. A pungent stench rose from the pit, and it was all I could do not to run in terror.

"You're going to kill them?" I asked him, my voice sounding just as dead.

"Not at all," Heillon said musingly. There was a fond smile on his face as he watched the beast slowly rise, its claws digging into the walls of the cavern. It pulled itself up inch by inch. "They will live long, odious lives, never knowing why their memories slip away so easily. Never knowing why joy and laughter and love are snatched by the darkness as soon as they appear." He hummed happily. "And the daemon will live among them, feeding and sharing its prey with its masters, as the natural order should be."

He was turning my village into a farm.

Part of me didn't even care; my body still reeled from the

confession. Not one of them had bothered to question it. Not one of them had bothered to ask if it was true.

And shouldn't they have?

If there wasn't something fundamentally unworthy about me, shouldn't they have questioned it? Shouldn't they have *seen* it?

Did they hate me that much?

My body shuddered, a convulsion racing through it. They must. They must have hated me that much, because otherwise one of them should have seen that there was nothing ill-fated about my destiny. That there was nothing *less* about me. But they didn't. They hadn't. They wouldn't.

Heillon began speaking in the fae tongue. I barely listened. He seemed to be repeating what he had said to me. The words were more than dramatic flare, it seemed. They were the ritual words. Magic unfolding piece by piece, in the proper order of a Bargain written in blood.

Promise to obey. Summon the demon. Kiss. Rise. Walk to my death.

Two steps down, three to go.

I frowned. Something wasn't right.

Something was nagging at me—an intrinsic understanding of the order of things, and its importance.

Heillon took my hand from where he knelt, looking up at me with those coal-black eyes as he raised my palm to his lips and kissed it. I barely noticed, my mind racing too hard.

Once more, the power flared all around us.

Promise to obey; I had said yes. I had agreed to the ritual and he had taken my blood as its first stage, mixing it with his own. Fair. Equal. Then, he kissed me goodnight.

Unbalanced, unequal, until the beast rose and I walked into its gaping jaws.

It was a Bargain.

A twisted, ancient Bargain. But just like the one I had made with Fynn, it felt familiar, because this Bargain was open. For these few scant seconds as the beast rose to its power, I had not completed the trade. *When the time comes, I will tell you to walk into the jaws of Hell and you will go.*

I turned to him, my heart hammering in my chest. Fynn had told me that no fae would be able to guess the truth of an open Bargain without being told, but he'd said nothing about humans.

Heillon didn't even bother to look at me. Didn't bother to see me as a threat. Underestimated and dismissed me, just as they all had.

But there was nothing less about me. There was nothing small, or pathetic or worthless about me, although I was beginning to think the same could not be said about them.

I was more than they had ever imagined, because I had just done what no human alive was capable of doing.

I had outwitted the fae.

In the fae tongue, I said to him: "I demand a favor."

It was as though time stood still. He lifted his head slowly, and when he looked at me, that hint of smug arrogance was gone. The dismissal, the disinterest—it all vanished. In its place was rage.

Aeons passed before, finally, he rose to his feet. Even the beast below had paused. With an elaborate flourish, Heillon gave three slow claps of his hands and bowed.

"My dear," he said softly, "No one has surprised me in a very long time."

I shook my head. He hadn't wasted a word telling me about his plans, and I wouldn't waste a word dueling with his ego. This was business—a Bargain to be concluded.

I opened my mouth, but before I could speak, he held up one finger.

"May I point out," he said, "that as noble as you are about to be, they will not thank you."

I froze. Something sick and heavy twisted in my gut.

He went on. "Even if they knew or cared what you did tonight, what you *will* do tonight..." Each word dropped like stones between us. "They will not thank you. You know this." He gestured widely. "Why not simply buy your own safe passage away from here? A different sacrifice may walk into the beast's jaws and complete the Bargain." He pulled a thoughtful face. "Your sister, perhaps."

My breath caught.

"You could have all you ever wanted, Bailey. You could make them pay for the suffering they put you through. And then you and your little boyfriend and his precious father can escape into a life of delicious, joyful, ecstatic obscurity."

The silence that fell when he stopped speaking eclipsed me. Consumed me. He was right. No matter what I did tonight, what I sacrificed for them, what I saved for them... They would never thank me.

They would never see me as anything other than the Offering—something they had simply decided they wanted me to be, and with their cruelty and their ego, had made so. An entire life was etched in that unwritten past, and I would never know it. A life I would never live, that had been robbed from me for no fucking reason.

I would never get that back, but I could demand reparation for what I'd lost.

Seconds dragged past, my breath caught in my throat. I knew what Fynn would have me do, if anything he had ever told me was true. I knew what Merelda would have me do, and I didn't even blame her.

But I had never wanted to make them pay. I had only wanted their love, and I would not get it.

Slowly, my shoulders straightened, my chin lifting as I stared down Heillon—another in a long line of people trying to claim my actions for their own needs. Trying to tell me what I should want. What was *right*. I could punish them all, like he suggested. By their own measure, it would be considered fair.

But was it fair to punish the people who had never met me, and whose only mistake was believing the lies they were told?

Was it fair to punish the children?

My teeth clenched, grinding together with an audible crunch. I was sick of living by someone else's measure of right and wrong. I had lived twenty-eight long years in this world suffering under one lack of fairness. I would not start my life in a new one living under the shadow of another.

"You will let me and the ones I love go safely," I told him, ignoring his plea. His eyes glinted, but he didn't interrupt. "You will let us free. You will neither harm nor capture us."

There was something flickering in his gaze, and I knew before I finished that he was too old and too clever for me to demand perfect safety from him. He would find a way to twist the Bargain against me. Because he was fae. Because he was Lumière. Because he was Heillon.

So, at the last second I changed tactics. I did not demand perfection, and I simply proved to him that I could be clever too.

"You will send the daemon back to Hell, leaving the village and all in it unharmed." My voice grew harsher. "And you must count every star in the night sky. One by one. Out loud, with only your voice, before you move from this spot or allow anyone else to do so."

A flash of fury coursed through me, and at the last second the demand for, if not questionable fairness, then at least *justice* overtook me. The need to remind this fae that humans were not toys for the immortals to play with, and what he had tried to do here tonight was unconscionable.

Before the madness could pass me by, in a low voice, I added, "On your knees."

The glittering emotion in his eyes surged once more into rage, although I swore something else was there alongside it. Something that looked almost impressed.

With a faint, reluctant nod, the favor was sealed.

The beast began to howl and the earth to crack, the rocks splitting in two. I didn't know whether it was the magic of my Bargain or Heillon's anger spilling out that made them shatter. He lowered one knee to the ground, then the other, to the accompaniment of raging thunder.

He could slit me from navel to neck in that position. My pulse hummed in my throat as I waited for him to pounce.

But he lifted his gaze to the heavens and said quietly, "One. Two."

With a hitch of my breath, I ran.

CHAPTER 39

Bailey

Sebastian pulled me along. "We have to go, Bailey. We have to get to water."

To water. Right. We had to get to a lake so I could use one of the arches and escape.

Stefan ushered us forward. No, not Stefan. I didn't even know his name anymore. Whoever he was—Sebastian's father—ushered us along. Merelda loped by my side, sending fierce, sharp-toothed grins at anybody who dared to step in our way.

And all around us the circus was rising, the fae's faces changing, twisting into what hid beneath the glamours. Oh gods, I couldn't believe I'd nearly trusted them. I'd nearly risked everything in a Bargain to cross with them.

We ran. We ran through the town as the people I'd grown up with my whole life laughed and sang and danced themselves into oblivion, with no idea what I'd just done. There would still be Bargains made tonight, Bargains I couldn't save them from. I couldn't stop them, and still I tried. I tried to throw the drink out of the hands that we passed, to smash the orbs that were appearing before every human.

In the shadows, it was worse. Human and fae alike danced together, bodies entwined in furious pleasure.

It was like nothing I'd ever seen before.

"Is it always like this?" I breathed. "Surely we don't forget this every year."

Sebastian looked at me, and, abruptly, I didn't want the answer. He gave it anyway.

"It's always like this, Bailey. The magic is strong. But..." He grimaced. "Never before have they left the bounds and hunted the entire town. I don't know why, or even how, they did that."

"Fynn," I spat out. "He decided to. He ran off with the ribbons and let them all into my town and, and—" I choked the words back.

I didn't even know why I was distraught. These people had never been nice to me, never wanted me, but I didn't want this for them.

"What will they do tomorrow?" I asked. "Will they know?"

"Some will," he said, barely sounding puffed out despite the chase. "For others, they'll simply be guided by an invisible hand, unsure why they keep returning to the same place, to offer the same service. Or why one of their memories is gone— why they can no longer recall the face of their first love or the name of their child." His eyes glinted. "But they won't be enslaved. They won't be living alongside a soul sucking daemon, and for that, they have you to thank."

I covered my mouth with my hand, too many emotions churning at once, and we ran faster. Then, I saw Sadey, leaning back against a cobblestone wall as dozens of witchlight balls danced over her head.

Her eyes were glazed with drink, and she poked the glass orb before her with a giggle. Its blue flame flickered in the night.

"No," I cried out, stumbling forward. "Don't agree, Sadey. Don't do what they say."

"Or what, Bailey?" she called out, the words lilting and dreamy.

I threaded my fingers with hers, trying to bring her back to me, but she only twirled me around in a dance.

"I'm to sing on the stages in the city, didn't you know?"

"That's—" I choked off my reply. "What does it cost, Sadey? Remember the cost! They're the Lumière, they don't give something for nothing."

Her laughter trilled between us. "No one does, but I don't care. Kindness, cruelty—it doesn't matter, Bailey. We're all happy here. We all agreed. And I..." She tilted her head. "I know your face, but who are you?"

I wrenched my hands free, and we ran and ran. Willow branches whipped us in the face, mud sinking around our boots, but we didn't slow. Soon the lake appeared before us, and I didn't waste any time. I pulled the pearl free and cast the arch above the water, ignoring the pounding of drums and strumming of lutes from the depths of the forest.

Just as before, the sprites appeared, and with them came that invisible wall surrounding us, protecting us from interference. I let out a sigh of relief: we were safe.

"Leaving without saying goodbye?" a voice called from behind me.

I stiffened. Fynn; of course he was there.

"Couldn't let me leave without one final twist of the knife?" I gritted it out without turning. I didn't want to see him; the darkness could keep him. He'd taken enough from me tonight.

He laughed. "I take it there'll be no goodbye kiss then."

Sebastian whirled with a snarl. "Keep your fucking hands off her," he said, eyes scanning the surroundings. Fynn must have been keeping to the shadows, even from Sebastian. But still I didn't look. If I could be strong about one thing, it would be this.

"Show your face, you coward," Sebastian called. "Show her who you really are."

"Oh, but she knows already, doesn't she? She knows how evil and wicked I am. You've told her in excruciatingly noble detail, I'm sure."

I gritted my teeth against the challenge in his voice, and still I didn't turn. He couldn't reach me within the protective circle. I only had to last a few more seconds. I'd never see him again.

One by one, four sprites emerged, and they reached for us with shimmering hands.

We didn't linger. Sebastian's father passed through first, followed swiftly by Sebastian, who glanced over his shoulder only once to make sure I was following. Then Merelda, who did the same. And finally, I stepped through the arch.

It was only when I felt the safety of that water surrounding me that I felt brave enough to turn, and although there was nothing to be gained from it, I did. I had no idea what possessed me, what I thought I would find. Maybe I just had to see his face one more time. To see who he truly was without the glamor, so I wasn't tempted to remember the beauty instead of the ugliness that he had shown me tonight.

So I turned, and I saw his face. *Watch their faces and see what changes,* Stefan had told me. The sharp twist of malice to their mouths, the fangs that would emerge from their upper lips, the gaunt shadows beneath their eyes; it would all reveal his true self to me, and I would finally accept how Fynn had lied. The final closure on the biggest mistake I had ever made, so I never made it again.

But... it wasn't there. Nothing about his face had changed. I grew still, frowning as he stepped a little further from the shadows.

"Why are you here?" I asked, my voice steady and cold even

as the power from the archway blazed, calling me toward Criera.

"Heillon needs to see you leave," Fynn said with a cold, bitter smile I couldn't understand.

I looked around, but Heillon was nowhere in sight. My frown deepened, confusion crashing through me. Was he hiding? He should still be counting stars.

But then Fynn tapped a single finger beneath his eye. I followed the movement on instinct—

And gasped, unsure if what I was seeing was real.

As if in a daze, the haunting words of the storyteller from the second night returned to me, sing-song, her crooning voice designed to delight and terrify her audience of children: *he traded his eyes.*

The power bloomed, and the arch began collapsing over us, my vision distorting in the water, but I knew that what I was seeing was true. Above the bitter smile twisted on Finn's face, those glittering, flame-like blue eyes were unlike any I'd seen.

Because they weren't eyes.

They were made of glass; two spherical baubles, embedded in his skull and lit with flame inside them.

Two Bargains, binding him.

CHAPTER 40

Bailey

EPILOGUE

It was night on the other side of the water. The stars above my head were unfamiliar—constellations I'd never seen before. Not in real life. Not in any book. I heard the sound of birdsong I didn't recognize, and large creatures rustling in the forest.

But I wasn't afraid. I was with two fae and an imp; people who knew this land back to front and would keep me safe. And none of us were bound any longer. None of us were trapped in any Bargain that might slowly drain our life or agency.

We cut through the dense forest quickly and soon emerged onto a brick path. No one spoke. With all that had happened, I didn't doubt we were all still reeling from what we had seen.

But they hadn't seen what I had. That last, final revelation.

And I didn't know how to tell them. I couldn't bear for Merelda to accuse me of being naïve, or for Sebastian to scoff and dismiss it as nothing. Because piece by piece, the puzzle was falling into place.

Fynn had told me he was trapped in a Bargain. Not with words, but with his actions. Again and again, he had told me, and I hadn't listened. But I was listening now, even though I barely wanted to, because my memories were slotting one by one into a new order, forming a terrifying story.

When I finally remembered the words that must have been the source of his Bargain, I crashed to a halt, my breath choking in my throat.

"Some of us may be bound by such a curse, but not you."

"Pick me instead."

"Say my name."

He was trapped until someone chose him. Until someone chose the hunter over the hero.

The shattering that I had felt when I had finally, truly, irrevocably turned from him as he stood there on the dais—when I finally walked away from him; it was his Bargain. The gate slamming shut.

He had tried to get me to choose him, and I hadn't. And when he had seen that Sebastian was who I wanted, he had done everything to push me away. To get me to safety.

Magic is not one size fits all, Bailey, even for the fae... I can create visions of people from nothing, but I cannot summon them.

The vision of my sister on the dais—her hand had trembled. Like an illusion.

My hands clenched into fists, but there was nothing to fight. Nothing to do but move forward, away from the land I'd left behind. The choice I had made.

For the first time, I had fallen for Fynn's lies, and in that moment when I had rejected him, I doomed him forever.

☾

END

Go
and
Be Blessed

Acknowledgments

I have several people to thank immensely, with profound gratitude, because this book wouldn't exist the way it does without them. But very quickly I want to first express gratitude for something else.

This book has been a test of my patience and resolve, and I'm happy to say I think I won. Before I started it, I'd made the decision to slow things down a lot. Everything in my life felt too rushed, too skimmed, and nowhere near deep enough for my tastes.

But that's the thing isn't it? So often in life, we relinquish our own tastes and choices for someone else's, and the indie world moves very fast. This time, I didn't.

So, even when this project ballooned from a planned 25k MF novella to a 140k book one out of a why choose duet... I stuck to the pace. I kept it slow, kept working in the way that I knew was healthy instead of rushing things, even though I knew it would mean my releases this year were fewer than I'd planned. I changed the intended release days, I committed to a beta read that would add months to the schedule, and I settled in to the extensions as they arose instead of losing sleep to beat them.

I think it was worth it; wait, no. I know it was worth it for me, and for how the book feels to my own creative spirit. I don't know yet if it was worth it externally, but I'm learning to let go of that pressure. I never had control over it anyway.

So, I guess this is gratitude for creative spirit and authentic choices. I'm grateful that we're beginning to create a world where personal growth and individual choices have value, and where we can lean into our own paths instead of being swept along with the tide. I don't know about you, but I'm getting sick of being shattered on the rocks.

Right. Enough of that.

I am so, so, SO grateful first to Kat, for being the support I needed when this precious new idea began to change shape. When Fynn started shaking his head and going off script, and the plot kept getting bigger and wilder. Your enthusiasm and cheerleading makes every book feel like the best project ever. Thanks, always, for being there for and with me.

To my new beta team who read this book first—Bre, Valynda, and Maycee—your feedback and heartfelt enthusiasm for the story, even raw and unpolished, was beyond incredible. Your unflinching support and honest insight was the missing piece I didn't know was absent in the writing process. I know in my bones that this book would not be what it is without your help and reflections, and I'm so grateful that you decided to join me in this beta venture.

To my ARC readers, and especially those who come back book after book; your support and enthusiasm means the world, and I love seeing your names and reflections return each time.

To my partner, for your unwavering support, kindness, sound boarding, and cheerleading. You make this beautiful life possible, and you make this life beautiful.

And finally, always, to you, the reader. I'm beyond grateful that you're here, devouring these worlds and meeting these characters with me. Whether this is your first book with me or your sixth, it fills me with joy to know there are people out there who enjoy the incredibly vivid and angsty daydreams that keep me occupied. Hope you keep finding new worlds to love.

<h1 style="text-align:center;font-style:italic">About the Author</h1>

Jade Bones is a fantasy romance writer who loves writing about delicious demons, magical worlds, and steamy romps. She is the author of the Hell's Fire Burning trilogy, a dark fantasy RH series following an escaped hellsoul and the demons stuck by her side. When Jade isn't writing, you can find her drinking tea, cuddling her dog, or taking tarot far too seriously.

https://www.jadebonesauthor.com

Desperate to know what's next? There are lots of wonderful projects in the works over here, and your best spot for updates is to sign up to my mailing list.

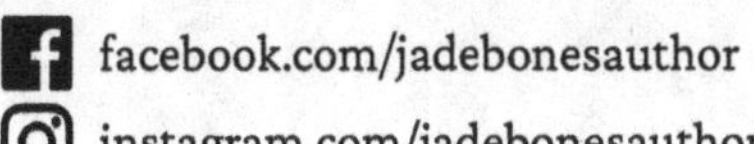

facebook.com/jadebonesauthor
instagram.com/jadebonesauthor